"

a

I

"

st

th

"

"

p

"

Books by Eileen Wilks

TEMPTING DANGER

MORTAL DANGER

BLOOD LINES

NIGHT SEASON

MORTAL SINS

BLOOD MAGIC

BLOOD CHALLENGE

DEATH MAGIC

MORTAL TIES

RITUAL MAGIC

UNBINDING

MIND MAGIC

DRAGON SPAWN

DRAGON BLOOD

Anthologies

CHARMED
(with Jayne Ann Krentz writing as Jayne Castle,
Julie Beard, and Lori Foster)

LOVER BEWARE
(with Christine Feehan, Katherine Sutcliffe, and Fiona Brand)

CRAVINGS
(with Laurell K. Hamilton, MaryJanice Davidson,
and Rebecca York)

ON THE PROWL
(with Patricia Briggs, Karen Chance, and Sunny)

INKED
(with Karen Chance, Marjorie M. Liu, and Yasmine Galenorn)

TIED WITH A BOW
(with Lora Leigh, Virginia Kantra, and Kimberly Frost)

Specials

ORIGINALLY HUMAN

INHUMAN

HUMAN NATURE

HUMAN ERROR

DRAGON BLOOD

EILEEN WILKS

JOVE
New York

A JOVE BOOK
Published by Berkley
An imprint of Penguin Random House LLC
375 Hudson Street, New York, New York 10014

ISBN: 9780399583155

First Edition: January 2018

Printed in the United States of America
1 3 5 7 9 10 8 6 4 2

Cover art by Tony Mauro
Cover design by Katie Anderson

LETTER FROM LILY YU

It had all started on a fairly normal day. Normal, that is, if your husband is a werewolf and the two of you are hanging out with your brother-in-law—also a werewolf and maybe the deadliest man in the world—and your best friends, who include a sorcerer, a Rhej, and a part-sidhe computer geek. We'd eaten chocolate chips cookies and talked about weaning and cussing and a device intended to absorb stray magic before being interrupted by a man who wanted to kill Rule.

Okay, that last part had been unusual. Not wildly so, but not an everyday occurrence. Things didn't really take a turn for weird, though, until we were summoned by the black dragon, who told us that Tom Weng wasn't dead. (I said that, didn't I? I kept saying he might still be alive, and everyone kept rolling their eyes at me.) Worse—it turns out he's a dragon spawn. Don't know what that is? Neither did we, until Sam told us.

Centuries ago, dragon spawn were created when a botched hatching resulted in baby dragons who were utterly mind-dark. Impervious to mind magic, they would never have been able to communicate, living their lives in terrible isolation. To spare them this, the dragons had permanently altered their forms so they could be raised as humans by humans, including learning our type of speech.

The dragons didn't get the outcome they were hoping for. Instead of reasonably well-adjusted imitation humans, they'd ended up with a crew of supersmart, sorcerous sociopaths with major parental issues. Fortunately for everyone else in the world, those spawn had died out a long time ago. They were supposed to be the only ones ever created, so Tom Weng's existence had come as a shock to Sam's crowd.

Another shock had interrupted the telling of this tale when someone fired two missiles at the black dragon's lair. Sam's defenses deflected one enough to minimize the damage; the other missile hit, but he somehow kept it from exploding.

The FBI Headquarters building in Washington, D.C., didn't fare as well.

It was bombs, not missiles, that took Headquarters down, decapitating much of the federal policing structure—including Unit 12. My unit. The only federal force composed primarily of magically Gifted agents. Martin Croft, who'd been running the Unit after Ruben was forced out, was critically injured in the blast. So were a lot of others. At least seventy-nine people were dead. People I knew. Probably a lot more than that, since there were a hundred forty-nine still missing the last I heard.

It sure looked like our Enemy had gotten tired of keeping the war under wraps and was coming after us with both barrels—and by "us" I mean the dragons, the lupi, the Gifted, and the Bureau. Anyone who might prove an obstacle to her plan to take over the world and remake humanity. The Great Bitch does not have a high opinion of free will. Too damn messy, all those people making their own decisions.

That night everything got worse. Much worse. They took Toby.

They also took Ryder—Cynna and Cullen's daughter, the nine-month-old prodigy who'd inspired our discussion of weaning. And eight-year-old First Fist, Diego, grandson of Ybirra Clan's Rho. Four-year-old Sandy of Czøs, son of that clan's Lu Nuncio. And a three-month-old baby named Noah, whose grandfather had been the Etorri Rho. The children had been snatched from their homes, where they should have been safe—homes that were all over the bloody continent.

They made one mistake, though. They didn't kill my cat.

Dirty Harry had been sleeping with Toby, as usual. Sam managed to extract Harry's memory of the snatch and share it with us. It was easy to ID one of the perps as Tom Weng. Easy, too, for some of us to ID the other perp: Ginger Harris. Ginger, Sarah's older sister. Sarah had been my best friend in the third grade and a big part of my introduction to monsters. The man who abducted the two of us had been fully human and fully a monster. He'd raped her because he loved her pretty blond hair. He'd killed her just before the police showed up and saved me.

We had a complicated history, me and Ginger. Two years ago, she'd tried to get Rule framed for murder. Now it looked like she was serving as avatar for the Great Bitch.

Because a dragon spawn was involved, the dragons were, too. With an assist from another dragon—Reno—Sam was able to determine where the children had been taken: Dis, the demon realm. Also known as hell. The dragons arranged for the best gate-builders in all the realms—that's what everyone kept saying about them anyway—to open passage for us. Dirty Harry was in serious-but-stable condition when eleven of us mounted up on motorcycles and went roaring off into hell.

One of our party used the gate, but not a motorcycle: Reno. Another one didn't need the gate. Gan, my short, orange, used-to-be-a-demon friend, had come here from Edge to help, and she was one of the extremely rare beings who could cross realms without a gate.

I'm not going to go into everything that happened in Dis. Most of it was bloody; all of it was terrifying. The short version is that Rule and I ended up separated, but we almost managed to reconnect while battling demons in the belowground palace of the former ruler of that region of *hell. Who was supposed to be dead, dammit. Instead Xitil was very much present and mad as hell—by which I mean crazy, Looney Tunes, nuts, 'round-the-bend bonkers. One of the last things I saw in that battle was two tons of Xitil looming over Rule, giggling merrily while the place burned around us. Rule had been standing over his brother's motionless body, armed only with a knife.*

I was trying to get to him when two enormous Claws caught up with me. One of them slapped the M4 out of my hand. The other reached out with huge, taloned hands.

That's when Gan grabbed me.

ONE

~

Lóng Jia

PAIN comes in many varieties. There's the crushed outrage of a smashed thumb and the *oh shit* rip of a twisted ankle. A bad tooth throbs, a headache pounds, and when a bone breaks, the bright shock of it shorts out your entire system, as intense as a climax. Then there is pain that swallows the entire world, admitting no presence beyond itself. Pain that goes on and on.

Rule woke to pain.

In the first few seconds or eons, there was no place to put the pain, nothing to assign it to, no sense it was lodged in this or that part of his body. Pain was entire, complete . . . until it wasn't. He grew aware of a voice. Not words, for the pain-universe allowed him no space to sort sound into words, but he knew this particular sound was a voice.

He was not alone.

Some instinct rose from a place so deep inside the pain could not shut it out. An instinct that said *quiet*. That said *listen*. He was hurt, badly hurt, and he was not alone. Not-alone was dangerous. His nostrils flared. He did not smell clan or Lily. He smelled . . .

". . . did you stop?" the voice was saying. It sounded scared.

"It's not enough to get him out of the water. We've got to get to cover. One of them could swoop down at any moment and . . ."

The word for what he smelled eluded Rule, but he knew the scent. No, two scents. The one that went with the voice was not-trusted. The other . . .

"Hey, why did you—what are you—eep!"

The other was very dangerous.

"Oh, right. The sleep charm. I forgot about that. I can put him in sleep and then he won't scream anymore. Okay. You can back off now. Please back off."

Very dangerous, but also . . . his. His, and trusted. Rule made a huge effort and opened his eyes.

The glare made his eyes blur, or maybe they'd already been wet. He panted, openmouthed, as pain threatened to white out his other senses. He blinked to clear his vision. All he saw was blue. After a moment he caught the word for all that blue: sky. Then a large head loomed over him, furred in orange and black with white above the eyes and on the ruff.

Tiger. That was the word for the one with the dangerous-but-mine scent.

The tiger licked the side of his head with a huge, rough tongue. And purred.

The tiger had a name. Madame Yu. Yes. He did not need to defend himself with Madame Yu here. His eyes closed in exhausted relief.

"How did Cynna say it worked?" the voice asked. "I hold it on him, but there was something else."

Memories flickered through Rule and landed on a name. Gan. The voice belonged to Gan, who used to be a demon and an enemy but was now a friend. She was not-trusted because her judgment was unreliable, not because she wished him ill.

"No, don't lick me! Lick him if you want, but I don't—oh, I get what you mean. I'm supposed to lick the charm to activate it."

Madame Yu was here. Gan was here. Where was his mate? Automatically Rule reached for Lily through the bond. Panic flickered, a hot little flame amid the vaster pain. So far. She was so far away—

Something damp and metallic pressed against his cheek.

Sleep swept in, soft and comforting as a blanket, and separated him from both thought and pain.

ONE second, Lily had been fighting two enormous Claws. Although fighting might not be the best term, since her M4 had run out of ammo and she'd been unable to get a new clip in before one of the oversize demons slapped it out of her hands. The next, she was waking up in this manicured garden. Trees surrounded the grassy area where she sat, interrupted in two places by paths. It was warm here, very warm, and a lot more humid than she was used to. Somewhere nearby, a bird sang. Water gurgled a happy-little-stream song. A stray sorcéri brushed against her hand, making the skin tingle faintly.

Lily sat motionless, her head aching, and looked up at the dead woman who'd greeted her.

Helen Whitehead was a small, birdlike woman of middle age who put the "white" back in Caucasian. Her skin was so pale she must have spent her entire life slathered with sunscreen, and her hair was the color of sun-bleached straw. Only her eyes testified to her body's ability to produce pigment— blue eyes that might have looked washed out in another face, but were vivid in this one.

Lily knew the face, the eyes, the hair. The last time she'd seen them, that uncolored hair had been wet with blood, the blue eyes clouded over in death. She reached the obvious conclusion. "I'm dead."

The woman tipped her head. "Did you suffer a blow to your head?"

As a matter of fact, she had. It ached, as did various other body parts. Bruises and contusions taken in the fight in the audience hall were reporting in, which spoke against her initial conclusion. So did the Glock in her hand—the one she'd drawn so automatically she hadn't noticed doing it. Lily didn't have a clue what the afterlife was like, but she doubted it included semi-automatic weapons.

Still alive, then. Which made her amazingly lucky, though it was hard to feel fortunate as she sprang to her feet with all the vigor of an arthritic eighty-year-old. Her ankle sang out in sharp rebuke when she put weight on that foot. Good thing she didn't plan to run anywhere right away. Her ankle might let her hobble away. Maybe.

Helen watched, mildly curious. "I understand head blows can induce confusion. Put the gun away, Lily."

"I don't think so."

"I do," said a voice behind her.

She spun—and something yanked the gun out of her hand even as she squeezed the trigger. The shot killed the hell out of a leaf or two without coming close to the man who'd come up behind Lily.

Her weapon whisked itself through the air to plant itself in the palm of the man's hand. He was tall and thin and clearly Asian—probably Chinese though his features were subtly different from the Han Chinese that comprised over 90 percent of China's population. Tibetan, maybe? His features were clean and elegant, his skin extremely pale, his hair black and pulled back in a tight bun. But his eyes were blue—sky blue— and brighter than any human eyes she'd ever seen. Brighter even than Cullen's, which she would have thought impossible. He wore a gold and black *shenyi*, the wraparound robe that had constituted formal wear for Chinese men for centuries. It hadn't been in style for a long time now.

Tom Weng had been wearing a *shenyi*. Weng had looked subtly different from the Han majority, too. She'd wondered if he might have a European ancestor somewhere, but maybe not. Maybe he came from the same ethnic group as this guy. There was a resemblance, wasn't there? He might be Weng's . . . cousin? Brother?

One way to find out.

Two months ago, Lily's mindspeech lessons with the black dragon she called Sam had finally paid off. An ability that had been dormant came to life. Mindspeech, she knew now, was only one way of using her mindsense . . . which was only logical, really. You had to sense a mind before you could speak with it. Lily's new sense was an odd meld of tactile and visual. Most of the time it slept in her middle, as much a part of her as her colon and as easy to ignore. When she wanted to use it, she gave it a mental nudge and it uncoiled, reaching out like a tentacle or probe—or like a mist, if that's what she wanted.

It was the mist she used now. With it, she could locate all the nearby minds at once. She nudged the coil sleeping in her gut, picturing it as a mist radiating out . . .

To her mindsense, the man simply wasn't there. That absence had only one possible explanation. He was dragon spawn.

"I've been wanting one of these," the dragon spawn said, turning her Glock over in his hands. He spoke clearly, but with a definite accent. "Later, you will instruct me in its use."

While she appreciated his use of the word "later" and the implied confidence in her continued existence, being somewhere else sounded like a great idea. Pity it would be so hard to put into practice. Dragon spawn were crazy strong as well as plain old crazy. He was probably also a sorcerer. Magic might not work on her directly, but she could be affected by what it did. Look at how easily he'd knocked her weapon out of her hand . . . which still tingled from the odd magic he'd employed.

A type of magic she'd touched before, she realized. "Telekinesis. That's how Weng was able to float or fly or whatever you want to call it. Not true levitation—at least, not the way dragons do it, which may not be levitation, either." Cullen thought dragons went out-of-phase with reality much the way demons did when they went *dashtu*, thereby reducing the effect of gravity on their huge bodies.

The thought of Cullen made her chest tight, as if she didn't have enough air. He'd fallen in the battle in the audience hall. She didn't know if he was still alive. She fought to keep the fear from her face, her voice. "Weng used a peculiar form of TK to move his body where he wanted it."

"I was told she wasn't as stupid as most humans," he observed. "Her initial response to you made me doubt this, but perhaps that was due to the blow to her head, as you suggested, Alice."

Alice? Was Helen using a different name here? Wherever "here" was. Lily's head ached. "Where are we?"

It was as if she hadn't spoken. "I will study her before we hand her over to our ally."

The woman—Helen or Alice?—spoke. "I have expressed my desire to make my own study of her."

"Be satisfied with the other one."

"Other one," Lily repeated. "You have another human here?"

For the first time, the man met her eyes. He even smiled. It was not a friendly expression. "We have a large number of them. Your people are limited in many ways, but you do breed well."

She had his attention. Good. Keep asking questions. "What's your name?"

"Surely even you know better than to expect an answer to such a question."

"Surely even you realize I meant a call-name."

"You will call me *Zhu*."

She snorted. "Master? Not likely."

"And yet you will do so. If not now, soon." Abruptly he switched to Chinese, but it was a dialect she'd never heard before. Not Cantonese or Taiwanese—neither of which she could speak, but she knew them when she heard them. Wu, maybe? Wasn't that the dialect spoken in Shanghai Province? He seemed to want someone to hurry up and . . .

What was that? Feet moving quickly and in unison. She turned.

Half a dozen ancient Chinese warriors came trotting out of the trees on one of the paths. At least they looked Chinese and their gear might have clothed the extras in a Genghis Khan movie, if Genghis Khan had been Chinese rather than Mongolian. Hollywood didn't pay attention to details like that. These men wore baggy pants, skimpy beards or long mustaches or both, and pointy leather helmets. Also what she thought were called cuirasses—two pieces of shaped leather strapped together to protect the chest and back. The sixth man's armor was made of something blue and shiny. Two of them carried swords, two carried bows, and two held . . . were those pikes or spears? Long wooden poles that ended in a pointy part.

She twitched with the urge to bolt. She wouldn't get far.

It wasn't until the six men formed up in a circle around her that she realized how short they were. Blue-armor was the only one taller than her, and he only had a couple inches on her. That armor was peculiar. Not metal, she thought, but she couldn't get a good look. Helen blocked her view.

The dragon spawn told them in that odd Chinese to "take her to the [gentle womb? fine bag?] with the other one" and started to walk away.

"What other one?" Lily called after him. He ignored her.

One of the warriors barked an order at her—not the guy with the blue breastplate. This one's face was weathered, wrinkled around the eyes. His armor was leather, but he had more of it than the others—winged pads on his shoulders, stuff that strapped onto his thighs. His order was simple enough that she understood it quite well: *come with us.*

"You are to go with them," Alice/Helen said tranquilly.

"Or else what?" Lily asked. "Are they going to poke holes in me with those big sticks?"

"No. As you perhaps have guessed, our ally wants you alive and reasonably intact. If you resist going with them, they will try not to damage you. If they fail in that attempt, you will be given medical care. You may find their version of medical care rather primitive."

Alrighty, then. Might as well go with the short warriors. Lily inclined her head regally at Shoulder Pads Guy and tried to channel Grandmother as she said in Chinese—Mandarin Chinese, that is, that being the only form of the language she could speak—"You will introduce yourself. Then I will go with you."

He scowled in what might be confusion. After a moment he repeated his order, but this time added that he was Li Po, *shǒu quán guī yuánsù de tiān Zhǔrén.* First something-something of the Heavenly Masters.

Lily lifted her eyebrows as if she doubted he'd gotten that right, but was too polite to call him on it. "I greet you, Li Po. I am Special Agent Lily Yu of Unit Twelve of the Federal Bureau of Investigation of the United States of America." *Nyah, nyah, nyah. My title's longer than yours.* "I will go with you."

They insisted on tying Lily's hands in front of her. Clearly someone thought she was a helluva lot more dangerous than she felt. They didn't search her—an odd omission, but maybe they assumed her bound hands would keep them safe from her. They were probably right.

Two guards walked ahead of Lily; one of them held the end

of the rope that bound her wrists as if she were an animal on a leash. Two more guards went behind, and the last two flanked her. *Dangerous prisoner here, folks.* She walked through another sorcéri, the loose bits of magic often found near nodes or the ocean.

The woman who wasn't dead and therefore couldn't be Helen didn't treat her as dangerous. Not-Helen strolled along beside her as if they were acquaintances out to enjoy the gardens on a hot summer afternoon. Maybe she was enjoying herself in her loose cotton clothing. Lily bet the guards in their leather cuirasses were almost as uncomfortable as she was in her leather jacket. Her ankle bitched at her with every step. She tried to ignore that, the heat, and the lingering throb of a headache and gather information.

All of the guards' minds were present to her mindsense. So was the woman's. Not dragon spawn, then. They were human minds, as far as she could tell—which, admittedly, was based on limited experience, but human minds generally reminded her of some yellow fruit. The guards' minds were yellow and fuzzy. The woman's was . . . odd. The color was mostly yellow, though with a blush of rose, but her mind was slick and the overall glow was tamped down in a way that reminded Lily of something. She couldn't think what, but the slickness meant she couldn't mindspeak the woman.

The guards, though—if she mindspoke one of the guards, would she need to think at him in Chinese? The black dragon didn't need to share a mutual language with someone to mindspeak him or her, but he could do all kinds of things that were beyond her. Like read minds. And how would it work if they replied? Most people had to vocalize for Lily to pick up their mental response. If they spoke in Chinese, would she "hear" them in English or in Chinese?

She resisted the urge to try it and find out. Far better if her captors didn't know about her little trick. Sweat dampened her hairline. They'd almost reached the trees and the shade they offered. A couple more sorcéri brushed against her cheek. There seemed to be a lot of loose magic here. "So what is this place? Where—"

The guard holding her rope gave it a jerk and barked out an order. Lily stumbled. She would have fallen if Not-Helen hadn't grabbed her arm. The woman let loose with a spate of that odd version of Chinese. It was like listening to someone speak English with a thick Scottish brogue. Lily recognized the language, but only understood bits and pieces. Not-Helen seemed to be chastising the guards for their stupidity, though, which was interesting on several levels.

After some back and forth between Not-Helen and Li Po, one of the rear guards trotted off. The woman turned to Lily. "What is your injury?"

"My ankle. A sprain."

"There is a rickshaw. These cretins left it on the other side of the bridge. It is true that wheeled vehicles are not normally allowed in the Xīnzàng de Jiā, but Li Po had the authority to bring it with him. I suspect he considers any sort of cart beneath his dignity. They will bring it now, but Li Po refuses to wait for it. He claims this is because he was ordered to take you to your cell and he cannot delay. In reality, he obeys me as grudgingly as possible. He disapproves of uppity women. Are you able to walk, or should they carry you until we reach the rickshaw?"

This woman had gone to some trouble to arrange transport for Lily. She might be kind by nature . . . or she might want something. Lily was putting her nickel down on the latter. "I'll walk. I'll be slow, however."

"Despite Li Po's claim, there's no hurry."

Lily started limping forward again. "I'm being taken to a cell."

"Of course. You will find it primitive, but at least it's one of those at the Justice Court. The jail in the town is much worse."

"Who's the other human? The one who's already in the cell?"

"Cynna Weaver."

Relief swamped Lily. Cynna was alive. Alive—and a prisoner. That was bad, but it meant that Lily wasn't here alone . . . a thought that swirled guilt in with the relief and dismay. She shouldn't be glad Cynna was here, but she was. Aside from the not-being-alone part, there was the fact that Cynna was a powerful spellcaster. They would have taken her charms away, and most spells called for components, but still, there was bound to be stuff she could . . .

"Do you know why our ally wants you?"

It took Lily a moment to switch tracks, and another moment to decide to answer. For whatever reason, the woman who looked exactly like Helen Whitehead was willing to answer questions—or to exchange answers. Best keep that going, if she could. "Unless she's changed her mind again, she wants to wipe my brain clean so she can imprint a copy of the Codex Arcana on it."

There was a slight hitch in the woman's stride. "She has the Codex?"

"I don't know. She doesn't keep me posted. What do *you* call that guy? The dragon spawn who wouldn't give me his name, I mean." Would this woman recognize the term?

"I advise you not to use that descriptive in his hearing or that of his brothers. They dislike it, and their emotional control is erratic."

"Is it better to call them *Lóng Luǎn*, then?" Lily used the Chinese phrase for "dragon spawn" to see if the guards recognized it. Sure enough, one of them gave her a sharp glance.

"No. They are addressed by honorifics rather than names. You refer to them as the Zhuren, plural, or Zhu in the singular. The one you met is Zhu Kongqi."

Lily's eyebrows lifted. "They're the Masters, and he's Master of Air?"

"The form of address they have chosen is not hyperbole. Each of them has studied and mastered a particular area of magic."

Not mind magic, though, she'd bet. "How many of them are there?"

"I'm told there used to be seven. There are now six. I suspect Zhu Shouyì was killed by one or more of his brothers, but it is possible he crossed to another realm. What do you know of the Codex Arcana?"

"It's The Book of All Magic, and it's a real thing, not a myth." They were trudging uphill now, surrounded by some landscaper's notion of what a forest should look like—uncrowded trees and not much undergrowth. Lily's ankle hurt too much for her to appreciate the setting. It hurt enough to drown out the ache in her head, if not the one in her heart. She wanted to ask if they were there yet, but that would be a dreadful waste of a question. Clearly they weren't. "Where are the children?"

"They aren't here yet."

Lily hadn't needed to explain which children she was talking about. Interesting. "But they will be brought here?"

"I cannot tell you more. Surely that is not the sum of your knowledge about the Codex—that it exists."

"Anything else would be speculation, not fact." Speculation based on fact, however. After trying hard for a year to have Lily killed, all of a sudden the Great Bitch had reverted to wanting Lily taken prisoner. She could see only one reason for that.

"I would hear your speculation."

"Can we be overheard by anyone who understands English?"

"No."

"If Zhu Kongqi is really a Master of Air, he might be able to listen in. Clairaudience is a type of Air magic."

"I have good reason to believe he will not."

And her tone of voice said clearly that she didn't plan to share that reason. Hmm. Either this woman was so interested in the Codex that she'd go behind the dragon spawns' backs to learn more, or she was playing good cop. No, Lily thought, she was definitely playing good cop. First the woman showed concern about Lily's ankle. Next she answered some of Lily's questions and offered advice on how to avoid offending her captors—and mixed her own questions in with her replies. Sound interrogation technique. The question was whether she was doing it on her own behalf, or that of the dragon spawn?

Assume the latter, play it safe, and say nothing? Or try stirring the pot?

What the hell. Playing it safe wasn't going to change anything. "I suspect the one we call the Great Bitch doesn't yet have the Codex—"

"Why not?"

"If she already had The Book of All Magic, she wouldn't need allies, would she?"

Not-Helen was silent a moment. "I interrupted you. Please continue."

"She doesn't have it now, but believes she can get hold of it soon. Why else go to so much trouble to obtain me alive? Why else make her big push for world domination now? Sure, she's always wanted to take over Earth, but all of a sudden she's in a hurry. This suggests two things. First, she knows the Codex is on Earth. Second, she either knows where it is or how to find it, and she wants it badly enough to push her world-domination plans into high gear."

The woman didn't respond. That was encouraging, as it suggested Lily had given her something to chew on. Lily tried to feel encouraged as they reached the top of the hill . . . and looked out on medieval China.

A high wall snaked out from the left side, partly encircling a large expanse of meadow turned garden that must have been groomed over generations. A tall gate in the wall was open, admitting traffic—foot traffic, mostly. There were carts, but they were pulled by people, not horses or donkeys. The wall continued to the right of the gate until it was interrupted by a small lake, its surface a placid mirror dotted by a few boats, none of them far from shore.

Centered in the meadow was an enormous courtyard, perfectly square. Three sides of the courtyard boasted ornate buildings wearing the peaked hats of Chinese architecture. One of those roofs must have been gilded, for it was a blaze of gold in the sunlight. The others were the dull red of clay tiles. The fourth side of the courtyard, the one nearest the gate, contained a structure, too, but it seemed to be an oversized gazebo, being composed of pillars and a roof. From her vantage she couldn't tell if there were walls set farther back, hidden from her view by the roof. There were people everywhere, but especially moving to and from the gazebo-like structure. A market, maybe?

In the center of the courtyard, a tower rose like a fat chimney that had lost its building, crowned by what, to her eyes, looked exactly like a giant Frisbee. The Frisbee was bright red. The buildings and the oversized gazebo were linked by tree-shaded walks. Several smaller buildings were scattered along those walks. The whole scene reminded her vaguely of pictures she'd seen of Beijing's Forbidden City—the wall, the wedding-cake architecture—but these buildings were stone, not wood.

On the other side of the wall lay a river that emptied into the lake. On the other side of the river was a town. The buildings closest to the river were stone—not as large and ornate as the buildings in the courtyard, but still with fancy roofs. None was more than two stories high. Away from the river they dwindled into what she thought were wooden buildings, though from this distance it was hard to be sure—substantial at first, then becoming what were likely shacks. There were a lot of shacks.

A couple spots within the town—city? Was it large enough to be called that?—were oddly blank, holding neither buildings nor vegetation. Beyond the buildings were fields of growing things, a dirt road, and hills. A couple of the hillsides had been terraced into rice paddies.

At least that's what she thought those stair-step fields might be. The hills were a long ways off, and she'd never actually seen a rice paddy. "What in the world is this place?"

"It's not in your world at all," Not-Helen said, amused.

"But the realm must have a name."

"It has had several names. The Zhuren call it *Wǒmen De*." Lily lifted her brows. "'Our Earth'?"

"They would translate it simply as *Ours*. Ah, there's the rickshaw. They were slow—on purpose, I'm sure. Li Po's men know how he feels about me."

Now that she'd pointed it out, Lily saw a small, two-wheeled cart halfway up the winding path, being drawn toward them by a single man between the poles. It was made from a mix of bamboo and wood and looked uncomfortable. "Thank you for obtaining it, ah . . . the man who stole my gun called you Alice, I think?"

The woman who could not be Helen didn't respond, though her pale lips turned up as if she were savoring some private joke.

Lily's heart pounded as if she were about to say something dangerous. How absurd. If she was right, the danger existed whether or not she stated her guess out loud. If she was wrong, no harm done. That didn't change the dread in the pit of her stomach. "Alice Whitehead, by any chance?"

"I am Báitóu Alice Li, though your manner of naming would make me Alice Báitóu. Báitóu, of course, means 'white head.'" That pale smile didn't change. "Helen Whitehead, whom you killed, was my twin sister."

TWO

~

WHEN Rule awoke again, pain was not the entire universe. More like a tidal sea that waned and waxed with each breath. He floated on that terrible sea and reached again for Lily through the mate bond.

Alive. She was alive, but how could she be so far away? Where was she?

Where was he?

Not Dis. He knew that instantly, for he felt the moon's song, distant but immeasurably soothing. He let that song ease him for a time, then gathered his thoughts to consider his situation. Lily might be inexplicably distant, but according to his nose, her grandmother was very close. And Madame Yu wasn't a tiger anymore. He remembered that. She'd been a tiger the last time he woke. If she'd returned to her weaker form, she must not be expecting attack. Not immediate attack, at least.

He also smelled smoke and cooking meat . . . a campfire? Yes. He did not smell Gan except for a faint, lingering scent that seemed to come from his own body, as if the former demon had handled him while he was unconscious. But Gan did not seem to be close now.

The ocean was. That mélange of scents soothed him, too, with its familiarity and timeless indifference. He hadn't noticed it the first time he woke, but only the wolf had roused then. Good thing Madame Yu had been with him. He might have killed himself trying to kill Gan or to escape. Lupi had been known to wake up in the operating room with unfortunate results for their would-be surgeon. To an injured wolf, almost everyone was an enemy.

That, of course, assumed he could have moved, which might be laughably optimistic. He was badly hurt this time. It wasn't just the pain that told him this, though that spoke convincingly, but the weakness, the woozy, out-of-control feeling . . . from blood loss? Probably, though his aching head suggested a concussion might be contributing. The pain in his head didn't worry him, though. Neither did that in his leg—a deep wound, he thought, but he hadn't bled out, so it would heal if he lived to heal it.

He might not. The worst pain came from his gut.

Rule had taken a bullet in the stomach not long ago. He'd needed surgery, an IV, a few units of blood, even antibiotics. Lupi normally didn't bother with antibiotics, given how easily their healing shrugged off unfriendly microbes, but gut wounds dump a nasty stew of bacteria into the system. His healing had been stretched enough, Nettie had told him, without having to fight off peritonitis, too.

This wounding was worse. The level of pain told him that. The location—below his stomach—suggested the reason, or part of it. And antibiotics, surgery, replacement blood, and IVs did not seem to be available here. Wherever "here" was.

Earth? The sky he'd seen earlier had been bright, sunny blue. Had he somehow been returned to Earth? What had happened to him?

With the question, a jumble of memory poured in. Fire. His brother's body, bloody and motionless. Lily on the other side of the cavern, nearly hidden in the smoke. No sign of Toby or the other children, and Cullen either unconscious or dead. Cynna trying to rescue Cullen. A mountain of pink flesh looming over Rule, giggling. Rule gripping his knife firmly as he faced Xitil, who had turned out to be insufficiently dead. She'd been about to kill him when . . . what? He couldn't think, couldn't remember anything beyond that moment when he'd faced off against the demon prince. But he remembered enough of what had happened before then to know that the only medical supplies he'd had were a roll of gauze and a tube of superglue.

No, just superglue. He'd used the gauze on Daniel.

Daniel, Mason, Max. Carlos, whom they'd left alone and wounded in the dark of a demon-infested tunnel. Jude. Gan. Benedict, Cullen, and Cynna. The names of those he was responsible for, those who'd come with him to retrieve the children, tolled through his head, adding to the ache of uncertainty about Lily . . . who was alive, but so far away. What had happened to everyone?

Troubled out of the privacy of his pain, he opened his eyes. Directly overhead was rock, but he was not underground, he saw with relief. Beyond the rock was sky tinted lavender by approaching dusk. He turned his head and saw a campfire and a naked woman.

She squatted by the fire, her back to him. A black-and-silver braid hung down the lovely curve of her spine, tied at the end with a scrap of cloth. She was not young, though he saw muscle in her slim shoulders; her skin held hints of the crepe of age.

Perhaps she felt him looking. She looked over her shoulder and spoke crisply. "You're awake. Good."

He blinked. The naked woman was Madame Yu. This should, of course, have been obvious. His brain wasn't working well.

"You need water," she said, and set something down—a stick with what might have been half a rabbit impaled on it. The source of the cooking-meat smell.

Rule lacked the human prejudice against nudity, but for Madame Yu to be unclothed . . . that was just wrong. But she'd been a tiger before, hadn't she? She didn't have her clothes with her, hadn't been able to bring them along when they . . . came here? Were brought here? "Where?" he croaked, meaning *where are we*. "The others. What—"

"Water now, then explaining." She unscrewed the cap on a collapsible canteen. It looked familiar. Probably it was. Probably it was the one he'd stuck in his belt after emptying it back in Dis. "I will lift your head. Do not try to help."

He was thirsty. Horribly thirsty, a truth that had been

obscured until this moment by his other hurts. He pictured the water sliding down his throat only to spill out onto the ground when it reached the hole where his guts should be. "I'll leak."

"I have glued you back together. Gan held you in sleep with one of the charms while I worked." She slid one hand beneath his head and lifted.

She'd superglued his gut? Did she know what to attach to what?

"You will not leak. Drink." She held the plastic bladder to his lips, giving him little choice.

The water was warm and tasted of dirt. He gulped it down eagerly.

She moved the canteen away before he was ready. "Not too fast, I think."

"How bad . . . am I hurt?" Enough that a little talking was painful.

"Most of the damage was to the ropy part of your intestines. I removed the worst mess and glued together what remained. I trust your healing can regrow what was lost." The last sounded like a parent's no-nonsense instruction: *brush your teeth, wash your face, regrow your intestines.* "There was also damage to the . . . bah. What is the word? The knobby intestine. *Jiécháng.* It was not severed, however. I glued it closed. I did not see damage to your other organs, but I was in a hurry. We were in the open. Drink again."

He did. The knobby intestine . . . the colon? Rule knew a little anatomy, enough for the kind of rough battlefield medicine he might have to use on one of his men. By "the ropy part," she must mean his small intestine. It sounded like he would have to regrow a lot of that.

"You also have a deep wound in your thigh. I used the last of the glue there, after Gan and I moved you to this spot. I did not have enough glue to seal it fully, but it is not bleeding anymore." She withdrew the canteen again. "I have been using a healing cantrip on you, also, but I am no healer. I cannot tell how much it is helping."

He licked his lips, dizzy. "Gan?"

"She has gone to steal some things. She can go *dashtu* here, so this should not be difficult."

"Steal from . . . who?"

"There is a village."

"Humans?"

"Yes. This is not one of the sidhe realms."

Was that good or bad? He couldn't think. "How did we get here?"

"Gan brought me and also Cynna and Lily. You, I believe, were brought here by Lily."

He started to shake his head and winced. Definitely a concussion. "Lily can't do that. And she is . . . far away." Much too far for his piece of mind or for her to have somehow brought him here, wherever "here" was. Madame still hadn't answered that one. Maybe she didn't know, either.

"You did not arrive in the same place as Lily because you did not leave from the same place in Dis."

"Lily can't cross realms." Much less bring him along with her.

"*Tch.* If Gan did not bring you, then how did you get here? You must have been pulled here by the mate bond."

That . . . made sense, actually. It had happened before, back when Gan was working for the other side and had dragged Lily into Dis. Rule had been pulled along with her, pulled by the mate bond. And he vividly remembered the Lady's voice saying *steady* back in Dis. Even more vividly he remembered what had followed. The mate bond had vanished, then returned, supercharged. At least that's what Cullen had said—that Rule was suddenly glowing with twice as much magic as usual. "The Lady," he said slowly. "She arranged it."

"Very likely. You are muddled from your wounds. This is not surprising. You were nearly dead. Is your memory bad?"

"I remember most of it. I don't remember receiving this." His hand lifted two inches to indicate his stomach. The tiny effort exhausted him.

"I think Xitil did that, but I was busy and did not see it happen. Do you remember Xitil?"

"Yes." A mountain of pink flesh towering over him. A band of blue eyes circling a round head. A mad giggle.

"Do you also remember that the children were not in the audience hall, as we had thought?"

He remembered the doppelgänger that he'd thought was his son and how it had felt to watch it *melt*. "He . . . they . . . the children must be in the cells . . ." He ran out of breath and drew in air slowly. Carefully. There were cells off the audience hall where they'd fought demons, a demon prince, and a dragon spawn. He'd seen Xitil emerge from one. "Cells sealed by rock."

"Not fully rock. When the false Toby melted, Gan thought to look for the children with her *üther* sense. It is hard to hide *üther* from one who can perceive it. Rock will block this perception, but Gan tells me the cells were sealed with something like the window we stepped through—ah, but you did not see the window. You may think of it as part-time rock. Part of the time it is rock, part of the time it is not. Gan discovered that, to her *üther* sense, this part-time rock flickers. When it does, she can perceive beyond it. She did not notice this earlier because the flicker does not happen regularly. Also, she was not looking in the right way." Madame shook her head, disapproval blending with forgiveness. "She is very young."

Rule had the impression the former demon was at least twice his age. But as an ensouled being . . . yes, in that sense Gan was very young. "The children? She found them?"

"The cells were empty."

All the air left the world. For long, terrible seconds Rule was pinned in a dark, airless void. Then his chest remembered its job and lifted, letting in air and sending pain ribboning through his gut.

"This does not mean they are dead," Madame informed him sternly. "You are not to think so. It is very likely they were taken through a gate. Drink again."

He let her lift his head again—hell, he probably couldn't have stopped her. But he wanted answers, not water. "Why likely?"

"There was a gate, although it was closed when we arrived. I perceived this. So did Gan. To her, gates feel like a wind that bubbles instead of blowing. This has little meaning to me, but she is very firm about it. Drink," she repeated, and this time gave him no choice but to swallow or let her dribble water over his closed mouth. She had pity on him, though, and continued talking as she administered measured sips. "Gan found this closed gate when she came out into the audience hall. She could tell what realm the gate opened onto. It was, she says, very bubbly. To her, this indicated it had been used very recently." She moved the canteen away slightly, letting him pause in gulping down the water. "She thinks this means the children were brought here through the gate. I think this, also."

His heart thudded sharply. "They're here?"

"Not yet. Drink. I will explain." She held the canteen to his lips again. "When Gan discovered the gate, she believed we would all be killed. I do not know that she was wrong; matters were not going well. Lily had told her she was not to cross until Benedict told her to, but Benedict was unconscious. She believed this made it her decision.

"She wished to live. She wished also for her friends to live. Cynna was closest, so first she brought Cynna here. She returned to the audience hall and grabbed Lily and crossed with her—dragging you along, as I said, to this realm, although not to the same part of it. When Gan came back the last time, she grabbed me. I do not believe she considers me a friend, but I was closest. She could not bring the others because she cannot return to the audience hall at any of the critical moments. She is already in all the other times she might cross to from here."

He took a last swallow and turned his head so he could speak. "That makes no sense."

"Obviously there cannot be two of her in Dis at the same instant. You have drunk it all? Good." She took the canteen away.

"How could there be two of her at the same time?"

Grandmother gave that disapproving *tch* again. "I have just said that could not be. You are not thinking well."

"Tired."

"Too much talking. Rest. I will get more water." She stood.

Madame looked even more naked when standing, though her dignity was unimpaired by the lack of clothing, just as her spine was unaffected by the tiredness he could see in her face.

"Wait. You said . . . the children are not here yet."

"Ah. Yes. Do you remember that many realms do not match with each other in time, even when they touch in place? Time is crooked between Dis and this place. This let Gan choose, a little, what time she crossed to. She is not sure what times she brought everyone to, but she is sure we all arrived here well before we left Dis."

He was too exhausted and hurting to make much sense of

that, but he thought he got the important part. The children
weren't here yet. They had some time. "How long?"

"How long until they arrive? One or two weeks. She is not
sure. They will not arrive where we are, however."

"How . . . d'you know?"

"Gan says the gate the children were taken through did not
lead to this location. She thinks she delivered Cynna near that
gate, and that she brought Lily somewhere near Cynna. But
not us. This is her area of expertise. I accept her opinion."

A gate. That stirred another memory. "Reno. Where is
Reno?"

"The question is when, not where. Reno left for this realm,
but he made a gate from the construct to do so. Gates are not like
crossing the way Gan does. They synchronize the time between
realms. Reno will arrive here at the same time he left Dis."

It was too much to get his tired mind around. His eyes were
trying to close. "Not . . . now. He will arrive . . . later. And
the children. Later." Rule was a week or two in the past. Toby
hadn't been kidnapped yet. A terrible tension eased. For now,
Toby was okay.

"Yes. I will get water now. This will take ten or twenty
minutes. There is a seep. It is not far, but it is necessary to
be cautious here when crossing open ground."

"Why?" he asked. Then, more sensibly—for there were
many reasons the open might be dangerous—he asked once
more, "Where are we?"

"*Lóng Jia.*" Her black eyes were remote, as if she looked
out on some private vista, one that held great meaning. Then
her gaze sharpened and flicked to him. "In English, you would
call it Dragonhome."

THREE

"**IT'S** *what?*" Lily stared at her friend, incredulous.

"The place dragons come from. Their home realm." Cynna leaned her head against the wall behind her and closed her eyes. "That's what they tell me anyway. The ones who speak English, that is, which is a really small group. Two, I think. Though the guards know a couple words—'come' and 'stay.'"

Alice Báitóu, aka Alice Whitehead, had been right. The cell was primitive. Not some horrible, slimy dungeon, however. They were on the second floor of one of the stone buildings she'd seen—the one called the Justice Court. They even had a window slit in the stone exterior wall to let in air and light, though that light was dimming now. It was late in the day, edging into evening.

But the cell was small for one person, seriously cramped for two, and unfurnished save for two buckets—one with a lid that she bet was their toilet; one with a tin cup for drinking.

In addition to the buckets, there were three paperback books—*A Tale of Two Cities*, *Huckleberry Finn*, and *The Norton Anthology of Poetry*. There was also a sleeping mat. Cynna was sitting on it. She was barefoot and wore dull black pants a lot like those the short warriors had worn. They were too short for her. Her mud brown top, on the other hand, was too large, but a tie at the neck kept it from slipping off her shoulders.

Her face was pale beneath the ink. She seemed thinner, as if she'd lost weight in the time they'd spent in Dis. Her right arm was in a sling. It had been splinted.

She had not been happy to see Lily, judging by her reaction when the guards delivered Lily to the small cell. "Oh, shit" wasn't her usual greeting. Lily had said something about Cynna not being very glad to see her here, wherever "here" was. And at last got an answer to that question.

"I saw a dragon in the sky, but I never thought—it didn't occur to me—" Lily stopped before she said something about Reno. She didn't think their captors knew about the green dragon, and she wanted to keep it that way. "This is the dragons' home realm?"

"Yeah. Sit down," Cynna said. "I'll tell you what I know. You're hurt?"

"Sprained ankle. I banged my head, too, but it isn't serious. Is your arm broken?" Lily limped the few feet between the door and Cynna's mat and lowered herself to the floor . . . the scrubbed wooden floor. The cell might be primitive, but it was cleaner than she was.

Cynna nodded without opening her eyes. "You ever had a broken bone?"

"Not since I was five. Broke my wrist when a tree ejected me."

"This is my first. Everything about it is deeply damn annoying." Cynna drew a shaky breath and opened her eyes. "Let me get through this, then you can ask questions. I know you'll have questions." The ghost of a smile touched her lips, then vanished. "They've been watching for you because I told them you might show up."

Lily nodded. "I thought you might have."

Cynna stared. "That's it? That's all you're going to say?"

"They were clearly expecting me. That might be accounted for by some kind of magical alert, but it seemed likely they'd been watching specifically for me—maybe through magic, maybe just with eyes on the ground. They knew who I was, though, so it was *me* they were watching for, not just random intruders. And they didn't ask the questions they should have. What about Rule? Cullen? The others?"

"What?"

Cynna seemed too staggered to think. More gently Lily said, "Did you tell them about the others in our party?"

"I . . . in a general way. You were the only one I figured might make it here, though."

"You had a reason to tell them."

"You could say that." Cynna's face twisted, a swift, unhappy clenching of mouth and jaw. "They killed a little boy. Broke his neck. I didn't answer fast enough, and one of them snapped his neck. I heard it break. He went all floppy and . . ." She shuddered. "Hell. I was going to tell this in order."

Lily leaned forward and grabbed Cynna's good hand—the one not connected to a broken arm—and squeezed. "Those sons of bitches. They threatened to hurt him if you didn't answer?"

Cynna's fingers tightened on Lily's. "They had a soldier grab three kids off the street. Zhu Kongqi—he speaks English—"

"I met him."

"He asked the questions, but it was Dick Boy . . . his name is really Dìqiú, which sounds like 'dickah,' not 'dick boy'—"

It did the way Cynna said it anyway.

"—but I like Dick Boy better, so that's what I call him. He's the one who killed the boy. I didn't answer fast enough, and he just . . . he's like a living lie detector. It's not mind magic—more like the kind of physical sensing a healer does, I think. Kongqi told me they'd kill the kids if I didn't cooperate, then he asked how I got here. I hesitated, trying to work out a way to tell the truth without giving them everything, but . . . but I didn't answer fast enough. Dick Boy waited maybe five seconds. He didn't give a warning, he just—" She stopped suddenly, squeezing her eyes closed.

"You're wrecked."

"I fucking am." Tears leaked from beneath those tight-shut eyelids. "He looked about four years old. Maybe I'm wrong about that. Maybe he was older. Everyone here is short, so he might've been older. Not that that would make it any better, but he was so damn little . . . the other two are still alive. At least I think they are. A girl and another boy. I think the second boy was the little boy's big brother. He cried and cried, but so quietly . . . I keep thinking about how I'm going to kill them. The two dragon spawn, but especially Dick Boy. I think about it a lot."

Lily didn't know how to respond. After a long moment she said, "Just before my ninth birthday, a pedophile snatched me and a friend. Ginger Harris's sister, actually. Her name was Sarah. He raped and killed Sarah in front of me. She was screaming and crying and he wanted her to be quiet, so he squeezed her throat while he . . . it surprised him when he realized she was dead." She'd never forget the look on his face. Startled, then embarrassed, like a kid who'd knocked over his milk glass and made a mess. "The cops came before he could do it to me. For a long time I thought about ways to kill him. It comforted me." Her mouth twisted. "Didn't comfort my parents."

Cynna glanced at her once, then away. "I didn't know about that."

"I don't talk about it." She hadn't talked to the therapist her folks sent her to. The only words that had made sense to her at the time had been, "I want to kill him," and she'd seen how that affected the adults around her. Most of them anyway. "Grandmother understood. She helped. She taught me about gardening."

"Gardening."

The disbelief in Cynna's voice almost made Lily smile. "When I told Grandmother I wanted to kill the monster, she patted my hand and said that of course I did, but I could not." Not that it was wrong or unsafe or illegal or that she should not think such things, but that she could not do it. She remembered the relief she'd felt. At last, a sensible response. "I could, however, kill all the grass and weeds I wanted, and she showed me where. That first year, I killed the hell out of a lot of Bermuda grass. I planted things, too. Planting stuff, that's leaning into the future." She'd needed both aspects of gardening—the vegetative murder and the leaning forward.

Cynna wore an odd expression. Not quite a smile, but

something more open, more like her usual self. A bit bemused maybe. "No offense, but I'd rather kill the spawn than a bunch of grass."

"You're not eight years old. You might be able to do it. Or you might get yourself killed trying, and we're going to need you, so don't make it your top priority, okay?"

"No." Cynna drew a deep, shaky breath. "No, my priority is Ryder. Ryder and the rest of the kids. But killing Dick Boy is pretty high on the list. If I get a chance . . ." She let go of Lily's hand and shook her head, but not as if denying something. More like the way a dog shakes after getting wet. "I didn't intend to fall apart on you. I might do it again, though. I'm not exactly at my best."

"I was told the children weren't here."

"No. Not yet." But Cynna put a finger to her lips.

In the silence, Lily heard the guards on the other side of their door. It was heavy wood with a tiny window not much bigger than a peephole. The hinges were iron, but there was no latch, the door being held in place by a wooden bar on the other side. Crude but effective. On the other side of that door, dice rattled on the wooden floor. One man exclaimed. Another complained about his ill luck.

She understood Cynna's caution. If they could hear the guards, the guards could hear them. Good thing they had another option.

Lily gave the glowy stuff in her middle a nudge and let it unfurl.

Cynna had some kind of mental shield, but not the kind that blocked mindspeech. To her mindsense, Cynna's mind was like a fuzzy, glowing kiwi. The green was unusual for a human, that being the color she associated with lupi minds. Lily thought it had something to do with Cynna being Lady-touched, Rhej to the Nokolai Clan. But it might have meant something else.

The fuzziness meant that Lily could mindspeak her. To do that, she had to touch a mind with a probe, then send pulses along the probe that corresponded with what she wanted to say. Those pulses sank into minds she perceived as having texture, but slid off the slick ones. She didn't know if the pulses carried her actual words or their meanings; people "heard" her as if she was speaking English, but maybe someone like Li Po would "hear" her in Chinese. There was a lot she hadn't had a chance to learn about her new ability before the world started blowing up around them.

Regardless of the content, though, she had to mouth words to create the pulses. At first she'd had to speak out loud, but she'd improved enough that mouthing them silently worked now. *Do you think the guards know more English than they're admitting?*

Cynna's eyes widened in what looked like relief. All Lily got back from her, though, was gibberish that reminded her of a baby's babble, word-like sounds without meaning. *That didn't work*, she sent. *Try mouthing the words the way I am.*

Possibly, Cynna mouthed. *Or they might [babble] translation device like they use in Edge.*

Lily's eyebrows went up. *Are these people trading with Edge?*

[babble] possible.

They could come back to that later, Lily decided. *What about the children?*

They haven't left Dis yet. They [babble-babble] time not congruous.

Lily's eyes widened. *What?*

The time here is earlier than when we left Dis. I don't know [babble] Sam said the [babble] not more than two weeks. Might be less.

You think it might be as much as two weeks earlier here? Lily repeated to make sure she understood—though that was not the right word. She didn't understand this at all.

It's not more than two weeks anyway. Technical reasons for that limit. Lily, we need to talk out loud some so [babble] suspicious.

Lily rubbed her head, hoping to rub some sense into it. But yeah, it made sense that they shouldn't just sit in silence. They didn't want anyone guessing they could communicate this way. "So how did you get captured?"

Cynna grimaced and answered out loud. "Easily. I arrived about fifteen feet in the air and fell. Fifteen feet might not seem like much, but I fell on . . . did you see any of Lang Xin? The town outside the compound?"

"Part of it."

"You maybe noticed that they like to build with stone. I smashed into a stone wall. I don't know if I broke my arm then or when I hit the ground because I'd passed out by then. Made it really easy for them to capture me."

"You hit your head?"

She shook her head. "I might have blacked out from pain, but I suspect it was from the crossing."

"Why would crossing make you black out?"

"When you cross to a realm with a major time incongruence, that can make you disoriented enough to pass out."

Lily frowned and spoke slowly. "I was unconscious when I first arrived. But I'd hit my head and thought that was why . . ." Her voice drifted off as the obvious rose up and smacked her. "You didn't break your arm today. You didn't arrive when I did, not even close. How long have you been here?"

"Six days."

Six days. Six days as a prisoner, with a broken arm, captors who didn't speak her language, and no way of knowing if anyone else had lived through the battle in the audience chamber. Six more days without her daughter, her baby. Six days alone in this small cell after watching the dragon spawn break a four-year-old boy's neck. "Shit."

"Pretty much, yeah. Do you . . . can you tell me anything about what happened after I left our little hell party?"

"They were all alive when I left." At least she thought so. Things had been pretty confusing . . . but why add to Cynna's burden with doubts? "But I think that wasn't very long after you left. Maybe five or ten minutes . . . shit. You've been here six days. Does that mean time passes here differently? Like a day here for every minute there?"

"I don't think it's that straightforward. I don't know for sure—this shit is way above my pay grade—but I think the time difference is because of something Gan did when she brought us. But it might be just that you and I crossed from different spots. Not that I understand how that works, mind— how spots ten feet away from each other in one realm can be linked to spots that are separated by days as well as miles in another—but then, I don't understand time. I know it's possible, though. At least, it is when the realms aren't time-congruent."

Was it her aching head that made it hard to follow what Cynna said, or was it the subject matter? Lily abandoned time incongruence for now. "They know about Gan?"

"Yeah. She fell with me—not onto the wall, lucky her, but I know she came through with me. People saw her before she vanished. Crossed back to Dis, I guess. I had to tell Kongqi about her." But Cynna shook her head as she said that.

Their captors knew about Gan—but not everything about her? Clearly they needed to get their stories straight. Lily's mindsense had coiled up in her gut again when she stopped paying attention to it. She gave it a nudge. *What do our captors not know about Gan?*

Cynna's mouth moved silently. *They know what Gan looks like and [babble] from Edge, that she's a crosser, and that dragons arranged for her to come with us.*

Mostly clear. Cynna was getting better at this. *They don't know that she used to be a demon? That she's a friend? That she's the Edge Chancellor?*

A head shake from Cynna.

Good. That's good. What about Reno? Do they know about him?

No.

That was really good news. *Have you heard from him?*

No, but he's probably not here yet. Then, out loud: "There's a lot I need to tell you. I've learned stuff about this place, mostly from Alice, so . . . shit. Do you know about Alice?"

"I met her," Lily said dryly. "She showed up almost as soon as I arrived."

"And you know she's—"

"Helen Whitehead's twin sister. Yes."

"She's some kind of bigwig here. I haven't figured out what her role is exactly, but she's got pull with the spawn so she must be useful to them. And she, uh—I'm her prisoner. Once the spawn finished questioning me, they gave me to her. She wants me to teach the peasants here more about how to use magic."

Lily was silent, trying to stretch her view of that cold, color-less woman to encompass . . . what? Missionary? Do-gooder? "She wants to educate the peasants?"

"I know. Weird, huh? But she's got a list of the kind of spells she wants them to learn. Practical stuff like purifying water and spells that promote healing. Anti-vermin spells—I already traded her one of those, one for fleas. No fire spells, though. For some reason that's forbidden." She huffed. "I've let myself get distracted again. I've told you two of the three things I wanted to be sure to say right away, in case they in-terrupt us. Here's the third." With that, she lifted the hem of her top.

For a second Lily was too startled at having Cynna flash her boobs to notice the golden cobweb clinging to her skin over her heart. It was round, about six inches across, and seemed to be made of very fine gold wire. "What in the hell is that?"

"They call it a magic cage. It traps my power. I can't do any magic that reaches beyond my skin. And it won't come off." As Cynna wrapped her top around herself again, her mouth kept moving, but silently.

Lily had stopped paying attention to her mindsense, so she had to nudge it out again. *Repeat, please. I wasn't "listening."*

I think that together we can blow this thing's circuits, but what I have in mind is kind of dangerous. Don't want to try until we're ready to act.

When the children get here. Yes. Lily's hands fisted. *But we'll need a way back. Can you make a gate?* Surely the an-swer was yes. Cynna had the memories and she'd participated in a gate-building once—and dammit, they had to get the chil-dren out of here, once they arrived. They had to go home.

But Cynna was shaking her head. *Not alone. Even gnomes don't try to build a gate alone, and they know what they're doing. Maybe Reno can help me when he gets here.* She switched back to speaking out loud. "I think the magic cage is sidhe work. That's based on what I can see of the runes incorporated in the web. Wherever it came from, though, it's old and it's sophisticated. It draws power from me—uses my own magic to block my magic, which is a real pisser. When I try to use magic, I get dizzy. If I keep trying, I pass out."

Lily frowned. "So does it really block your magic? Or does it just react to an attempt to use it by knocking you out?"

"The first, I think. Far as I can tell—and damn, but I wish I had Cullen's vision!—it's like a magic vacuum. It sucks up my magic, and not just the amount I'm trying to use, either. It doesn't matter if I'm trying to do a Find, throw a mage light, or cast a powerful spell. Same result. I get dizzy almost instantly, the depleted kind of dizzy. If I keep trying anyway, in a few seconds I pass out."

"Nasty."

"Yeah."

"Tell me about this place. What have you learned?"

"A lot. Um . . . first thing you should know is that this is a high-magic realm."

"I thought it might be. Lots of sorcéri." Though she hadn't had any brush against her since being brought inside . . . maybe the stone walls blocked them?

Cynna nodded. "It's like Edge in some ways. The magic isn't dangerously high everywhere, but there are large areas humans stay away from. Unlike Edge, though, there isn't a single band of territory that's safe, but a patchwork of safe and not-safe. Mostly people have settled near moving water. That has to do with the way Water holds on to magic—better than Air, but it doesn't grip as hard as Earth does. And Fire, of course, doesn't hold on to magic at all. Fire magic is really misnamed. When that type of magic is released suddenly, you get fire, but calling it "fire" is like calling cows "milk" because you get milk from them. The product isn't the same as . . . damn." She rubbed her face wearily. "I'm going all Cullen on you. Explaining too much. Sorry. It's just so damn good to have someone to talk to."

Every time Cynna spoke Cullen's name, Lily felt a little stab of hurt. *He's not dead*, she told herself. "I know what you mean. When I learned you were here, I was glad. Then guilty because I was glad."

"Yeah." Cynna sighed. "Yeah, it's like that. I'm glad you're here. Maybe I shouldn't be, but right now I don't care about 'should,' I just . . . part of me hoped Gan would bring Cullen, but that's stupid. If they'd captured him, they'd have killed him right away. A sorcerer is too dangerous to keep around."

It sounded like Cynna was sure Cullen had been alive to be captured. Either that, or she was in denial. Lily decided she didn't care which it was. She saw a lot of value in denial herself right now. She sent a probe out again. *You knew Gan would bring someone else, but you didn't know who?*

We didn't have a chance to chat. She grabbed me and zap—we were here. And falling. Cynna rubbed her arm as if remembering the result of that fall. "Where was I before I wandered off-topic?"

"This is a high-magic realm. People settle near water, where the ambient magic isn't as high. Though I thought the ocean raised ambient magic levels, not lowered them."

"They settle near running water, not the ocean. The ocean's where magic gets dumped when the rivers empty into it. Big lakes can be a problem, too, though that probably isn't the case in Lang Xin because of the spawn. Who we are not supposed to call spawn. I should warn you about that. They like to be called Zhu in the singular, Zhuren in the plural, and if you forget, they'll hurt you. But like dragons, they're sponges, able to soak up a lot of magic."

"Is everyone here human? Except the spawn, I mean. And are they all Chinese?"

"Well, there aren't any lupi." Cynna smirked briefly. "According to Alice—almost all of this is from her, so grain-of-salt it—China's the only part of Earth that abuts this realm in a way that causes fall-throughs. Beings from other realms do turn up, but they don't have descendants. Or haven't so far. Living in a high-magic realm inhibits fertility, and most races are nowhere near as fertile as humans. Of course, most of the races from sidhe realms can interbreed with humans, but there's a big taboo about that here. Far as they're concerned, all nonhumans are demons."

"Chinese folklore is full of beings that get called 'demon' in English," Lily said absently, "but they aren't what we mean by the term. What about real demons? The ones from Dis?"

"Oh, they fall through sometimes, but they're usually killed pretty quickly."

Lily's eyebrows lifted. "Demons are hard to kill. These people do it with, what—bows and arrows? Swords?"

"Humans aren't the only ones doing the killing."

"The spawn?"

"Sometimes, I guess, but there are a lot of scary predators here. Top of the list are the dragons, but according to Alice there are plenty of other big, bad beasties, though we don't have to worry because Lang Xin is warded."

"Warded, hmm? The whole city? By the spawn?"

"Yes, yes, and I think so."

"Are there a lot of . . ." A sudden increase in the chatter on the other side of the cell door made Lily pause and look that way, as if she might be able to see through the solid wood if she just tried.

"Shift change," Cynna said—but she was looking at one of the walls, not the door. After a moment Lily realized she was checking the angle of the sunlight streaming in through their window slit. "Or maybe not. I think it's too early for that, but telling time by the sun is not my thing. Can you understand them?"

"Not when they're all talking at once like this. I've never heard this dialect before, and it—" She broke off at the barked command from right outside their door. "I understood that. We're to get away from the door." Since they were already as far from it as was possible in the tiny cell, she didn't move.

An eye peered in the tiny window, then retreated. There was a scraping sound—the bar being lifted—then the door opened.

It was the guard with the blue breastplate or cuirass or whatever. He'd brought a couple friends along—men who held cocked bows, the arrows pointing straight at Lily. "See-nah Wee-vah stay," he ordered. "Li-li Yu come."

"They're taking you more seriously than they do me," Cynna observed. "When they come to get me, they don't use drawn bows. My broken arm robs me of that dangerous edge, I guess."

Lily rose slowly to her feet. "They do come for you sometimes, though?"

"Yeah, sometimes Alice sends for me. Also I'm taken out of the cell every morning so they can scrub the cell and I can scrub myself. They're big on cleanliness."

"It's not morning." Which meant this was probably interrogation time.

"Come!" Blue-Armor repeated.

Lily summoned her Grandmother imitation. She stared at him haughtily and spoke slowly, using her best Mandarin . . . and sending her mindsense out. "I come, but how do I address you, honorable sir?"

To her amazement, he offered her a short, stiff bow. "This one is Fang Ye Lì, a Fist Second of the Zhuren. You may address me as Fist Second."

The word he used—*quán*—was pronounced differently in Mandarin, but this time Lily knew it meant "fist" because she heard him in her head, too. In English. Pleased, she limped out of the cell as if this were all her own idea.

FOUR

～

ON the other side of the cell door was a large open area defined by three interior walls that were studded with barred doors. Cells, in other words. No windows here; mage lights floated near the ceiling. The fourth side held the stairs that seemed to be the only way in or out, shelves crammed with an interesting miscellany of items, and what Lily thought of as a holding cell that projected out into the room. It had bamboo bars instead of walls and was a lot bigger than her cell. Inside it, four men sat or lay prone in attitudes of boredom or despair.

In the middle of the open area was a big, scuffed table and several wooden stools. She'd stood next to that table when they searched her before sending her into the cell, leaving her pockets empty even of lint. For some reason, though, they hadn't taken her rings.

Her wedding ring still circled the third finger on her left hand. The ring that held the toltoi rested on the matching finger on her right hand. She ran her thumb over that one now, wondering why. Maybe they thought it was wrong to take a prisoner's jewelry? She tried to remember if Cynna still had her wedding band . . . yes. She'd felt it when she'd squeezed her friend's hand.

But they'd left Lily the toltoi, too.

She'd been given the little charm when she was ritually made part of Nokolai Clan. The toltoi wasn't magic. It had something, yes, but not magic. *Arguai*, the sidhe called it. Spirit, according to others. Even Sam said he didn't understand spirit, so maybe the spawn couldn't sense it, didn't know there was anything to the ring but a pretty design.

Pity she didn't know how to use it. Sure, it might have helped her mindspeak Rule if he'd been a few hundred miles closer, but he wasn't.

The man who'd summoned her from her cell stood watching her. Fang Ye Lì suited his name—his surname anyway. One of the meanings for Fang was "square," and he was built like a block, husky and squared-off at every angle. His eyebrows were thick, and a drooping mustache framed a mouth too small for that lantern jaw. No beard. And that blue armor . . . as she got her first good look at it, she blinked in surprise.

Could that be what it looked like? "I greet you, Fist Second. Where are we going?"

"We go first to the women's bathhouse."

She lifted her brows. "That will be pleasant."

His cheeks darkened—with embarrassment or anger? In some men, they looked much the same. "We are not barbarians. Please hold out your hands."

She did, positioning herself so she could see the three walls with barred doors. Five, six, seven . . .

"It is not one of the better bathhouses," he said stiffly as he gripped her hands, began wrapping her wrists with rope . . . and gave her a surprise. The Fist Second had an Earth Gift. A pretty strong one. "It is used by women who work in the compound. They, ah, they are not of high status. I have sent for a proper attendant, however, and the bathhouse will be reserved for your use."

Lily shrugged, copying the way Grandmother responded sometimes to minor offenses from those who clearly did not know better, and decided where she wanted to fit in this man's worldview. "I understand that women here are not allowed into the warrior caste. It is not important. I know what I am."

His eyebrows shot up. "You claim to be a warrior?"

Grandmother, she decided, would not bother to respond to such foolishness. So she didn't. "Your armor intrigues me. Can it be made from dragon scales?"

His chest didn't quite puff out, but his shoulders grew even more square. "It is. My grandfather was among those who killed the Great Blue in the third generation."

"Impressive," she said, and meant it. "If you have time later, I would enjoy hearing that story. Where else do we go? You said the bathhouse was first."

"To Zhu Kongqi. There is a rickshaw waiting outside."

The phrase he used for "rickshaw," translated literally, was "wheeled reed packet." At least, that's what it would mean in Mandarin. But because she was picking up the meaning with her mindsense, she knew what he meant. What was interesting, though, was that Fang didn't seem to have trouble understanding her Mandarin. He should have. Even native Mandarin speakers sometimes did. Her accent sucked. "Why does he want me?"

"I do not know. He allows you time to bathe first. You are able to walk? To descend the stairs?"

"Certainly." Warriors didn't show pain, so she went down the stone stairs as if her ankle wasn't screaming at her to *cut that out*. Good thing it was only one flight.

The sun was down, but not out. If she'd been home, she would have said it was seven thirty or eight on a summer evening. The temperature suggested it might be summer here, too. Lily settled into the rickshaw—"wheeled reed packet" was a good description—and asked about the other cells and their occupants.

"Currently," the Fist Second told her, "we are holding thirty-one violators of heavenly law."

She'd counted twenty-five barred doors. That included the cell allotted to her and Cynna. Thirty-one violators of heavenly law plus her and Cynna—assuming the two of them weren't part of Fang's count—minus the four men in that holding cell equaled twenty-nine prisoners behind those twenty-five barred doors. They were full up. "I don't think I've violated any laws, heavenly or otherwise."

Fang Ye Lì agreed that probably she had not, but of course

if one of the Zhuren wished for her to be locked up, then she must be.

As she seated herself in the rickshaw, she considered the numbers. Some of the other prisoners must be doubled up, but they could still have split up her and Cynna easily enough by putting her in with someone else. They hadn't. Maybe they were just really considerate and wanted her to be with her buddy. Or maybe they wanted her and Cynna together so they'd talk. Maybe, like Cynna thought, one or more of the guards knew more English than they were admitting.

The rickshaw's wooden wheels were noisy on the cobbled path and the ride was bumpy. Turned out the women's bath-house was on the other side of the compound, and they'd be going the long way, following the paths rather than cutting directly across. That was okay. It gave her time to ask questions.

By listening to Fang's mind as well as his speech, Lily understood everything he said when he was addressing her. When he spoke to someone else, the flow of mental speech cut off. She didn't learn what the Frisbee-topped tower in the center of the courtyard was, save that it was "of the Zhuren," but the oversized gazebo was a combination of market and check-in point. Everyone who visited the city had to register their presence and the reason for their visit. Did Lang Xin have many visitors? Yes, for was it not the bright heart of the world? And of course all who visited came to Xīnzàng de Jiā—literally, Heart's Home, which seemed to mean the courtyard and all the governmental buildings.

More to the point as far as Fang was concerned, the law was born in Lang Xin and flowed outward like a heart pumping blood. And the law was his passion.

There were two levels of law: village law and heavenly law. Village law varied, being enacted and administered in the various villages. Heavenly law came from the spawn. Magistrates were appointed by the Zhuren and sent to the larger towns, where they were responsible for approving village law and arresting those believed to have broken heavenly law. Anyone accused of violating heavenly law was brought to the Court of Heavenly Justice for trial, hence the cells on the second floor.

The spawn rotated all of the key administrative positions

among themselves, including that of judge—a position they called Father of Law. Some of them weren't very keen about that particular duty. Not that the Fist Second put it that way, but that's what he meant. Depending on which of the spawn was serving as Father of Law, months might go by before someone was brought to trial. The prisoners probably didn't mind the delay. Almost everyone accused of breaking heavenly law was found guilty. Guilty meant dead.

"What is heavenly law? Can you give me examples? I would not wish to break it out of ignorance."

"Paying the annual tax is first. Most of our prisoners are guilty of failure to pay, but we do have one man accused of killing a prostitute who displeased him. She was pregnant."

"Murder is against heavenly law?"

"Murder in general is a matter of village law, but it is an offense against the Zhuren to cause the death of a pregnant woman or an unweaned babe. So, too, is lying to the magistrates. Rebelliousness. Failure to present deformed infants. Failure to educate—"

"Your pardon, Fist Second, but what was that one about deformed infants?"

"Infants born with visible deformities must be presented to the magistrate, who will determine if they should be killed immediately or allowed to live until their third birthday, when they will be evaluated more fully. This is an important law." He spoke sternly, as if he expected argument. "Many deformities do not prevent a person from contributing."

"Hmm." High-magic realms produced more mutations. Deformities might be common here—and something to hide, out of shame? Or something to be killed, out of fear. "What about failure to educate?"

"You needn't worry about breaking that law," he said as if making a mild joke. "It applies to village elders or councils, not individuals. Children must be taught courtesy, after all, as well as history and heavenly law. We have arrived."

The building in front of Lily was small, stone, single-story. The roof was thatch. A woman stood outside, bowing as they came to a stop. She was shorter than Lily by a good four inches and looked like a strong breeze would blow her away. She wore what Lily thought of as traditional Chinese women's garb: a wraparound top with a long skirt sashed high. Top and skirt were a light blue linen with dark blue bindings on the sleeves and lapels. No shoes, Lily saw, but she wore a straw hat shaped like a flattened pyramid that shaded her face . . . her white, wrinkled, Chinese face. White as in lacking pigment entirely. Her eyes were so pale a blue that the irises almost vanished. Her eyebrows, too, were all but invisible.

She was an albino. A true albino, not an imitation like Alice Báitóu. A world worried about mutations might not be kind to albinos.

To Lily's surprise, the Fist Second ordered one of his guards to remove the rope binding her wrists. As the guard did that, Fang looked at her. "We will await you here, by the door. Understand that it will not help you to harm the attendant or attempt to take her hostage. We would regret her death, but it would be laid on your account, not ours."

The attendant bowed to Lily and whispered that she was honored to serve the Zhuren's . . . what? Lily didn't recognize the word she used and her mindspeech wasn't as clear as Fang Ye Lì's. Given how soft her voice was, maybe she didn't really want to be heard. Was this tiny woman supposed to guard Lily inside the bathhouse? Lily tried to picture her as some kind of aging ninja, capable of guarding dangerous out-realm prisoners. She failed.

Why was she being treated to a bath anyway? Cynna had said their captors were clean freaks, but there were easier ways to make sure prisoners didn't offend their captors' noses. Lily shook her head at all the unanswered questions and followed the tiny woman inside.

It was a single room, dim and hot and humid. She caught a faint whiff of sulfur in the heavy air. Heat, humidity, and that sulfuric tang came from the pool that occupied much of the space. A natural hot spring, Lily thought, and wondered if hot springs were common here. Not that she knew what it would mean if they were. She had the vague notion that hot springs were associated with seismically active areas, but that might be wrong.

Low wooden stools were placed around the pool. The attendant pushed her hat back to dangle from its cord, revealing hair the color of sun-bleached winter grass. She bowed and whispered that perhaps the honored *lái* would remove her clothes and sit?

Ah—that was the word she'd used before: *lái*. This time Lily caught the meaning that went with it—"new arrival." A term for fall-throughs, maybe? "Tell me your name first, please."

"This lowly one is called Ah Hai."

Surnames came first here, as they did in China. Lily commented that "Ah" was not a surname where she came from.

"I have no family name, honored *lái*."

The absence of a family name suggested a tragic lack of standing—bastardy, maybe? Or slavery? Did her bare feet betoken her lowly status? They'd taken Cynna's shoes away. What did that mean here? Lily wanted to ask, but she needed this woman to feel comfortable answering questions, so she turned the conversation to a less fraught topic—namely, how this bath was supposed to proceed.

Ah Hai was comfortable talking about her area of expertise, and her mindspeech became more intelligible. The basic procedure sounded similar to the way brownies bathed, a communal affair in which you soaped and rinsed off before you got into the hot water to soak. Or to play, if you were a brownie. This bathhouse was usually used by female servants who worked in the compound. Servants didn't rate a bathing attendant, so Fang had requisitioned Ah Hai, who worked at an upper-class bathhouse in town.

Lily was a prisoner, yet Fang had gone to some trouble to obtain a temporary servant for her. That had to be a status thing. But why? What about Lily made her status high enough that she was supposed to have a bathing attendant?

Ah Hai was happy to show Lily the things she'd brought for Lily's comfort that weren't available at a servants' bathhouse: soft, scented soap; heavy linen toweling; hair oil; three kinds of lotion and two salves. Also a small bamboo flute.

It seemed that Lily was receiving the deluxe treatment. This made her deeply suspicious, but she couldn't see that it would make any difference for her to refuse the attendant's services. They needed her alive to give to the G.B., right? Anything else they might do . . . well, they could do it whether or not she cooperated with her bath. Might as well go along and see what happened. She wasn't crazy about getting scrubbed by someone other than Rule, but he was so damnably far away . . . injured? Alone? Still in Dis? She hated that idea, but it might explain why he felt so distant.

No, that was wrong. If it was a week earlier here than it had been when she left Dis, he wouldn't be in Dis yet. He wouldn't even be in California. A week ago they'd still been at Leidolf Clanhome in North Carolina. A week ago, Toby had been at Nokolai Clanhome with his grandfather. He hadn't been kidnapped yet.

She went very still at the thought, possibilities and improbabilities tumbling through her head. Finally she quit trying to sort them out and sat on one of the low stools to pull off her boots. They laced up the front like combat boots, so she expected them to come off okay in spite of her ankle, which had to be swollen. The first one did; the second did not.

She persevered and ended up with a badly throbbing ankle, two grimy socks, and two bare feet. The blasted ankle would probably swell up even more now. She sighed, stood, and began stripping. When she was naked and uncomfortable about it, Ah Hai snatched the pile of dirty clothes off the floor along with Lily's boots and socks and hurried to the door.

"Hey!" Lily's ankle slowed her enough for the attendant to pass everything to one of Fang's men outside. The door slammed shut again. "Why did you do that?"

Ah Hai bobbed in a nervous bow. "They are dirty, honored *lái*. They must be cleaned."

"Is that what the Fist told you? That my things would be cleaned?"

"The honorable Fist Second told me to give them to his man, but surely they will be cleaned."

"And returned to me?"

"Oh, yes, surely that is so." She sounded anything but sure. Her frightened smile attempted to placate Lily.

Lily stared at the closed door in frustration. For a long moment she considered storming out of there and demanding the return of her things. But while Grandmother might be able to pull that off, she doubted her own ability to impress armed warriors when she was buck naked. Not in a way that added to her status anyway.

"Your ankle is hurt, yes?" Ah Hai said timidly. "When you

are finished soaking, I will wrap it for you and apply salve to your other hurts. I have good salves. If you will sit, honored *lái?*"

Lily sighed, limped back to the nearest stool, and sat. "Tell me about the Zhuren."

"They are very great," Ah Hai whispered.

"Very powerful, yes," Lily agreed, and began unfastening the braid she'd put her hair in roughly one day and two worlds ago. "We don't have Zhuren where I come from."

The woman sucked in a breath in startled sympathy. "I will pour the water now, if you will tip your head back." She did so, wetting Lily's hair thoroughly, then began working some of the soft soap into her scalp. Her fingers brushed Lily's skin and Lily's lips parted in surprise. Ah Hai was an empath, God help her. It was a very minor Gift, though, so maybe it didn't cause her too much misery. The little woman might have to touch someone to pick up their emotions clearly.

Not that she'd pick up anything from Lily. Her own Gift blocked all magic, the helpful along with the harmful, although for reasons she didn't understand, the kind of body sensing healers used did work on her . . . but Ah Hai's empathy wouldn't. That must seem very odd to the woman.

Half a dozen questions pushed into Lily's mind. Her fingers itched to jot them down, but she didn't have her notebook, a pen, or anything else, and she had to set priorities for this interview. So as Ah Hai lathered Lily's hair, Lily coaxed her to talk about the Zhuren. Nothing secret, she assured the woman. Only those things that everyone here knew.

"Would you know our history?" the woman asked hesitantly.

"That would be good."

Most of what Ah Hai told her came through clearly to Lily's mindsense, suggesting the woman was on comfortable ground with the tale. For long and long, people here lived primitive lives. So many things wanted to eat them, and the people had so little! Without a village, a community, how could a person survive? And so they gathered in tiny villages, but life was hard. Most of the *lái* knew little when they fell through, after all. A man who had grown rice his whole life might know how to dig, plant, irrigate, and harvest, but he did not arrive here with all his tools. He might know how to make a bucket, but not how to make the tools he needed to do that.

Ah Hai rinsed Lily's hair and applied hair oil, combing it through. She began lathering Lily's body now. Lily did not hiss or flinch when the soap stung the shallow cut on her forearm. Warriors didn't do that sort of thing.

That was the First Age, Ah Hai went on, and none knew how long it had lasted, for the people had neither the time nor the knowledge to make paper to write down their history. Then one day—oh, many generations ago, many-many—an entire village fell through. A large village.

No, Ah Hai did not know how such a thing could happen, but it had. Some said the earth shook so hard it broke open, revealing the intact village, but that was only stories, not part of the official teaching. But the earth did shake sometimes, did it not, when the great worm asleep at the heart of the world rolled over in her dreams? (The "great worm" bit didn't sound Chinese to Lily, though she had the vague idea there was something similar in Greek mythology. Or was it Egyptian? Never mind, she told herself. She could chase mythological clues later. Of more interest was the idea that earthquakes were common enough to have birthed a myth.) So perhaps the world had shaken on that day, shaken so hard that the seal between worlds was broken, allowing a whole village to fall through.

This village had tools, everything needed to make life good, including a forge and a smelter, and with them arrived those with knowledge of basic metallurgy and metalworking—bronze, copper, and iron. Paper-making, too, and many other things. That village became Lang Xin, the bright heart of the world, and thus began the Second Age. People lived better, much better. Villages grew larger; famine grew rare.

Yet many beasts still hunted them. Life remained precarious until the dawn of the Third Age . . . when the Zhuren came.

Ah Hai grew downright animated talking about the arrival of the Zhuren. She poured water over Lily as she spoke, describing many portents, none of which sounded reasonable, but the core of her story was that the Zhuren had sailed along the Great Serpent to arrive at Lang Xin's gates at dawn on that great day. Lily had not seen the gates? They were on the east side of the city and very old, very beautiful. She described the Zhuren as seven tall and beautiful boys. Not adults, no, Ah Hai said in response to Lily's question, not when they first arrived, but each as tall as an adult man. They had been raised by the Kanas, inhabitants of a distant village, who had kept their existence a secret until it was time for them to take their places in the wider world. Many shrines had been raised to the Kanas, Ah Hai added.

"Shrines?"

Ah Hai sighed. "So sad. The dragons had been kept away from the village by the Zhuren. This angered them. It is said that when the Zhuren left, dragons flew over the village and burned it to the ground. We are told that not one escaped."

"Tragic," Lily agreed. And possibly convenient, if someone didn't want it known just how the Zhuren came to exist. "The Zhuren must have been deeply grieved."

"Oh, yes. They wore white for an entire generation to show their mourning. Honored *lái*, we have finished now with washing and rinsing, if you wish to soak in the hot pool."

An entire generation? Lily stood. "How many generations have passed since the Zhuren arrived and the Third Age began?"

"We are in the fifth generation of the Third Age. Is your ankle very sore? Shall I help you into the pool?"

"No, I can do it. My people count a generation as thirty years. Is that how you count it?"

Ah Hai suddenly reverted to her earlier uncertainty. "This worthless one does not know numbers very well, honored *lái*."

"It is not important," Lily lied, and lowered herself gingerly into the water . . . the really, really hot water. Not boiling, she assured herself. If it were boiling, she'd see bubbles. Her skin was unconvinced by this logic, but if servant women did this all the time, a warrior could, too.

The soft, high notes from a flute sounded from behind her. Gradually the heat began to feel soporific instead of life-threatening.

The spawn were not immortal. Lily knew that much, though now that she thought about it, Sam hadn't told them how long the spawn lived, just that the ones born on Earth had long since died out. These spawn had still been boys when they arrived five generations ago. If a generation was thirty years, five generations would be a hundred fifty years. If it was twenty years, five generations would be a hundred years.

Is that how old the spawn were? Between one and one-and-a-half centuries? And did that matter?

Not immediately, she decided. What mattered more was how the spawn had arrived in this realm. Or had they been born here? Hatched, that is.

However human the spawn looked now, they'd hatched from eggs like any other dragon—small, brightly colored, and wingless. Unsurprisingly, Sam hadn't said much about the spell needed to turn their bodies human, save that it had taken him at least a couple centuries to devise it. A complex and sophisticated spell, then. Who had performed it on these spawn? One of the dragons? If Sam could develop such a spell, another dragon might have thought of it, too.

The dragon she'd seen had been mind-dark, but there must be plenty here who weren't. His presence did suggest that these dragons weren't very careful about their hatchings . . . but this was Dragonhome, the place where dragons originated. Bound to be a lot of dragons here, so based on sheer numbers there probably were more botched hatchings. Maybe the question was whether or not someone other than a dragon could create a spell to change baby dragons into the human-shaped spawn . . . and get close enough to the babies to use it. That seemed really unlikely. Sure, she had played mental midwife at a hatching, but that situation had been wildly unusual, maybe unique.

Reno might know. He was bound to know more than she did anyway. Was he not here yet, as Cynna had suggested? What about Gan? And Rule, dear God, and Rule . . . and what did the spawn want from the Great Bitch? What was *her* role in this realm? Everyone she'd met so far practically worshipped the spawn. None of them had said one word about a female goddess or Old One, so where did *she* come into the picture?

The questions tumbled in her head, mixing with the heat, the soft sound of the flute, and the exhaustion of a long and terrible day. Lily blinked, trying to stay awake, to stay on her guard . . .

She was running. Running in the darkness. They'd taken away her shoes and every footfall hurt, but she had to keep going. This was no sprint, but a marathon, with miles and miles still to go. Rule. She had to get to Rule, but he was so far away . . .

Some sound jerked her awake. She jolted—and nearly fainted, her head light and swimming, and—shit, how had that happened? The thread of mind-stuff stretching away from her was gossamer thin, stretched out so far it was almost gone.

She'd tried to reach Rule in her sleep?

". . . not good to stay too long in the hot water, honored *lái*, please, if you will come out now—"

"Yes." The thread of mind-stuff snapped back into her gut. It still felt thin. *She* felt thin, as if she'd used up some of herself along with the mind-stuff. "I stayed too long in the hot water and am dizzy. Help me out, please."

The tiny woman was stronger than she looked. With her assistance, Lily was able to climb out without falling flat on her face. She stood carefully still while Ah Hai patted her dry, and after a bit her head stopped spinning and she realized something.

She was starving. Ravenous. "Is there any food?"

Ah Hai was desolate to say that there was not. It was not the custom to bring food into a bathhouse, but perhaps a drink of cool water? She was further distressed to have to tell Lily that the Fist had expressed impatience and wished them to hurry.

At least, that's what Lily thought she said. She didn't dare unspool her mindsense to find out for sure. She did not get the massage with scented lotion the little attendant had planned to give her or any salves. She did get a drink of water and wrappings for her ankle, along with a pair of loose trousers and a sleeveless tunic. No underwear.

She did not get her boots back. Nor was she offered some other form of footwear. "You may tell the Fist I will be ready to go as soon as my boots are returned."

Ah Hai was suffused by embarrassment. She bowed several times, but was finally able to stop and go whisper through a cracked-open door. Whoever she reported to passed the word on to Fang Ye Lì.

Lily didn't catch everything that happened next, but either her ear for their dialect was improving or volume helped. The Fist was not happy. He demanded to know why Lily did not wear the sandals provided, then learned that no sandals had been provided. He asked someone outside the bathhouse if that were true. Someone tried to explain, saying that the other woman (Cynna?) had had her shoes taken away, and they had taken Lily Yu's shoes just now. That's when Someone got knocked to the ground. Someone, it turned out, was an imbecile.

The rest was harder to make out. Fang stopped yelling, and the dialect confused her when she didn't have her mindsense to sort it out. But it sounded like Lily had a different status than Cynna. Not that of a warrior, like she'd tried to claim, but *xi qi*. The word or phrase didn't tell her much. Depending on intonations she couldn't hear with a wall between them, *xi* had at least four meanings, *qi* had dozens, and the combination might refer to something only poetically related to its components. But it didn't seem to mean prisoner.

This culture was based on that of ancient China. Face mattered. Status was only one aspect of face, but it was one she could try to shift in her favor, and going barefoot here meant you were a slave, not just a prisoner. In the end, Lily limped out of the bathhouse in her own boots. The second one had been hard to pull on over her swollen ankle, but she'd managed. She might be exhausted, magically drained, and starving, but by God, she was wearing boots.

She wished she knew if it made a difference to anything except her feet.

FIVE

~

IT was full dark now, but mage lights bobbed over the paths. Lily glimpsed a few people on those paths, but no one moved through the central area. She allowed one of the guards to retie her hands and climbed back into the rickshaw and told herself to sit up straight. They did not need to know she moved through a gray fog of exhaustion, or how cold and clammy that fog felt.

She was on her way to the *Qī Jiā*—the Home of the Seven—where Kongqi awaited her.

He wouldn't kill her. She thought he wouldn't damage her too badly, either. The Great Bitch might only need her brain, but that brain required a reasonably healthy body to maintain it. But there were plenty of nonfatal ways to cause pain . . . only they hadn't pulled out Cynna's fingernails, had they? What would she do if Kongqi had three little kids with him to use as incentive?

She'd answer his questions.

That was so clear and obvious that some of her fear drained away. She'd answer and she'd do it quickly.

With that settled, she'd better think about how she'd respond. Should have already thought about that instead of drifting off in the hot water. Should definitely not have drained herself so badly reaching for an impossibly far-away Rule, because now she was too depleted to mindspeak Cynna to make sure she didn't contradict what Cynna had said. Though how she was supposed to stop herself from doing stupid shit in her sleep—

Shut up, she told herself. All those shoulds did not do a damn thing to help. Think. What did she most need to keep from Kongqi?

Her mindspeech. It might be AWOL due to overuse at the moment, but it would return. A sorcéri drifted across her cheek at that moment as if to underline that thought, which made her think of Cullen, which made her heart squeeze in her chest. Cullen liked to collect sorcéri. He could see them. He—

Shit. Cullen saw sorcéri because he was a sorcerer— meaning that he saw magic. The spawn were sorcerers, too. She'd been moaning about not being able to use mindspeech while she was with Kongqi, but that would be about the worst thing she could do. He'd *see* it.

Maybe he already had. She'd already used her mindsense in his presence, hadn't she? To find out if he was a spawn.

Lily forgot to play stoic warrior and scrubbed her face with both hands. She might have already given Kongqi a big, fat clue about her mindsense, and there wasn't a damn thing she could do about it. The best she could hope for was that Kongqi hadn't been paying attention to his Sight at that moment. It wasn't an unreasonable hope. Cullen kept his awareness of his Sight dialed down much of the time. It could be distracting, he said. Kongqi might, too.

She sighed deeply, then forced herself to straighten. What else did she need to keep from Kongqi?

Gan. The things about Gan that Cynna had kept hidden, that is. Kongqi knew Gan was a crosser and had brought Cynna and Lily here. He didn't know Gan used to be a demon and therefore could go *dashtu*. Gan might be nearby even now, waiting for a chance to help—and dammit, why hadn't she looked for Gan's mind while she was bathing instead of . . . never mind. What else?

The mate bond. She was used to keeping that secret. The bond was as much a spiritual construct as a magical one, so there was a decent chance Kongqi wouldn't notice it despite his sorcerous vision. Better be sure she didn't try to use it while she was in his presence, though.

Last but far from least: Reno. Very much, Reno.

If she and Cynna had a secret weapon, it was the green dragon. Who probably wasn't here yet, but would arrive at some point. Whose abilities were largely a mystery to her, but they included mind magic on a level that could hide itself from an Old One—at least for a while—and blowing up nodes. Or coming so close to blowing them up that it took everything the Great Bitch had to stabilize them . . . which she had done, just as Reno had expected, thereby preserving the life of her avatar. And the construct? Had the G.B. saved it, too? That enormous and enormously powerful magical construct that had been draining all the magic from a region in Dis in order to do God-only-knew-what . . .

And that's what she had to learn. That was the key question: what was that magical construct supposed to do? The only people here who might know were the spawn. Well, maybe Alice Báitóu, too . . . Alice, whose role she did not understand. Why was the woman here? Was she the G.B.'s agent or emissary? That would explain her clout with the spawn, but then why had she been so worried about the G.B. getting hold of the Codex? If she—

Lily emerged from her thoughts with a jolt. They'd halted in front of the largest of the stone buildings in the compound, the one with the gilded roof. Directly in front of them, three broad steps led to a narrow veranda and a pair of ornately carved doors. Lily's mouth went dry. On this hot, humid evening, her hands felt cold. Showtime.

"Come," Fang said.

They did not go up the shallow steps to the fancy doors. Instead they took a gravel path to another entrance off to the right, one partly hidden by tall shrubs—an entrance reached by descending a narrower set of stairs heading below ground level. Lily's mouth twisted when she saw those stairs. Bad stuff happened every time she went underground.

She halfway expected some kind of dank dungeon. Instead they entered a small anteroom carpeted in rush mats where two more guards waited. Those two saluted Fang by thumping their chests with their fists. Fang gave them a nod and led Lily and his original pair of guards into what might have been an up-scale office hallway, albeit one lit by clusters of mage lights instead of fluorescent tubes. The walls were white and plastered, the floor wooden and spotless—and being kept that way by a woman who was washing it on her hands and knees. Recessed doorways punctuated both walls at regular intervals. Some doorways had doors; some did not.

The doors were not like the ones she was used to. No doorknobs. Instead they had round iron rings that reminded her of knockers. "How do those doorknobs work?" she asked. Fang glanced over his shoulder at her, his face puzzled. Wrong word, maybe? She tried again. "The latches. The rings on the doors."

He paused, then looked at her again and spoke in a voice so low she barely heard him. "Lily Yu. I do not [something]. Your kinship with the Zhuren is remote, but [something-something] courtesy. But the Zhuren are not [something about questions or problems?]. You would do well to remember that." He turned and continued down the hall.

Lily followed, frowning. Had she understood any of that right? Damn, but she missed her mindsense. Her kinship—if that's what he'd said—with the Zhuren was certainly remote. Nonexistent, as far as she was concerned. Her magic might be descended from dragons, but she wasn't. And yet Tom Weng had called her cousin when they met, and the only way Fang Ye Lì could have gotten the idea that she was some kind of kin to the Zhuren would be if one of them told him so.

Why would they do that?

The hall appeared to bisect the entire basement level of the building. About halfway down it they turned into another hall. She glimpsed a stairwell in the direction they did not take—one with stairs leading both up and down. This was not the lowest floor, then. The second hall traveled about fifteen feet before turning right. Fang didn't go that far, stopping at one of the doorways that lacked a door. He motioned for her to go in.

She did, trailing the other two guards. This room was small, white, and bare except for a single wooden bench on the wall to her left. In addition to the open doorway, there were two closed doors: one on the wall with the bench, one opposite it.

"You will sit, please," Fang informed her from the hall. "Your guards will not speak to you unless they must give you instructions." He left.

More thinking time? That would be good . . . if she could stay awake. She ought to be too terrified to doze off, but mostly she felt like sludge—slow, oozy, and miserable. She would have killed for a cup of coffee.

No coffee here. She mourned the loss, then prodded her reluctant brain to focus on what she did have. A fistful of secrets to keep, an exhausted but mostly intact body, no allies, no weapons . . . unless she considered her mindsense a weapon. Maybe it could be, but it wasn't usable at the moment. How long would it take for it to recover?

Well, she'd depleted her magic once before by reaching too far with her mindsense. How long had it taken to refill that time? Her sludge-brain oozed through that memory, eventually delivering an answer: she wasn't sure. She'd been pretty busy at the time, her ability still very new, and she hadn't really noticed. But roughly two hours after almost passing out, she'd been able to mindspeak Mika.

So, two hours or so to refill enough to use mindspeech with a nearby dragon. But that was the easiest mindspeech of all. Plus there was more free magic available here, and how did that affect her refilling? She'd felt several sorcéri just traveling from the bathhouse to this place. Had she absorbed them entirely because she was depleted? Or had she gotten only the tiny sample her Gift automatically collected? She didn't know—but even if she had soaked up every bit of every sorcéri she'd encountered, that wouldn't be a lot of power. They were just wisps.

But mindspeech wasn't the only thing she could do, was it? Twice she'd used her Gift to actively drain magic.

Both times had been extreme situations. Both times, she'd used it on living beings. The first time she'd drained the magic permanently from a Gifted woman who'd been trying to cause an earthquake. That had shaken her pretty badly. The ability to turn a Gifted person into a null . . . she wasn't sure anyone ought to be able to do that. The second time, she'd been in a life-or-death battle with an immortal and only partly corporeal being. She'd nearly killed herself that time.

What would happen if she tried to drain a spawn?

The thought startled her into something like alertness. That would be a weapon, all right. But one that hurt the spawn, or her? The spawn must soak up magic the way dragons did. The way she did, too. How much was their magic like hers?

She'd never touched one of the spawn. She had shaken hands with another touch sensitive once, though. He'd fainted. No, that was wrong. Fagin had said later that he hadn't lost consciousness. He'd looked unconscious, though. He'd looked like someone who'd been magically depleted, in fact, but that wasn't what he thought had happened. He'd said that their Gifts had tried to sample each other, and when hers won, his had recoiled or snapped back—that he'd been knocked on his ass by his own Gift, not hers. Fagin knew a thousand times more about magical theory than she did, so she'd accepted his version.

What if he'd been wrong? What if she had partially drained him? She hadn't asked at the time. She hadn't known enough to ask. But if the spawns' magic was like hers, just touching one of them might knock her out—either by her own Gift recoiling or by his magic draining hers. That assumed spawn were more powerful than she was, but it seemed a valid assumption. They were the offspring of dragons and dragons were vast.

Of course, that wasn't what happened when she touched dragons. She didn't pass out. They didn't pass out. She felt the seethe of their magic just like she felt any other magic she touched. The question, then, was whether the spawns' magic was like hers or like dragon magic. It seemed as if it must be more like dragon magic. They were dragons in human bodies, after all, so probably she could touch a spawn safely. But if they could drain magic the way she—

"Zhu Kongqi will see you now." Fist Second Fang Ye Lì stood in the doorway, his square face grim.

This time they took the right-hand turn in the hall. It was easy to see where they were headed—a pair of guards stood on either side of a pair of doors. The guards saluted Fang with that chest-thump thing. Fang marched up to the doors, knocked, and spoke his name and title.

A faint scraping sound and the door opened all by itself.

Okay, that was weird. Telekinesis, she supposed, of the finicky, show-offy sort. A quick glance at Fang's impassive face suggested he'd expected this response. Maybe Kongqi always opened doors in that look-Ma-no-hands way. Lily followed the Fist Second into the room.

And was hit by a massive wave of magic. A wave that came at her from every direction at once. Every inch of skin on her body vibrated, even the skin covered by cloth or hair. Toes to nose to scalp, her skin buzzed like she'd been plugged into an electrical socket.

Maybe she reacted the way she did because she'd just been thinking about it. Or because this felt like an attack, and years of martial arts training dictated a certain type of response. Or maybe it was as instinctive as hunger. For whatever reason, when that power wave hit, she *pulled*.

It lasted a second. Two seconds. Three. Then the magic shut off.

"Interesting," said a cool voice.

Lily blinked, disoriented—by the attack, her response, and what she'd sensed in those three seconds. One thing was clear, though. The sense coiled in her gut felt plump with power again.

"Your defenses are as complete as I'd been told," Kongqi said in English. "I was not told, however, that you can eat power."

"No?" Lily looked around the room. She didn't see any other spawn. Just Kongqi. Did that mean the one Cynna called Dick Boy wouldn't be part of her interrogation?

The room itself was long, narrow, and utilitarian. Shelves and trunks lined the wall on her right. Opposite it, three large windows in the exterior wall were dark mirrors, bouncing back reflections of the myriad mage lights bobbing around the ceiling. Glass windows, then. Surely only the wealthy had those here. A long table in the center of the room had been built at counter height. It held a wide assortment of objects: tools and gadgets whose purpose she couldn't guess; bowls and jars containing fluids, seeds, roots, and unguessable substances; a few scrolls; a small knife; three gray stones set one atop the other; a branch from some conifer; a candelabra with three unlit candles; wooden boxes of various sizes; and a small bamboo cage with a sleeping finch perched inside.

All in all, the room was a lot like Cullen's lab. A sorcerer's lab. She looked at the self-titled Master of Air. "There are probably a great many things your ally hasn't told you."

"Of course." Kongqi sat in a wooden armchair at the far end of the room next to an empty hearth. Beside him was a small table holding a teapot; a second wooden armchair faced his. He paused to sip from the teacup he held. He'd removed his *shenyi*—a quick glance found it hanging from a peg on the wall—and wore only the kind of loose trousers and tunic she'd seen here on most people. His were black, made from what looked like linen, and lavishly embroidered. "However, she appears to be under the impression that you have no conscious control of magic, only the automatic response of your Gift. Eating power is an intentional act."

Lily shrugged. "For you perhaps."

"You would have me believe it is different for you?" Skepticism lifted his brows over those shining blue eyes. Those eyes kept making her think of Cullen, and that made her mad. "And yet your power derives from dragons. It should be similar to mine, though more limited."

"My Gift may be descended from dragons, but I'm not. I'm human. Unlike you."

"That proves nothing." He switched to Chinese, directing it at Fang. He spoke quickly, and unable to use mindspeech, Lily didn't understand all of it. Something about binding her. Something about "the other" and waiting.

What other? Or had he said others, plural? Not children. Please, no children.

Fang gripped Lily's arm. "Come."

She was getting really sick of that word.

SIX

~

LILY got about five steps farther before Kongqi said, "Stop. Lily Yu, what do you see when you look at the bird in the cage?"

Lily glanced at the little finch. It wasn't moving, hadn't reacted at all . . . "It looks dead."

"Touch it," Kongqi said.

She gave him a wary glance, shrugged, and reached out. She could just get one finger through the cage to stroke the bird's feathers. "Huh!"

"What do you feel?"

"Something odd." She continued to stroke the motionless bird with her finger. The texture reminded her of . . . "Netting. That's what it feels like."

"That is also what the spell looks like."

He saw magic, of course. But maybe he couldn't feel it the way she did? Maybe he was curious about her Gift. "You've put a spell on a dead bird?"

"It is in stasis. Reptiles are the easiest creatures to place in stasis. I have not yet discovered their upper time limit for that state, but have revived them with no ill effects after thirteen months. Birds do not tolerate it as well as reptiles, but can be revived after six days with few or no ill effects. Mammals do not tolerate it at all. They begin to suffer deficits almost immediately, and cannot be revived at all after three to twelve minutes. I do not yet know why."

"I've never heard of a stasis spell. Is it anything like that freeze thing some sidhe can do that stops a person from moving?"

"No. That is simple body magic. The stasis spell is more complex. Come, Lily Yu."

There was that damn word again. She came. She didn't have a lot of options at the moment. She sat in the damn chair. Fang picked up the coil of thin rope from the floor, knelt, and began tying her right ankle to one chair leg. "Is this really necessary? I can't be much of a threat to you."

Kongqi was watching her closely. "Your magic intrigues me."

Was he ignoring her question, or was that intended as an oblique response? His expression gave her no clues. "Oh?"

"I cannot perceive it clearly. It obscures itself."

Cullen had no problem seeing her magic. Did the spawns' Sight work differently than his?

"I will learn more about it," he said. "Would you care for tea?"

"Is it drugged?"

"No."

"Then yes, thank you. I would love a cup of tea."

"Fist Second, leave her left hand free."

Lily watched her enemy pour her a cup of tea while Fang finished securing her to the chair—save for her left hand—then left the room. Dragons didn't lie. So she'd been told anyway, and her experience backed that up. But that might be because it was so hard, maybe impossible, to lie in mindspeech. A spawn wouldn't have that problem.

Kongqi set the small, handleless cup on the table beside the teapot. After a brief hesitation she picked it up. Maybe he was lying. Didn't matter. If he wanted her drugged, she was going to end up drugged. Might as well have some tea. She took a sip. And raised her brows. "A potion?"

"Can you tell what type?"

"Not really. Mostly I just feel the water magic involved." She took another sip. The buzz of magic was distracting, but otherwise it was good tea.

"You do not expect it to affect you, although your Gift only wards your surface."

Shouldn't he know all this? His magic ought to act the same way. "My Gift is not a ward. There isn't a part of me, inside or out, that can be affected by magic. Was I allowed a bath and an attendant because I'm considered kin to you?"

"Yes. It would not do for humans to think they can offer discourtesy to one who is kin to us."

But no humans would know about their supposed connection if Kongqi hadn't announced it. Or had one of the others made that claim? What benefit did any of the spawn get from claiming her as kin? Maybe she was wrong to think of them as a group with similar motives. Dragons were singular beings, not often given to group action. And the spawn were sociopaths.

It all made her head hurt. Lily drank her tea and wished it were coffee.

"We will discuss altruism now."

"Altruism." This was not the direction she'd expected her interrogation to take.

"It is an interest of mine. Humans seem to place great value on the quality or practice of altruism in the abstract, yet in the specific their actions are seldom what could reasonably be considered altruistic."

"People are a mess," she agreed automatically, then thought about what she'd said. "And yet most of us try to do the right thing. Not everyone, and not all the time, and we often disagree about what the right thing is. But we try."

"Is that how you define altruism? As 'doing the right thing'?" His eyebrows lifted in scorn. "Extremely sloppy thinking. It offers no parameters for action."

"I used to be big on well-defined parameters. Now, though . . ." Lily thought about some of the lines she'd crossed. Some of the things she'd done or left undone. "Now I think that learning what is and isn't right action is the job of a lifetime. The real answers, the true ones, have to come from within. Rules can guide us, especially when we're young, but not all the way. Even if we think a lot about the rules, what they mean, why they exist, that only takes us so far. When you come right down to it, the rules are made out of words. Words are . . . they're signposts pointing at the thing, not the thing itself. And the thing *moves*. It changes. What the words point at looks so different by the time you're thirty than it did when—" She broke off, surprised and alarmed by how much she'd said. What was wrong with her?

She gave her tea a suspicious look. She didn't feel drugged. Dizzy with fatigue, but not drugged. "I'm surprised by your interest. From what I've been told, you aren't concerned with right action. Only with what benefits you."

He didn't look insulted. Or bored. Or anything else she could decipher. Lily had dealt with witnesses whose faces gave away little, but this guy beat them all. "All beings are interested in right action. We merely define it differently. Pursuing my own interests is rational. Placing the interests of others above my own would be irrational."

"Sam wouldn't agree."

"Do you expect the opinion of this Sam to weigh with me?"

"It might. He's also known as Sun Tsao—in your manner of naming, Tsao Sun—or the black dragon."

"Ah." At last, a reaction. He sat back slightly. His eyes were so bright. Intense. They made her think of a summer sky, of sunlight ping-ponging off air molecules until the air itself shouted blue. "You know him well?"

"Not well, but . . . no, that's wrong. I don't know all of him, but what I do know runs deep."

"And you believe he espouses altruism, just as you do."

"I don't think his values are the same as mine. Or maybe I mean his priorities. He is a dragon, after all." Sam didn't place much stock in community, for example, or in kindness . . . no, that didn't feel quite right. Dragon kindness arrived with teeth and claws, forcing you to fight your way past some trouble rather than rescuing you from it. "But he does believe in a higher good. He doesn't act only to benefit himself."

"What you perceive in him is enlightened self-interest."

"I've seen that, sure, but I've also seen him act in ways that go beyond any self-interest. How do you know anything about the black dragon?"

"What do you see as the difference between enlightened self-interest and altruism?"

"Why don't you answer my question, then I'll answer yours?"

"Because I have no need to please you. You, however, may wish to please me, or at least delay the unpleasantness to come. What do you see as the difference between enlightened self-interest and altruism?"

"When you talk about unpleasantness, you make it hard for me to focus on other subjects."

"Make an attempt."

Might as well. He hadn't asked her for anything that touched on the secrets she wanted to keep. "I guess the difference is that you have to reason your way into enlightened self-interest. Figure out the pluses and minuses of helping someone. With altruism, you help them for their sake, not your own. You don't expect a benefit."

"You would say, then, that altruistic actions are not the result of rational thought, but arise from an innate desire for the well-being of another?"

"I don't think we can eliminate rational thought altogether. Sometimes humans have to lean on rules because we . . . well, we haven't yet seen where they point, you might say. Not clearly."

"Let us test that hypothesis. Have you finished your tea?"

"Not quite."

"Finish it now and hand me the cup."

She no longer wanted the damn tea. Throwing it in his face sounded good. She suppressed the urge. "Why?"

"So I can tie your arm to the chair. I can do so without your cooperation, but you are surely intelligent enough not to waste strength struggling when it serves no purpose. Also, I would prefer to not break either the cup or your arm."

She was intelligent enough to not want to get into any bad habits, either. Such as obeying him just because he scared the shit out of her. Still, she didn't want the damn tea, and she did want to find out something. He'd have to touch her to tie her up, wouldn't he? Skin to skin.

She handed him the cup.

He took it in his left hand, set it down, stood up—and seized her wrist, lizard-quick, holding it immobile.

Neither of them passed out. She'd pretty much decided that wouldn't happen, so no surprise there. Mostly she'd expected his magic to feel like dragon magic, order and chaos tumbling together in a complex dance that created a tactile sensation like no other. Or she might not have felt anything. Grandmother had said that magically the spawn were more of an absence than a presence, and Kongqi's mind was invisible to Lily. She thought that maybe his magic would be, too.

Instead she felt ice, slick and cold. So cold.

"I have had to amend my usual test," he was saying as he tied a tidy knot that pinned her arm to the arm of the chair. "Your magic precludes the use of *jùdà téng*, which I have used on my other experimental subjects."

Wait, what? He wanted to test her, conduct some kind of experiment, not question her? That made no sense. "What are you talking about?"

He stood looking down at her with those bright blue eyes and no expression at all. "*Jùdà téng* is a form of body magic that causes agony but no physical damage. Clearly I won't be able to use that on you, which is less than satisfactory. Nor can I use traditional methods of inflicting pain without risking a breach of our agreement to deliver you as undamaged as possible. Still, I've contrived a decent substitute for *jùdà téng.*"

Lily's mouth was horribly dry. "What in the hell are you trying to test?"

"Altruism. It is a curiously persistent and widespread delusion among what are called sentient species. I wish to determine whether it is a purely social delusion that develops because it is useful for weak mammals such as humans, who must gather in packs to survive, or if there is some biological basis for it. So far my results have been ambiguous, but I've recently adjusted my methods. I believe my current test accounts better for outside variables."

He was mad. Hadn't Sam said the spawn were insane? She hadn't realized, hadn't understood . . . "Where I come from, scientists have MRIs to look at brain activity. I don't see how you can find out much without being able to see what's happening in the brains of your test subjects."

"Pain," he said simply, turning away to move to the table. "If there is an innate altruistic response to find, I must first break down your executive function so that your response will be unthinking and not a product of social conditioning. Previous tests have shown that high levels of pain do this quite effectively."

Her executive function was trying to shut down already, being filled with *oh shit oh shit oh shit.*

"Earlier you referred to my decision to allow you time to bathe. My reply was accurate but incomplete. It was necessary to delay testing you anyway, so why not allow you a bath? I had to be certain I could achieve a degree of pain similar to *jùdà téng* by other means." He turned back to face her, a large glass jar in one hand. "My brother assured me I could, but I needed to conduct my own tests. That took time. I had to revive two of the subjects before I could question them about the experience."

Lily frowned at the jar. It seemed to be full of small, black, squirming . . . "Ants? You're threatening me with ants?"

"Perhaps you are not familiar with *téngtòng mǎy*. I do not know if they exist in your realm." He unfastened the lid of the jar. "Their venom contains a potent neurotoxic peptide that affects sodium ion channels in a way that produces a remarkably pure pain, yet causes no lasting damage. I will demonstrate."

He returned in a few unhurried strides, stuck a stick in the jar, and removed it. A single black ant clung to the end of the stick. He lowered the stick to Lily's bare forearm and shook the ant off.

It looked like any other ant—bigger than some, sure, about the size of a fire ant. Maybe it was a fire ant, or this world's version of them. Lily had been stung by fire ants before, and it wasn't fun, but "sting" was the right word. One hot prick of pain, unpleasant but nothing to—

Acid poured over and into her arm. The shock of pain was pure and brilliant, a pocket nova going off in her flesh. And going off. And going off. It didn't *stop.* Lily's arm burned with a bright incandescence that subsumed everything she'd thought she knew about pain. The rising crescendo of it burst through thought and reason and wound itself around her tighter and tighter and . . . and then a hint of coolness, washing the pain back a bit. Not gone, no. Her forearm throbbed and burned, reminding her of when she'd been shot, only mixed with the aftereffects of the time she'd been brushed by mage fire.

The spawn was rubbing a sticky paste on her arm. "Nothing but magic can truly banish the pain from a *téngtòng mǎyǐ* sting, and I cannot use magic on you. But this helps, does it not? A folk remedy."

Her eyes were wet. Her cheeks were wet. She didn't remember crying.

"The pain from multiple stings is truly agonizing, I'm told. I didn't test that personally, as the pain from a single sting was enough to make it difficult for me to focus sufficiently to rid myself of the venom. There is also some degree of temporary paralysis around the envenomed area, which is why I will be using your left arm. You are right-handed, I believe, so the paralysis should not cause undue difficulty. It will pass in roughly one day, as will the pain. The tremors may be annoying, as they linger longer, but there will be no lasting damage."

Paralysis? Tremors?

He straightened and glanced at the door. It opened. Fist Second Fang came in . . . with Ah Hai.

Fang held the albino woman's arm. Lily couldn't see Ah Hai's face; she kept her head down. Fang's face was easy to read, with that fierce frown . . . or was it? Maybe that was more of a professional scowl than a real one. *Hiding something behind that scowl, are you, Fist Second?*

Kongqi spoke to the Fist Second in rapid Chinese. The words slid through Lily's distracted mind without registering. The Fist Second brought Ah Hai across the room and stopped about five feet from Kongqi with the little slave in front of him, his hands gripping her arms to hold her in place.

"What is your name, claimed one?" Kongqi asked in Chinese. This time, Lily understood him.

Ah Hai darted a single glance up at the spawn, her eyes

wide with fear and confusion, then looked down again. Her whisper was so soft Lily barely heard her. "Ah Hai, Zhu."

Lily's forearm burned and throbbed, burned and throbbed . . .

Kongqi looked at Lily, his expression unchanged . . . and yet suddenly a switch clicked in her head and she could read it. He wasn't hiding his feelings. His face showed nothing because he felt nothing, not a jot of satisfaction or regret, pity or sick excitement—nothing but a keen and monstrous clinical interest. If giving her candy had worked better for his test than giving her pain, he would have given her candy. Her pleasure would have had no more effect on him than her pain. Her feelings were not part of his world.

He spoke then. Clinically. "My first round of experiments suggested that offering to torment a stranger instead of the test subject does not elicit a dependable altruistic response. With the second round I explored the other extreme, offering close family members as the alternative. Those results were so variable as to be useless. My third round also produced inconclusive results. It was suggested that I erred in offering children to those test subjects. After reflection, I concurred. The instinct to protect your own young does generalize in humans to protectiveness for all human children, but the intensity of that generalized instinct varies from one individual to the next. This variability could account for the ambiguous nature of those results. With the current round of experiments, I offer test subjects an alternative who is known to them as a source of comfort or pleasure, but who is not related to them. Hence, Ah Hai."

He stuck the stick back in the jar. "You now know what to expect in terms of pain from the *téngtòng mǎi*. The experience is extremely unpleasant. If you wish to avoid this unpleasantness, tell me to use the ants on Ah Hai instead of you. That is all you must do. Choose her pain instead of yours."

Revulsion swept over her, along with a sticky sort of fear, sour and unholy. She didn't speak.

"No?" He withdrew the stick. This time a whole swarm of ants clung to it. "I control the ants. They will sting you one at a time, as I dictate. I will stop between stings to ask if you wish me to hurt her instead of you. Once you agree, I will move the ants to her, then I will put salve on your bites. She will be stung but not damaged, and your pain will be eased. Who should I put the ants on?"

She went on saying nothing.

"Ah Hai is not a child or a relative. She is older than you, timid, and a slave. She is unable to offer you any benefit as an ally or threat as an enemy. You should feel free to choose her pain over your own."

Lily licked her lips and tasted salt. "No."

SEVEN

∽

CYNNA looked up from *The Norton Anthology of Poetry* for the fourteenth time. Lily still wasn't back. She bit her lip.

She didn't think about how good Cullen's arms would feel right now. She'd done that at first, but it had ceased to be a comfort when she could no longer believe she'd feel his arms again. She might. She clung doggedly to that. But "might" didn't hold back the fear.

Idiot, said a dear memory. *Put down the goopy poetry—*

Hey, she thought, *you like poetry! You quote it sometimes!*

Sure, but you don't, and you're just using it to avoid thinking. Which is what you really need to do.

Her mouth crooked up. She might not be able to believe she'd hold Cullen again, but she could argue with him in her mind just fine. And the annoying man was right, even if he was just her imagination. She did need to put down the poetry and do some thinking.

Suppertime had come and gone. Lily's bowl of rice-and-whatever sat in one corner of the cell, waiting for her return. So did the second mat and blanket the guards had tossed in. There was no light left outside; a single mage light bobbed in her cell. That was Alice's doing; Cynna couldn't use her own magic for a damn thing. Alice had arranged for the guards to provide a mage light every evening. Cynna sat on her mat as darkness gathered and thought about her plan for removing the be-damned magic cage. She thought about the questions she hadn't had a chance to ask Lily before they took her away, and about how Cullen *was still alive*, dammit, and that however endless the last six days had been for her, Ryder had only experienced about one day without her momma and daddy, plus Ryder had Toby with her so she was *not* feeling terrified and abandoned. Cynna thought, and did not give in to despair.

Been there. Done that.

They couldn't damage Lily, right? They needed her body and brain in good shape to give to the Great Bitch. Pain magic was out, too, since it wouldn't work on Lily, so whatever was happening shouldn't be too horrible.

It wouldn't be good, though. She knew enough about the spawn to be sure of that. But it did no good to try to guess what particular kind of nasty might be happening, so she thought about what she knew and what she needed to know. What she wanted to ask the next time she got a chance. She thought hard and did not pray. She hadn't prayed since she watched Dick Boy kill that little boy. She couldn't pray when she spent all her time wanting to kill . . . not that she was going to fantasize about that anymore. To hell with that shit.

Though God knew she still wanted to. She wanted the spawn dead, especially Dick Boy, and preferably by her hand. She wanted to personally rip apart the two people—a dragon spawn and the avatar of an Old One, a goddamned self-proclaimed goddess—who'd stolen her baby. But fantasizing about murder just sank her deeper into the frozen pit where she'd spent the last few days. Fantasy didn't do a damn thing to get her out of that pit. Or this cell. Fantasy just kept her mind busy, kept her from thinking about Ryder every damn second. Thinking about Ryder hurt more than every other pain in her whole life rolled into one. It was bigger than she was, a swallowing emptiness. So she'd fantasized about murder and hadn't even noticed that she'd given up. Until Lily came limping into the cell, she hadn't realized that she had fucking given up.

Lily never gave up. She didn't know how.

Cynna thought of Lily as a bullet. She didn't mean that in a bad way. Lily had killed, yeah, but she wasn't violent the way

Cynna could be—used to be—back in the bad old days. Even after she started turning her life around, on bad nights she'd still gone looking for a fight. Nothing else seemed to help, and she hadn't known why she was so angry, or how to let go of her anger, or even that she'd used anger to protect herself. Except that it hadn't. It had only left her unbearably alone, making her angry all over again at a world that shut her out. Angry at herself for being too flawed, too wrong. For screwing up. For, in the end, shutting out the world.

Lily didn't have that kind of anger. She wasn't a bullet because she was violent, but because she shot for her goal. Period. It never seemed to occur to her that she might not reach it. Maybe "guided missile" was a better description. If Lily rammed into something she couldn't get through, she immediately started figuring out how to get around it.

Cynna couldn't see how they were going to get out of this cell. She didn't see how they could rescue Ryder and the rest of the children with six dragon spawn and an entire realm trying to stop them . . . then somehow get the children to safety. Somehow stop the Lady's enemies from doing something godawful with that magical construct. Somehow get back to Dis at the right time to save Cullen and Rule and the rest of them . . . and go home. That had to be the final goal, to get home again. Doing all of that—shit, doing any two out of three—was clearly impossible. Thinking you could do the impossible had to be a fucking delusion.

It was a delusion Cynna meant to hold on to with both hands, both feet, and her teeth. She just wished she had better teeth to clamp down with, like a wolf's or a tiger's or—

The bar lifted on the other side of the door. She sat up straight. Lily?

But it was one of the guards silhouetted against the light from the other side of the open door. "Come," he said.

The guards all seemed to know two English words: "come" and "stay." Which, give them credit, was more than she knew of Chinese. She was not good at languages. She could order beer or curse in Spanish. That was about it. And Chinese had to be the weirdest-ass language ever, as she'd figured out when, curious, she'd looked up some stuff about it online. What seemed like one word was really lots of words depending on how you said it, but it wasn't like the difference between "caw" and "cow." More like the difference between "cow" and "cow," only you put a bit of lilt into one and left the other flat. Or stressed one more, or said one faster, or something. She couldn't tell. She didn't have the right ears for Chinese.

Not that she'd been trying. The last six days, she hadn't tried to do much of anything.

She grimaced and got to her feet. It hurt. Mostly her arm—broken bones hurt a lot more, a lot more continuously, and for a lot longer than she'd realized—but also all along the side of her body that had bounced off that stone wall. She had a fine set of bruises, but her arm was the only thing that had been broken. Or ruptured. Organs could do that, and hers hadn't. That probably meant she'd been lucky. She probably ought to be grateful.

Hell with that, too. Slowly, moving like she was an old, old woman, Cynna left her cell.

A scattering of mage lights bobbed along the ceiling. The guard who'd summoned her joined three more in standing around, looking stuffed and official. They couldn't sit at the big table like they usually did because Alice Báitóu was sitting there. So was a woman Cynna hadn't seen before. The new woman had the kind of round, chubby face that doesn't wrinkle much with age, but her skin had that tired look skin gets after a few decades if its wearer hasn't invested in some dermatologist's retirement plan. Her black hair was streaked with gray.

"Join us," Alice said, nodding at a stool across from her and the new woman.

Cynna lowered herself carefully to the stool and sighed for her aches. "Hello again."

Alice wasn't much for small talk. "You said the healing spells you knew weren't of use to anyone but a healer."

"All but one of them, yes." Not that Cynna really knew the spells. You can't really know a spell you can't cast. But she knew about them. They were from the memories, those incredibly vivid mental creations that had been passed down from Rhej to Rhej for over three thousand years. Searching them was draining, both emotionally and magically, but the magic involved didn't extend beyond her skin so it wasn't affected by the damned magic cage.

"The spell that blocks pain, you mean?"

"Yeah. The no-pain spell can be learned by anyone with a Gift, and by some with innate magic that isn't a Gift." Lupi, for example. "Though it's kind of the opposite of a healing spell." It blocked pain, but it blocked healing, too, and it was set up on a loop so it drew more and more power. Cynna had learned that the hard way.

"I will want it eventually. Today I am interested in the one that allows a healer to focus in more clearly on whatever bodily problem she is assessing. This is Ah Li," Alice said with a nod at the other woman. "She is one the finest healers in Lang Xin."

"I don't guess she speaks English."

"I am quite capable of translating."

"Please tell her I'm glad to meet her."

They went through a brief three-way greeting ritual. According to Alice, Ah Li was honored to meet Cynna. Then Alice said, "Ah Li is owned by the city."

Cynna's eyebrows shot up. "Owned by?"

Alice said something to Ah Li. The healer set one hand on the table. It had six fingers. As soon as Cynna saw that, the woman pulled it back out of sight.

"Children born with a deformity or mutation used to be killed at birth," Alice said. "The Zhuren do not allow this except in cases of extreme deformity, when it may be considered a mercy. If such a child survives to the age of three, he or she is assessed by a magistrate. If it is determined that the child can grow up to be a contributing adult, he or she can either be claimed by the Zhuren or sent back to live with their family. The claimed children are trained to serve. Among them are many with Gifts, such as Ah Li."

"They're slaves," Cynna said flatly.

Alice shrugged. "In your world they would be called slaves. Here they are the *yāoqiú*, the claimed. It is an honorable status. Ah Li was given to the city of Lang Xin after her training. She now runs a house of healing. The wealthy generally use more prestigious healers, so most of her patients come from the poor, who are either treated for free or for a nominal payment. She has three apprentices and two journeymen who are also healers. You met one of those journeymen. He set your arm."

"I remember."

"Ah Li is ideally situated to teach others what she learns from you. Today I want you to teach her that focus spell."

Cynna shook her head. "I can't teach her the spell. You keep saying it that way, but to properly teach a spell I'd have to demonstrate it. With this damned magic cage I can't do that. Even without the cage, I couldn't demonstrate a healing spell. I don't have that Gift. You want me to pass on a spell, not teach it."

"Use whatever language you like to describe the process. You know what I mean."

"The language matters. Teaching a spell implies that the student will be able to use it. I've told you about how hard it is to translate a spell from one discipline to another. The symbolic language of the spells I know may not work for someone whose mental landscape is furnished with a whole different set of symbols."

"I understand that." A touch of impatience flickered through Alice's usually passionless voice. "We worked that out with the flea-killing spell. The version we arrived at functions as it should."

"Yeah, well, I knew three versions of that one. Comparing them let me figure out what kind of symbolic language to use. I only know one version each of the healing spells, and they aren't simple constructs. I'm not saying it will be impossible to make them work. Just that it won't be easy and may take a long time." Longer than Cynna wanted to be here.

"That is why I brought Ah Li with me. She can attempt the spell and ask questions if she encounters a problem."

If? More like when. Alice thought she understood, but she didn't. Translating spells from one discipline to another was tricky as hell. Cynna was better than most at that because she'd had a lot of practice. She stored spells on her skin. To do that, she had to be able to translate every component of a spell into a pattern, then make that pattern blend properly with every other portion of the spell. Sure, there were a few spells that worked for pretty much everyone, no matter what discipline they'd been trained in. Or even those with no discipline at all. Mage lights, for one. That stupid pain-blocking spell, for another. But most spells harnessed a practitioner's internalized understanding of the world through symbols to shape the user's intent, both conscious and unconscious. You needed the two to work together. You could concentrate like crazy on setting a fire ward, but if your unconscious mind was playing with fluffy pink bunny rabbits at the time—or with daggers dripping with your enemies' blood—you were going to get your eyebrows singed. If you were lucky, that is.

But Cynna had already figured out that Alice had no real grounding in the craft. Whatever her Gift was—and Cynna was sure she had one—she wasn't a trained spellcaster. "Okay. You want two things from me. First, you want me to pass on the spell for focusing a healer's sensing. Second, you want me to work with you and Ah Li to try to translate the spell into a form Ah Li can use."

"I want you to succeed, not simply try."

"I can't guarantee that."

"You must make every effort to succeed."

Cynna nodded. "That's three payments, then. One for the spell itself. One for making every effort to translate the spell into a form your healer can use. And one—call it a bonus—for succeeding. Let's talk about that payment."

Alice nodded and the dickering began.

The pale Alice was an odd duck. She had no problem using the guards to enforce her ownership of Cynna, but she didn't use pain—or the murder of children—to force obedience. She was willing to bargain for Cynna's spells. That's how Cynna had learned almost everything she'd passed on to Lily.

It was not how she'd obtained a visit from Ah Li's journeyman, however. Alice had sent the healer to Cynna before coming to talk to her new property. Had she done that out of compassion or for practical reasons, to assure herself her property was in decent shape? Probably the latter, but Cynna couldn't be sure. Alice didn't seem to feel anything strongly enough to make her easy to read.

Cynna wished she could have talked to Lily before opening negotiations. Lily was the queen of questions. But at least she'd started thinking again, and some of her thinking time had been spent figuring out what she might ask the next time Alice showed up.

She started with big asks, stuff she wanted but didn't expect to get. Sure enough, Alice wouldn't tell Cynna why the spawn wanted the children or when the children would arrive. She wouldn't admit she knew anything about the magical construct on Dis, either. She wouldn't remove the magic cage, not even briefly. Cynna couldn't get her to say one word about whatever arrangements existed between the Great Bitch and the spawn, though she did admit that Lily was part of those arrangements. That admission Cynna got gratis.

That's about all she got, other than frustrated. They did manage to agree on the first payment. Alice would tell her more about wild dragons in exchange for Cynna passing on the spell verbatim. They'd agreed on that much when Cynna heard sounds on the stairs.

Feet, sounding heavy. Booted feet, she thought. And words barked out in a crisp voice. Chinese words, of course, so she didn't know what the hell she said.

A moment later Lily arrived, wrapped in a blanket and carried by one of the guards. Her face was pale as pus. Her gaze darted around wildly. She was shaking, little tremors that traveled from head to toe. Cynna shot to her feet. "What the hell have you done to her?"

The guard with the blue armor came up the stairs behind the guard carrying Lily, issuing orders Cynna couldn't understand. Another guard followed him. A small, odd figure brought up the rear, a tiny woman as pale as Lily, though her pallor looked permanent. Her hair was the same color as Cynna's, but her features were Chinese.

Cynna strode forward. "Lily." She reached out to touch her friend, but the man holding her knocked Cynna's hand away, barking something at her. Lily's lips moved, but Cynna couldn't hear what she said.

"Fang does not want you to touch her arm," Alice told her.

After that, a lot of Chinese flew around as the guard who held Lily carried her into the cell. Blue-Armor—whose name seemed to be Fang—Alice, and the healer all spoke, sometimes right on top of each other, though everyone had to pause when the pale little woman answered a question directed at her by Ah Li, because no one could have heard the woman's whispers otherwise.

They didn't all fit in the cell. Cynna managed to shove her

way in. She was taller than any of them, after all. Or maybe it was the pure blind panic that did it. She fell to her knees beside Lily, who was still covered by that damn blanket. "Jesus, it must be eighty degrees in here! Are you trying to give her heat stroke? What the hell did you do to her?" As she spoke— yelled—she pulled back the blanket.

Lily jerked like she'd been shot, her eyes flying open. "No!" It came out hoarse, like she'd already shouted her voice away. "No, no, no . . ."

Her forearm was badly swollen. "Did you break it? What's wrong with her arm? What—"

Hands on Cynna's shoulders. "Come."

Something in her snapped at hearing that damn word. She shoved to her feet and spun, aiming a blow at whoever—she couldn't see right with her eyes all blurry and wet—but her goddamned arm, the splinted one, bashed into someone else's body in the crowded space. Pain ricocheted through her. Her knees damn near buckled.

"Come," the voice ordered again. It was Blue-Armor, she thought. Fang. He had hold of her elbow now.

Alice spoke in her maddeningly calm way. "Ah Hai believes the blanket necessary. She thinks Lily is in shock. Come out of the cell and let Ah Li see to Lily. She is a healer."

"She can't—Lily's Gift—" Cynna's voice hiccupped to a stop on a sob.

"She cannot heal Lily, but she can help. The Fist Second will remove you if you do not remove yourself. He does not want her to die."

Cynna allowed herself to be propelled out of the tiny cell, but she stopped just outside it so she could look in. Alice had preceded her and Fang, leaving the two barefoot women in there with Lily. The healer knelt on the floor, running her hands along the length of Lily's body without touching her and humming—a weird, atonal sound that shifted pitch unpredictably. She said something. Fang said something. One of the guards hurried off, heading down the stairs. The healer said some more things. The little blond Chinese woman was kneeling beside Lily, too. She replied in a whisper.

Cynna, too, whispered. "What happened to her? What's wrong with her?"

Alice answered. "She was stung by a type of ant that may not exist in your world. The sting causes great pain—indeed, common lore has it that people can be driven mad by the pain, though I suspect this is hyperbole. I have not experienced it myself as the *téngtòng mǎyǐ* are not found here, but in the jungles to the north."

Cynna licked her lips, which felt oddly numb. "Then how did they get here to sting Lily?"

"The sting, while painful, does not cause any lasting damage. Shock is not—"

Cynna rounded on her. "How the hell did those ants sting Lily?"

A fraction of a second's hesitation. "Zhu Kongqi was conducting an experiment."

Hate boiled up, so strong it made her shake. A tsunami of hate, pure and total, demanding action, a goal, a *target*—

The guard who'd been dispatched came trotting back carrying a pile of blankets and mats. He trotted right at Cynna. Her heart pounded so hard in her ears she couldn't hear him, but she saw his lips move. Belatedly she realized she was blocking the doorway. Those blankets were for Lily.

She stepped aside. She was shaking.

The guards passed his load to the tiny blond-haired woman. She and Ah Li began rearranging Lily, propping her legs up, rolling one mat to create a support for her arm. Lily keened when they moved it. The sound made Cynna's shaking worse. The two barefoot women murmured to each other some more, then the healer glanced over her shoulder at Cynna. She spoke.

Alice translated. "She wishes to know if Lily has diabetes."

"No!" Cynna said, startled. "That is . . ." Could Lily have diabetes and not ever have mentioned it to Cynna? Even if that were true—and Cynna was pretty sure it wasn't—if she had diabetes, she'd have brought medication with her. And she hadn't. "No, I'm sure she doesn't." She thought a moment longer. "It's been a long time since she ate, though." They'd had some jerky before going into the small audience hall. At least Cynna had. She assumed Benedict had made sure Lily ate, too. Before that . . . Cynna wasn't sure how long they'd been in hell. She didn't know when or if Lily had eaten in the long day leading up to their departure. She dimly remembered that someone had forced her to eat at one point. Isen, yes. He'd threatened to tie her down and feed her if she didn't eat. He'd probably meant it. She had no idea about the others. She'd been oblivious to everyone and everything except the need to get to Ryder. "A long time since she slept, too, if that makes any difference."

More Chinese from Ah Li, followed by a curt instruction from Fang, and the guard trotted off a second time. Then there was some back-and-forth in Chinese between Alice and Ah Li.

At last Alice spoke in English again. "Ah Li is not trained in Western medicine. Neither am I. It is difficult to translate what she perceives into terms you would understand. She has never personally treated someone suffering from the sting of *téngtòng mǎy*, but is aware of how they are to be treated. Lily's reaction does not match what she has been taught. She does not know if this reaction is the result of the amount of venom involved—Lily was stung many times—or of some subtle physiological difference in Lily's body. It may even be an allergic reaction, although if so, it is atypical. She considers Lily's condition to be similar to shock, yet it is not truly shock. I'm afraid I do not understand the distinction. It has to do with the circulatory system."

"I've had some EMT training." Not enough to be a real EMT, but Cynna had needed to know some of the basics. A lot of the Finds she'd done for the Bureau had involved people who were missing. Sometimes they'd been injured or suffering from exposure. Or both. She'd usually had real medical people along to treat them, but she'd wanted some first aid training just in case. "What we call shock is circulatory shock. It means the organs aren't getting enough blood. That happens for lots of reasons, usually involving blood loss, but sometimes snake bites. The venom of some snakes keeps the blood from coagulating, which makes the victim bleed internally, and—and is that what's happening to Lily?"

More Chinese flew back and forth. Fang chipped in at one point. Finally Alice said, "Ah Li is aware of this bleeding problem with some snake bites. She does not think this is happening with Lily because of the lack of other symptoms typical of such bites and her failure to detect any large-scale bleeding. If bleeding were occurring on a very small scale, she would not be able to sense it. This is why we need the focusing spell."

"Skip the commercial. Is Lily going to be okay or not?"

"Ah Li is reluctant to offer a prognosis when she can neither alleviate the symptoms directly with her Gift—she is quite frustrated by that—nor determine their cause. She hopes that palliative care will prove sufficient. She has sent for a syrup made primarily from sugar and water, infused with strengthening herbs. It is used here very commonly."

"Sugar water and hope," Cynna said flatly. That must be why the healer had wanted to know if Lily had diabetes—so she could give her sugar water. "That's it. That's the best you can do."

"Ah Li will also give her a sleeping draught, as sleep is probably the best restorative. She will remain here until Lily is out of danger."

"Out of danger?" Cynna snorted. "Guess Ah Li will be moving in with us, then."

"You quibble with my wording, but understand my meaning. None of us want Lily Yu to die. I certainly do not wish to lose my best healer."

"Your precious Zhuren would kill Ah Li if she can't keep Lily alive to give to the Great Bitch?"

"That is one possibility. Another is that Zhu Kongqi's brothers would be angry with him for possibly upsetting their arrangement with the Old One. That could lead to considerable destruction."

From inside the cell came Lily's voice: "No!"

Cynna took a step toward the cell door. Fang grabbed her good arm and said something in Chinese. Alice answered in the same tongue. Then he used that damn word again: "Come." He tugged on her arm—away from the cell.

"I need to be in there," Cynna said, trying not to sound frantic. They wouldn't listen to frantic. She had to sound firm, certain. "I need to be with her."

Alice shook her head. "You lack medical training. There is no room in there for someone who can't help."

"That other woman, whoever she is—the blond one—"

"Ah Hai was sent by Zhu Kongqi to help with Lily's care. We cannot send her away."

God knew no one here would go against one of the Zhuren's wishes. Or whims. "I'm Lily's friend. I can keep her calm. I can . . ." Tell her everything would be all right? Cynna avoided lying these days, but she used to be good at it. Even at her best, though, she didn't think she'd have been able to pull that one off. "I can let her know she isn't entirely surrounded by enemies."

Alice hesitated. Nothing showed on that damn pale face. Nothing. "Very well." She spoke in Chinese briefly.

Cynna didn't wait. She slipped back inside the cell.

The two women tending Lily shifted enough for Cynna to kneel with them—Ah Hai on her right, Ah Li on her left. She ignored them.

Lily's right arm lay alongside her body, outside the blanket. Her left arm lay propped on a couple of folded blankets. It was swollen up like an overstuffed sausage with red dots marring the skin like measles. Her complexion looked awful, with a gray cast beneath the light tan. Her hairline was damp with sweat, her mouth slightly open. Her eyes were closed, but as Cynna watched, she could see movement beneath the lids, as if she were in REM sleep. Or hallucinating?

Back in the bad old days, a lot of Cynna's friends had tried drugs. She hadn't. Her mom's alcoholism had given her a horror for ingesting anything that might take her over. But she understood the lure, the need to feel *good* for once. One night, one of the dancers she'd worked with at the club had smoked some weed laced with PCP just before going on. She'd done that a lot; the weed mellowed her and the PCP made her feel strong. This time, though, she'd passed out. Too much PCP maybe, or maybe it hadn't been PCP at all. Cynna had stayed with her to make sure she kept breathing. When she woke up, she'd sworn she'd been awake the whole time, but hallucinating.

Her eyes had moved beneath her lids just like Lily's were.

"Hey, Lily." Cynna put a hand on Lily's cheek. Her skin felt cool and clammy. Her eyes didn't open, but her right hand twitched. "This is Cynna. You know my voice, right? Ah Li is with me. She's a healer. She can't heal you, of course, but she can tell things aren't right with your body. And they aren't, are they? Something is messed up. It would help if you told us about it. What's going on right now, Lily?"

A shudder traveled down Lily's body. Slowly, as if she had

to push each word out with great effort, she spoke. "Bloody. Burns. Melting. Things melting. All globs. Globs burning." A pause, then a single, angry word: "*Him!*" As if startled by her own vehemence, her eyes popped open. Her gaze darted around, passed over Cynna's face without recognition, then jerked back. She stared right in Cynna's eyes. "*No.*"

Then she gave a little nod, a ragged sigh, and passed out.

EIGHT

RULE came awake suddenly, his heart pounding. "*No.*"

"What is it?" Madame Yu said.

He licked lips that were dry and cracked. He was thirsty. He hurt. It was dark now, with no fire to warm him, yet he was hot. Overhead was the same dull rock of the outcrop he'd been lying beneath before. "Something's not right."

"Many things. You are feverish. Fevers often bring bad dreams."

He shook his head. That wasn't it, wasn't what had woken him . . . he'd been dreaming about Toby. He remembered that much. A scent dream, which meant it was his wolf dreaming, for wolves dreamed in scents the way humans dreamed in images . . . but something had broken in, broken through. Something terrible.

"Since you are awake, you should drink some more."

Once he'd drunk as much as he could, he said simply but with feeling, "Hungry."

"The healing cantrip I have been using speeds healing, but draws from your flesh to do this. It seems to be working. You will be hungrier than this before you have healed enough to eat."

"Bad for . . . wolf to get . . . too hungry."

"I will not allow you to harm anyone."

He accepted that as readily as if she had been a Rho and truly able to prevent him. In his current state, this didn't strike him as odd. "Where's Gan?"

"Asleep. She is very tired. She did well in the village. We now have a pan, a knife—dull, but it can be sharpened. Clothes. Two blankets."

Oh. Yes, he was covered by a blanket now, and she wore clothes—a loose tunic top and trousers. He hadn't noticed. "I'm not thinking straight."

"You have a fever."

"I'm not going to die." Not now, not from these wounds. He was suddenly sure of that. It was a directionless certainty, having arrived from nowhere and without any reason to back it. He felt worse now than he had the last time he'd woken. But he was not going to die.

"Good."

Her acerbic tone made him smile. It faded quickly. "We have to go to Lily."

"Perhaps she is on her way here to us."

"No. We have to go." He was as sure of that as he was that he was not going to die of his wounds.

"You will not be fit to travel for at least three days."

"Can't wait for me to be fit. We have to go to her."

"We will do so when you have healed a bit more. The village where Gan stole your blanket is on a well-traveled river. The people there appear to be Chinese, from Gan's description. She is not sure what language they speak. Her translation disk does not give her that information, but it is probably one of the Chinese dialects. I hope to be able to make myself understood."

He absorbed that. "Rivers flow to the sea. Which way is the sea?"

In answer she pointed.

"We have to go the other way."

"There are boats that travel upriver. I do not know how. Perhaps sails. Perhaps they row. Gan did not observe these boats, but she heard of them. Once you are able, we will go to the village and barter for passage on a riverboat."

"Barter . . . what?"

"Gan brought an assortment of gems with her, an act of foresight that makes her very pleased with herself."

He'd forgotten that. "Yes. Good. We will leave—"

"In three days. You cannot walk so far yet."

"I'll Change. The wolf can do what the man cannot." And the wolf . . . yes. That's where both his certainty and his urgency came from. The wolf knew. He had to go to Lily.

"You will not waste what little energy you have Changing."

"That is not your decision."

A moment's silence. "Do not Change tonight, at least. Go back to sleep. Heal some more. We will talk again in the morning."

They would leave for the river in the morning. Rule didn't tell her that, however. No point in wasting energy arguing. He let his eyes close and drifted off into a hazy, feverish doze, and for some measureless time he slid between fretful sleep and fogged waking.

Every time he rose to something like wakefulness, he heard Madame's voice, chanting.

NINE

~

Earth
A hotel suite in Boston, Massachusetts
Eight days and seven hours before
Lily, Rule, and the rest went riding off to hell

"I'M bored." The girl slumped on the couch thumped her iPad down on the cushion. She was clearly preteen, though it was hard to say how much "pre" was involved. She still had the rounded cheeks of childhood, but her red T-shirt revealed other rounded shapes beginning to take form. Her hair was brown and straight and might or might not have been brushed that morning. She wore glasses and a dissatisfied scowl.

The man seated at the table in front of a laptop paid no attention. He was a fit man whose black hair had a dramatic white streak. He might have been anywhere from forty-five to fifty-five—though if it were the latter, his taut, tanned skin suggested he'd had work done.

"I want to get out of here. Do something. I never get to do anything."

Robert Friar sighed and looked away from his laptop. "Amanda. You know why we need to stay in the hotel."

"I don't care. And anyway, this is stupid Boston. Everyone here's a tourist, so they won't notice you."

"People in Boston do have the Internet," he observed mildly. "Even law enforcement people. While it's unlikely I'd be recognized, it's a chance we don't have to take. So we won't."

She crossed her arms. "You could wear a hat. Or dye your hair. I don't see why you won't dye it. And you have to go out sometime, don't you? To give Mr. Weng's pills to whoever is going to dose the FBI guy. I could go with you and—"

She stopped speaking and straightened, the movement graceful in a way foreign to preteens everywhere. Her expression flowed into something *other*, something vastly larger than the bored girl who'd been there a second ago. "I have bad news, Robert."

The man's expression changed, too. From amused tolerance to reverence tinged with worry. "Mistress?"

"Most of the team I sent to retrieve the beacon have been killed."

"But the beacon? Did they—"

"They retrieved it, yes. But only three survive." A pause, then a sigh. "No, two now. Their attackers are only partly corporal, which I had expected. This makes it difficult for my team to strike back effectively. They are penned up now in what you might call a culvert. The Xuandon is blocking the entrance to that culvert for now. They can't get past without killing him."

"I . . . have seen the Xuandon. I can't imagine what could kill him, short of a nuclear explosion."

"It is a very strange realm. Fortunately, the Xuandon has followed orders. The beacon is in the hands of the little crosser."

Relief relaxed the man's shoulders. "It has the beacon, then. That's what counts."

A chill note entered the voice that, despite its pitch, did not sound like that of a young girl. "What counts, as you put it, is getting the beacon into *my* hands."

He bowed. "Of course. But if the crosser has the beacon, surely—"

"It should have left already. It hasn't. My inability to communicate with it is . . . frustrating." Yellow flashed in the depths of the plain brown eyes—a flash timed in such a fraction of a second, the man might have missed it.

He didn't. He dropped to his knees, lowered his head. "Mistress."

A delicate sigh. "Rise, Robert. I am not upset with you."

He rose, hesitated, then said, "Surely the crosser won't linger there with all the others dead save one."

"It is not very bright. Like you, it doubts the Xuandon can be killed."

He accepted this rebuke with a duck of his head.

"If it survives long enough to realize its error, it will not be able to cross where it had planned, so will not arrive where we expected. Transit in and out of that realm is tricky and I won't be able to monitor the little crosser's path. Two of the realms it must pass through to reach Earth are closed to me." Another sigh. "One of the things I look forward to learning once I have the Codex is how it was able to cross from *that* realm directly to Earth. That should be impossible."

"Will you know where the crosser arrives, once it does?"

"I will know the nearest node. I should be able to locate the beacon itself shortly after that, assuming it has not become activated. If that happens, it may be able to hide itself from me, at least for a time."

His eyebrows lifted. "Do you mean that hiding is one of the beacon's innate properties, or that it will decide to hide?"

"It is a complex artifact which has resided in *that* realm for a long time. It is undoubtedly alive, and probably possesses some degree of sentience. Given the paranoia of its maker, it will have ways to hide. Not that it could do so, not from *me*, if we were in the same realm. That, alas, will not be the case."

"Then I'll need to get in touch with the squad who was supposed to meet the crosser, let them know they have to be ready to travel at a moment's notice. Should I go myself, once we know where? Amanda and I could return to Boston after—"

"I will postpone that decision until I know more. The time of the crosser's arrival is as uncertain as the location. I am fairly sure it didn't arrive at a time previous to now, but cannot say at which future moment it will reach your realm. I would prefer for you to complete your task here before—" She broke off. Erect young shoulders went rigid. Brown eyes flashed yellow. And stayed yellow.

Friar didn't move. He might have stopped breathing.

After a few seconds, the rigidity eased and the eyes were brown once more. She didn't clench her fists or give any obvious show of anger, yet somehow radiated fury. "Unfortunate," she said in a flat voice.

"Mistress, what has happened?"

"The crosser was wounded by that cursed fool of a Xuandon—a totally unnecessary swipe of his tail in reaction to being wounded. The crosser has finally fled the realm, but—ah, the Xuandon is down now." Satisfaction mellowed her voice. "A messy death, but he deserves it."

Friar waited. When she said nothing more, he asked, "And the crosser?"

"Is not here yet. When it arrives, I will let you know which node it uses. In the meantime, remain here but move up your timetable for dosing the FBI agent. Oh, and Robert?"

"Yes?"

"Once Amanda and I have finished instructing the agent, take Amanda to the New England Aquarium." She smiled a mother's indulgent smile. "She'll enjoy the penguins, and I think she deserves a treat, don't you?"

A nature preserve near San Francisco, California
Seven days and nineteen hours before
Lily and company left for hell

Ed Minsky did not care for exercise, but he'd made the mistake of telling his wife what the doctor said at his last checkup. Not that he'd had a lot of choice. That woman could get a Mafia don to confess. So here he was, huffing and puffing along a damn nature trail. He hated running. He hated nature. He—

What the fuck was that?

A flash of pink, bright pink, in those bushes halfway down the slope. It had moved.

He stopped. Stared. And thought of the hot pink sweatshirt his neighbor's little girl loved so much. The one with a glittery cat on it. The kid wore that thing when it was eighty degrees outside.

Nothing in nature was that shade of pink. He started down the scrubby slope.

Ed might hate running and nature, but he wasn't a clumsy man. His profession demanded a certain level of agility. He made it down to the bushes where he'd glimpsed that flash of pink with no worse injury than a scratch from a stupid damn bush with thorns an inch long. The bushes that were his goal were not equipped with armament, thank God, but they were thick. He could see bits of pink through the leaves, but not what they belonged to. "Sweetie?" he said in the voice he used with cats and kids. "You hurt?"

No answer. She'd moved earlier, though, hadn't she? God, he hoped he wasn't about to find a tiny little body. Heart pounding, he circled the bushes, looking for a way in. And found it, along with a trail of drying blood leading in. "Oh, hell."

The entry to the shrubby cave was sized for a kid, not a grown man. He had to crawl and still got stabbed and scratched by limbs and twigs and it was a good thing he'd didn't have to go far, because . . . "What the *fuck?*"

For a second he thought he'd climbed down here to rescue a stuffed toy. It was all that pink fur. Nothing real, nothing living, had fur that color. Plus it had a tail, bushy like a fox's. It was about the size of a fox, too, but it was emphatically not a fox— too chubby, wrong head, wrong . . . everything. It lay curled up in a ball, the bushy pink tail wrapped around it as if for warmth.

The fur didn't cover the face—a black-skinned face with all the smushed-in cute of a Pomeranian. The huge, dark eyes in that cute little face blinked up at him.

"Son of a bitch," he said reverently. He hadn't seen any of the creatures that had been swept into Earth during the Turning, but he'd heard of them, seen a few photos. This must be one of them—a creature from another realm. And then, with emphasis: "Son of a *bitch!*"

It wasn't just a creature. It had hands. The palms were hairless and black to match the face, and the thumb was in the wrong place, but otherwise they looked almost human. Especially since one of those small hands was gripping a small knife.

The other hand held something, too. Held it out to him. Gingerly he took it.

It was a little silver disk. There was writing on it, but it was weird writing. Some other kind of alphabet, he guessed. Why did—

It peeped at him in a squeaky voice. His ears heard "Meep-ha" or something like that. His mind heard "Translation charm."

"Whoa." He almost dropped the disk. That was so weird.

Meep-re-hi. "I am dying."

And at last he noticed how wet the ground was beneath the not-a-fox. Wet with blood. He couldn't see where it was coming from—maybe the fluffy tail hid the wound?—but that was a lot of blood for such a small body to lose. "Shit," he said sympathetically. The knife had persuaded him the not-a-fox was an adult, so he didn't feel all wrenched about its upcoming demise, but he did sympathize. After a moment he offered, "I could get help."

Mreep-meep-meep. "No time. We make deal."

"What kind of deal?"

Meep-mreep-ma-mreep-meep. "Bury me. You get my things, no curse."

Ed was not a superstitious man. He didn't put much stock in curses ordinarily, but this creature was hardly ordinary. Still, he was sure it couldn't curse him after it died. Before, maybe, but not after. Dead was dead.

Not that it mattered. If Ed Minsky made a deal, he kept it. Maybe he was getting the short end of this one—far as he could see, the dying not-a-fox didn't have any things to trade other than that little knife. It had already given him the charm thing. Though maybe there was something hidden under that bright pink body . . . oh, well. It wouldn't hurt him to bury it. "All right—no, wait a minute. Does it matter where you're buried? I don't have anything with me to dig."

"No. Bury deep. So . . . nothing eats me." The shudder that went through the small body might have been horror. Might have just been pain.

"Okay, then. We've got a deal."

". . . deal . . ." The big eyes closed.

That was the last word the not-a-fox said. Ed waited. He wasn't comfortable, stretched out like this. There wasn't room to sit up. But he was a patient man. He spent the wait figuring out what to do with the body. Carry it out wrapped up in his jacket, he figured. If anyone saw him, he'd tell them it was his wife's little poodle that got out and got torn up by coyotes. He'd seen poodles whose idiot owners dyed them funny colors, so if any of the pink fur showed, it wouldn't matter. Take it home so he could get his shovel. Trish would not want him burying the not-a-fox in their backyard, though, so where . . . just come back here, he decided, after dark. His place wasn't far. That's why he'd come here for a stupid run in the first place.

About the time he got that settled in his mind, the small hand holding the knife went limp. The blade tumbled to the ground. He reached out and held his hand in front of the smushed-in muzzle. Still breathing.

After a moment the eyelids lifted, leaving a half-moon of white showing. The not-a-fox continued to breathe for a couple more minutes. Then it stopped.

Ed waited another minute out of respect and to be sure. Then he stuffed the silver charm in his pants pocket and squirmed out of his jacket—not easy in the close confines— and started to roll the limp body onto it. He saw two things that surprised him. First, the not-a-fox was wearing a belt, half-hidden in the fur. It had a couple pouches and a sheath for the knife. Second, when he moved it, the tail fell away, revealing a huge, gaping wound. How had the little son of a bitch lived long enough to make a deal? He shook his head . . . and wondered what had made that wound.

Best if he didn't linger here.

He finished getting the limp body onto his jacket, stuck the creature's knife in its sheath, and backed out of the bushes, dragging the jacket and its burden with him. As soon as he was out, he sat up and stretched. Damn. He'd gotten blood on his pants. Some on his hands, too.

Couldn't be helped now. Should he check his take here, or wait till he got home?

A quick look wouldn't hurt, he decided. Only those two pouches to check out, and they . . . no, wait. Was that a necklace?

It was. Simple thing, he saw when he tugged it off over the dead thing's head. Silver chain with a disk like the not-a-fox had given him. Another of those charm things. He stuck the necklace in his pocket with the first disk and tried to unfasten the belt. The catch wasn't like anything he'd ever seen, though. Might have to cut it off later. For now, he dug a couple fingers into one of the little pouches and pulled out . . . how about that. Five big, round pearls. Looks like he'd been wrong. The not-a-fox had had some pretty good shit, after all. Five pearls was no treasure trove, but these looked like good ones.

He stuffed them back in their pouch and nodded his thanks at the not-a-fox. "I'll bury you nice and deep, don't worry." Then he dug his fingers into the other pouch and pulled out a small silk bag. It took a moment to unknot the tie so he could spill the contents out onto his palm.

He whistled. Could that be what it looked like? He'd never seen a ruby that big. The color was right, though. Cabochon cut, which might mean there was a flaw, something that made a faceted cut unwise . . . he reached for it with his other hand so he could hold it up to the light.

As soon as his fingers, still damp with blood, touched the gem, it flashed.

Startled, he almost dropped it. Then, thoughtfully, he did drop it—back in its little silk bag, which he knotted again. Better be careful. If this was some kind of magical shit . . . well, he knew who to talk to about that. Didn't want to sell this to any of his regulars if it had magical shit on it. Might be dangerous.

Might also be worth a whole boatload of money to the right person. Jasper knew who some of those people were. He'd want a cut, but if this was worth what Ed suspected . . . grinning, he shoved the silk bag into his pocket.

Looked like this was his lucky day, after all. Who knew nature could be so profitable?

A deserted cove fifteen hundred miles south of San Francisco near the tip of Mexico's Baja Peninsula

As yachts went, this one was a baby at a little over forty feet long. That was a decent size for a trawler, though, and this boat was more trawler than yacht, though it was made for living aboard—bedroom and head in the aft, lounge in the middle, galley tucked up near the bow. On the rear sundeck, a curvy redhead in a tiny bikini sat on a cushion in the shade provided by a canvas awning.

She was cute in the way some women are, no matter what their age. She had the body of a thirties pinup girl and the skin of a true redhead, generously sprinkled with freckles. Her tip-tilted nose was peeling, as were the tops of her shoulders. Her hair was a short froth of curls and her attention was fixed on the screen of the laptop on the low table in front of her.

The man who came out of the aft cabin wore less than she did. Nothing, in fact. If she was cute, he was a young Adonis—tanned, fit, a perfect blend of sleek and muscled. His hair was that shade of dark brown that looks black in some lighting; it was as curly as hers and about the same length. His eyes were pale blue and smiling. "Ready for our swim?"

"Almost," she said without looking up. "Michael, there was another incident involving violence against one of the Gifted. This one was in Arizona. It seems like a trend, but I can't find any common thread among the victims, the perpetrators, or—well, anything, except that Gifted people are being hurt."

"You need a break," Michael said, bending to run his hands along Molly's arms and kiss her neck.

She made a pleased sound. "Well . . . maybe. Do that again."

He did, but this kiss was a noisy smack. "If I do much more, I'll be diving into you instead of the ocean."

She turned to smile at him. "And you don't want to do that because . . ."

"I . . ." He stopped, frowned. And straightened, his eyes going distant. "Oh." He stood very still. Inhumanly so. After a long moment he said, "That's not good."

"What is it?"

"A bit of my old home just showed up here, and it's . . . damn. Molly, we have to go."

Her eyes widened. "Immediately? There's a node—"

But he was shaking his head. "I should have said I have to go. You—"

"Now you're just being stupid."

A smile, but fleeting. "I have to go, but I don't have to go quickly. We'll take the boat."

TEN

~

Dragonhome

LI Lei walked on rough ground beside an enormous wolf, led by a former demon with an abundance of pockets in her clothing and a tie to one of the most powerful artifacts ever created.

Her joints hurt. Her feet hurt. Her eyes were gritty from lack of sleep. The spell she'd used to stay awake last night cleared the brain, but it did not banish tiredness, only sleep. It was very tempting to turn tiger. The tiger's bones would not hurt. The tiger did not age.

Not that it mattered. Sometimes—rarely—the tiger called her. More often, she called the tiger. When the tiger called her, it took no time, no magic, and no effort to slide into her powerful body. When she called the tiger, it took time, pain, and a great deal of magic to do so.

The tiger was not calling her now, and she had but little power after last night.

She had taken a risk, using that healing cantrip on Rule. It was a brownie spell that worked only on those of the Blood, feeding power into the pattern their innate healing held for their bodies. Lupi healing was, to her sensing, very like that of brownies, so she had thought it would work . . . but while brownies could use that cantrip safely on other magical races, she was not a brownie. Her power was very different from theirs. Very different from Rule's, too, and it had been her power the cantrip fed into his healing. There had been a possibility she would damage his healing instead of boosting it.

But Rule had been in bad shape. Despite his assertion that he would not die, he had been sliding in that direction.

She had taken a chance. Not, however, a blind chance. She could not sense his body directly as a healer would, but she could sense the magic that sustained it and read the pattern in its song. That had assured her the cantrip was working as it should, and so she had continued to employ it throughout the night.

And he had clearly been better this morning. Far from healed, but several steps along in that direction, no longer sliding backward. That made it worth the power she had spent, a wild squandering she would not have dared in a less magic-rich environment. She had no affinity for body magic. What a healer could do with ready efficiency, she spent much power and time to accomplish.

Ah, time. Like gravity, its constraints molded everything, imposing costs, curtailing choice. There was magic enough here to replenish what she'd lost, but that replenishment would take time. She did not dare draw directly from a node or ley line. Both could be monitored. That required a high order of spellcasting, but she did not assume her enemies lacked skill. Decency, yes. Compassion and integrity, yes. But not skill.

"This way," Gan called, and scrambled down into a ravine. "We follow this east for a couple miles. Easier walking."

Li Lei advanced to the edge and paused, eyeing the steep side of the ravine with displeasure. "And if it rains, we swim."

Gan rolled her eyes. "If it rains, we'll climb out."

Her left knee did not like going down. Most actions did not trouble it, but going down hurt. "Can you manage this?" she asked the wolf beside her.

In answer he started down the slope. She huffed and followed. Perhaps it was as well she was depleted. She might otherwise be too tempted to change forms, and it was best she did not. There was a reason for the tiger's agelessness.

The walking was, indeed, easier at the bottom of the ravine. The ground was firm and mostly lacked vegetation. Perhaps it flooded too often for plants to grow.

"How come you let him do this?" Gan piped up. "I mean, I'm glad we're going to the village, even if I will have to stay *dashtu* a lot. There's nothing good to eat out here. But you said it was a bad idea. That he was too hurt."

"Yes. And he said that I could not stop him."

Gan snorted. "He's not thinking very well right now."

"This is true."

The wolf beside her snorted, too. She looked down at him . . . not, admittedly, very far down.

The weight Rule had lost was not obvious in this form, and walking on three legs instead of four did not slow him greatly. The gut wound did. The pain must be fierce despite the boost she had given his healing.

He had woken this morning ten or fifteen pounds lighter than before he'd been wounded, but without a fever. This had given him too high an opinion of his plan. If he survived until tonight, he would be feverish again. And Gan was right. She could have stopped him. He could have been sound asleep right now instead of forcing his wounded body to move. "He has a connection to an Old One. Perhaps his Lady is speaking to him without words and we truly must leave now. Perhaps he is mad and will die. We will find out."

"But why did you let him?"

"Because I do not make his choices. Only my own."

"I don't understand."

"That is obvious." The corners of her mouth tucked up slyly. "I also permitted it because we will not walk the whole way."

Gan turned to face her, walking backward now. "Are you going to make him float? Can you do that?"

"No. There will be farms as we draw closer to the river. You saw them. We will stop at one and I will ask questions."

Rule grunted. It sounded like an objection.

She looked at him. "Do not mistake my identification of this realm for familiarity. What little I know of this place will be as helpful as scholarly knowledge of prehistoric America would be to a visitor to the modern United States. We go to a town strange to us. I may look like the people here. Gan thinks I do. I know nothing of their customs, laws, money, culture, or even what language they speak. And you will stand out. In either form, you will startle them. We need a way to explain our oddities. We also need a cart."

"Oh, a cart," Gan said, disappointed, and faced forward again.

Rule, of course, did not argue. That was one advantage to his being four-footed.

The footing was better, as Gan had claimed; Rule was not. They proceeded slowly, but his breathing grew rough.

The ravine they traveled angled away from the ocean. This was good, for the village they sought was set well back from the shoreline. Li Lei had given that some thought. She had seen odd paw prints on the sand of the beach. Large ones. She had not seen any fishing boats. Perhaps the ocean was especially dangerous here and people did not settle too near it. Certainly it both held and released much more magic than it did on Earth. Too much, perhaps, for the purely human? It was hard to tell. It had been a long time since she had been purely human.

Li Lei did not sense magic the way her granddaughter did. For her, magic was a call, a song in her blood and bones. She knew Lily thought dragons possessed the Sight, like human sorcerers. This was wrong. Sun had allowed Lily to continue in her error, so Li Lei had not corrected her, either. Sun had reasons for what he did and for what he did not do. But dragons—and Li Lei—perceived magic more directly than that, a sensing that had no analogue among the other senses.

Although song came close. She wondered sometimes if the visceral song of magic was anything like the moonsong the lupi heard.

Rule stumbled. She paused, frowning at him. He continued walking. After a moment, so did she. She did not wish to worry so much about him. She did not possess the discipline to stop. It was very annoying.

But Rule needed to live for so many reasons, some of them having nothing to do with the war or saving the Earth. He carried her future grandchildren in his loins. She knew this, even if he and Lily did not. And she did not want . . . well, there were many things she did not want to happen, most of them beyond her control. Here and now, she could do little but keep walking and hope she absorbed enough power along the way to use her cantrip again when Rule collapsed.

Here and now. Her mouth tightened grimly. She had hoped never to be here, nor in this particular moment. Not that she'd ever imagined being in this place, in this lost realm, under these circumstances. But she'd known for long and long that a day like this might come.

It had not been inevitable. The Great Enemy might have been stopped any number of times, in any number of places, along the way, or at least delayed for another millennia. She had tried. She had fought against the Enemy for more years than humans normally received. Sometimes she'd won, sometimes she'd lost . . . so many battles over so many years, most of them fought in the smallest of ways. Most of them—maybe all?—about choice.

People feared choice. With it marched change, and people feared change more than either death or taxes. Easier to do things the way they had always been done. Easier, even, to surrender choice, let others make the decisions, and complain when things went wrong. Easier, for many, to assert that God was in charge, so everything must turn out all right in the end, no matter how bad things looked.

Eh! Did people not understand that the vastness they called God reached into this world only through them? That choosing to do nothing when evil walked among them gave God no way to act?

But then, most people did not understand evil. Often it arrived cloaked as habit. In the privacy of her thoughts, Li Lei admitted that she was not immune to the comforting allure of habit. It could still capture her in spite of the lessons of over three centuries of living. Habits of thought, in particular . . . right now what she longed for most was her own familiar bed. That and Li Qin's dear familiar voice. Her son's wry smile. The garden her namesake granddaughter had helped her make . . .

But she was not going to think about Lily. Lily was alive. That much was certain. She knew nothing else about Lily's situation or condition. She would live with that unknowing because she had to. She would not speculate.

Rule stumbled again. This time, he wobbled as he regained

his footing. His head hung low. His sides heaved as if he'd been running. She stopped, studying him with more than one sense. "Gan," she said crisply. "Stop."

She dropped to her own knees. Rule was usually reasonable, but he was a lupus. A dominant, badly wounded, and very hungry lupus. Best if her head did not loom over his while she told him what to do. "Rule. You are stubborn enough to kill yourself, but this does not help Lily. You may lie down now and rest. Gan will stay with you. I will go ahead. We must be near a farm by now."

Rule growled at her. He did not raise his head.

"Do not be impertinent. I am quite capable of obtaining a cart or some other transport." But logic, she could see, was not penetrating his thick, addled head. Too much stubbornness. Too much pain.

The former demon had gotten well ahead of the two of them, but she was trotting back now. "Is he okay?"

"No." If logic did not work, try something else. "Rule. You made us leave, pointed us in the direction you want us to go. Very well. We will go to the village and seek a boat to carry us to Lily—if you live. If you die, who will lead us?"

The big wolf swayed . . . then slowly sank to the ground.

She laid a hand on his shoulder. "Good. That is good. I will be back with a cart as soon as I can."

"Will you bring some food, too?" Gan asked hopefully. "Something sweet?"

Li Lei did not snap at Gan. It was something any child might say, was it not? The former demon might have had about as many years as she had, but her soul was very new. "We will see." She creaked to her feet. "You will stay with him. You have the water. Dig a little bowl in the dirt and fill it so he can drink."

Gan eyed the wolf warily. "He'll try to bite me again, like he did yesterday."

"His thinking is clouded. Tell him what you are doing. Remind him of who you are. Move slowly. I must go now."

With that, she left her charges and climbed the eastern embankment to look around. It was a fair, sunny day, neither hot nor cold, with clouds piling up to the south over the unseen ocean. It would rain later, she decided. By tonight, certainly.

Well, they had been lucky so far. Perhaps their luck would extend to finding a boat or some other shelter by then.

Far off to the northeast, she glimpsed a twist of the river they sought, shining in the sun; the rest was hidden by the rolling land. Much nearer, the orderly green of cultivated land beckoned. And yes, there was a house or barn—a low, small building almost hidden inside a small grove of trees. Sensible. Trees might shelter one from attack from above. That was likely important in a place where wild dragons flew.

That building was her starting point. If those people did not have a cart, they would know someone who did. Li Lei headed toward the building at a much brisker pace than before, moving into a trot after a few minutes. Her knees did not tolerate running for long, but she could travel a long distance by alternating walking with trotting.

Li Lei understood her limitations. Some were physical, such as her inability to run for miles as a lupus could. Some were magical. She was not good at body magic, nor could she use mindspeech as her granddaughter did. But she did have a few tricks.

One in particular would help them now. It was not the most moral way to obtain what they needed, for it interfered with free will. But sometimes one must settle for what worked . . . and she was very good at ensorcellment.

ELEVEN

~

AN invisible net tightened on Lily and dragged her through muddy waters toward the glittering surface, that interface between dark and waking: *here there be pain.* She wriggled and flopped like any captive fish, unable to escape, until she broke through to air, eyes still closed but mind awake, aware . . . and amazed. The Pain was gone. Oh, she hurt, but it was a normal hurting, a mere distraction of pain. Enough to make her grouchy, but not crazy.

Had she been crazy?

Yes. Yes, she was sure she had been, for she'd seen impossible things. Terrible and impossible.

Was she still?

When the sharp spurt of fear flooded her, she reached instinctively for comfort in the way that required neither hands nor sanity. Reached for reassurance, for hope, for a reason to take the next step. And felt Rule, distant but alive. Still alive.

Okay, then. Time to open her eyes.

She saw sunlight on a wall, bright and buttery. A wall that didn't writhe or grow teeth, didn't convulse or collapse or drip ants. Just . . . a wall.

Relief nearly sank her back into sleep, but warmth near her feet distracted her with thoughts of Dirty Harry, though she knew it couldn't be him curled up there. He was back on Earth, either wounded or dead . . . but that hadn't happened yet, had it? How could she remember things that hadn't happened yet? She didn't know how to think about this shit. What did "now" even mean if it wasn't the same now everywhere? Here a now, there a now, everywhere a different now.

The hell with thinking. She needed to pee, needed to in a way that defined urgency. That meant she was going to have to sit up. Stand up, too, but first things first.

As she gathered her resources for the effort, someone said something in Chinese. Her fuzzy brain did not want to think in Chinese. She frowned and moved an arm—the one that didn't hurt—and used it to prop herself up.

Her head swam. She squinted through the dizziness and saw Ah Hai kneeling near her feet, surprisingly untidy; a couple strands of hair had worked their way out of the neat plait and her clothes were wrinkled. She spoke again.

Reluctantly Lily's brain disgorged a translation this time. Li Hai wanted to know how she felt. She managed to answer in Chinese. "Weak. Better. Not all the way better, but you don't have tentacles anymore." That was a definite improvement. Lily had a dim memory of Ah Hai with slime-dripping tentacles and a long, black, forked tongue like a snake. Or had the snake tongue belonged to someone else? "I need to—"

"She's awake?"

That was Cynna's voice, coming from outside the cell. What was Cynna doing outside the cell?

"Lily!" Cynna burst through the open cell doorway and came to a halt, looking worried. "How do you feel? Is the pain gone?"

"Like crap. Mostly. I need to pee," Lily said firmly.

Unfortunately, she had to have help. She was too dizzy to walk the three steps to the bucket then crouch over it. Cynna exited again, either to give her privacy or because there wasn't room in the tiny cell for all of them. Ah Hai supplied the assistance, whispering at Lily as she kept her from toppling over. She would be better soon, oh yes, it was only the drug making her dizzy and that would pass soon. What drug? Oh, one for sleeping. Ah Li had given it to her last night.

Lily wondered if Ah Li had been the one with the snake tongue. Back on her sleeping mat, she experimented with sitting up and leaning against the wall. It worked okay if she stayed still. Now what? What was the next damn step?

"Lily?" Cynna sounded worried.

She realized her eyes had drifted closed again and opened them. "Why is the cell door open?"

"It's temporary. Alice is out there"—she nodded vaguely behind her—"waiting for me. We're dickering for an exchange of information."

"What kind of information?"

"I want to learn more about the spawn. She wants a healing spell I know—really it's more of a diagnostic spell, but it can only be used by a healer. We've sealed the deal on passing on the verbatim spell, but it probably won't work for anyone from this realm. Wrong symbology. We're negotiating about what I'll get for translating it into something her healer can use. I get two payments for that—one for the effort, and a second if I succeed."

"She has her own healer?"

"Not exactly, but that's how she thinks of Ah Li. You met Ah Li last night."

"I don't remember last night very well." Lily licked lips that were dry enough that a grin would have split them. Good thing she didn't feel like grinning. "Does she wear shoes?"

"What?" Cynna looked worried again.

"Ah Li. Does she wear shoes? The slaves here don't, and I think slaves use Ah in place of a family name."

"Oh. Yeah, she's owned by the Zhuren, but they gave her to the city." Cynna's lips thinned. "Alice insists it's an honorable status."

Maybe it was, to them. "Ah Li gave me a drug to make me sleep?"

"It seemed like a good idea. You were in so much pain, plus I was pretty sure you were hallucinating even when you seemed to be unconscious."

She managed not to shudder as memory threatened to yank her down. "The pain's a lot better now, more like a bad sunburn. The crazy seems to be gone."

"Good. Excellent. That part confused everyone. Ah Li said the ants that stung you aren't supposed to cause hallucinations. None of them could figure out why you reacted like that."

Since Lily had no idea, either, she asked for some water.

Ah Hai brought that, but the cup had a willow twig in it. Ah Hai giggled, covering her mouth, and explained that the twig was soaked so it would expand into a vaguely brushy shape. It was for cleaning her teeth—but later, after Ah Hai fed her breakfast.

Lily refused that particular service firmly. Her hands were a little shaky, but not that bad. Breakfast turned out to be cold sticky rice with pickled vegetables, eaten without the benefit of utensils. Maybe they were afraid their prisoners would stab them with a chopstick.

It was unutterably delicious. She was starving. She ate quickly. Her arm, the sore one, worked fine. No lingering tremors. It looked puffy and was dotted with angry red spots, but it worked. She kept staring at it. No ants. Every so often she'd twist it around to make sure of that.

When her bowl was empty, Ah Hai offered her a damp rag to clean her hands and some salt to go with the wet willow twig. Apparently you were supposed to scrub with the salt as well as chewing on the twig. Lily did that, then glanced at Cynna and said in English, "Ah . . . she's been here all night?"

"She won't leave. She says she's yours."

Lily jerked. "What?"

Another voice came from just outside the cell, speaking Chinese. "Zhu Kongqi told her to care for you. She may consider herself on loan to you." Alice stood behind Cynna. Since she was nearly a head shorter than Cynna, Lily couldn't see her well. Alice switched to English. "I have waited patiently, Cynna, but it is time we finished our discussion."

"Yes, but . . ." Cynna frowned at Lily.

Ah Hai had taken advantage of Lily's distraction to take one of her hands and start rubbing it with scented soap, combining cleaning with massage. It felt really good. "Go on, Cynna. I'm all right." That was at least half true. Physically she was much better. The food had helped clear away the lingering effects of the drug.

Cynna grimaced. "I was hoping for some input from you. You're good with questions."

Ah. "You know the sort of things I'd ask for." As she spoke, Lily poked at the sense coiled up in her gut. Its ready response surprised her. She might be a mass of aches and weakness temporarily knitted together by sticky rice, but her mindsense felt springy and powerful. *I'll listen in*, she told Cynna.

Cynna nodded and followed Alice out of the cell. Lily could see one end of the wooden table through the cell doorway; Alice sat at it. Cynna probably did, too, but she'd moved out of Lily's line of sight. This wasn't a problem for her mindsense, which followed Cynna's glowing kiwi mind easily.

Ah Hai released Lily's hand and whispered something Lily didn't catch. She looked at the little woman and, reminded, brought her mindsense back to touch Ah Hai with it. "Pardon?"

"If you would put your hand in the bowl, please?" Ah Hai held out a wooden bowl filled with water.

Bemused, Lily rinsed her hand. The water was tepid and made her want more of it. A bath. She needed another bath.

Li Hai set the bowl down and began drying Lily's hand with a scrap of linen. She whispered so softly that Lily barely heard her. "The honorable Báitóu Alice Li is wrong, honored *lái*."

"What do you mean?" Without intending to, Lily had lowered her voice, too.

For the first time, Li Hai looked up, looked Lily right in the eye—and her uncolored eyes shone with fervency. "You took my pain. The pain intended for me. The pain the Zhu would have given me, not for any wrong I had done, but because he wished to. I am yours now."

Well, shit. What did she say to that? Did she try to explain? How could she, when she didn't understand herself? She'd *had* to keep saying no. Even when she couldn't pluck the real bits out of the hallucinatory ocean, even when she couldn't remember what she was saying no to, much less why, she'd had to keep saying it.

"All right," Cynna said in the outer room. "We're agreed about the first payment. You'll tell me all you can about the wild dragons. For the second payment I've asked for several things, but you keep turning me down. Why don't you make me an offer?"

Quickly Lily sent her mindsense back to the other room. *Cynna*, she sent, her lips moving soundlessly, *I want to know why Alice is here.* And then, as Ah Hai began washing her other hand, changed her mind. *Cancel that. I'll find out elsewhere.*

"Very well," Alice said. "In return for your honest effort at translating the spell, I will give you your freedom in three years. If you succeed, I will free you in one year."

Silence. Here in the cell, Ah Hai finished washing Lily's hand and retrieved the bowl of water so Lily could rinse.

Cynna spoke slowly. "You think my freedom will mean much to me without my baby?"

"I cannot offer you your baby. I can offer you freedom."

"No deal."

That's what Cynna said. It was not what Lily's mindsense "heard." *Go fuck yourself* came through loud and clear. Lily's eyebrows lifted. That hadn't been directed at her. Maybe Cynna wanted to shout that at the whole world, wanted it badly enough that she broadcast it in a way Lily could pick up.

"You still believe you'll be able to affect what happens when the children arrive," Alice observed with all the emotion of the airport voice that warns people "unattended baggage will be removed immediately."

You better damn well fucking believe it.

Another really clear thought. Before Cynna could shout out loud what she was screaming mentally, Lily sent another question. *Ask her what day and time it is in our realm right now.*

"What day and time is it in my realm now?" Cynna asked. "And does a day here equal a day there? If not, how does the time rate differ?"

Good addition, Lily applauded. They needed all three answers. If time here passed faster or slower than it did on Earth, knowing the current day wouldn't tell them how long it would be until the children arrived.

"That is three questions, but you have only two payments remaining."

"I want all of that answered as my second payment. Translating the spell is going to be difficult. It deserves ample payment."

A longish pause. "I am unable to answer the first question, as simultaneity across realms that are not congruent in time is not a rational concept. I believe, from the nature of your questions, you are attempting to determine how time passes here in relation to your home realm?"

Cynna hesitated.

Yes, Lily sent.

"Yes," Cynna said.

"I can tell you that a day here does not, at this time, equal a day in your home realm. The amount of variance is itself variable, however, so any answer I give you today would be inaccurate tomorrow. I could tell you what the general range of variance is."

"How general?"

"It will be based on sixty-seven years of data. For the first fifty-five years such data was obtained through an imprecise mechanism, but we believe it to be accurate to within seven minutes. The data obtained in the past eight years should be accurate within three seconds."

That works, Lily sent, *if she'll also tell you every day what that day's variance is, starting today.* This way they'd get some idea right away.

Cynna relayed that, adding, "And you need to tell me all of this—the general range and the daily variation—in terms I understand. Hours and minutes, that is."

"I am accustomed to using those units, so that will not be a problem. However, I will not always be available to give you the daily variation. I can see that you receive the information."

"Agreed," Cynna said.

"Agreed," Alice said. "And your third payment, should you earn it?"

See if she'll let you save that one for later.

"I'd like to settle that later. I want a chance to talk to Lily about it. The translation will take time, so there's no rush."

"I prefer to settle it now."

"I don't."

Another silence. Lily imagined Cynna sitting out there in grim quiet, determined to outwait the other woman. Finally Alice sighed. "I can see you will not cooperate on this point. Very well. What do you need to begin your translation?"

"Right away, something to write on and with. And next, Ah Li. I'll have questions for her and I'll need her to try various versions as I work them up. I'll need you to translate."

"Ah Li's time is very full. Can Ah Hai answer your questions? She is already here, and she is of the same culture."

"Probably, for now. I'll still need Ah Li eventually."

"Very well. I will not be able to translate for you, however. I have other duties. Lily Yu seems to be fluent enough to handle the translating."

"Wait a minute," Lily called out. "If you want my help, I should receive a payment, too."

Alice turned to look into the cell at Lily. "Your assistance would be a convenience for me, but is not a necessity. I do not object to a small payment, but it will be material rather than informational."

"Okay. I'll accept the payment that you, in all fairness, believe would most benefit me without exceeding the value of my assistance." This way she got paid twice—once in whatever Alice deemed fair payment, and again when she learned what Alice thought would "most benefit" her.

Alice blinked slowly, then smiled her faint smile. "You have dealt with dragons, haven't you? Very well. Agreed." She stood. "The time variance now is approximately seventeen minutes, seventeen seconds. Cynna, I will send over writing materials."

"Hold on," Cynna said. "What's the general range for that variance?"

"You will receive that portion of your payment upon completing your efforts, not before you have started. About the verbatim spell . . ."

When they started discussing the specifics of the spell, Lily stopped listening. Much more interesting that Alice had been able to cite the time variation right off the top of her head. Lily thought about that, frowning.

"Honorable *lái*?" a timid voice said.

Lily blinked and looked at Ah Hai, who still knelt nearby. "Doesn't that hurt your knees?"

"My . . . oh." She flushed slightly, as if Lily had commented on something extremely personal. "I am old now and sometimes stiff, but I can still adopt correct posture."

"Hmm," Lily said, borrowing one of Rule's favorite

responses. "Well, if you're kneeling because you think it's proper, that's your business. Just don't do it because you think I want you to, okay?"

Ah Hai looked confused.

"Never mind. What did you want?"

"Oh, a silly thing. I wondered if you would be going to the bathhouse today? And if I might go there ahead of you and bathe?" She blushed. "I am not very fresh, I think."

"I don't know if I'll be allowed to go the bathhouse today, but you can go whether or not I do. I guess we can ask Alice if I get a bath today. Ah . . . there's something I've wondered that you might help me with. How long has the, uh, the honorable Báitóu Alice Li lived here?"

Ah Hai's eyes widened in surprise. "She was born here."

Lily blinked. Born here? But . . . "She's not Chinese."

"Her mother was a *lái* from another land. I do not know what land," she whispered apologetically, "but she had yellow hair like your friend."

What about her father? Alice's pale face showed no signs of an Asian heritage. "What is Alice's position? Her rank? I don't like to ask her directly. It seems impolite."

"You did not know? She is *xi qi*, like you."

Xi qi. Lily had heard that phrase before, but her mindsense hadn't been working then. It was now. To Ah Hai, *xi qi* meant "like the Seven," and also meant . . . "Another way to say it would be that she is dragon kin?"

Ah Hai nodded, smiling.

Dragon kin, but descended from dragons in a literal way, unlike Lily. Alice was the daughter of one of the Zhuren. Or granddaughter? But that would make her three-quarters Asian, and she looked wholly European. And was her parent or grandparent the reason her mind was shielded? No, that didn't make sense. The Zhuren were simply not present to Lily's mindsense. Alice had an actual shield, which meant she could use mind magic.

Lily shook her head, impatient with her own confusion. One thing was clear. If Alice was descended from one of the Zhuren, then her twin sister had been, too. Helen, whom Lily had killed. That was not likely to make Lily popular here. "I suppose the Zhuren have had a great many children."

Ah Li ducked her head. "Not a great many. Few women can hold their seed properly. It is very powerful."

Powerful in that it carried power, yes, and magic interfered with fertility. Still, hadn't Sam said that the spawn back on Earth, the ones he'd created from a botched hatching, had had a lot of descendants? Maybe she wasn't remembering clearly. An awful lot had happened since then. "Still, it has been five generations. Even if their children are few, those children have had children, too. There must be many who are dragon kin."

"Oh, no. I have not been clear. Not all children born to those who lie with one of the Zhuren are *xi qi*. All have magic, you understand, but not all have magic in a way that is like the Seven."

Ah. That made more sense. It was the magical lineage the Zhuren traced, and they only claimed those offspring or descendants who possessed dragon-style magic. But what would the spawn consider dragon-style magic? They were mind-blind, but according to Sam, that wouldn't be true of their descendants. "The children are tested to determine what type of magic they possess?"

Ah Hai shook her head. "I do not know if there is a test, only that such children are announced as *xi qi*. Although sometimes one is not announced until he or she is almost grown."

Telepaths often didn't come into their Gift until puberty. Human telepaths, that is. Helen Whitehead had been a telepath. Would the spawn have recognized Helen's Gift as dragon magic when they themselves were blind to it? They'd recognized Alice, called her *xi qi*. "Can you tell me what Alice Báitóu's Gift is?"

Ah Hai looked puzzled.

"What type of magic does she possess?"

"I do not know. She is much favored, however, so she must be powerful."

"How is she related to the Zhuren? Whose child or grand-child or—"

Ah Hai was so distressed she interrupted. "Honored *lái*, I am glad you asked me instead of the honorable Báitóu Alice Li. It is considered very rude to ask this of one of the *xi qi*. The

Zhuren do not consider it proper to—to speak of which of them fathered a child."

"That's very dragon of them." Dragons considered parentage a deeply private matter. Maybe that was instinct rather than a social dictum. It might seem odd to think of such solitary beings as having social rules, but they did—generally geared toward making them less likely to kill each other.

"Pardon?" Ah Hai asked hesitantly.

"Never mind. Thank you for your guidance. I have a question about the sister of—"

"The hell he is!" Cynna cried.

Lily had mostly tuned out what was going on in the large room outside her cell. Cynna's angry outburst jolted her attention that way, and she realized she'd heard but not heeded a new voice in the conversation between Cynna and Alice: Fist Second Fang Ye Lì.

He said something in Chinese. She caught a few phrases—"yellow-haired" and "tell her"—but not the significant ones.

"Be still," Alice said firmly, "or the Fist Second will have you restrained. How will that help?"

Lily sent her mindsense back into the other room. Cynna's mind was the easiest to spot, being that light, glowing green. Alice's mind was distinctive, too. There were four unknown minds clustered together—guards?—and one she thought she recognized. That mind was close to Alice and Cynna. She reached for it.

The Fist Second spoke again, but he wasn't addressing her, so she didn't get a mindspeech assist in catching the meaning. She didn't need it. The words were simple. "Bring Lily Yu out now."

A moment later one of the guards stood in the doorway and used that hated word: "Come."

Ah Hai must have understood that English word, if she didn't know any others. She helped Lily rise to her feet. Lily felt stupidly weak, but her ankle wasn't as bad as it had been . . . it was wrapped, she realized. Someone had wrapped it while she slept. Ah Hai, most likely—she'd wanted to do that before, and now she considered herself Lily's . . .

Lily gave her helper a sudden, sharp glance. How had Ah Hai known that Lily had accepted The Pain in her stead? The spawn and Lily had been speaking English, not Chinese. "Do you understand English, Ah Hai?" she asked casually.

The tiny woman replied in Chinese. "Pardon, honored *lái?*" She sounded neither puzzled nor comprehending.

"Come!" the guard barked again.

Lily managed to walk out of the cell on her own. She didn't start trembling until she'd left the little cell and Fist Second Fang told her that Zhu Kongqi required her presence.

TWELVE

~

IT was the *Qī Jiā* again. The Home of the Seven. Where Kongqi kept his lab.

Lily couldn't hide her fear. It swamped her, creating a physical tide she could not control. As she walked down the hall beside Fang, her legs seemed strung on rubber bands instead of bones—twitchy and unreliable, apt to collapse. No doubt her skin had turned an interesting shade of pasty. Her arm throbbed. The guard who'd bound her hands in front of her had tied the rope too tightly. It hurt.

". . . early for monsoon season, but rain seems likely soon," the Fist Second was saying as they walked toward the door flanked by a pair of guards. "Is your home subject to monsoons, Lily Yu?"

She clenched her jaw. He'd been doing this all the way here. Talking to her, asking questions. It might be an effort to gain information when she was rattled, but the questions were so trivial . . . which could mean they were intended to lower her guard. Or his chattiness might be what it seemed: an effort to distract her from her fear. She took a slow breath, trying to calm her racing heart, and checked the mate bond. The feel of Rule steadied her. "Some parts of Earth have monsoons, but where I live is dry. San Diego is the name of my city."

"What does *San Diego* mean?" The city's name sounded odd surrounded by Chinese.

"It's named for a saint." The Chinese word she used for "saint" meant holy or sage.

"Does your city venerate the wise?"

"My city is filled with people," she said dryly. "People venerate many things, most of them not wise."

A small snort. "Many here venerate alcohol."

"Many in my home realm do, also."

The guards at the door saluted Fang with that chest thump. He gave his name and title as he had before. Again the door swung open without the assistance of a hand. Lily thought she might throw up. Did she really have to just walk inside? Screaming in terror sounded like a better idea.

She swallowed bile and stepped into Kongqi's lab.

The dragon spawn sat in his comfy chair again, a teapot and two cups on the table at his elbow. "Lily Yu," he said in Chinese. "Take tea with me."

She wanted to say something clever. She couldn't think of anything. She wanted to reach for Rule again. She didn't dare. The mate bond had a spiritual component, but it was magic, too. She couldn't risk Kongqi becoming aware of it. Alone and silent, she walked toward the horrible parody of hospitality waiting at the far end of the room.

"Fist Second," Kongqi said as Lily sat in the chair where she'd been tormented before, "you may remove her bonds, then leave us."

Fang banged his chest with his fist, then bent to untie Lily's hands. Her fingers tingled as the rope fell away. She opened and closed her hands to restore circulation and tried to ignore her fear and the way her arm burned.

A moment later, the door closed behind Fang. She forced herself to look at the room's other occupant.

Kongqi's incongruously bright blue eyes studied her. "You are very frightened," he observed in English.

"It is natural to fear pain."

"You have made an illogical assumption." He said that reprovingly, like a disappointed tutor, and poured pale tea into one of the cups. "Why would I subject you to the stings of the *téngtòng mǎyǐ* a second time? Either I already have the required data from my first test or the test failed. If it failed, subjecting you to it a second time would introduce a variable that would taint any data I obtained."

Lily licked dry lips. He wasn't going to use the pain ants on her. No, he said he wasn't, but that might be part of his experiment. Maybe he thought he'd get all kinds of interesting data if she weren't expecting the pain. She breathed carefully and managed to say, "Which is it?"

"The latter. Some of the ants that stung you have mutated."

She got out another word. "Mutated?"

"Unfortunately." He held out the cup.

She took it, hating the tremor in her hand.

He went on as he poured himself a cup of tea. "The *téngtòng mǎyǐ* come from a high-magic region. Mutations are common. Most are readily discerned with a visual examination, but some are not. That was the case this time. It took me several hours of examination to discover the variance."

Lily raised her cup to her lips. The tea smelled so familiar. Like home. Like Grandmother. She inhaled for a moment without sipping and was able to express a complete sentence this time. "What form did this mutation take?"

"Their venom." He sipped his own tea. "It contains a neurotoxic peptide that affects voltage-dependent sodium ion channels. The principal effect of that particular peptide is intense pain. Among some of the most recently imported ants, however, the venom contains a second peptide that acts differently on the dorsal root ganglia. It produces hallucinations." He sighed. "Most disappointing. The mutated venom introduced a variable not experienced by any of my other test subjects. I will not be able to include your data."

"How appalling."

"I find it difficult to ascertain the difference in human usage between sarcasm and irony. Most of my brethren will not make the attempt. Irony is acceptable, but all of us dislike sarcasm."

"Is that an oblique threat?"

"I thought it fairly straightforward. Who is Rule?"

Her heart jumped. "I beg your pardon?"

"Rule. I thought at first you were calling for some sort of rule or ruler, then realized it was a personal name. Rule. Who is that?"

"My husband." She took a sip of tea. It wasn't coffee, but it was welcome. "I called for him?"

"While you were in distress, yes. You do not remember?"

"Mostly I just remember pain. Pain and monsters." Another sip. Should she believe him about not using the pain ants? God knew she wanted to. "How do you know the scientific language used in my world to describe the effects of the venom?"

"Why do you think I would answer that?"

"I don't think that you will or that you won't. I wish to find out."

He took another sip of tea, watching her. Saying nothing.

She tried again. "Why do you begin these sessions with me with tea?"

"It is appropriate. You are *xi qi*."

Xi qi. Of the seven. Kin. What did that mean to Kongqi? "It's appropriate to drink tea with kin," she agreed. "Is it also appropriate to cause kin great pain in order to satisfy your curiosity?"

He shrugged. "As kin, you are due some dignity. As my captive, you are in my power. We will now discuss integrity."

"Will we?" Her arm felt too sensitive, like a sunburn, the skin stretched sore and taut. It also tickled.

"Why do you keep looking at your arm?"

She hadn't realized she'd done that. "An illogical reaction, I'm afraid. My arm itched, and my hindbrain thinks that means there's an ant on me."

"What is this hindbrain?"

"One way of referring to the part of my brain not under my conscious control."

"Humans control very little of their brains. Do you consider yourself a person of integrity?"

"Hmm." She sipped again, wanting time. Wanting to be somewhere else. Almost anywhere else. "Our last philosophical discussion was followed by great pain for me. Do you plan to test my replies to your questions?"

"Not in the fashion I used before. How would you define integrity? How does it encompass or differ from honesty?"

God. She was not up to handling this kind of discussion right now. Her arm itched. She fought the urge to look for ants or scratch. "Honesty is a component of integrity, but it's not . . . just telling the truth isn't the same thing as integrity. Elves don't lie, but they love to deceive."

"Is integrity, then, the lack of deception?"

Lily rubbed her arm and thought about integrity. The people she loved all possessed it, but how to define it? What would Grandmother say? Or Rule, or Isen or . . . Benedict. Yes. If anyone she knew embodied integrity, it was Benedict. "Integrity means you're grounded in larger truths, so firmly grounded that you will die before you are untrue to what you know is right."

"If that is so, then integrity is conditional upon knowing what is right."

She frowned, trying to follow both logic and feeling. "No. It's possible to possess great integrity and be wrong. To do the wrong thing for the right reasons. Integrity is—it's about being true to what you believe is true and good."

"You've spoken twice about 'being true.' Do you believe, then, that fidelity is an aspect of integrity or a synonym for it?"

"I'm not sure. Probably it fits in there somehow, but I need to think about it some more. How do you define integrity?"

"Self-honesty."

That was pithy. And unexpected. "There's a saying in my realm that you can't be true to others unless you are true to yourself."

"Humans are not always fools," he observed, turning to pick up the teapot. "Would you care for some more tea?"

"Ah . . . yes, thank you."

The tea he poured was still hot. Lily's hand didn't shake this time, but the urge to check her arm for ants remained strong. She tried another question. "Why do you want to discuss integrity?"

"It is an interesting concept. The religions and philosophical constructs of species in several realms all place a high value upon integrity. They do not all define it the same way, but the variance is no more than might exist between two individuals of the same culture speaking the same tongue. I am told this includes the sentient dragons."

Wait, what? Did Kongqi think some dragons weren't sentient? Lily phrased her question carefully. "You are referring to the dragons in my realm?"

"Yes. Do you disagree?"

"Ah . . . no. Though I suspect they wouldn't define it the way I do. More like you do, maybe."

His gaze sharpened. "What do you base this on?"

"Sam possesses great integrity. Surely he couldn't have built up that much if he didn't place a high value on it. Integrity isn't something you accumulate by accident, like fat cells. It's the result of intention." She hadn't known that until she said it, but the insight pleased her.

"The one you call Sam is the black dragon."

"Yes." More interested in Sam than in the topic of integrity, wasn't he?

"You claim to know him well."

"That wasn't what I said."

"How did you come to know him?"

Lily took a slow sip of her tea. "I could tell you about that," she decided. "But I'd want something in return."

He leaned back in his chair. "You will tell me about all the dragons you have met—what you know or believe you know about them, what you have observed, what you have been told."

"Are you planning to hurt me if I don't?"

"Not physically. I am limited in the type and amount of pain I can cause, due to the need to keep your body in reasonably good condition. Also, I have not found that torture produces reliable results, and the physical duress involved makes it difficult to judge the accuracy of the response. However, you have demonstrated that you possess an altruistic instinct, one that is capable of overriding your aversion to pain. If you refuse to cooperate, I can harm others in your stead. That would cause you emotional anguish, would it not?"

"I'd probably tell you all sorts of things to keep that from happening," she agreed. "But how would you compel me to tell the truth?"

"While I lack the expertise of my brother, I am able to sense such crude physical reactions as typically accompany lies in humans."

"I've lied to you twice since we met. Were you aware of those lies?" Lily wondered if she was giving off any of those "crude physical reactions" right now . . . because that was the first outright lie she'd told him.

He was silent for several moments, sipping tea and studying her. "That was a lie."

"Was it? Maybe you're right. Maybe I've only lied once, just now. Or maybe I've lied several times. Or I might have spoken the truth, but as the elves do, misdirecting you. Or I might still be suffering from enough anxiety about the pain ants that you can't be sure when I'm telling the truth, because my heart rate shoots up every time I think you might use them on me again." That much was true, and Kongqi couldn't smell a lie the way Rule did. He had to be relying on things like heart rate.

Another long pause. "I am considering offering you an exchange of information. Alice has found that to be a relatively simple way to learn what she wishes from your compatriot. She can easily determine if she receives fair value, however. Either a spell works or it does not. I cannot subject what you tell me to such a ready test, and humans do not hold their pledges sacred."

Was that why they'd started by talking about integrity? To give him some idea of whether she'd honor a deal? "I am human. I'm also *xi qi* and a member of the Nokolai Clan of lupi. Lupi consider their pledged word inviolable."

"You are not lupi."

"And yet I am a member of a lupi clan."

"Are you saying you consider your pledged word inviolable?"

"My saying so would not prove it was true, would it?" Her tea was cold. She drank some anyway and thought. "If we did make a deal, we'd have to agree to limits on what I'm obliged to tell you. There are things that I cannot, in honor, reveal. What do you propose to offer me in return for information about dragons?"

"First you must give me your word you will not reveal my proposed deal to anyone."

She didn't have to think long before shaking her head. "That won't work for me. Too all-encompassing."

He shrugged. "Then we cannot make a deal. I do not wish my brothers to know I am considering revealing this information to you."

"I could promise not to reveal it to anyone who was born in this realm."

He considered that. "That will work, with the proper wording, as long as you exact a similar promise from any to whom you reveal this information."

He went on to suggest specific wording. Lily considered it, decided it said exactly what it seemed to, and used it. "You have my word that I will not reveal to anyone born in this realm the terms or existence of the deal you are about to propose. Before I reveal anything regarding this deal to someone not born in this realm, that person must give me the same promise."

"Very well. In exchange for learning all you can tell me about the sentient dragons, I will tell you why the lupi children were taken."

Lily's breath caught and held. After a second she exhaled. No point in pretending he didn't have her full attention. "Let us discuss this further."

THIRTEEN

~

BY the time Lily stepped back outside the Home of the Seven, her arm had gone from bad sunburn to mad itching to an aggrieved tenderness, a neural shout of "Don't touch me." The day had turned to dusk, a dimming due to weather as well as the hour. The sky was a furrowed mat of gunmetal clouds.

She and Kongqi had discussed the hell out of their deal. There'd been plenty to hammer out, but the hardest part turned out to hinge on the definition of the word "captive."

They had, with difficulty, agreed on the basic terms before hitting that hitch. She didn't have to reveal everything she knew about dragons, but she would answer his questions honestly and as fully as honor allowed. As far as Lily was concerned, honor required her to hide all kinds of shit from an enemy. She did not mention this. In return, he would tell her why the children had been taken—and it had to be real information, not just "because the Great Bitch ordered it." To guarantee that, he would go first. Today and every time she was brought to him for questions, he would go first, answering a single question from her.

It was a badly lopsided deal—one question for her, multiple questions for him—but the best she could get. She'd agreed in principle, then told him they needed a clause that vacated their deal if she freed herself. She wasn't going to consider herself honor-bound to remain his prisoner so she could fulfill their deal.

At first he was amused, then annoyed when she insisted. She'd pointed out that if he handed her over to the Great Bitch like he planned, she'd no longer be able to fulfill their deal. Death, he said, voided all deals. And yet, she'd said, neither of them knew how long she might be the Great Bitch's prisoner before her Enemy got around to brain-wiping her. He'd drummed his fingers, an oddly human action. Very well, he said. The deal would cover only the time period in which she was his captive.

That's when they started trying to define "captive."

The meaning seemed obvious. Captives were people who'd been captured. But a few seconds' thought told her she couldn't use that definition or she'd be a captive forever. She'd been captured; she couldn't go back in time and uncapture herself. She'd suggested it meant that he controlled her movements. He rejected that on the grounds that it would allow her to declare their deal void if he failed to direct her every movement. It was simple enough, he'd said, looking bored. Being his captive meant she was under his control. She'd snorted. If he controlled her, why did he have to negotiate a deal to get what he wanted?

That had pissed him off. She'd thought he was about to forget about not damaging her. Instead he'd told her coldly that he wished to eat, and he'd summoned Fang.

The Fist Second had tied Lily's hands and escorted her to the waiting room where she'd been taken before. The spawn, he told her, did not dine with others, but he would see that lunch was brought to her. This time the small room hadn't been empty. An old couple, very finely dressed, sat on one of the benches. They were accompanied by a young woman whose clothing suggested she was a servant rather than a daughter or granddaughter. All three had looked dismayed by her.

A servant had brought her meal on a small, lacquered tray, complete with more tea, chopsticks, and a damp napkin. This time she'd gotten a version of fried rice with fresh vegetables, not pickled, and meat—a small roasted bird of some sort, sticky with a sweet glaze. Pigeon, maybe, or some kind of fowl that didn't exist on Earth. Fang had untied her hands long enough for her to eat. The food was a lot better than what she'd gotten at the Court of Heavenly Justice, and when Fang took her back to Kongqi's lab—which he called a workroom—the spawn had gotten over his snit. He'd proposed a definition she could accept. Lily could consider herself no longer his captive when it was clear to any reasonable person that he could neither have her confined nor order her freed. With that settled, they'd formally agreed to the terms.

Then they'd begun fulfilling them.

With a creak, the rickshaw's wheels turned. The wind was up. It tugged at Lily's hair, which someone—Ah Hai again, no doubt—must have braided for her while she slept. It hurried the scattered pedestrians along the paths and whipped a few big, fat drops of rain on ahead of the coming deluge. Thunder rolled. A flurry of pigeons erupted from the Frisbee atop the mystery tower, making Lily think of her lunch. This was not a happy memory, given the way her stomach was churning. Swallowed rage did not digest well.

She'd had to swallow and keep swallowing.

She knew now why the Zhuren wanted the lupi children. And it *was* the Zhuren who wanted them, not the Great Bitch. Toby, Ryder, First Fist, Sandy, Noah . . . a babe of three months all the way up to a boy of eleven. They were the deal the Zhuren had struck with *her*. Them, and what she would do to them.

Not death magic, no. That was too simple an abomination.

She was going to have to tell Cynna. She dreaded that. She was pretty sure she could find Cynna's mind from this far away, but maybe she shouldn't use mindspeech for this news. Cynna would react. No way she could keep herself from reacting, and they didn't want anyone wondering why Cynna suddenly started throwing things or trying to pound a hole in the wall or whatever. They had to keep the mindspeech a secret.

If they weren't already aware, that is. Lily had used her mindsense when she first met Kongqi. And the spawn could surely see her Gift . . . but did they understand what they saw? Did they know what to look for? Telepathy, sure, they must know about that, given the likelihood of people like Helen Whitehead showing up in their descendants. The spawn must know that dragons communicated mentally, but they might assume that was all telepathy.

Mindspeech was not telepathy. It was a separate ability, a learned skill, not innate. The spawn clearly knew a lot about Earth—Kongqi knew about peptides and ganglia, for God's sake, which was more than Lily could claim—but mindspeech was all but unknown back home. However, they apparently had contact with one or more of the sidhe realms as well. There was that thingie that blocked Cynna's magic—what had she called it? A magic cage. Plus Cynna thought that the guards might have a translation charm, which meant some kind of traffic with Edge or another of the sidhe realms. Those charms relied on mind magic; the spawn wouldn't be able to make them.

She needed to ask Cynna why she thought that. Her fingers twitched with the urge to jot that down. Damn, but she missed her notebook.

Lily had the vague notion that those in the sidhe realms were aware of mindspeech. Their tech was magic-based, after all. So maybe the spawn had heard of mindspeech through their sidhe contacts. Had Kongqi indicated any awareness of it in their long discussion this afternoon? Not that she'd noticed. She'd told him about her first sojourn in hell, when she'd met Sam, and he'd asked questions, but carefully, concealing how much he already knew about "the sentient dragons."

And there was a term that raised a whole lot of questions. Hadn't Cynna said something about getting info on the wild dragons as part of her deal? Lily was guessing that "wild dragons" referred to the ones from botched hatchings, the mind-dark dragons, but what if—

An explosion of birds burst out of a nearby tree, startling her. A second later, she saw what had startled them—and yanked her mindsense back inside her.

The man who floated down to land between two trees wore a red-and-gold *shenyi* that was as impervious to the wind as the ornate hat on his head. His black hair was in a braid down his back. His mustaches were braided, too, twin ropes that ended in gold beads at the jawline. Husky build. A hooked nose, like a raptor. Small, deep-set eyes dark as raisins gave him the appearance of peering out at the world through slits.

The rickshaw bearer stopped. Everyone stopped.

The man stepped closer, eyeing Lily as if she were up for sale but he had grave doubts about the price being asked. "I am the Zhu Dìqiú," he declared in a voice deeper and less musical than Kongqi's. "I am told you speak the Tongue of Heaven."

Zhu Dìqiú. Master of Earth, aka Dick Boy. Better be careful with this one. She bowed over her bound hands. "I speak some Mandarin, *qiānsùi.*" The honorific literally meant "you of the thousand years" and had been used to address empresses and crown princes in imperial China. She and Beth used to call their oldest sister *qiānsùi.* Drove Susan crazy. Lily had no problem using it for one of the spawn, who wouldn't know how sarcastically it was meant. "I do not know the dialect spoken here, but I can understand some of it."

"You were with the Zhu Kongqi for several hours. You will tell me what you spoke of with him."

Lily expected rivalry among the spawn, but this was appallingly direct. Kongqi would hear about this confrontation. Was that the point? Did Dick Boy suspect Kongqi of making a deal with her? Lily hid her confusion with another little seated bow. "Of course. Is this one permitted to ask a question?"

"No."

Damn. She'd wanted to know if Dick Boy thought of her as Kongqi's captive. Kongqi certainly seemed to. He'd used the possessive repeatedly, and when dragons said "my," they meant it.

"What did he want from you?" Dick Boy demanded.

She needed Dick Boy to think she was cooperating so he didn't start breaking other people's necks to motivate her. Best thing, then, was to cooperate like crazy, burying what she didn't want to say in a deluge of information. God knew she'd had perps do that to her sometimes. "We drank tea," she began. The raindrops were falling thicker and faster now. "It was very good tea. He explained why the sting of the pain ants had caused me to hallucinate. I am afraid I do not remember the correct terminology, but it had something to do with peptides and ganglia—"

"Stop. He did not [unintelligible] to talk about ants."

"Your pardon, *qiānsùi.* Perhaps I misunderstood. Do you wish me to speculate on his motives?"

"You annoy me. This is not wise."

"I am trying to respond as you require. If you do not wish

to hear about the ants' sting, I will skip that. We also discussed integrity. Should I tell you about that discussion?"

"No. What else?"

"He asked me questions. I told him about my first trip to Dis, when I was split in two by—"

"You were what?"

It was raining steadily now. That didn't seem to bother Dick Boy, probably because it didn't touch him. She couldn't see the rain bending around him or anything like that, but he looked dry as a bone. "I was split in two when a realm-crossing demon, assisted by the power of the Old One who bargained with you and your brothers, tried to bring me into Dis. A demon prince of that realm had made a deal with *her*, you see. Do you know about Xitil? Should I tell you about her? Demon princes have extraordinary powers within their realms, and she was also called Earth Mover, so—"

"Fah! I cannot [something] your speech. It is very ugly." He looked at Fang. "What did she say?"

Fang rattled off what seemed to be a recount of Lily's words in his dialect, although she couldn't be sure when she didn't dare use her mindsense. She did not cry "Aha!" or grin in triumph or allow her eyebrows to shoot up, but it was satisfying to have at least one question answered. Fist Second Fang must have some kind of translation charm. It was way too unlikely that he'd know both English and Mandarin.

Fang finished. Dick Boy looked back at Lily. "You claim to have been split in two."

"That is right. Half of me remained on Earth. Half was taken to Dis, which those in my realm call hell because it's the home of demons. Both halves of me were embodied—that is, each of me had a body. An identical body, as far as I could tell, though the me that went to Dis didn't get any memories and the me that remained on Earth didn't have my Gift."

"Fist Second," he said. "Translate."

Fang did. Dick Boy frowned. "That makes no sense. You believe it to be true, but you are mistaken."

"I report on my experience. There were two Lily Yu's for a time. I think my soul was split in two."

"Your soul." His mouth twisted in derision. "How human of you. Your mind may have somehow been split in two. I do not see how that [unintelligible], but it is more [something] than [something] your soul. I have never seen any evidence that souls exist."

Lily was delighted. She could talk about souls and such for hours if it would keep him away from the subjects she did not want to discuss. "I would have said something similar before half of me died and I—"

"Stop. Did you discuss souls with the Zhu—"

A gong sounded, so loud it might have been struck right next to Lily.

Crimson light flooded the wet air.

Dick Boy shot straight up.

Fang issued rapid-fire orders, the words piling up too quickly for Lily to understand. He took off at a run. So did the rickshaw's human motor and the guards, but not in the same direction as Fang. The wheeled-reed-packet bounced and jounced over the cobbles. Lily cursed her bound hands, which kept her from grabbing on to the sides, and tried to see what in the hell was going on.

The crimson light came from the red Frisbee atop the mystery tower. It pulsed slowly like the heartbeat of some great beast. Lily tipped her head back and spotted Dick Boy hovering at least a hundred feet up, barely visible in the rain-curtained air. A tease of motion in the corner of her eye had her head swiveling in time for her to see a second figure shooting up. A moment later, a third figure rose into the sky. Then the rickshaw jolted to a halt and nearly flung her out face-first.

They'd stopped short of the entrance to the Court of Heavenly Justice, and for good reason. Guards were pouring out of those doors at a run. Then a pair of men trotted out, each with one end of a huge iron spear on his shoulder, followed by more spear-bearing pairs. She could tell they were iron because they were rusty. The officer she'd met when she first arrived—Li Po—stood with his hands on his hips, glaring at his men as they assembled.

"Come!" barked one of her own two guards. "Come, come!"

Getting out of the rickshaw was awkward with her hands tied in front of her. She made the most of that to slow things down, wanting to see, to watch what happened. The moment she had both feet on the ground, though, her guards grabbed her arms and hustled her to the open door.

It was noisy inside. Frightened cries and pleas came from the cells on the upper floor. Usually there were a few people on the benches in the entry hall. Not now. The stairs to the upper floor lay on the right side. Her guards did not take her there. Instead they dragged her toward another set of stairs at the back of the entry area, one she'd seen but hadn't taken. One going down. More voices came from below.

"Lily!"

That was Cynna. Lily twisted as much as the hands on her arms would allow. Cynna was being propelled down the stairs from the upper floor by a guard who held her good arm in an armlock. Alice was with her.

"What's going on?" Lily called. The guard holding her left arm jerked her forward. She stumbled and would have fallen if the guard on her right hadn't steadied her. Pain shot through her bad ankle.

"Cretin," said her right-hand guard. "She cannot go so fast."

"Dragon," said Alice calmly as she reached the bottom of the stairs. "A large one, judging by the timing of the pulses. The red again, probably."

Dragon? Hope jolted through Lily. She sent her mindsense out and up . . . up . . . but there was no dragon mind nearby, compelling her attention.

Meanwhile her guards forced her onto the stairs, where her inattention to her feet caused her to stumble again. Lily drew her mindsense back, touched it to the mind of the right-hand guard, and switched to Mandarin. "Honorable Fist, I thought the wards kept the dragons out."

The one on her left muttered what sounded like a curse. The one on her right said, "No wards can keep dragons out. Beasts, yes. But dragons . . ." He shrugged. "The Zhuren will deal with it."

The other guard said something Lily didn't understand, then added something she did: "The red knows too much."

At the bottom of the stairs were people. Lots of people. They filled the wide hallway that ran off to the left and right, and they all seemed to be talking at once. Several called questions to Lily's guards. "Move back," said the left-hand guard. "Make way. Do not block the stairs. Move back."

"A dragon, yes," said the other. "Move back. You know the rules. Move to the walls and sit. The path to the stairs must be clear."

"You two guards—halt," Alice called.

The guard on Lily's right stopped right away. The one on her left didn't. By the time he did, she was stretched between them like a tug-of-war rope. A really wet tug-of-war rope, for the rain had left her clothes sticking to her, wet and clammy. She looked up the stairs. Alice was coming down, calm as ever, with Cynna and her guard right behind. Quickly Lily switched her mind-sense to Alice—shit, she'd forgotten that the woman's mind was slick to her.

Shielded. She was pretty sure that Alice's mind was shielded rather than naturally off-limits. It felt more like the shields Cullen used than like the natural slickness of brownie minds.

Fortunately, Alice's words were intelligible even without an assist from mindspeech. "Where do you take Lily Yu?"

"To the small cell off the interrogation room."

"Good. Cynna Weaver can be placed there also."

Lily's guards exchanged glances. "The Fist Second did not say—"

"But I do. Do not [unintelligible] with argument. If the Zhuren decide to hunt the red this time, I may be wanted. I do not want my captive to burn." She gave the guard holding Cynna brisk instructions and headed back up the stairs a lot faster than she'd come down.

There was confusion enough in the next few minutes that Lily thought about trying to escape. Everyone around them thought the guys in uniform had to know more about what was going on than they did and refused to take "I don't know" for an answer—proving, in Lily's mind, that civilians were much the same everywhere. Her guards were distracted by the questions, the demands, the crowding. They kept hold of Lily's arms, true, and her hands were tied. But they should have used an armlock the way Cynna's guard was. Armlocks gave you much better control. Plus Lily had boots. Bring her heel down hard on Right-hand Guard's foot and jab him in the diaphragm

with her elbow. He was the perfect height for that. Drop, pulling Left-hand Guard off-balance . . . what came next would
depend on how Left-hand Guard reacted, but she'd trained for
this sort of thing. She had a decent chance.

If her ankle had been in better shape, she might have tried
it. And that would have been a mistake. Even if she pulled it off
and got away from the guards . . . if she somehow got her hands
free and made it into the city . . . what then? What could she do
better while hiding out in the city? The information she needed
was here. She'd acquired a chunk of it today, a stomach-
churning chunk. But not enough.

Besides, it was likely that one or more of those ifs wouldn't
pan out. She'd end up recaptured after putting them on notice
that she needed to be handled more carefully. That would make
a second escape attempt much harder when the time came.

None of that made it any easier when she saw what the
guards meant by "the small cell off the interrogation room."

"My coat closet is bigger than that," she told her guards in
English.

Their response was to shove her inside. Her and Cynna.
The door slammed shut.

FOURTEEN

~~~

IT was dark. Really dark. Lily dripped on the floor and reminded herself that she did not suffer from claustrophobia.

"No doorknob on this side," Cynna said. "Are you okay?
Did he—what did Kongqi do?"

"Talked. Asked questions. I'm fine." But she wasn't. It felt
like her only options were screaming and punching out the
wall or collapsing. Screaming sounded okay, but punching out
the wall would hurt.

Let the floor hold her up for a while, she decided, and put
her back to the wall and slid down it, using mostly only one
leg because her ankle hurt, dammit. It was awkward. She
wanted her hands free. Would it have killed them to untie her
hands before shoving her in here?

Once she was down, she was hit with a wave of pure tired.
Tired in every way. She drew her knees up close, folded her
arms over them, and rested her head on her arms. Longing had
her checking with her mate sense . . .

"You're not okay." That sounded like an accusation.

"I'm considering trying Arjenie's technique."

"Uh—which one?"

"The fall-apart technique. Go ahead and fall apart and get
it over with." And there was Rule. Far away, but she could feel

him. That settled her some. Not entirely, but some. Cynna didn't have that, she reminded herself. She only had Lily. Lily roused herself to lift her head. "How about you? You okay?"

"I can't pace." Cynna's voice was taut, as if she were a lot closer to the screaming and wall-pounding than Lily. "It's not right to put me where I can't pace. Otherwise, I'm as okay as I can be, here and now. This seems to be an expected thing. Hiding belowground from a dragon, I mean. Alice acted like it was routine."

"Maybe it is. I asked one of the guards. He said their wards don't work on dragons."

"Yeah, I kinda figured that out while I was talking with Alice. See, I copied out the spell she wanted, and she was paying me for that by talking about wild dragons when we were interrupted by . . . well, by one of the wild dragons, I guess?"

The questioning note in her voice confused Lily briefly. "Oh. Yes. They talked about it being 'the red.'" She sent her mindsense to Cynna. *It's not Reno. I checked.*

"Damn."

Aloud Lily said, "The spawn are dealing with the wild dragon—whatever 'wild dragon' means, and I really need to know what you learned from Alice, but maybe not right this second. But there is a dragon, according to Alice, and Dick Boy took off when the alarm—oh, about that. You know that tower in the center of the courtyard? The one with the Frisbee on top? The Frisbee thingie is the alarm."

"What about Dick Boy?" Cynna's voice was sharp. "What about him?"

"He dropped down to chat with me when I was on the way back from Kongqi's workroom. Flew down. He wanted to know what Kongqi and I had been talking about all afternoon. When the alarm went off, he shot straight up. Is telekinesis an Earth magic thing?"

"Huh? Why do you ask?"

"I just wondered. His title means Master of Earth, and he's clearly good at that flying thing they do, which uses TK. Did I tell you that earlier? I can't remember. They use a form of telekinesis to fly. It made me wonder if telekinesis was connected to Earth magic. It doesn't feel like Earth, but it doesn't really feel like any of the elements."

"Oh. No, TK is a really rare Gift for a reason. It's balanced."

"I don't follow you."

A sigh, then Cynna lowered herself to sit on the floor, too, her back against the opposite wall. That put her calf up against Lily's thigh. Lily felt Cynna's foot tapping restlessly. "Balanced means that it draws on all four elements equally—Earth, Air, Fire, Water. Gifts usually draw on one or two elements, not all four, and people usually have an affinity for one or two elements and aren't as good with the others. That's one reason complex spells are performed as rituals. A ritual lets you balance the elements within the spell instead of within yourself because hardly anyone can do that. It's kinda the holy grail for practitioners—learning how to truly balance the elements. The closer you come to real balance, the more power you can work with. Theoretically, if you could balance them perfectly, you could do really complex shit without a ritual. Some people think that's where the legend about power words comes from—that in the old days adepts were able to balance the elements so perfectly they could pack a zigaton of power into a single word."

"But TK is naturally balanced?"

"Pretty much. Not perfectly balanced—that's not possible, or that's what everyone says, and by 'everyone,' I mean it's the common wisdom in every branch of the craft I've studied."

Lily thought that over. "Cullen had to balance the elements when he opened that gate, didn't he? The one the Edge gnomes tricked him into building."

"Yeah. Opening a gate requires a really tight balancing, and he had to hold that balance himself because it was ley line energy."

"Ley line power has to be balanced by the practitioner?"

"Technically no, but ninety percent of the time yes, because—well, that's complicated. Do you need to know that part? Okay, then, we'll just call it mostly yes and move on. Balancing that much power is one reason using ley line energy directly is so dangerous, and Cullen is not naturally balanced. Trust me on that. But sorcerers have the advantage of being able to see the power they're directing. I'd guess that dragon spawn have the same advantage." She paused. "Did you get me talking about craft to calm me down?"

"No, that's a happy accident." Cynna's foot hadn't stopped its jittery tapping. Did she think she was calm? And Lily had to quit putting off sharing what she'd learned. She reached for Cynna's hand. Physical contact made mindspeech easier. *Cynna, I need to tell you what I learned from Kongqi. We made a deal. One of the terms of the deal is that I'm not supposed to reveal its terms or its existence to anyone who was born in this realm. Before I tell you, you're supposed to promise that, too.*

Cynna's foot stilled briefly. Her reply came back clearly. *That's a nice, big loophole. Okay. I promise not to reveal the terms or the existence of your deal with Kongqi to anyone born in this realm.*

Lily continued. *In exchange for me telling him stuff about dragons—about sentient dragons, that is. That's what he calls our dragons. In exchange for that, Kongqi told me why they stole the children.*

Cynna went utterly still.

There was no good way to say this, or else she was too tired to think of one. Straight out would have to do. *The spawn want to Change the way lupi do, only between human and dragon, not wolf. The Great Bitch has taught them some rite or ritual they can use to steal the children's ability to Change.*

Silence. Cynna was so still . . . "Are you breathing? You're not breathing."

Cynna gulped in air. "I am now. I'm fine. I'm okay, except for being a fucking mess and there's no one to shoot when I really want to shoot someone—which is certainly some kind of messed up, but I'm okay. What you said . . . that makes sense, doesn't it? These spawn want to be full dragons just like the ones Sam told you about, but they're not quite crazy enough to give up being able to communicate, and they're mind-dark, so that means staying human-shaped. But they want it both ways—able to be dragon when they want and human when they need to. Best of both worlds for them. And I shouldn't be talking. Not out loud. Shit. Shutting up now."

"It's probably okay. I'm ninety-nine percent sure Fang has a translation charm, but Fang's not nearby. No one is." She could tell because she checked with her mindsense. "They're all off enjoying their emergency, which is why we're stuffed into a coat closet. A really small coat closet."

"Where I can't pace, which is just wrong." Cynna sucked in another shuddery breath. "That's their deal with the Great Bitch, isn't it? Their half of it, I mean. They get to be dragons, only with the Change so they can be humans, too. What does *she* get?"

"I don't know. Kongqi wouldn't even discuss making that part of our deal." Which she shouldn't mention out loud, just in case someone did wander by or have a clairaudience spell or Gift they could use to listen in . . . the "not reveal" part of the deal meant she had to make every effort not to be overheard. She switched back to mindspeech. *Think at me. Don't speak.*

A pause, then: *Right. Why children?*

What?

Did Kongqi say why they needed children for this power-rape they've got planned? Was it because kids would be easier to handle than adult lupi, or does their ritual require lupi who haven't Changed yet?

They need children, Lily sent grimly. *Children too young for First Change. Once a lupus has Changed, the ability can't be stripped from him.*

"Shouldn't be possible at any point," Cynna muttered. Then said silently, *Did he say if this power-rape would kill the kids?*

I didn't ask. I assumed . . . but I can ask next time. I get to ask a question every time he sends for me for a chat.

A moment's brooding quiet, both physical and mental, then Cynna sent, *I want to say hell yes, ask that, but there might be something else we need to know more.*

Lily had a dozen questions she wanted badly to have answered. *Yeah, we'll need to talk about that. About what I should ask. Cynna, they stole five children. And there are six spawn.*

"Shit. Yes. So—" Cynna stopped the out-loud part of her speech. *They tried for more but they got stopped, so they've only got five kids, which means one of them is left out. That's got to make trouble. Trouble among the spawn has to be good for us, if we can just figure out how to make use of it.*

That's what it looks like, Lily agreed. *I don't have any suggestions yet for how to do that, but we can keep it in mind. Look for opportunities. Another opportunity might be the dragons.*

What? How?

If we can get in touch with one of the dragons here—not the mind-dark ones that they call wild dragons, but a regular dragon—

"Lily, they're all wild dragons."

"All?" Lily stared as if her incredulity might let her see through the blackness. "That doesn't make sense. Do you mean that they're all mind-dark?"

"Like the spawn, you mean? Putting together what Alice told me with what I know about dragons, I'd say yes. They don't use mindspeech. They don't seem to communicate with each other or with the humans here. The people here think of them as beasts—huge and scary and not sentient."

"All of them." Lily's mind was well and truly boggled. "But that would mean that every dragon in Dragonhome is the result of . . ." Dammit, she could not speak about botched hatchings to Cynna. That was the dragons' deepest, darkest secret, and she'd given her word not to—

The ground shook.

Earthquakes were familiar territory for California-born-and-bred Lily. That didn't make them welcome, especially when she was locked up underground. Automatically she reached for Rule again. The connection, however dim and remote, soothed her. "Shit. What are they doing out there?"

"Might be the dragon, not the spawn."

"Can dragons do that? Cause earthquakes?"

"I don't know."

"This place is probably seismically active. They've got a myth about a great serpent who sleeps deep in the earth and—" Lily stopped abruptly.

"What?" Cynna demanded. "What is it?"

"Nothing." *Nothing important,* she sent.

Tell me.

It really is nothing. I just noticed that Rule's moving. He's been staying in the same spot, or at least it seemed like he was. It's hard to tell when he's so far away. It startled me when I realized he was moving, that's all.

Cynna spoke slowly. "You're talking about the—"

"Not out loud, I'm not."

Right, Cynna sent. *The mate bond. You feel Rule through it?*

Of course. He's really far away—or it feels like he is, but that might be because we aren't in the same realm.

But that means he is in the same realm as us!

Lily shook her head, angry that she had to explain the obvious. She didn't want to be angry with Cynna. She was just so tired. *Your Find worked on Ryder when she was in Dis and you weren't, didn't it? And when Rule was in Dis and I wasn't—or part of me wasn't—anyway, the part of me that wasn't in the same realm as he was still felt him through the mate bond. I knew where he was geographically, just like I do now.*

Cynna gripped Lily's arm. *For you to locate Rule, to feel him in a specific location, he has to be either in this realm or in one that's physically congruent with it. Probably needs to be time-congruent, too, but I can't swear to that. We know this realm is not congruent with Dis, so . . . he's here. In this realm.*

Lily stared into the darkness at what might be Cynna's face—a slightly paler shape. "Are you sure?" she whispered, forgetting about mindspeech. Forgetting everything except that maybe, just maybe . . .

"Eighty percent sure. Ten percent I'm-no-expert. Ten percent who-the-hell-knows." A long pause. "I don't think you're listening to me."

Lily realized her mindsense had curled up inside her again when she stopped paying attention to it. Once more she nudged it out. *I am now.*

We don't know where Gan went, do we? Cynna sent. *After she delivered you here, we don't know where she went. Maybe she brought more people here than just you and me. She just didn't bring everyone to the same spot.*

It was just as well Lily was already sitting on the floor. Otherwise she might have hurt herself collapsing under the flood-tide of emotion that hit.

He was coming. The knowledge was utterly sure and solid, however irrational. Rule was coming to her.

FIFTEEN

~~

The town of Bolilu
Two days later

THE map was a gorgeous thing, perhaps eight feet long and four feet wide, covering the entire table where it rested beneath squares of glass. It was hand-inked in four colors, and if it was more illustrative than accurate, it did provide a fair amount of detail about the settled areas. Those were concentrated on or near the river they'd been traveling, which the people here named the Huang He, although it was not yellow—at least not the stretch she had seen—but villages dotted three of the river's tributaries as well.

It should be a fine map. Viewing it had cost Li Lei a full five yuan. She did not have a good understanding of local currency, but she knew that five yuan would have bought a night's lodging at a much better place than the one she'd rented when their boat arrived here last night.

She did not look prosperous. This was annoying. The clothes Gan had stolen for her were old, not as clean as she would like, and had not been of good quality to start with. Shopkeepers did not treat her with respect, and people on the street expected her to step aside for them. That, of course, was only partly due to her clothing; she was keeping her power veiled. Even nulls responded to one who held great power, although they were usually unaware of this.

But it was best if people took no notice of her, and so she hid her power and paid for the privilege of standing in this man's shop and looking at his fine map. The robber who owned the shop would not even sell her paper, quill, and ink to make a sketch of it. He preferred to sell his own copies, and very dearly, too.

Had Li Lei been of a mind to be fair, she might have acknowledged that the mapmaker had invested a great deal in his goods. In a preindustrial society such things were luxuries. Paper was expensive here. No doubt the glass that protected the map had been costly as well. Windows were mostly shuttered or covered with hides, and few people could read. Many would never see a book in their lives—if, indeed, they had books here. Bookbinding had existed in China for two thousand years, give or take a few centuries, but this place was not China.

It had been a long time since Li Lei had lived in a preindustrial society. She did not have a good opinion of them.

"Honored guest, will you be much longer?" The robber who had taken her five yuan sounded annoyed. "It is time for lunch."

"A few more moments." At one time she could have precisely preserved an image of the map in her mind. She remembered the technique, but alas, it did not work with a human brain. She also knew three spells to preserve an image . . . well, two. Most of two. Which meant that really she knew only one, and it required components she did not have.

Ah, well. It would have been conspicuous to perform it here anyway. "Do you have a small map for this area?" She tapped the glass above one of the tributaries.

"A very fine map, oh, yes." He went on to describe it to her in glowing superlatives.

She had no trouble understanding him. It had been a shock when she first heard the dialect they spoke here, for it had been a long time, a very long time, since she had spoken it herself, and that had not been one of the better periods of her life. She'd reacquainted herself with the sound of it on the way to this town, encouraging the boatmen to speak with her. Her ears remembered it better than her tongue—the tone sandhi were almost as complex as those of the Min dialects—but that was not a major problem. She spoke it well enough, and to these people she was a *lái*, a fall-through, albeit one who had fallen into this realm many years ago. They did not find it odd that she stumbled now and then in their language.

What had her name been when she first learned this dialect? Hu, yes, she recalled the surname, but not the given name. Of course, she hadn't lived under that identity for long. Very difficult years they had been, though, which was perhaps why she didn't—

". . . seventeen yuan," the mapmaker finished.

"Seventeen yuan?" Li Lei had no trouble sounding scandalized.

He told her about the fine quality of the paper. He showed her the map. He reminded her that he would subtract half of her viewing fee from any purchase. She looked at it, and at three additional maps of various sizes, and bargained with him strenuously before finally buying one of the smallest maps for three yuan.

It was not a map of the place she intended to go. This man would remember her. She could have ensorcelled him into forgetting, of course. She had done something like that with the people she'd questioned at the farm, then again in the village where they'd found passage on the first boat. But this way was more virtuous . . . and had the advantage of steering any who watched for her in the wrong direction.

It was always pleasant when one could combine virtue with advantage. Li Lei left the shop, smugly pleased . . . and a tickle of something like song made her look up.

The dragon whose silent song had touched her flew too high, however, for her eyes, hidden by the wispy clouds. She stared up anyway, wistful now. Life was never fair. She knew this. It still made her sad. Sun had sacrificed much, remaining on Earth to do what needed doing there. If she lived to return— and she had every intention of doing so, despite the odds—she would share the memories she'd gathered of this place where his ancestors had been born. But she could not share a memory she did not have. She could not give him the memory of flying in the skies of Dragonhome.

He, of course, would deny any sacrifice. That was not a

dragon concept. One considered costs and potential costs, risk and benefits, in light of one's goals. Then one acted. Sacrifice was a foolishly emotional term for choosing to act in support of one goal over others.

She snorted softly to herself and walked on. Sun was very wise, but some things he did not understand.

As Li Lei made her way down the street, she set part of her mind to watch for trouble. She could not truly segment her mind as dragons did. Human brains did not accommodate such division. But she was not purely human, was she? And setting a sentinel was an old, familiar task.

It was a busy street. Most of the people she passed possessed some magic—often just a trace, but Gifts were common here. This was not surprising in a high-magic realm. She passed sellers of oranges, sellers of cloth, sellers of spices, tin, pottery, and several sellers of glass. Glass drinking vessels of all shapes and sizes. Glass vases, pitchers, and urns. Decorative glass. A tiny shop that sold only mirrors. No windowpanes, but likely those had to be special-ordered. The town of Bolilu was known for its glassworks, thanks to the high-quality sand nearby. Hence the glass in the mapmaker's shop; even that robber could probably not have afforded glass to top his map if he'd had to import it.

Most of the people around her wore hats. She would need to obtain one. They also smelled bad. Li Lei had forgotten what it was like to walk amid so many people who lacked deodorant and were not able to bathe daily. She did not have to blend in with others in that respect, she decided.

"I could've stolen that map for you," said a voice from roughly elbow height. "You didn't have to pay for it."

Li Lei's glance flicked over and down. She didn't precisely see Gan. She sensed her in the way she sensed all magic. She could, with an effort, construct a visual image from that sensing—it felt rather like crossing her eyes inside her head—but it was a blurry, flickering thing.

Unlike her granddaughter, Li Lei could not see into *dashtu*. Sun believed that Lily's ability to see into *dashtu* meant that in time—by which he meant a few decades—she could learn to go *dashtu* herself. He ought to know. It was he who had first mastered the trick of it when he realized the dragons would have to emigrate to the demon realm until magic returned to Earth in sufficient levels. He had taught it to the other dragons, knowing they would need the ability in Dis. *Dashtu* was innate to demons, not dragons.

"Shh," she said.

Silence for a few moments, then: "I'm bored."

Li Lei considered enlivening Gan's day by lighting one of her toes on fire. The former demon might be invisible to those around then, but she was not inaudible. As she knew very well. "Shh," she said again.

As they neared the market, the smells from the food stalls made her hungry even as they flooded her with memories. Most of her life had been spent where the world smelled like this. She had already made some purchases before going to the mapmaker's shop; at the market she added to them.

They had reached the town of Bolilu yesterday after changing boats three times. The only boats available so far had been sampans—shallow-draft boats suitable only for short distances. These were plentiful, as most travel took place on the river, but Rule said their journey would not be short. Nor did they have a great deal of time. They needed a faster vessel. Here, in this larger town, they hoped to find a *chún-chún*.

Translated literally, *chún-chún* meant ox-ox. The boats were named for the beasts that drew them. These beasts were not oxen. Li Lei had not seen them, but no team of oxen could pull a boat upriver as rapidly as these boats were said to travel. *Chún-chún* carried official mail to and from the capital, for they were the fastest means of transport here, and so the fastest means of communication. But they were not owned by the government and made much of their income by taking on cargo, private mail, and even passengers. For a large enough fee, they might be willing to forgo their usual stops for cargo. Should they be reluctant, Li Lei was willing to encourage them . . . once a *chún-chún* arrived. There were none at dock now.

She stopped at a booth that sold footwear and inspected a pair of men's sandals. After they'd rented a room yesterday, Rule had Changed. At first she thought this was temporary so he could communicate, and indeed he had been very ready to speak. First had come a question: Could Li Lei create a gate when the time came?

Gan had pointed out that she could carry people with her when she crossed. Rule had pointed out that there would be five children and four adults to evacuate—too many for Gan to take with her. Li Lei had pointed out that they did not need to create a gate. The children had been (or would be, to use their present frame of reference) removed from Dis through a gate; they needed only to reopen one already constructed. Gan was sensitive to gates. She'd sensed the one they used to remove the children and thought it was a permanent gate.

What if Gan was wrong? Rule has asked. Didn't temporary gates cease to exist after they had been used?

Yes and no, she'd said. Temporary gates lacked what might be called an anchor, that part of the structure that kept them from dissipating. Such anchors took months to build, so it was possible their enemies had not bothered. Yet even without such an anchor, the gate's structure would linger for a time. He might think of it as the ghost of a gate, neither solid enough to use nor entirely gone. This structure could be awakened, reopening the gate, which was much simpler than building one from scratch. Still, they must hope Gan was right. Reopening a permanent gate would be much better. The nodes had been destabilized when Reno flew through the magical construct. They would not be as unstable here as they were in Dis, but a temporary gate tied to even slightly unstable nodes would collapse quickly.

No, she did not know how quickly. And no, she could not open either type of gate herself. She did not explain why. However, she should be able to instruct Cynna Weaver in what was needed. Or Reno could do so if he arrived in this realm at the right time. The green dragon was very knowledgeable about that sort of thing.

But Reno could not create a gate himself? Rule had asked.

No, she had said. And refused to say more.

There had followed much discussion, in the course of which she learned that Rule intended to travel as a man for the rest of their journey. He had argued that a wolf was a difficult traveling companion to explain, even harder than a tall European man. This was true. She had discovered that they did not have dogs or wolves here, while Europeans were rare but not unknown. He could be a *lái*, he said, like her. She would have preferred that he return to wolf. He could move on three legs much better than on one. Also, for reasons she did not understand, her healing cantrip worked best when he was wolf. But it was his choice, and he chose to go on two feet.

Therefore, those feet had best be shod. Li Lei completed her bargain and slid the sandals into a net bag. Rule wanted boots, but boots needed to be fitted to the foot. He would have to wait until he could visit the shops himself. He was not yet up to that.

He might not be up to eating, either, but he believed that he must. The wolf was too hungry, he said. Li Lei trusted his understanding of his own limits, so last night had permitted him to eat some noodles with his broth. It had not seemed to harm him. Today he would have more substantial food. No meat yet, which was what his wolf craved, but meat would be too hard on his incomplete gut. At the market Li Lei purchased *ci faan*, *baozi*, and *jianbing*, placing the foodstuffs in one of the string bags she had bought, then set off for their room.

The nature of the street and the people changed as they neared the river. Fewer shops, shabbier people, not so many women. Not so many Gifts in passersby, either. Nulls did not prosper where magic was prized. She let her shoulders droop and moved differently—see, just an old woman, not rich, neither threat nor target—and added a smear of *look-away*. Not a strong smear; she could use only a trickle of magic without breaking the inversion with which she hid her power. But her string bags were full and she did not wish to be delayed by some hungry thief.

Li Lei turned off into a narrow alley between a sturdy warehouse and a disreputable building made of wood. The ground floor of the wooden building was a bar, although its proprietor referred to it as a teahouse. At the back of the "teahouse" was a set of ramshackle stairs.

"That will break if you lean on it," she told the not-a-demon behind her as she climbed the stairs.

Gan immediately rattled the railing. "Huh," she said as part of it came loose in her hand. "You're right. Not a bad club, though. Or maybe Rule can use it for a walking stick."

"It is too short for a walking stick for him." Many things were too short for him in this world. The pants Gan had stolen for him last night, for example. They looked very silly on him. She would be doing more shopping later.

At the top of the stairs was an untrustworthy balcony, which gave access to three doors into the building. She went to the middle door and knocked. A moment later she heard the bar on the inside lift. The door opened.

Rule looked terrible. His face was pallid and beard-stubbled. With his shirt hanging open, both his wound and his ribs showed. But he stood on two feet without wobbling—which he should not have done. His healing had quite sensibly prioritized his gut wound, leaving the one in his thigh entirely unhealed. "I was hoping for pizza delivery."

"You are feeling well enough to joke," she informed him, approving.

The small room they'd rented was empty save for a single cot with a straw-stuffed mattress and the meager possessions they'd acquired: three blankets, three drinking cups, and three bowls. It was also empty of fleas and bedbugs. She'd seen to that. She could tolerate squalor if she had to. She saw no point in tolerating bugs.

"You did bring food, even if it isn't pizza." His nostrils were flared.

He would be unable to focus on anything else until he ate. She delved into one net bag. "This is *baozi*. It is a steamed bun with vegetables inside. Eat slowly. If you can digest it, you may have more later. And sit. You should not walk on that leg."

He promptly folded to the floor more gracefully than should have been possible with a single usable leg and bit into the *baozi*.

"I'm hungry, too," Gan said hopefully, flickering into full visibility.

Li Lei handed Gan two *jianbing*—crepes wrapped around eggs and vegetables with a spicy sauce—and took a bite of the third one, enjoying the hot brightness of the chilis. She had not purchased one of these for Rule. Spicy food would not be good for him. "I think you are right."

Gan's eyes widened in astonishment. "I am?"

"Yes. It will not work for you to stay *dashtu* on the next

part of our journey. It is likely we would be observed speaking to someone who is not visible, and there is the problem of food. You can steal it, but on a longer voyage such thefts are likely to be noticed."

"Good! Only I don't look like anyone here."

"No. You will be a mutant."

"I'm not a mutant."

"You will pretend that you are. Mutations are common here, and not all mutants are killed. That will explain your appearance. You will be the . . . bah. English does not have the proper word. The daughter of my husband's sister's son."

"I'm not that, either."

"We will lie."

"Oh!" Gan beamed. "I like lying. I'm not very good at it yet, but I can lie if I try."

"This will be good practice for you, and easier than many lies since you won't have to utter an untruth. You cannot speak."

"Of course I can!"

"That will be part of the lie," Rule explained. He'd finished the *baozi* and was trying not to stare at the bag holding the rest of the food. "You'll pretend you can't speak. Since you can't use the language here, it's important that you not speak to anyone."

Gan nodded. "That makes sense." Then shook her head. "But if I can't talk, how can I explain why I'm not talking?"

"We will explain for you," Li Lei said. "Before you allow yourself to be seen, however, we must dye your hair. Even mutants here do not have blue hair."

As she had expected, that produced a torrent of protests. Gan was very proud of her hair. But the change was necessary. Li Lei could ensorcel a few people into finding Gan unremark-able, but not everyone all the time. Gan must either dye her hair or remain *dashtu*. The little one heaved a great, sad sigh, and agreed.

Li Lei had bought the dye in the market. Unlike her visit to the map shop, that purchase had not made her conspicuous. Old women had been trying to hide their white hairs ever since there had been old women. But they needed water and a tub, and while such things should have been simple to obtain, the proprietor of the teahouse was not a pleasant man. Nor did he have a proper respect for elders. She could have ensorcelled him, but to do so, she would have had to touch his slimy mind. Sun had always told her she was too fastidious . . . but then, had he been forced to deal with such a one, he might well have cleaned up that rotting carcass of a mind so thoroughly that all that was left was a smiling idiot. Sun did not tolerate insult.

It would have been a *pleasant* smiling idiot, however, Li Lei thought wistfully. But changing the proprietor into a pleasant idiot would be conspicuous, and so she bowed and bowed and paid too much and planned the spell that would send every flea and bedbug for a mile around to the proprietor's bed.

When she returned to the room carrying the empty tub, Rule was sitting on the cot. He had eaten the other two *baozi* while she was gone. She did not chide him. Most people living in the United States in these days had never known real hunger, the kind that builds over days, not hours. She had. She should not have left the food in the room with him. "Are you in pain?"

"No. I probably will be." He sighed. "It was hard to stop."

She studied him briefly with her other sense. It did not tell her enough. "While your head is still clear, you may wish to study this." She pulled the map from her pocket and handed it to him.

Gan hopped onto the cot beside Rule. "We went to this map shop with—hey, that's not the one you bought!"

"No," Li Lei agreed. "I bought the other map to mislead the robber who owns the shop. I stole this one. The boy will bring water soon. You need to—"

"I didn't see you do that!"

"You weren't supposed to." Li Lei had been pleased to learn that she still possessed some skill. She did not recommend thievery as a profession, but in a life as long as hers, one had both opportunity and need at times to pursue less desirable occupations. "You will stop interrupting for a time, Gan, and return to *dashtu* while we await the water I paid too much for." She sat on Rule's other side. The cot creaked. "Rule, this map is unlike those you are used to. It is not drawn to scale. This is where we are now." She tapped the hanzi for Bolilu. "This is north." Another tap. "Where are we going?"

Rule closed his eyes for a moment, then opened them and pointed. "Here, I think. This direction, at least. I can't tell about the distance."

"That is Lang Xin. It is the capital."

He flicked her a glance. "Where the spawn live?"

"Yes, although that farmer said they do not all live there at all times."

"I don't know what that farmer said. I don't know what anyone here says, and that isn't going to work." He looked at Gan. "You have a translation charm. Perhaps you could lend it to—"

"No." Gan flattened a hand on her chest as if protecting the necklaces she wore inside her shirt. There were three: one with the translation disk; one with the charms Cynna Weaver had made, one of which she had used to keep Rule in sleep; and one that seemed to be a heavy gold chain with no pendant. "I need it."

"We might work out some trade," Rule persisted. "At least we could take turns."

If one watched the chain, however—as Li Lei had done when Gan bathed last night—it swung as if it carried an invisible weight. This was very interesting, as Li Lei could not sense any magic whatsoever attached to it. Whatever link the Chancellor of Edge had to the medallion, which was one of the greatest magical artifacts ever created, was invisible to every sense.

"It's mine," Gan said stubbornly. "I need it. And you don't have any chocolate, so what could you trade?"

"You both need such a charm," Li Lei announced. "With your permission, Gan, I will attempt to copy yours."

Gan looked dubious. "You can do that? The gnomes make them hard to copy. It's called a monopoly. That means they want to get paid for making the charms instead of someone else."

"I am not greatly skilled with charms," she admitted. "I know the basics, however, and I will be able to read the spell on your charm. If I can read it, I should be able to duplicate it."

"Will you, now." That was Rule, looking interested. "Cullen says only adepts can fully hide spells, but the gnomes seem to have hidden the one on their translating charms."

"There are three ways of hiding spells placed on an object. Two of them do not inconvenience me." Because they affected the Sight, not the type of sensing she used. Very few beings sensed magic directly. "The third can be used only by one capable of creating a Great Artifact. Gan's charm was not made by such a one. I will read the base spell, which will be a form of mind magic. I am good with mind magic. I will need to . . . ah. *Dashtu*," she reminded Gan briskly when a knock sounded on the door.

It was the boy with the water. Once he left, Rule offered to help dye Gan's hair. Li Lei turned him down. She could remove the dye from her hands the same way she removed dirt; he could not. Not without Changing, at least, and that was an unnecessary expenditure of power he needed for healing. While she applied the inky dye, they discussed how to go about exchanging more of Gan's gems for cash.

Gems were in demand, as one might expect in a magic-driven society. The corundum-based gems—rubies and sapphires—were more common here than back home, so their value was not as high as one might expect. Topaz was surprisingly rare, however; the one they'd sold had brought them this far. Emeralds were so rare they did not dare try to sell one. It would make them too conspicuous.

Diamonds would be best, they agreed. They were highly desirable, yet not so uncommon as to draw attention. Plus there were stories about a huge diamond deposit on the same coast where they'd arrived in *Lóng Jiā*.

Li Lei had learned some of those stories in the village where they first bought passage on a sampan; she'd learned more from the boatmen. The diamond deposit was said to be several days' walk from the nearest village, a trek that was extremely hazardous. To go by water might seem better, but no one ventured onto the ocean. Even dragons, she was told, avoided tangling with the great beasts of the sea. Still, there were always some desperate enough to make the attempt by land. Most were never seen again, but now and then one returned with a handful of diamonds—or with empty pockets and a hair-raising tale of survival. It was enough to keep the stories alive.

Those stories would become their story, Li Lei explained as she rinsed the dye from Gan's hair. They were going to draw attention. There was no getting around that. She could blend in, but Gan and Rule could not.

Rule had interrupted her then. "I don't suppose you can cast illusions on us?"

"I am not an elf," she had snapped, adding with some reluctance—for she disliked committing herself to a process which might well end in failure—"I may be able to concoct an ointment that will make you less distinctive. I do not know, and it will take time. I think you do not wish to remain here for several days while I attempt it?"

He did not, and she had continued her explanation. People who looked as odd as they did would be regarded with suspicion. Any story they told to explain themselves would be suspect; therefore, they must make sure people had a good story to make up about them.

They would not claim to be adventurers who had somehow survived terrible hazards to dig up diamonds. They would, in fact, deny this. It was unfortunate that none of them knew anything about mining diamonds. They would have to display real ignorance rather than the calculated sort, but she did not consider that a major handicap.

She would say that they came from a very small village near the coast—too small for anyone upriver to have heard of it, and in quite the opposite direction of the fabled diamond deposits. Their diamonds—which she would allow one or two people to glimpse—were an inheritance. Rule had simply shown up one day, as the *lái* do. She had taken him in out of charity, and also because he might be helpful on her trip to the capital, but the foolish man had gotten himself injured and was no help at all. And the odd-looking Gan was the daughter of her nephew-by-marriage and had no special Gifts. Li Lei would insist on this.

No one would believe her, she finished with satisfaction as she plaited Gan's damp, ink-black hair. They would believe their own stories.

Gan did not understand. ". . . and you don't want them to believe this one thing, but you tell them that because you think they'll believe this other thing that you tell them isn't true, only you want them to think it is true, and I don't see how that makes sense! How can you keep track of it all? It doesn't make sense!"

"It is a lie inside a lie," she said. "You are too new at lying to understand."

"How do you put one lie inside another?"

Rule was eyeing her with a slight smile. "You are a frightening woman."

She snorted, pleased, and tied off Gan's braid with a scrap of cloth.

Rule spoke to Gan. "People believe the stories they tell themselves more readily than any other sort of tale, truth or lie. Madame Yu knows how to get them to tell themselves the story she wants them to believe. You don't need to understand how she does that."

Gan twisted to look at her, eyes wide. "You can make people lie to themselves?"

She snorted again, more loudly. "That is no great accomplishment. People enjoy lying to themselves. They do this all the time."

"Withholding information is not a lie," Rule said evenly. "But it's not precisely honest, either."

"Why not?" Gan asked curiously.

"Rule is annoyed because he thinks I have not told him everything," she explained. "This is true, of course. I know many things he does not. I am nearly three hundred years older than he is."

"I can see that," Gan said seriously, "but why does it annoy him?"

This time her lips did twitch.

"Annoyance aside," Rule said dryly, "I do have questions. First, about our cover story. It's unlikely the spawn know I exist, much less that I'm here. The time difference means that, at this point back home and in Dis, I haven't yet left for Dis, much less traveled from there to Dragonhome. But we are dealing with an Old One. If the Great Bitch somehow foresaw that I might end up here and warned the spawn ahead of time to watch for me—if they distributed an alert or arrest order for someone of my description—"

"Then we are, as Lily's generation would say, screwed."

That made him laugh, as she'd intended. On the whole, she avoided vulgarity. It bored her. But like the jeans she'd worn to travel to Dis, vulgarity had its uses. She chose to explain a bit more. "The Enemy can read patterns, but it is extremely difficult to read patterns across realms. If she had a large body of devout worshippers here . . . but from all I can learn, she does not. Nor is she truly prescient in the manner of your Ruben Brooks. It is therefore highly unlikely that she foresaw your presence in this realm."

"All right. Next question. At first I thought the dragons here must be like those in ancient China—rare, and mostly willing to coexist with humans. That isn't the case, though, is it?"

"No." She cocked her head, thinking it through. "Perhaps it is time for me to speak of certain secrets about dragons. Gan, do you wish to stay and hear them?"

"Yes!" She bounced in excitement. Then stilled. "Wait. Dragon secrets?"

"Yes."

"Will the dragons be mad that I know their secrets?"

"Yes."

"I'm going to go get some sweets."

SIXTEEN

~

MADAME went to the door with Gan, giving her money and instructions. Rule sat on the cot and hurt.

The pain in his gut wasn't bad. He could ignore it. His leg was harder to overlook. That wound hadn't healed at all, from what he could tell. Or maybe it was healing at a purely human rate . . . which gave him a new appreciation for the sheer guts it took for humans to risk themselves.

Humans like Lily. Why hadn't she contacted him through mindspeech?

Too far away. That was the answer he'd been giving himself, and it made sense. Lily could only reach so far with her mindsense, and he was beyond that limit. But there were other possibilities. Had she been injured? Was she currently healing some terrible wound at this horribly slow rate? Had she connected with Cynna, or was she alone? Gan had tried to take Lily near the same spot she'd taken Cynna, but she didn't know how close she'd gotten. She was sure she hadn't taken both women to the same time. She couldn't. So Lily might have arrived quite a bit earlier or later than Cynna, so the two of them might not have found each other. Lily might be alone. She might be injured, even unconscious. He had no way of knowing unless—

"*Tch.* Whatever you are thinking, you need to stop."

He scowled at Lily's grandmother, who had retrieved the last net bag she'd brought back from her shopping. One she hadn't yet emptied. "Do you worry about her at all?"

"Very seldom. Do not berate yourself. You will get better at not worrying when you are older."

That startled a choked sound out of him. His wolf was amused, even if the rest of him was not. He scrubbed his face with both hands and dragged his mind away from the what-ifs. "You have dragon secrets to tell me."

"Yes. First we will take tea."

This didn't surprise him, as the items she was removing from the last net bag included a teapot, a pitcher, and two small bowls of the type he knew were used to drink tea. But the small bamboo scoop gave him pause. "Not the full tea ceremony?"

"Of course. It will not be a proper ceremony." She had saved some of the water brought by the boy; she poured it into the teapot now. "I do not have proper implements. But we will do what we can. You may fold two of the blankets to cushion our knees."

"Madame," he said with strained courtesy, "I do not think my leg is up to kneeling."

"Then do not kneel." She paused to glance at him, her dark eyes bright with humor. "I have had my hands in your guts. I think it is time for you to call me Grandmother."

"Ah . . . very well." She meant it as an honor. At least he thought she did. Or did she want him claiming kinship to strengthen her right to tell him things the dragons didn't want him to know? Or was she asserting her authority as his elder?

All of the above, probably. He folded two blankets, sat on his with his bad leg outstretched, and waited with what patience he could muster as she set out the tea things. Lily did not enjoy the tea ceremony. He did, but this was hardly the time or place for it. Still, he understood why she needed the ritual. It was a way of formalizing what she was about to tell him . . . though what that might be, he couldn't guess. He was already up to his ears in dragon secrets.

Top of that list was their bizarrely convoluted reproduction. Dragons had a little genetic hitch: they were born male. All of them. The transformation to female involved them eating gold—hence their reputation for collecting treasure—and possibly the help of their brethren, although that was a guess.

After a newly female dragon mated and laid her eggs, she began reverting to what the brownies called primitive mind, ruled by instinct and unable to use almost all mind magic. When those eggs hatched, the babies had to be named in a process that required the assistance of someone who could mindspeak them. Without that, the babies' minds would be closed to mind magic forever, mute and deaf to the only speech possible to them. That was where dragon spawn came from. They were the products of a botched hatching, one without a midwife capable of mindspeech, who had been transformed. In human forms, they could use human speech and not be locked in mental solitary confinement.

Unfortunately, this didn't seem to keep them from being sociopaths.

At last Madame knelt on her blanket. If the position was hard on aging joints, she gave no sign of it. Before she could begin, he spoke. "I know I'm supposed to clear my mind, to focus on the ceremony. Before I do that, I have a question about these secrets. Will you—"

"There are two secrets." She moved one cup a fraction of an inch. "One is very old. It is about all dragons. The other is more recent. It is about one dragon. Lily is entitled to know these things because of her heritage. You are not. I will tell you anyway."

That almost answered the question she hadn't let him ask. "Is that going to get you in trouble?"

"We are in a great deal of trouble already. Do you ask, like Gan, if the dragons will be angry?"

"I want to know if they're going to come after you."

"Dragons are not all one thing. Even more than humans, each is his own. Humans feel a need to agree with their group, whatever that group may be. Dragons . . ." She shrugged.

"Feel a need to disagree?"

A small smile. "Perhaps. In any event, there are very few subjects upon which they agree sufficiently to act jointly. This is not one of those subjects."

She did not say they wouldn't be angry, he noted. "And if one or more of them decides to act on his own?"

"It is unlikely any of them would attempt to rebuke me, as that would annoy Sun. But if so, I will deal with them. No more discussing. We begin. I will heat the water."

There was nothing here to heat the water with. He did not point this out.

She folded her hands together under her breasts and sat for a moment in a stillness so palpable he could almost smell it. Then she reached out in a sure, graceful gesture to lift the large teapot . . . which was steaming.

First she filled the small teapot and swirled the hot water around in it. Her movements were slow, as stylized and graceful as a kabuki dancer or a ballerina. When she poured hot water into the cups, one hand supported the other arm as if she were holding back the long, draping sleeve she wasn't wearing.

Having filled the pot and cups, she promptly emptied them into a bowl set off to one side. She opened the paper holding a small cake of black tea with a pungent aroma and broke off a piece, crumbled it, and placed three pinches in the bamboo scoop. It was now, he knew, time to appreciate the tea. She danced the scoop around, pausing near him so he could enjoy the sight and scent of it, then brought it back. Each movement was precise and slightly exaggerated, with subtle flourishes added to enhance the sense of a dance. Rule found his shoulders easing, his muscles relaxing into the moment.

She poured a little hot water into the small teapot, using a brown napkin to catch any drips. Even the way the napkin was held was part of the ritual. Then she slid the tea leaves into the pot. When she filled the pot with hot water, her arm lifted so the sight of the flowing water became part of the ceremony. As water united with tea, scent bloomed.

She immediately poured from large teapot into small, and from small teapot into cups—then, one by one, emptied all of them into the bowl at her side. The first pouring was never drunk. Then she rested, hands under her breast, allowing the tea to steep.

Rule's mind drifted. He was hungry. The rolls he'd eaten were more of a snack than a meal. No meat, and he *needed* meat, but that need seemed a consideration for later, not for this moment. Other thoughts floated in, most of them all too familiar, like the image of his son's empty bed. But in this moment, Toby was all right. He remembered seeing that empty bed, remembered the tidal wave of fear and rage, but that hadn't happened yet. He *would* get to his son in time. He could let that thought go. Thoughts of Lily were harder to set aside. She might be suffering now, in this moment.

. . . or she might not.

That thought snagged his attention, striking a spark of surprise. He'd forgotten that not-knowing meant that *he didn't know*. Lily might be doing well. She might be badly hurt. She might be somewhere in between, anywhere in between. He didn't know, and he didn't have to keep reacting as if one thought were more real than the others simply because it frightened him.

His wolf chuffed at him, amused and annoyed, for his wolf had known this all along. Ah, well. He let that go, too, content with the moment, the smell of tea, and the company of the woman who wanted him to call her grandmother. He was, he realized, calm. Truly calm. He smiled, realizing something else. She hadn't insisted on the tea ceremony because *she* needed it.

At last the tea was poured, large teapot to small, small teapot to cups. This time they drank. Neither spoke for a long moment, then Rule said, "Thank you . . . Grandmother." The word felt odd in his mouth. He had never used it in a personal sense before.

"*Búyòng xiè*," she said, and paused. "That is a phrase used when an American would say, 'You're welcome.' It does not have the same meaning. Literally, it says, 'Do not be formal.' It has been interesting to be surrounded again by the culture of my youth."

"Interesting in a good way, I hope."

"Interesting," she repeated. "You did not ask if these secrets are dangerous to you. I will answer anyway. It is unlikely any of the dragons will be angry enough to kill you. This would create a schism with an ally they need to defeat *her*. And on that, dragons are united: *she* must be defeated. I will now tell you why."

"You haven't asked for my promise not to repeat it."

"You have better sense than to spread information that dragons consider intensely personal. I will suggest that neither you nor Lily tells Cynna Weaver. She might feel a duty to include it in the clan memories. This would be unfortunate."

"Yes, I can see that."

"Very well." She abandoned her kneeling posture with a soft grunt, bringing her legs around to sit tailor-style. "This is a tale of the distant past, so distant that even the sidhe have no record of it save a few tales spun into myth. Such myths, like those told by humans, hold kernels of truth wrapped in gauzy invention. They speak of godlike beings who enslaved other races. That much is true.

"In this long-ago time, a race arose much gifted in mind magic and much devoted to conquest. To ownership. I could tell you they saw other races, other sentient peoples, the way humans see cows or horses or pigs, but this makes them seem more human than they were. Humans often form attachments to animals. This race of owners formed attachments only to their own race. With others, they were not cruel for the sake of cruelty. They were indifferent. This was their reality: they were people. All other beings, sentient or beast, were to them as a stone or the wind. Part of reality, but things, not people. Things to be destroyed, ignored, or owned."

"Selective sociopaths," Rule murmured.

"You would see them so, but this seeing makes them seem like damaged humans. They were not. Their minds were alien to yours. To mine, also. You and I could better understand demons than we can these owners.

"Some things came easily for this race, such as mind magic. But they were not innately powerful. Canny and Gifted, yes, but not with great power. Because of this, some places were able to withstand them. This was, to them, intolerable." She sighed faintly. "The memories of dragons are long and can be passed down, in part, to their offspring. Yet even dragon memories do not tell how the race of owners found this realm we are in now. It may have been by chance rather than design. Nor do we know with precision how they first enslaved dragons."

Rule felt the jolt of that bomb. "They *what?*"

"Do not interrupt. What I tell you next is deduction, since dragon memories do not extend so far back. The owners would have seen that dragons possessed what they did not. Power. Great power. But at that time all dragons were mind-blind, impervious to mind magic . . . except, as you know, at one time. Through a naming ritual, the owners took control of the minds of newly hatched dragon babies.

"Once they had a sufficient number of hatchlings, they left this realm. Nor did they ever return here. We do not know why. It may be that they knew from the start that they would need to alter their new slaves, and therefore were not interested in harvesting additional unaltered dragon babies. The owners were not themselves skilled at body magic, but one of the races they had enslaved was. It is thought this was a sidhe race, but that is speculation. Still, we know that at some point they took their mind-slaved dragons to these experts, who altered them at a genetic level. Female dragons are difficult to control, you see. Even the owners could not fully control an adult female, for dragon instinct is too strong. Also, they wished to control the reproduction of their property. The easiest way to do so was to make dragons all male."

"Before that, they weren't always born male?"

She snorted. "You cannot believe that evolution resulted in a race that is entirely male. One in which none can become female without a great deal of tinkering. Of course dragons were not originally so." She paused, then continued. "The owners raised their stolen babies and, at some point, changed them as I have said. When the babies became adults, they used them. With the power of dragons behind them, they became unstoppable. More realms fell to their ownership.

"This went on for what humans would consider a long time, but dragons live a long time. These stolen dragons lived for hundreds of years *knowing* what had been done to them. And they learned. They learned much about magic, especially mind magic. Their owners encouraged this, for they wanted the use of those great minds along with their magic. This was a mistake. At some point one of the dragons—not of the first generation, we think, but the second—learned a new thing. Something the owners could not do. Something they did not know was possible. He segmented his mind."

Rule's eyebrows lifted. "Humans who do that are considered insane."

"Humans do not understand minds. This dragon is remembered by several call-names. The most common is Yì Sĭwáng.

When Yì Sïwáng segmented his mind, the set-apart portion was not controlled by his owner."

"Were the owners telepathic?"

"In a manner of speaking, yes. They did not experience the thoughts of others, but they perceived thoughts in their own fashion. Because of this perception, Yì Sïwáng had to not only segment his mind, but shield the segmented portion and hide his shielding."

"All at the same time? At his first attempt?"

"He was," she said simply, "a genius. The first task he set for this new segment of his mind was to find a way to secretly teach this skill to the other enslaved dragons. There is a long story about how he did this. It is useful for teaching young dragons, but you are not a young dragon. I will skip it. The result of Yì Sïwáng's teaching you can, I think, guess." She stopped abruptly. "My mouth is dry." She waved at the teapot, then picked it up and poured more hot water over the leaves still in the small pot.

Rule asked softly, "What does Yì Sïwáng mean?"

Her smile was small, tight, fierce. "A Thousand Million Deaths."

And that almost answered his next question, but he still had to ask it. "What happened to the owners, Grandmother?" She'd never named them. She'd carefully avoided naming them.

"They do not exist. Their cities do not exist. Their language, history, and culture do not exist, and their name has been wiped from the history of all beings everywhere, save for those whispers lingering in the myths of the sidhe." She lifted the teapot, poured, and held out a cup. "More tea?"

He accepted it but did not drink, his mind tumbling with implications. The most adamantly sovereign race in existence had been born in the most complete slavery. Slavery of the mind. When they found a way to lift that bondage . . . genocide had not been enough. They had needed to destroy every trace of those who had enslaved them. "A thousand million deaths must be an understatement."

"Oh, yes." She sipped. "You understand now why I say dragons agree about stopping *her*. The one you call the Great Bitch wishes to subjugate entire races. Dragons have long memories," she said as she had before. "They do not forget.

They do not forgive. They hate *her* with a depth you cannot conceive."

Rule looked at the teacup in his hand. He drank it quickly to get rid of it, then he set the cup down. "I see why you insisted that Reno could be trusted not to act in a way that helped *her*."

Grandmother nodded. "And now we come to the other secret."

His eyebrows lifted. "We do?"

"Have you never wondered why many dragons chose Earth, out of all the realms, to settle?"

"Many times," he said dryly. "They do not encourage questions. I've also wondered if they—our dragons—were all the dragons there are."

"No. Dragons are not numerous, but their numbers are not so thin as that. Many live in the sidhe realms, but Earth held an appeal those realms did not." Her sigh was faint. "It is not so much that dragons want to go home as that they want home to be possible."

"The fall-throughs here," he started—then stopped and thought it through. People had fallen into this realm from Earth often enough to populate it. Demons had fallen through from Dis sometimes. A few had fallen here from other realms, too, but not many. "Have there been any fall-throughs the other way around? People—or beasts—falling into China or Dis from here?"

She shook her head. "This is unlikely. One does not fall up, only down. It is a matter of entropy. Magic is disorderly, so greater magic means greater disorder. Beings fall from a low-magic realm to one with greater magic and so greater disorder."

"I thought Dis was fairly high-magic."

"It has more magic than Earth, but it is not a true high-magic realm. Dragonhome is. We are traveling through what is probably the lowest-magic region in this world, and there is more magic here than anywhere on Earth and most parts of Dis. Humans cannot live in most parts of Dragonhome. Some places here even the sidhe could not survive for long."

He considered that, decided it didn't take him anywhere useful, and brought the conversation back to what she'd said earlier. Or had she just implied it? "The dragons—some of them anyway—came to Earth to be closer to their home realm?"

"In part. Theory made them think Earth had nodes in common with Dragonhome. Also, they were curious about humans. Curiosity is a driving force with dragons. It wars at times with their territorial instinct; they do not love travel. But a chance to learn about their ancient home was very interesting to them. A chance to find their lost kin was, for some, compelling.

"The chance seemed slight. They knew little of their original realm, you understand. Certainly not how to find it. They found a few hints, but these were tenuous. Many dragons concluded that either the realm itself or access to it had been destroyed by the owners long ago, possibly in one of their ritualistic wars among themselves. They were a quarrelsome people," she added. "But dragons did not forget their distant kin. They did not forget that there was, or once had been, a world where all dragons were mind-blind. They did not," she concluded dryly, "agree about what to do, but some wanted to find those kin, or at least determine that such a finding was impossible."

Curiosity stirred. "How did they manage to get to Earth when they can't build gates?"

"Who do you think taught the gnomes how to build gates?"

"Ah . . . I see. I suppose they wouldn't have passed on that knowledge for free?"

Her response was a soft snort.

"Is that how we got our gate into Dis? Because of some ages-old deal between gnomes and dragons?"

"All gnomes everywhere must build a gate or see that one is built if two or more dragons require it of them."

He considered that. "And yet they needed Lily, and the gate she carried at the time, to leave Dis."

"There are no gnomes in Dis. You are running after shiny things, leaving the real subject behind. Stop this. Several dragons came to Earth not long—I speak in dragon terms—before the Great War. Yes," she said, no doubt reading his expression, "you see that this changed matters."

The Great War she referred to was not World War One, but a cataclysm that had engulfed pretty much every realm in existence over three thousand years ago. At its heart, it had been a battle of ideas . . . opposing ideas held by two camps of Old Ones. One side fought for self-determination for the younger races. Sovereignty, in other words. The other side fought for the right to help the younger races develop into the best they could be—with those Old Ones determining what each race's "best" ought to look like. That side had made themselves into gods in order to better help—or interfere with, or dictate to—the younger races. That side had been mad.

It had been largely a proxy war, with the two camps of Old Ones battling through intermediaries. Largely, but not entirely. In some realms, Rule had been taught, Old Ones had fought in person. Those realms didn't exist anymore.

The Great War was the reason the Great Bitch couldn't simply enter Earth and take over. Her side had lost, and the winning Old Ones had fixed things so no Old One could enter any realm. But the realms were not equally protected. The Great Bitch could have an avatar in Dis—and currently did—but if the woman now serving as her avatar entered Earth, most of her power did not enter with her. Rule didn't understand that. It had to do with the amount of *her* that could enter Earth. Apparently that was quite small, thank all the gods.

The Great War was also the reason Rule existed. His people had been created to oppose *her.* "A lot changed with the Great War."

"A lot of dragons died," she said grimly. "Proportionately more than any other surviving species, if one does not count the constructs."

His eyebrows lifted. "Do you consider lupi a construct?"

"Do not be touchy. I referred to the chimea, dworg, and ti'tel."

"I've never heard of the ti'tel."

"You would not have. I do not know if any still exist. We will hope not. Two aspects of the Great War affected the search for Dragonhome. First, certain events in the war convinced Sun that Dragonhome could best be accessed from Dis."

"Why Dis?"

"Dis is unique in some ways. It touches on more realms than any other. You do not know enough for more explaining to be useful. Another outcome of the War was the closing of

Earth. Not that 'closing' is the correct term, but it will have to do. This closing was necessary, for Earth was the most unprotected of the approachable realms, but it meant—"

"What does that mean—approachable?"

"You interrupt," she said sternly. "I mean the realms in ready contact with each other. The sidhe realms had their Queens to protect them. The singular realms other than Earth had various types of protection against *her* and the other two Old Ones who retained their godhoods. Earth did not."

His eyebrows flew up. "Other two? Who were, or are, they?"

"You may discount them. They were never worshipped by humans."

"While Lily and I were on our honeymoon, Earth was visited by a god who hadn't been worshipped by humans in the past but wanted to change that. He wanted to crack open our realm in a way that would have allowed *her* to enter before it fell apart entirely."

"Dyffaya." She sighed, shrugged. "He was a special case, but I will explain more. Sun believes one of the Old Ones who still holds a godhead is active in one of the singular realms and has agents in two or more of the sidhe realms. He is not ours to deal with; the Queens will do so. The other Old One I refer to fell into sleep at the end of the Great War. The patterns strongly suggest It sleeps still. You are very distractible."

"You are seldom this willing to offer information."

"I will cease to do so if you continue to annoy me. As I was saying, one of the results of the Great War was that Earth would be mostly closed to the other realms. The nature of this closing meant our realm would grow depleted in magic as time passed. Some of the dragons left Earth then. Some stayed. Some who stayed hoped to find a way to access the home realm from Earth. If they did not, when the magic grew too thin, they would cross to Dis. There they could test Sun's belief that it offered better access. In the meantime, there was much to be learned."

"No doubt." Rule shifted. His wolf was growing restive, impatient with the man's questions and the woman's convoluted stories. What did any of it have to do with getting to Lily? With taking his son back from their enemies? With returning to that audience chamber in Dis to rescue his people?

"So the dragons hung around on Earth, but they didn't find access to their home world."

"They did not find a safe way to access Dragonhome from Earth," she corrected him.

"They found an unsafe way?"

"The time discontinuity is too great and the strata too brittle. I will explain later, if you wish. As you say, the dragons 'hung around.' When the time came, they left for Dis. After some exploring and a great deal of fighting, they claimed a large region for themselves. It did not have any shared nodes with Dragonhome, but it bordered a region that did."

"Xitil's territory."

"Yes. At the very heart of her territory, as you know. Near the twin nodes."

"Difficult to use that access when it's part of Xitil's palace, and yet . . ." He paused, considering. "And yet they are dragons. And they lived in Dis for a couple centuries without finding a way to Dragonhome? Perhaps dragons are distractible, also."

That elicited a sharp crack of laughter from Grandmother. "You want me to come to the point, wolf? Very well. I told you one secret so you would understand why we can trust Reno to act against our enemy. I will skip the details and tell you the other secret so you will understand why we cannot trust him to act against the dragon spawn who rule here. One dragon did find a way into Dragonhome and, eventually, a way back. You know him as Reno. These spawn are his children."

SEVENTEEN

~

"I was right," Li Lei announced. "Those are not oxen."

It was a warm, sunny day. The river was swift and muddy, the brown water casting friendly glints back at a sky drenched with color. Seagulls swooped and called, proving that their species did, indeed, end up everywhere. Men and women bustled about, loading or unloading the sampans docked at all four of Bolilu's piers. Those piers were anchored by pylons made from the trunks of huge trees that had been spelled to resist rot. The river was not always friendly.

"Are you ever not right?" Gan asked curiously.

She cast the little one a glance. Gan was visible today. She wore servant's clothing. It had been difficult to find garments in her size. "It is rare, but it does happen. The next time it occurs, I will be sure to mention it to you, if you are still alive."

Gan's eyes widened in alarm. "You think I'm going to die?"

"It's a joke," Rule said. "She means that she's wrong so rarely that you're likely to die of old age before it happens."

"But she's really old now, and I won't start getting old for—oh!" Gan's eyes lit up. "That's why it's a joke, right? Because she'll die before I do." She burst into laughter.

Li Lei's lips did not twitch, but inside she laughed, too. If you could not laugh about death, you were missing life's biggest joke.

She and Gan stood at the land edge of the long pier. Rule did not stand; he sat on one of the pylons, recruiting his strength so he could continue to pretend he was not in pain. At least he had crutches now. Not the primitive stick things that people here used, either. Rule needed better. So did everyone else, and so she had spoken with a woodworker yesterday, who had made a pair to her specification with a proper handgrip. Perhaps the design would spread.

She and Gan had packs containing all their worldly belongings—this world, that is. Rule did not. He had not liked letting two females do the carrying but had been forced to admit she was right. No warrior here would encumber himself with packs when there were others to carry them.

Abruptly Rule pushed to his feet—or rather, to his foot and crutches. "Let's go."

They headed down the longest pier. Their goal was at its far end. *Chún-chún* could not come close to shore due to their deeper drafts—they had keels—and also their means of propulsion, which frolicked in the water nearby.

In size and shape, *chún* lay midway between a dolphin and an orca. In coloring, they varied from olive green to greenish gray. They were clearly domesticated, as they wore harnesses. They were just as clearly mammals. As Li Lei watched, one farther out in the river blew water from its air hole. The *chún*'s head did somewhat resemble that of a hairless ox. The eyes were set opposite each other like those of a fish, but the beast had visible ears and its snout had the look of an ox's muzzle. This resemblance was heightened by a pair of horns that evolution had surely not provided.

"I wonder who made them?" Li Lei asked thoughtfully.

Rule looked at her. "You think someone did?"

"That is obvious." The magical imprint on those creatures sang out their engineered status clearly to one who knew what to listen for. To be fair, one also had to be able to sense that magic in the first place. "You may take my word for that," she added graciously so he would know it was not his fault he was unable to perceive what she did.

"Hmm," he said.

Rule was in a better mood today, no doubt because they were in motion once more. They had been forced to wait over a day for a *chún-chún* to arrive. Rule had not handled the delay well. He might be on two legs again, but he was a very grouchy wolf. Gan had avoided him by wandering around *dashtu* for most of the day yesterday.

The time had not been wasted, however. Li Lei had sold four diamonds, allowing them to obtain additional clothing and supplies, including what she would need to copy the translation charm and what she hoped might work for the disguise ointment.

Yesterday she had studied Gan's charm. Not surprisingly, the Chancellor of Edge had the very best translation charm available—one that the beautiful Cullen Seabourne would have said was not a charm at all, but a minor artifact. It was both self-renewing and what was known in Gnomish as *gvortikh*, and in Elvish as *á hemambri*. Dragons knew it, also, although the thought-engrams that served as words in their speech did not translate precisely into other languages. Human languages did not have a word for it, unless you counted "artificial intelligence." Li Lei did not count it. *Gvortikh* mimicked sentience, but had little in common with the processing of computers.

The translation spell itself was a lovely bit of work, tricky but within her abilities. Imprinting it upon a charm would be challenging. The difficulty lay in weaving the pseudo-sentience into the charm along with the spell. Process mattered, particularly with such high-order magic. She rather thought it would take her more than one attempt.

The delay had also allowed them time and privacy for her to use the healing cantrip on Rule again. She was depleted now, but she would fill up quickly on the river. That was an excellent place to absorb power, if one knew how. Water did not hold tightly to power the way Earth did, and this river had drained magic from all the land it had passed through.

They advanced slowly along the crowded pier. Today people did not expect Li Lei to step aside for them. This might be because she was dressed with more prosperity, but she did not think so. No, more likely it was the man with her who made a difference. Rule was tall and thin, strange-looking and wounded—and not at all the sort of man people expected to

step aside. He moved as if the crutches were accessory, not necessity. And, of course, there was the very large knife now
sheathed on his hip, a blade close in size to a machete. Another
recent purchase.

They reached their goal—a long boat with a pointed bow
widening to a flat stern, which held a small cabin. Its deck was
crowded with crates, which two men were moving into tidy
stacks. No doubt they had sold or taken on cargo and needed
to redistribute their load. Both men were Gifted and . . . her
eyebrows shot up.

Rule bent and whispered near her ear. "What is it?"

"I will explain later," she said in English, raising her voice
slightly as she switched to Chinese. "I would speak with the
honorable *chuán fùqīn*." The title she had been told to use
translated as "boat father."

The older man glanced at her, frowning, and set down his
box. His eyes were an odd topaz color. "I am the boat father.
How may I help you, madame?"

"I am told you go to Lang Xin."

He gave her a small bow. "That is so."

"I wish to buy passage for myself, this *lái* and the daughter
of my late husband's brother's son."

His gaze flicked to Gan. "That one is related to you?"

His face was stony. His body was alarmed. Li Lei caught
his gaze and spoke clearly, putting force behind her words.
"She is harmless. You do not find her appearance startling."

The tension eased out of his shoulders. After a pause he
shook his head sadly. "But only look at my poor, small boat,
madame." He gestured, indicating the tidy but crowded deck.
"You see how little room we have. We could not properly accommodate such worthy passengers."

Pleased to deal with someone who knew how to do things
properly, Li Lei settled in to bargain, dropping the ensorcelling gaze. It would not be fair to use it for this. It would not be
as much fun, either.

"HE'S a what?" Rule repeated.

Li Lei shrugged. "'Beastmaster' is the term I know. I do
not know what they call them here."

Rule's voice was developing a growl. "It's not a term I know."

She looked at him. "Perhaps you should have more meat." She had allowed him chicken yesterday after receiving his promise to report accurately on his reaction. His temper had improved despite the painful cramping that hit later, and there had been no blood in his stool. A good sign.

"I am stretched, madame," he snapped, forgetting he was to call her Grandmother. "I am not out of control."

She chose to ignore his forgetfulness and his temper and looked out over the cheerful brown water.

She and Rule sat on their packs near the sun-warmed pier, waiting for the boat owner and his sons to finish loading and unloading. Gan was swimming in the river. The little one was fond of swimming, especially if there were "fishies" to chase. Li Lei had cautioned her not to allow anyone to see her eating what she caught. Human people did not consider live fish a delicacy. Raw fish, yes, for some. Live ones, no.

After a few moments Rule spoke carefully. "I am not accustomed to having someone else make decisions for me. I would like to have been consulted before you agreed to terms with these beastmasters."

"That was not practical. The person I am supposed to be would not consult her hired guard. I obtained the terms we sought. They will make only a few stops on the way to the capital—those stops they must make to pick up official mail."

"Couldn't you . . . persuade them not to stop at all?"

She gave him a withering glance. "You are not thinking. First, the boat father's honor is involved. Using ensorcellment to cause an honorable man to do something he considers dishonorable would damage his mind. Second, if this boat does not abide by its contract with the government to carry mail, its owners would be arrested. This would not help us get to Lang Xin."

Rule ran a hand through his hair. "All right. I get it. I take it this Mei Bo controls the *chún* through his beastmaster Gift."

His pronunciation was not bad. Unlike many Westerners, Rule had an ear for tones. "Mei Bo and his children, yes. It is a rare Gift and not normally found in humans, but the boat father and his family all possess it. This disturbs you?"

"Mind control disturbs me. The charms Cynna made should shield me and Gan, but—"

"No and no. The beastmaster Gift does not work on human minds, and it is not mind control. It is . . . bah. I could say this properly in Dragon. In English, it is hard. This Gift is not constructed in a way that allows it to control minds. It suggests. It does not compel. Such suggestions may be weak or strong. A strong suggestion reaches almost the same result as true control, but it arrives there through a different means. Even weak suggestions work well if the animal is stupid."

"Is it a type of ensorcellment?"

She snorted. "It is nothing like ensorcellment. It is closer to mindspeech."

That startled him. "It's animal mindspeech?"

"It is not mindspeech, and we are all animals."

"But it's similar to mindspeech. You just said so."

Trying to explain minds to the mind-blind was frustrating. "Yellow is more like blue than it is like a caterpillar, but yellow is not blue. The beastmaster Gift is more like mindspeech than it is like ensorcellment, but it is not mindspeech. It cannot carry words. It touches minds on a primitive level, so only works on very simple minds. Nonsentient minds." She was not reaching whatever worried him. She tried again. "Think of sentient minds as onions. A beastmaster cannot affect sentient minds because his magic cannot reach through the layers of the onion to its core. This is a bad image," she added. "It misleads as much as it helps. Do not lean hard on it."

One corner of his mind twitched up. "You sound like Sam. So the beastmaster can't affect human minds. What about a wolf's mind?"

"That is what troubles you?" She clucked her tongue and shook her head. "Foolishness. Your wolf is as sentient as your man. You know this. You aim your worry in the wrong direction."

His eyebrows climbed. "Where should I aim my worry?"

"Given a strong Gift and some training, a beastmaster can sense sentient minds, even if he cannot influence them. It is not the type of sensing Lily does." Nor what Li Lei did, for that matter. "It would be . . . muddy. Unclear. But it may be enough. These beastmasters may be able to tell that you are not human."

He frowned, then said slowly, "Nonhumans are very rare

here, from what you've said. But we've already told them I'm a fall-through. A *lái*. No reason I couldn't be a *lái* from one of the sidhe realms."

She shook her head. "How, then, would you and I know the same language? No, you must be from Earth. These people do not know about our realm, however. A little about China, but nothing of the West. We may be able to—"

Several feet away from shore, Gan shot to the surface of the river, water streaming from her newly black hair, and began splashing quickly toward shore, grinning. Her swim had cheered her.

"We will discuss what to say about you—and what to imply—later," Grandmother said in a low voice to Rule. "Gan deals better with clear instructions than with the muddle of deciding."

Gan plopped down beside them and whispered rather too loudly, "Hi, Rule! Hi, Grandmother! I met someone. She's a good swimmer, faster than me, but I hold my breath longer. Ask her what her name is, okay?"

A moment later a second head broke the surface of the water. Her hair was black, too, but the effect was totally different as she stood on the river's sandy bottom, water streaming down her sleek female body. She was not naked. She wore the same sort of linen tunic and trousers that most women here wore. But wet linen did not conceal.

She was in her late teens and as naturally beautiful as most young creatures. She was obviously related to the boat father and his sons, and like them, she was a beastmaster. A powerful one, stronger than her father and brothers. Her eyes were as yellow as citrines and fixed on Rule. Her lips parted as she stared at him, transfixed. Her hard nipples might have been due to cold, but Li Lei did not think so.

She sighed. The beastmaster's beautiful daughter was going to be trouble.

EIGHTEEN

∽

San Francisco, California
Five days and twelve hours before
Lily, Rule, and company set off for hell

THE office at the back of the antique store was small, window-less, and tidy. The desk was either Louis XVI or a very good imitation. The file cabinets were standard office bland, but the tall shelves opposite them held an interesting miscellany. In addition to a large number of impressively bound books, there was a pair of carved ducks; a wireless printer; a small ceramic urn painted in Picasso's distinctive style; an enthusiastic spider plant growing in an old chamber pot; and a velvet Elvis.

The man sitting at the Louis XVI desk was long and lean with a wide, flexible mouth. He ran a hand through his hair—dark and curly, flecked with gray—and spoke into his phone. "Look, Ed, I don't know how you got this number—"

"Friend of a friend," Minsky said vaguely.

"But I'm not in the business anymore."

"Right, right. Everyone knows that. I'm just hoping for a little advice from an old friend. A few minutes of your time. I've always been straight with you, haven't I? I helped you with those coins you needed to move a few years ago."

"You helped," Jasper said dryly. "For a commission."

"Sure, and if you're wanting a commission, we could dis-cuss that. I wouldn't object if you wanted to handle the sale. You've—"

"I'm not in the business anymore," Jasper repeated patiently. He liked Ed, but he really needed to get back to the quarterly taxes. Didn't much want to, but need and want often sped off in different directions.

"So don't handle the sale. That's fine," the other man said promptly. "Just let me buy you dinner tonight so you can take a look at it. If you could give me a couple numbers to call, that'd be great, but mostly I just want you to have a look, give me some idea what to ask for it. I don't know the magic trade, and even if I did, I've got no bloody idea what—"

The office door swung open. "Hey, did you forget that we're supposed to go to—whoops. Sorry. Business?" The man in the doorway smiled crookedly.

That was Adam—crooked smile, crooked nose, all part of the charm of a face with the warm, lived-in comfort of a favorite chair. Adam, who loved puzzles, World of Warcraft, and the theater; hated television, Brussels sprouts, and intolerance; and had only to walk into a room to magically multiply the mess. He was neither short nor tall, fat nor thin, a nice-enough-looking guy who didn't stand out in a crowd until you looked at his eyes. Big, soulful brown eyes with absurdly long lashes for a man who'd turn fifty in another year.

Angel Eyes, Jasper liked to call him. Pissed him off every time. "We don't need to leave until seven."

Adam made a point of glancing at his watch. "Which usually comes pretty soon after six fifty-two."

Damn, was it that late already?

"Is that Adam?" Minsky said. "Bring him with you to dinner. My treat. Wherever you like. Does eight o'clock sound good?"

"I haven't agreed to meet you," Jasper said, amused in spite of himself. Very few of his old associates knew about Adam. Very few even knew Jasper's real name. Ed knew both, and he had never shared that information. A bit twisty in some ways, Ed Minsky. He'd lift your wallet without an ounce of shame, but he'd never rat you out or renege on a deal.

"Come on, Jasper. Won't do you a bit of harm and you'll get a good meal out of it. Just take a look at the ruby, see if you can tell me what it does."

"Why are you so sure it's magic?" Ed had no trace of a Gift.

"The provenance," Minsky said promptly. "If you'd seen the not-a-fox I got it from, you'd understand."

"Seen the what?" Curiosity stirred. Jasper told himself not to be an idiot.

"Not-a-fox. That's how I thought of him, her, or it. Bright pink fur and the cutest little face. That's quite a story, how I got this ruby. I'd be glad to tell you all about it over steaks. Or pad Thai? If I remember right, you like Thai."

Jasper was hooked and he knew it. He put up a show of resisting, but his heart wasn't in it. He wanted to hear about the not-a-fox. Reeled in, he finally said, "Okay, but it has to be tomorrow. I've got plans tonight."

"But those plans must include eating. Let me buy you two—"

"I've got plans," Jasper repeated firmly.

Reluctantly Ed accepted that he'd have to wait an entire day to get what he wanted. They settled the when-and-where, and Jasper disconnected.

Adam was frowning. "That was one of your old business associates. The kind you don't have anything to do with anymore because you're not in that business anymore. You're having dinner with him."

"Want to join us?" Jasper shut down his laptop. He'd have to finish the estimated taxes in the morning. He emphatically did not want to come back to them after his vacation, and the play tonight wouldn't let out until after ten. Too late for his tired brain to deal with governmentese. "He asked me to bring you. I think you'd like Ed."

"He knows who you are?"

"Long story," Jasper said, rising. "But yes, he does. I'm not getting back in the business, Adam. Just giving an old friend a quick, informal appraisal."

Jasper's office opened into the shop's storage area—a crowded space kept navigable through meticulous organization. There was a bathroom to the right. Next to the bathroom was a large, antique safe that was a good deal harder to get into than it looked. If someone did get it open, there was a good chance they wouldn't notice the hidden compartment in the safe's thick, heavy door.

Adam spoke as they walked past the safe. "You miss it sometimes."

"Sometimes." He thought about his last big job, though, and that put paid to any wistfulness. He'd pulled it off, sure. Stolen a magical device from a place he shouldn't have been able to get into, much less escape from. But it hadn't been a thrill. It hadn't even been profitable. He'd been forced to do it because Adam had been held hostage by one of the baddest bad guys Jasper had ever encountered. And he'd run into quite a few, back in the old days.

At the back of the building, Adam unlocked the door while Jasper engaged the security system. It was a decent system, enough to deter the stupid thieves without being too advanced for the average antique shop owner to invest in. A smart thief could get through it in under ten minutes, a real pro in under five.

Jasper's own time had been a minute-fifteen.

"I don't like to think about you longing for the old days," Adam said as they stepped out into the narrow loading area behind the shop. "I'd rather think I added to your life, not that I took something important away from you."

"You know better." Jasper shut the door, which locked automatically. Just as automatically he glanced at the cameras to make sure they covered the area properly. "It's a good thing we didn't meet twenty years ago—"

"When I was still so deep in the closet I wouldn't have dared even look at you, you mean?"

"And I wouldn't have considered giving up my profession. I wasn't ready then. Now . . . do I miss it? Sure, sometimes, the way a retired athlete misses competing. But it was time. I knew that, or I wouldn't have agreed. It's a bad idea for an aging ex-quarterback to come out of retirement in an effort to re-create his glory days. Wouldn't work out for an aging thief, either."

"Aging?" A warm hand slid down Jasper's butt. "Hmm, let me see, now . . ."

Jasper grinned, turned, and found Adam's arms and his smile ready for him. When they kissed, there was more heat—and more tongue—involved than he'd expected. By the time the kiss ended, he was thinking about stepping back inside the shop. There weren't any really good spots, but he and Adam were creative.

"I should at least act as if I trust my fiancé, shouldn't I?" Adam murmured. "Sorry."

Fiancé. Such a wonderful word. "If that was an apology kiss, makeup sex ought to be right around the corner. By which I mean back inside the store, not up against the door."

Adam shook his head mournfully. "But then we wouldn't have time for supper, and I'd have to listen to your stomach growl all during the play."

And they would be going to the play, come hell or high water. Adam had dragged him to each and every play put on by the highly experimental acting troupe his friend Mark had been part of. Jasper wasn't a strictly *My Fair Lady* type, but neither did he think Shakespeare was more authentic when performed nude. And the play with the dead chickens . . . but Mark had finally landed a part in a production at Magic Theater. Magic put on a lot of new plays, but they were the real thing. No dead chickens tonight unless they were on Jasper's plate for supper. "I'm pretty sure that's your stomach growling, not mine."

"Hmmm, no. Might be your brother. Did he drop in for a visit?" Adam made a point of peering behind Jasper, as if he might have overlooked the extremely large wolf Jasper's half brother turned into upon occasion.

"Idiot."

"Arithmophobe."

"Flap-mouthed geek."

"Scurvy snob."

They grinned at each other. With a touch, Jasper activated the shop's secondary security. He didn't know how to set a ward himself, but he could activate the one his brother's friend had set and renew it as needed.

They set off down the narrow street that backed the antique store, tossing out cheerful insults both Shakespearian and modern. Jasper couldn't stop smiling. They'd earned their happily-ever-after, he and Adam. And hard as it was to believe, it looked like they'd be getting it.

*   *   *

SUPPER was good. They'd gone to their favorite Vietnamese place, where they knew they'd be served quickly. And the play was excellent.

"Mark's always had great stage presence," Jasper commented at intermission. Supposedly they were in line, but the mob at the concession stand was large and not at all linear. Jasper put their chances of actually getting a couple of beers before they had to return to their seats at less than fifty percent. "But I never realized how good he could be until now. I forgot it was him onstage."

"He just needed a decent vehicle." Adam was beaming. Nothing made him happier than seeing a friend succeed. Adam liked to think he was tough and cynical—and he was a survivor, no doubt about that, and tough in the ways that counted. But he had a heart of marshmallow fluff. "I—oh, look, Michele's here. Who's she with?"

"I don't see her. Where . . ." Jasper's voice drifted off as a crawling sensation rolled up his spine to his scalp. It felt like his hair was trying to stand on end.

"What is it?" Adam frowned. "You've got the weirdest look on your face."

"Someone just broke into the shop."

Adam glanced at the pocket where Jasper had put his phone. "How can you—oh. It's the *other* alarm."

"I'm afraid so. Adam, I have to go."

"No, you have to call the police, then *we* will go."

Jasper lifted one brow. "And tell them that my ward just alerted me to an intruder?"

"Why not?" Adam demanded. "You sure as hell aren't going to check it out yourself!"

Well, yes. That was exactly what he was going to do, though for the first time he felt a mild regret that he'd insisted that his brother's people stop following him around "for his protection." Being watched every moment had driven him crazy. But he'd admit that a lupi backup might have come in handy tonight. "Can you get a ride home? I could take a cab myself, but—"

"That's not the issue, dammit!"

Jasper did not call the police, but he didn't go alone, either. Adam went with him. Jasper didn't like that, but not because he thought either of them would be in danger. If someone was good enough to break in without setting off his regular alarm, he or she was a professional and would be gone before Jasper could arrive. That would take at least twenty minutes, even at this time of night. Probably closer to thirty. But he hated for Adam to miss the last part of the play.

"Forget about the damn play," Adam said when he voiced that concern for maybe the second time. Or third. "This is your livelihood. But I don't get why you're so sure they'll be gone."

"Don't worry, they will be. Unless they're after what's in the safe." He'd sold almost all the things he'd obtained in his previous profession as quickly as possible. Almost, but not all. A couple of the items in the safe would be extremely valuable to the right person . . . or to the wrong people. He might have been a thief, but he drew the line at making certain objects available. "I hope they aren't trying to get it open, because that will take awhile. Even for a pro, that safe is not easy to open."

"That did not answer my question."

The sound of a siren moving up from behind him made Jasper grimace and pull over to the side of the road. "Only a professional could get past the regular security system, and pros don't linger. They get in and out fast. They'll have already picked out what they want, so it won't take long."

"Cased the joint, you mean?"

"You're cute when you talk thief. Yes, and I've been going over which of my recent customers might have been interested in my stock for the wrong reasons." He watched in his rear-view mirror as a cop car, lights flashing and siren blaring, sped past, then pulled back out into traffic again. "Tonight they probably pulled up their van at the rear—there's never much traffic on that street—and took things out through the loading door." He sighed, thinking of the lovely 1880 writing desk he'd gotten just last week. Victoriana sold well in San Francisco, which was why he specialized in it. Worth eight grand, easy, though the thieves would be lucky to get more than a couple thousand. Illicit antiques weren't hard to move, but you never got full value. "Though it's possible they went for the small stuff, especially if 'they' is really 'he.' Or 'she,' I suppose. A lone thief would have trouble moving furniture out quickly."

"And yet the police could have gotten there a lot faster than we will. They might have caught your thief or thieves if you had called them right away. You didn't."

"Hmm."

"Don't hum at me. That's your 'I'm not arguing even though you're an idiot' noise."

Jasper grinned at the weave of headlights ahead. And didn't argue.

"You could have come up with some reason for the cops to check your shop other than mystical, magical wards. You didn't want to call them because you didn't want the thief or thieves caught."

"I'll call the cops when it's time."

"After the bad guys have gotten safely away with your possessions."

"It's just stuff," Jasper said mildly. "Insured stuff at that."

"And . . ."

Jasper sighed. "I don't like prisons. I understand the reason for them. We can't afford to have everyone behaving the way I used to. I just don't want to be responsible for . . . did you know that the average prison cell in the U.S. is six feet by eight feet?"

"It's their own actions that would put them in prison, not yours."

"Six feet by eight feet," he repeated. "Imagine living for a decade or more in a room smaller than a lot of walk-in closets. Being locked up in that room. Allowed out only to shower or, if you're lucky, to exercise in an enclosed area without so much as a blade of grass, surrounded by men who are at least as stir crazy as you are, and half of them are gang members."

Adam was silent a moment. "You really didn't retire just for my sake, did you?"

"I've been telling you that."

"Yeah, but you also insisted there was nothing to worry about, that you were too good to get caught."

"Well," Jasper said modestly, "statistically speaking, I had reason to believe that. I never did get caught."

Adam took his hand. "Pusillanimous braggart."

"Self-righteous knave." Jasper squeezed the hand in his.

JASPER stared down at the ruby in his hand . . . which he'd found tucked away inside his safe. He spoke softly, almost reverently. "That son of a bitch."

"What?" Adam called from the shop proper. He knew Jasper's stock almost as well as Jasper did and had been looking through it while Jasper checked out the storage area. "What's missing?"

"Nothing. You don't need to keep looking. I know who broke in tonight, and he didn't take anything."

"What are you talking about?" Adam appeared in the doorway between shop and storage area. "How can you be sure?"

"It was Ed. Ed Minsky, the guy we're supposed to have supper with tomorrow. He left this in my safe." Adam lifted his hand, which held a silk scarf along with the ruby. He'd handled enough magical items in his time to know better than to touch one that was active . . . and this one was.

Jasper had never thought of himself as a sorcerer, not until a real sorcerer told him that's exactly what he was. According to Cullen Seabourne, the common definition of sorcery—the legal definition—was nonsense. It wasn't being able to use magic outside yourself that made you a sorcerer. It was the Sight.

Jasper's Gift was fairly weak. Unless there was a ton of power involved, he had to work at it to see magic. He'd seen the glow from this gem while it was still inside the safe, and he hadn't been trying.

Adam frowned at the gem in Jasper's hand. "How do you know it was Ed?"

"First, because the item he wants me to look at is a ruby. Second, because he's one of a handful of people in the world who could have opened my safe, left this, and gotten away before we arrived."

Adam's eyebrow's shot up. "He's a safecracker?"

"The best, he'd tell you, but Ed exaggerates sometimes. He's in the top five, though." He'd worked a job with Ed once. Normally he'd worked alone—you really can't trust thieves—but that particular safe had been beyond his skills. The job had gone smooth as silk, and Ed had taken his cut in gems, as agreed. Jasper's share had included a very old book. A spellbook, to be precise. His specialty had been magical items, usually contracted for in advance. A smaller market than the gemstones Ed preferred, but a lucrative one.

"Why would he do that?"

"The reason that occurs to me does not make me happy. Give me your shirt."

"For what?"

"It's silk, isn't it?" Jasper wrapped the gem in the scarf. It was a large scarf; as he finished, the glow dimmed, but did not disappear.

"Yes, but—"

"Whatever this is, it's powerful. Powerful means potentially dangerous, and I don't want it leaking all over the place. The only thing I know of that can block magic is silk."

"It's a magic ruby?" Adam asked, intrigued. He started unbuttoning his shirt. "What does it do?"

"I don't know. That's part of the problem. The other part being why Ed broke into my shop to plant it here."

"You think he's trying to frame you or something?"

Jasper shook his head. "Not Ed. It isn't the police we need to worry about." Though he was damn glad now that he hadn't called them. "It's whoever Ed wants to hide this from."

"Huh." Adam shrugged out of his shirt and handed it over. "So what do we do?"

"Put it back in the safe for now, I guess." Jasper wrapped the shirt around the wad of scarf. The glow dimmed still more. He could still see it if he tried, though. "And ask Ed some questions tomorrow night."

BUT Jasper didn't get to ask Ed any questions. Ed didn't show up to buy him and Mark dinner, so they ate pad Thai without him. A couple hours after they got home, a homicide detective knocked on their door. Edward Robert Minsky's mutilated body had been found in a Dumpster about a mile from the shop. His phone had been in his pocket, and Jasper's number was the last call made from that phone.

Naturally, the detective wanted to know everything Jasper could tell him. No doubt the subsequent interview was frustrating for the man, since there was almost nothing Jasper could say. An old friend had called to ask him and his fiancé to dinner, but hadn't shown up. No, he didn't know what Ed had wanted, other than the chance to catch up. No, he didn't know where Ed had been staying, or anyone who might have had it in for Ed. Some thief, no doubt, Jasper had told the man. Ed dealt in gems, after all. Maybe he'd had some with him, or the thief thought he did.

The San Francisco Police Department later determined from the video at Jasper's shop that he and Mark had gone there less than an hour after the detective left. They'd entered the premises at 12:10 and left again at 12:17, after which—as far as the SFPD could tell—they vanished.

NINETEEN

~~

Dragonhome

FIVE glistening gray-brown bodies leaped through the water, churning out water-diamonds to sparkle in the sun. All wore harnesses, the rigging that hitched them to the boat. One had a rider.

Physical contact wasn't necessary for the Siji to use their Gift; it was simply easier that way. The rider controlled the lead beast. *Chún* were herd animals and not very bright. Instinct told them to follow the leader, and that's what they did, needing only an occasional nudge from the Siji acting as backup. The boat father and his daughter did most of the riding—her in the morning, him in the afternoon, with his sons taking turns in the backup spot. They had the strongest Gifts.

It was afternoon now. Had they been in a world with clocks, Rule would have guessed it to be between three and four o'clock. In this world, the slant of the sun and the growl in his stomach said it had been too long since lunch . . . which had not included meat. People in this world did not eat much meat. It made him want to go hunt his own.

"I need a few drops of blood," Lily's grandmother said.

He turned to look at her. "My blood, I assume?"

"It will activate the ointment and key it to you." She held out a small pottery bowl. "Hold this."

The substance in the little bowl looked like dirty Crisco and smelled like fat, flowers, and herbs—chrysanthemum and honeysuckle, ginseng and licorice, plus others his nose couldn't pick out in this form.

"Give me your other hand," Grandmother said.

He lifted his lip at her in a silent snarl. "I am not Gan, to be given orders."

"No, you are a very touchy wolf who should show more respect for your elder."

He inhaled slowly. Exhaled. "My apologies." After a pause he added, "I dreamed of my brother last night. All day, it's felt as if he rode the boat with me. It makes me feel . . . hasty."

"A difficult dream?"

"They all are lately." Another pause. "He's still alive. Not just in the sense that we're in an earlier time here, one before he was hurt. He was still alive when we left."

"So Gan said."

"So is Cullen."

She didn't respond to that.

"I won't grieve for him," he told her fiercely. Gan had been sure Benedict was alive when she started grabbing people and crossing with them. She had not been sure about Cullen. She sensed life directly, if Rule understood what *üther* was, so he could trust what she said about Benedict. But in all the commotion, she hadn't had time to sort out the *üther* she'd sensed where Cullen fell. Some had been from demons. Maybe all. Or maybe not.

"That is a good decision," she told him crisply. "Even better if you would stop worrying yourself ill over what has not yet happened."

He barked out a single laugh, ran a hand over his hair, and held out his hand. "You wanted blood."

She took his hand, folded his fingers back out of the way, and jabbed his thumb with a needle, then held it over the bowl and squeezed out a few drops of blood. Releasing his hand, she used a small bamboo paddle to stir the mess. "I could not find any kesum. People here do not recognize my descriptions of it; I believe it does not grow here. I have substituted another form of coriander. The ointment accepted the spell, but I think it is not stable. Smear it on your face now."

He grimaced, disliking putting the smelly stuff near his nose, but did as she'd bidden him.

"Hmm." She stared at him, her eyes narrowed. His wolf did not like being stared at. "It worked."

"You don't sound happy about that."

"I was right. The spell is unstable. It will break apart too quickly." She handed him a damp rag. "You may as well wipe it off. I will try again."

He scrubbed his face. "What did I look like?"

"You looked as I expected you to look."

"And that is helpful in some way?"

"*Tch.* It is mind magic, but it is not illusion. I told you that. It does not change your appearance, but the reactions of those around you. Anyone who sees your face when the ointment is working will think you look familiar. The way you *should* look. One person may think you look like his neighbor, who is very tall. Another may later be unable to recall what you looked like, but will swear he knows you from somewhere. Another might believe you look a bit like his uncle."

"So if I looked in a mirror when this stuff was smeared on me, I'd just see my own face because that's what I expect to see."

"Yes." She sighed. "But only for a few minutes. I must try again."

Two days later

The western sky blazed crimson. The eastern sky was already dark. Dusk wrapped the *chún-chún*, slightly dispelled by mage lights set fore and aft. An owl's call floated out upon air scented by river and the nearby forest. Water lapped against the boat's hull.

Rule did not find the liquid music of the water soothing. He wanted to hunt. Needed to hunt, to run on four legs, to—

"The moon will be full soon," Li Lei Yu observed.

He could not have what he wanted. Not yet. "Not that soon.

Four more days. How is the disguise goo coming?" She'd gotten the last batch to last thirty minutes.

"I do not think it will stabilize further without the kesum, and I do not have the time or ingredients to devise a completely different medium to hold the spell. It will have to be invoked at the last moment. Are you jumpy because the full moon draws near? Or because your lady is urging you to hurry?"

He shrugged. "I'm too jumpy to tell why I'm jumpy."

"Ah."

He ought to be going over the plan again. He'd had little enough to do on this journey but think, think and plan, and come up with possible scenarios, potential problems . . . and in the end, what happened wouldn't follow any of the possible scripts he'd considered. But considering those possibilities helped him avoid the obvious pitfalls and kept his mind fluid.

At least he hoped he was avoiding the obvious pitfalls. A great deal depended on Madame—on Grandmother, he corrected himself. He didn't like that part of the plan. He had great confidence in her, but what she proposed to do . . . though at least she knew what she was getting into. Knew a great deal more about that than he did, he admitted. It had been her idea.

Grandmother interrupted the downward drift of his thoughts. "The boat father says we will reach the capital in two or three days."

He glanced at her. She was looking out over the dark river, her gaze unfocused. "Or four, if the magistrate at our next stop is especially dilatory." The magistrate of Liangzhou often kept the boat father waiting while he finished preparing his official correspondence. "You haven't read all of the last magistrate's papers."

"I will finish tonight."

They'd had an unpleasant surprise two stops back. An official had tried to detain Gan when they left the ship to purchase supplies, including more ingredients for Madame to try in her disguise goo. Madame had promptly ensorcelled the man. Turned out that the government *had* sent out an alert—but for Gan, not Rule. Gan had been seen when she brought Cynna to this realm, and the spawn had sent out a directive to detain "an unusually short female being of demon heritage with orange skin and blue hair." Gan's hair might be black now, but her height and skin color were harder to disguise.

Madame had told the official that "this is not the being you are looking for," which had damn near made Rule burst out laughing. He couldn't get her to admit she'd quoted Obi Wan on purpose. Her eyes had twinkled, though.

So Gan was restricted to the boat when they were docked unless she went *dashtu*, and Madame had decided they needed additional intelligence. She was gathering that by raiding and reading the official mail their boat picked up, which was kept in a magically sealed pouch and locked up in a trunk in the cabin. Neither the magical nor the mundane lock was a problem for her, but the reading was a challenge. The characters were not written the way she was used to, making it slow going.

She'd gone through the official correspondence from two magistrates and was working on the third batch . . . in full view of the beastmaster family. They didn't notice. She'd told them not to. She hadn't found anything suggesting that officials were watching for Rule. She had found references to preparations the spawn had directed their magistrates to make. Those references were maddeningly vague.

Rule asked, "But you've seen nothing interesting? Nothing related to those mysterious preparations?"

"These documents are much the same as the others. A long report about a project to drain swampy land. A reply to a question about the tax rolls. Another related to the number of mutant births. Copies of various documents that are routinely sent to the capital—official commendations and reprimands, summaries of legal cases. And a request for clarification regarding 'those preparations upon which we embarked per decree number 37, Year of Heavenly Guidance 137.'"

"Does the request for clarification clarify anything for us?"

"The magistrate wants to know if there was a clerical error involved in the number of casks of rice to be secured. He is politely incredulous and does not think the number stated could be correct."

Casks of rice. "Does he say what that number is?"

"No."

Rule shook his head. "Not much help, then. It suggests they may be stockpiling food, but without knowing why . . . the spawn could be expecting a bad crop year, or engaged in natural disaster planning. They might want to drive up the cost of rice. They might intend to start distributing food among the poor."

Madame said nothing for several moments. Then she spoke crisply. "The problem is that I am reading correspondence going the wrong way, from the magistrates to the spawn. I need to see what the spawn are telling their magistrates."

He shrugged, impatient. Restless. "This boat is going to the capital. It can only pick up official documents traveling to the spawn, not those coming from them."

"Perhaps we should steal some of the magistrate's incoming mail at our next stop."

"You're joking."

"You are very nearly rude. If we must wait a day or more upon the magistrate, there will be time to arrange a theft. Gan can go *dashtu*."

"And I suppose she will have no trouble finding the documents we wish to see? And if she does find them, no one will notice that they're gone?"

"You are very grouchy tonight. Perhaps you should go for a run."

His eyebrows flew up. "And risk being seen as wolf?"

She snorted. "More risk of being eaten, I think. Some predators here are very large. You would need to give a reason to spend the night on the shore instead of the boat."

"If there were a village here . . . but there isn't." The *chún-chún* usually tied up for the night at a village, but in keeping with their passengers' desire for speed, they'd pushed on until they absolutely had to stop and rest the *chún*. "I'll think on it." Gods knew he wanted to run—to hunt—but should he?

She patted his arm. "If a run clears your mind, it is worth some risk. Do not use your injured leg."

He had to smile. Madame tried to remember not to give him orders. She forgot. Frequently. Ordering others around wasn't just a habit for her. It was the way she showed love. He understood. He, too, was a dominant.

He was deeply glad she was here. First, of course, because

he feared they'd have no chance of rescuing the children without her, much less those they'd left behind in Dis. Then there was the way she'd been able to speed his healing. He hadn't known a nonhealer could do that. His gut should have taken a month to grow back, yet his healing was now repairing both his gut and leg. That meant the gut must be nearly or fully regrown.

All of that mattered greatly, but he'd known Madame Yu was fiercely capable. He hadn't known she would also make such a comfortable companion.

Not soothing, no. Intermittently maddening . . . and yet comfortable. She was wise and canny and powerful, and that was surely part of it. But mostly, he thought, it was the trust. Even with clan he didn't feel this sort of trust, for with clan he was always aware of the need to be strong, capable, in charge. No one but Madame Yu was in charge of Madame Yu. Then there was her gift for silence. That could be aggravating when he learned she'd withheld some bit of information—she loved secrets as much as dragons did—but some of her silence came from a deep quiet within her, a quiet that seemed to render her immune to worry. One he could rest in along with her now and then.

They sat together in easy silence now, their backs to the piled crates in the middle of the ship.

In the deepest channel of the river, a large body splashed. The *chún* were feeding. It took a lot of fish to fuel those powerful bodies, but the *chún*'s masters could send schools of fish their way, allowing them to eat their fill in a relatively short time. The boat father's sons were out there now, making their fishy suggestions. The boat father himself sat atop the cabin's roof in the stern, relaxing with his pipe. His daughter was preparing the evening meal.

Cooking was done in a cast iron box on legs with a louvered grate on top—louvered to allow control of the airflow, and so the heat of the fire. The rice was already cooked and waiting in a large tin pot shaped to fit the grate. Mei Ling's knife flashed with brisk efficiency as she cleaned the last of the three large fish Gan had brought her. They would be chopped fine and stir-fried with some vegetables.

Gan herself was still in the river, like the boat father's sons.

Frequent renewal of Grandmother's magically powered suggestions kept the beastmaster family from finding her behavior strange, but the river was not safe at this time of day. She lacked the young men's ability to turn aside predators with mental suggestions. She claimed that her ability to see *üther*— a type of energy produced by living creatures—would let her avoid them.

He hoped she was right. "Why do you allow Gan to swim so late in the day? Many predators feed at dusk."

For some reason that amused Madame Yu. She actually chuckled. "You think it is for me to allow or not allow?"

"She won't listen to me. She'd obey you."

"Perhaps."

"No 'perhaps' about it. She's afraid of . . . no, that's not it." He frowned, mostly at the realization that he couldn't put words to what he'd seen, but didn't understand. "She was afraid of you at first, but not anymore. Fear wouldn't be why she obeyed, but she would obey."

"It is simple enough. I am her first parent."

"She—" He cut that off to stare at the old woman sitting placidly beside him. "You think she sees you as a parent? A mother figure?"

"Mother, grandmother . . ." She shrugged. "The little one has no model for either. I create them in her. This is a serious responsibility. I am careful with my ordering."

If anyone else had said that, he would have laughed. Gan might not be a demon anymore, but she was long past the age when she could be parented. "What about the gnomes? They're guiding her, surely."

"The ones she respects are guides, yes. A guide is not a parent."

Their supper arrived, carried by the girl who'd cooked it. She knelt gracefully and held out both bowls, smiling shyly. Her name was Mei Ling. She was a daughter of the Siji, which was the name the beastmasters gave themselves. They were a tribe or family group descended from a nonhuman *lái* from the sidhe realms—or so Madame said. The beastmasters said their *lái* ancestor had been human, but there was strong prejudice here against racial mixing. They would wish to claim a purely human ancestry whether or not it was so.

Mei Ling was seventeen and very lovely, and Rule was only too aware that she'd decided to be in love with him.

Madame—Grandmother, he corrected himself—accepted her bowl with a regal nod. "*Xiè xie,*" Rule said as he accepted the other. *Xiè xie* meant "thanks" and was one-fourth of his readily available Chinese. He could also say "please," "ox," and "madame." Along with the thanks, he gave Mei Ling a particular kind of smile. The kind he had no right to offer her.

She giggled, possibly at his pronunciation, possibly because she was seventeen. And glowed with pleasure at his smile.

A quick spate of Chinese from her father made her turn, scowling. She shot something back at him, but rose in reluctant obedience.

Mei Ling's father had told her to attend to her charges, meaning the *chún.* She'd told him that he knew very well her brothers were doing that. Rule knew this because a voice had murmured the translations in his ear as they spoke—a voice that sounded disconcertingly like Madame Yu. After two unsuccessful attempts, Madame had presented him with a working translation charm that morning. It hung around his neck with the charms Cynna had made before they left Earth. It was not self-renewing like Gan's charm, she'd informed him with a tartness meant to mask either chagrin or frustration. She had decided to omit that element, as every time she tried to weave it in, the harmony was disrupted. But it should last through the full moon. She could renew it for him after that, if necessary.

It might be. The moon would be full in four days. They would reach Lang Xin in two or three days—or four, if the magistrate at Liangzhou was especially difficult and kept them waiting two full days. The children would arrive in this realm between three and six days from now, or so Gan guessed. They didn't know exactly how displaced in time they were compared to Dis, but they might reach the capital at the same time his son did. Or a few days before that. Or a day late.

That was one reason for Rule's tension. There were others.

Madame clucked her tongue. "She courts you."

Rule took his chopsticks out of the inside pocket on his tunic. He was fairly good with chopsticks, fortunately. Not as good as a native, but no one expected him to act like a native.

"She flirts, that's all. Isn't proper courting supposed to go the other way in a patriarchal society?"

She snorted. "A proper courtship would take place between her father and yours, though I might act on your behalf since you are a *lái* and I am presumed to have authority over you. Her courtship is about mating, not marriage."

Rule had just popped a bite of fish in his mouth. He did not choke on it. He was, however, startled to feel a dull flush creep up his neck. He hadn't been embarrassed by sex since he was thirteen. "She can't expect that."

"Seventeen is old enough to expect exactly that."

"I was thinking of the lack of privacy." Counting on it, in fact. "She's never more than a dozen yards away from her father and brothers, even when she's riding one of the *chún*. They're not about to let the two of us wander off alone even if she wanted to, and I'm not convinced she does. Flirting with me when we can't be alone together is safe. Not that her family likes it. They'd rather she didn't speak to me."

"Her father has not made up his mind about you. If he decides he approves, the lack of privacy will not be a problem."

"I assure you it would. Not that I . . . dammit."

"Your face looks very funny. Perhaps you do not know that Mei Ling will not be allowed to marry. Daughters of the Siji do not marry."

Rule's new translation charm could not make up its mind how to translate "Siji." It whispered three options in his ear: drivers, four seasons, and—rather disconcertingly—dead ones. "Drivers" was probably right, for that was what the Siji did. They drove their beasts.

Madame went on, "Marriage would take Mei Ling into her husband's family, and her Gift is too valuable to lose that way. Her family does want her to have children, however." A sly glance. "It will be awkward for you if her father decides you should sire his grandchildren."

"If you're right about her," he said slowly, then stopped.

"Yes," she said, understanding him even though he hadn't said the rest of it. "You will need to handle her carefully, Rule."

Grimly, he ate a few more bites before replying. "There

aren't any Siji in China. You didn't know they existed until we met these people. How do you know so much about them?"

"People tell an old woman all manner of things."

This time he snorted. "I'm certain people told you things long before your appearance fit their notion of 'old woman.'"

"You are not wrong. However . . ."

When her voice drifted off, Rule glanced quickly at her. She was frowning at the lingering blaze of sunset. "What is it?"

"Dragon."

TWENTY

RULE shoved to his feet.

Madame continued to frown absently into the west. "He may be only curious. So far he's only . . . no." All at once she was on her feet, too, shouting in Chinese, which his charm rendered as, "Dragon! Take cover! Dragon!"

Rule's night vision was better than a human's, but it didn't do him much good now. The dragon was coming at them from the west, where the sky was bright with sunset, preventing his eyes from adapting. Then all at once it was visible, a dark blur hurtling down at them, neck outstretched and wings folded as he dove with shattering speed.

Rue's mind clicked over into *certa*, the battle state. Even as he saw clearly how impossible it was for a single man, lupus or not, to stand against a dragon, his body was in motion. As the great beast's wings shot out, breaking his fall and the air in a small explosion, Rule crouched. And leaped.

The boat father hadn't been quick enough to react to Madame's shouted warning. He'd risen, but still stood atop the cabin's flat roof as the dragon's talons reached for him. Talons a bright, improbable blue, as were the rest of the dragon's scales that gleamed in the mage lights. Talons that part of Rule's mind noted were much smaller than Sam's.

In *certa*, observation, calculation, decision, and action flow in a single kinetic stream, so as Rule landed on the cabin's roof and drew the long knife he'd acquired in Bolilu, he knew many things. He knew the heat of that great body overhead and the shock of impact on his damaged leg. He knew the overwhelming smell of dragon—meat and spice, metal and musk. He knew the boat father was about to hurl himself off the cabin's roof, and that he wouldn't make it. And as he twisted his torso so his swing would carry all the strength of legs, back, and shoulders, he knew he struck at a dragon perhaps half of Sam's size. Which meant that if he were very fast and very clever, the dragon might not kill him right away.

The boat father leaped.

One talon closed around the man's arm, stopping his flight with a jerk. The other reached for a leg.

Dragon scales are hard. According to Cullen, some of that hardness was magical. Those on the belly a few feet above Rule's head were the size of dinner plates and would have bounced his blade back at him. Those on the feet were the size of quarters and correspondingly thin. But he could reach only one foot, the one wrapped around the boat father. So he aimed above it, where the scales were smaller and thinner than on the belly, but not as small as those on the foot.

Rule's knife connected. The blade sank deep, jarring him as it lodged in bone.

Blood stinging with heat splattered his face and chest.

The dragon screamed, a sound like a pipe organ exploding, every chord played at once with impossible volume.

The boat father fell into the water.

The great wings beat once and again, carrying the dragon up and away. And to Rule's amazement, he didn't circle around and come back.

"*Tch*," Madame said. "You have let him take your knife away with him."

IT was much later when he learned why the dragon left.

Their hosts had been very excited about the near calamity. They'd needed to tell the tale over and over, to compare it to other tales of miraculous survival. Beastmasters could turn aside the other great beasts that wandered this world, he learned. But not dragons. None of them had ever heard of someone surviving such an attack by a dragon, so the boat father was as much lauded for his luck as Rule was for his courage.

Lauded, that is, by everyone but Grandmother. While bandaging Rule's leg—the wound had reopened—she informed him that he had been very foolish.

He didn't argue. How could he, when she was right? He'd acted without weighing the consequences. Did he have the right to risk himself when his son's life was at stake? To risk sending Lily into mate shock?

Not that there had been time to weigh consequences, he thought as he unrolled the blankets that served as his bedding. Everyone was finally quieting down for sleep. He just wished he knew for sure he'd acted to save a life, and not just because action—any action—had felt so damn good.

And he'd learned something, hadn't he? Something that had his mind clicking away at his half-formed plan, adding to it. He lay down on his folded blanket and stared up at a sky brilliant with stars and knew it would be a long time before he could sleep. So it didn't much matter that Gan would not stop talking. She had missed the brief battle, having had the sense to dive deep underwater when she heard Madame's warning, and intended to rectify that omission by discussing it endlessly.

There was just enough room for the boat's passengers to lie head to foot between the side of the boat and the cargo neatly stowed on its deck; not enough room for them to lie side by side. Gan sat up in her own bedding near Rule's feet, chattering away. Madame lay near Rule's head. Rule wasn't really listening to the one-sided conversation until Gan asked a question and Madame answered it.

"You did *what?*" he asked, low-voiced.

"I showed him who he was dealing with," Madame repeated.

"Good for you!" Gan said cheerfully.

"Yes," Rule said, "I heard what you said. But I don't know what it means."

"You did realize that the dragon was an adolescent?"

"I knew he was smaller than other dragons I've seen, but . . . a teenage dragon?"

"Is this such a surprise?"

Yes, somehow it was. "His age has something to do with you showing him what he was dealing with?"

"All teenagers are difficult. Teenage dragons especially are not sensible. They want only to hunt, fight with each other, and burn things. This is why European stories of dragons are so different from Chinese stories of dragons."

Wait, what? "European stories are about teenage dragons?"

"Of course. Adult dragons send their adolescents away until they are old enough for sense. In the old days, this meant sending the adolescents away to Europe. Sometimes Africa, but mostly Europe. You lupi do something similar."

"We send our teens to the *terra tradis* until they learn to control their wolves. We don't wait for them to become sensible."

She gave a snort of amusement. "That would be too long to wait, I think. But this custom of sending away the adolescents is why I stopped hiding my power and gave this teenager a pinch."

Rule's eyebrows lifted. "You've been hiding your power?"

"What kind of pinch?" Gan asked.

"The kind adult dragons use to rebuke their offspring. It is a small tweak in the . . . bah. I do not know the English words. It hurts, but does no damage. And of course I hide my power. We do not wish for the spawn or someone with the Sight to know what manner of threat I am."

Gan was literally bouncing with excitement. "So the dragon thought you were a dragon, too. An adult dragon, who could send him away. That's why he didn't come back?"

"I treated him as an adult would treat an adolescent who intruded on his territory. The youngster responded properly. I do not know what he thought."

"So Rule didn't need to be a hero after all?"

Madame didn't answer immediately. When she did speak, her words came slowly. "It has been a long time since I pinched a dragon. That is body magic, and I have no great affinity for it. It took several moments to find the place to pinch. Had Rule not caused the dragon to release his prey, he would still have flown off because he had been rebuked by an elder . . . but with the boat father clutched in his talons. This does not make

Rule's action wise," she added sternly. "But I do not deny that he made a difference."

"Thank you," Rule said dryly.

"The girl will be even more silly now that you are a hero," she informed him. "And the father will not stand in her way. He may urge you to mate with her."

"To fuck her, you mean?" Gan didn't sound as if she liked the idea, which surprised Rule. Gan was generally in favor of fucking anyone, anytime, anywhere. "Rule's not supposed to fuck anyone but Lily Yu. They got married."

"Yes," Rule said even more dryly. "Which may be difficult to explain to the young lady. Madame, I need to ask you about the limits of ensorcellment. You heard what the beastmasters said about the—"

Rule! Rule, can you hear me?

"Yes," he whispered as the world shuddered and shuddered. "Yes. Lily. You're all right?"

I'm with Cynna. We're captives, but we're okay. We're in Lang Xin. You?

"Lang Xin. Yes, we knew—we guessed—we're fine. We're all fine, and we're coming."

All? Who's with . . . Her mental voice faded out, then came a last whisper. *Too far away still. We'll talk when you're . . .* And it was gone.

"Rule," Madame said sharply. "It is Lily? She is mind-speaking you?"

He couldn't answer, not right away. Not until he stopped weeping.

Two hundred miles away, Lily wiped the wetness from her cheeks, then woke Cynna to tell her.

TWENTY-ONE

~

HE was fast and he was pissed. He came up off the ground, bounced on his toes—had no one ever told him not to telegraph his moves?—and swung into a powerful roundhouse kick.

Lily swayed out of the way, her bent arm shooting up so her forearm connected with his calf—and shoved. He went down hard. Again.

"*Tíng!*" Second Fist Fang called out. Halt.

She straightened. Sweat stung her eyes. It was too damn hot for this, she thought, then could almost hear a remembered voice asking if she intended to invite people who wanted to kill her to step into a nice, air-conditioned building first. Benedict's voice. The memory brought a grimace to her sweaty face.

He was alive, dammit. He would be alive when they—somehow—got back to the audience hall and rescued him and the others. She wiped the sweat from her forehead with the back of her hand and believed that as hard as she could.

The man she'd sent tumbling glared up at her. He'd been fast, but angry. She was faster. A genetic gift, she'd always thought, from Grandmother, which put her at the upper end of human reflexes. Not lupi fast, no, but she'd been sparring with lupi for the last couple years. She was no Bruce Lee, but she was pretty good. She had a bruise on her left hip from yesterday's bout, but that opponent had more bruises. And today's match had ended even faster.

Her ankle seemed to be completely healed. It had stopped hurting two days ago, which seemed awfully quick, but the sprain must not have been as bad as she'd thought. The hardest part today had been to limit her responses so her enemies wouldn't know too much about her capabilities. She'd tried to stick to judo, which had been her martial art of choice for years, but not any longer. After she joined the clan, Benedict had insisted she learn others. Variations of kung fu, mostly.

When it came to combat, Benedict was always right. You could cripple or kill with some of the strikes in kung fu. That's why she hadn't studied it originally . . . and why she'd needed to. The bad guys she went up against these days were really bad and often not human. She'd needed more options, and along with kicks and punches, kung fu taught flexibility. To use what worked.

The guard she'd put in the dirt twice got to his feet. She bowed. He bowed, though his scowl suggested that was not the move he would have preferred. Fang strode toward him, face impassive. And without any warning—no tells there—gave a perfect example of the kick Lily had just avoided. The difference was that this kick was exhibition-style, the power withheld so it didn't maim or kill. Fang's foot still slammed into the other guy's head.

Down he went again.

"You were told to spar," Fang said dispassionately, looking down at the man sprawled in the dust. "You were told the *xi qi* is not to be damaged. Had she failed to evade your kick, she would be unconscious now. Or worse."

"I did not mean to disobey," the guard whispered without moving.

"And yet he did, didn't he?" Alice said, approaching them at an easy pace. She spoke Chinese, like Fang—whom Lily had understood because she had her mindsense out. That didn't work on Alice, but she was getting pretty good with the dialect they spoke here. Listening while using mindspeech to get the meaning seemed to print it into her brain. "It made him angry to lose to a woman. Foolish." She added three words that were not Chinese, words Lily didn't know, accompanied by a complex gesture.

The man screamed. His back arched, held for two long seconds—and he collapsed, his face pallid.

"Perhaps I should not have disciplined your man for you, Fist Second," she said to Fang. "But I arranged this. I feel some responsibility for the outcome." She turned to Lily and continued in English. "You are enjoying your exercise?"

"Very much." Alice had proposed a daily exercise period as Lily's payment for translating between Cynna and Ah Li. Lily had wanted to run. Alice had nixed that, but to Lily's surprise had suggested sparring with the guards. Supervised, of course. An interesting choice, Lily thought. Apparently Alice thought that staying combat-ready would be of most benefit to Lily without exceeding the value of her translation. "What did you do to the guard?"

"A form of *jùdà téng*. One of the Zhuren could have done it directly. I lack their precision, so I use a spell. There will be no lasting damage."

"*Jùdà téng* is body magic that brings agony."

"You have heard of it? Yes. Was that Fist incompetent or are you unusually competent?"

"He's not bad, but he lacks control. Anger works against you in combat."

"The Fist Second has been pairing you with his best men. You keep winning."

Lily started to argue—because really, the men hadn't been that good. A sudden thought stopped her. She'd been sparring with lupi for two years now. Maybe she'd gotten better than she'd realized. It was an oddly disquieting thought. "I imagine my training has been different from theirs. I know some moves they don't."

"Hmm." Alice cast her a speculative glance. "You go to the bathhouse now."

She seemed to want an answer, though she hadn't made it a question. Lily obliged. "Yes. Ah Hai waits there for me."

Ah Hai had refused to return to the bathhouse where she'd worked before. Humbly, apologetically, even tearfully she had refused, even when directly ordered to do so by Alice. The Zhu Kongqi had said she was to take care of Lily Yu. The Zhu had not told her to stop taking care of Lily Yu. Therefore, she must continue to do so. Alice had given up, even arranging for Ah Hai to sleep in one of the cells at night.

Lily's days had fallen into a bit of a routine. First a translation session with Cynna and Ah Li. After that came her workout, followed by a bath so she wouldn't stink if Kongqi wanted to talk to her. Which he almost always did. All this busyness meant she hadn't been able to mindspeak Rule again after that wonderful but fleeting contact last night. Not that she hadn't tried, but—

"Let us walk together awhile," Alice said. "You can cool down. I can ask you questions. I am curious about my sister's death."

"Ah . . ."

A small smile. "I am not interested in retribution. Walk with me." She turned and started walking.

It grated to obey, to follow along like a well-trained hound. Lily shoved the annoyance down and caught up with Alice— partly because she did not need to offend the woman, and partly because she, too, was curious. She did not understand Alice Báitóu.

Fang barked an order. He and two of his men fell into place a few feet behind them. They didn't bind her hands. They'd stopped doing that yesterday.

The day was bright and hot, but there was a bit of a breeze. It felt good on Lily's sweat-damp body. There were a lot of people out and about, but everyone stepped aside for Alice . . . who wasn't saying a damn thing. Who continued not to say a damn thing long enough for Lily's mind to return to its obsession.

They were running out of time. The children would be here soon. How soon, they didn't know. Tomorrow? The day after? Five days from now? And she and Cynna didn't have a plan.

Oh, they had half of one. They knew how to break out of jail. They could do that pretty much whenever they wanted. They had some ideas about what to do next, but no *good* ideas. Nothing that made their breakout more than the preliminary to a baroque form of suicide. She needed her weapon, dammit. She could toss guards on the ground if they came at her one at a time, but for any real action, she needed her weapon. She needed Rule and Grandmother and some damn way to leave Dragonhome once they got the kids.

She'd tried to reach Rule again last night. And failed. Oh, she'd managed to brush his mind. But whether because of depletion, distraction, or pure weariness, she hadn't been able to establish a solid connection. He was at the very limit of her range, even with the mate bond to help, even using the toltoi to give that bond a boost. It had been like standing on tiptoe, trying to turn a screw overhead with nothing but her bare hands when she could barely brush it with her fingertips.

What she needed was a damn screwdriver.

She frowned, wondering if that was possible. Not a screwdriver, but a mental . . . something. A construct. Was that how Sam and the other dragons could mindspeak lots of people at the same time? Did they keep bits of mind-stuff handy, already formed into something that could connect with other minds?

She couldn't imagine how to do that. Her mindsense always collapsed back in on itself when she wasn't actively using it. Fact is, she just wasn't very good with it. She'd improved, sure, especially when it came to translating. She no longer had to give that process her undivided attention to get the gist of what someone was saying. But she couldn't send words along that connection without concentrating hard. She'd had to trance herself to send it far enough to reach Rule.

He was coming, though. Headed her way. He'd be closer when she tried again—hopefully while taking that bath. If her day followed its usual pattern, she'd have some quiet time in the bath and could try again. She wanted that contact, needed it . . . and not just to make herself feel good. She didn't suck at tactics, but Rule was better. He might be able to pull together a plan that gave them more of a chance.

Though too much of their chances depended on Reno. Surely he—

"I did not love my sister."

Alice's words startled Lily as much for the interruption of her thoughts as for their content, which took her a couple seconds to process. She replied with careful neutrality. "Families are complicated."

"I was surprised by how difficult her loss was for me. I had expected to be relieved. Relief was present, but it was not the whole of my reaction."

"Families are complicated," Lily said again, "and not all bonds are based on love."

"The bond between Helen and myself was based on her need. She was a vampire—metaphorically speaking, of course. She did not eat blood. She ate me."

Lily did not know what to say to that. She fell back on an old interviewing technique. "I'm not sure what you mean."

"I understand that most telepaths do not come into their Gifts until puberty. This was not true for Helen. She was born telepathic, although at first only with me. Her tie to my mind kept her sane. By sane," she added, "I mean that she did not devolve into catatonia."

Which was the usual outcome for telepaths, Lily knew. "She used your mind to stay in touch with reality? How?"

Alice gave her a reproving look. "That is a personal matter."

And the rest of this wasn't? Alice puzzled Lily, puzzled her greatly. "So from the moment you were born, your twin was in your head?"

"Yes. This caused developmental problems for me. From my reading, I know that many twins have trouble differentiating, especially when young. To a young twin, 'we' is as important a pronoun as 'I.' Also, there is usually a dominant twin. Helen was certainly that. As far back as I can remember, she was in my head and *feeling*."

"She was an empath as well as a telepath? A projective empath?" Empathy wasn't a terribly unusual Gift. Projective empaths, however, were about as common as snow in the Sahara.

"The empathic element existed only with me—a quirk of our twinship, I believe. Helen felt very strongly. I do not. Her emotions, her desires, overbore my own. I conjecture that I failed to develop a normal range of emotions because my role in our conjoined sense of self was to balance Helen's excessive emotions. However, the telepathic component exaggerated existing differences. It did not create them. Helen's emotions were strong from the beginning, and mine were not. It is surprising, is it not, that two genetically identical beings could differ in important ways?"

"Such as in your Gifts?" Lily hazarded. She still hadn't managed to touch Alice, learn what her Gift was.

Alice made a small, dismissive gesture. "It is impossible for twins to have the same Gift, so that is not surprising. Experts in your realm often cite environmental factors as the causative agents for the variations in personality, behavior, and skills in what are called identical twins. I consider that explanation accurate but insufficient. My opinion is based in part on my own experience, which of course is subjective and therefore difficult to quantify. But I believe that differentiation is caused by an innate drive to differentiate. That each sentient being is instinctively driven to establish an identity distinct from all other sentient beings. I wasn't able to do so until I was thirty-two. That is when the Old One you consider your enemy formed her own bond with Helen, and Helen no longer needed her bond with me. So she broke it."

A telepathic bond, she meant. The Great Bitch had had a telepathic bond with Helen . . . which had supplanted the one with Alice. And suddenly Lily understood. Alice hadn't loved Helen. She'd been subsumed by her, then all of a sudden she'd been cut loose. "She ate you, you said. You mean that she ate your sense of self."

"That is one way to put it."

"But you had some sense of self. You must have, to survive having that tie destroyed."

"If, as I propose, the drive to differentiate is innate, it must also be self-renewing. The effort to establish oneself as a distinct self would be continual and therefore could not be extinguished."

"A drive you think is common to all sentient beings. Not just to humans?"

Another small, dismissive gesture. "That is a theory. I may be extrapolating too widely. I have not collected data on every type of sentient being."

"But you didn't want to limit yourself to speaking only about humans. Do you consider yourself human?"

"I am partly human, of course." Alice stopped and glanced at Lily for the first time since they started this peculiar conversation. "Are you curious about my ancestry?"

"Yes."

"I am willing to speak of that, but first you will tell me how you killed Helen."

Shit. "You, ah, weren't telepathically linked to her at the time, I guess."

"No."

"Well. Okay. She'd tried to open a hellgate to Earth so she could let the demons in and shove me back through that gate so the Great Bitch could wipe my mind. You know about that part?"

"I do not require context. I simply feel a need to know the exact manner of her death."

"She and I fought. She was whacking me with an ancient staff, trying to kill me. I banged her head against the stone floor until she quit. It killed her."

"You bashed her brains out."

"That would be one way to put it."

Alice was silent for several paces. Lily had no clue what was going on in her head. The woman didn't seem to have expressions.

Finally she spoke. "I will bathe with you today."

Lily really couldn't think of a damn thing to say to that. It wasn't as if she could tell the woman no, but—what the hell?

Alice's pale lips turned up the tiniest amount. "You may relax. I did not intend that as a sexual overture, and I repeat that I am not interested in retribution. You put an end to certain possibilities when you ended Helen. Most of those possibilities were abhorrent to me."

"But not all."

"Not all, no." A long pause. "I did not realize that until later. It came as quite a surprise."

ALICE and Helen Báitóu—Whitehead in English—had been physically altered by the Zhu Shēngwù, Master of Body Magic, to look European. Lily learned that as they headed for the bathhouse. She also learned the names of Alice's mother, who was dead; her father, still alive but senile; her three half siblings through her father, all of whom lived in a village three days' journey to the south; one grandfather, dead for many years; and both of her grandmothers, also dead. Her mother's mother—her *lái* grandmother—had lived to a ripe old age, however, being over a hundred when she died. Alice's voice took on a ghost of warmth when she related that, as if the woman's longevity was a source of pride.

That grandmother had been named Alice; this Alice was named for her.

Lily did not learn the name of Alice's other grandfather. The one still alive. The one who was a dragon spawn. That, she was informed, was too personal.

Alice had strange notions about where to draw boundaries, Lily thought as she entered the dim, steamy bathhouse. Or maybe she found it convenient to assert that some matters were "too personal." Maybe she didn't want Lily to know who her grandfather was because . . . what? Because Lily wouldn't approve? Not likely. She might not understand Alice, but she knew the woman was not an approval junkie.

Ah Hai was waiting. She bowed to each of them, but Lily got the first bow. "Ah—the honorable Alice is my guest today," Lily said in Chinese, "so she should go first. With the lathering and rinsing, I mean." Let Alice get naked first. She'd insisted, hadn't she? Switching back to English, she looked at Alice. "Why change your appearance to look European?"

"So we would blend in." Alice began stripping as matter-of-factly as she did everything.

"When you went to my realm, you mean. To the U.S."

"Yes." Naked and unconcerned about it, Alice moved to sit on one of the stools. She was in good shape, Lily noted. Amazingly good shape for a woman her age . . . not that Lily knew her real age. Helen had supposedly been fifty-one when Lily killed her, but Helen had also supposedly been born in Sacramento. Her age might have been as much of a fabrication as the rest of her personal history.

Ah Hai had begun the scrubbing on Alice's shoulders. It must have felt good. Alice's eyes closed. Lily persisted with the question Alice hadn't really answered. "I don't understand. There are lots of Asians in California. Why change your appearance?"

"The goal was to attract little notice. Therefore, it was thought best for us to appear to be part of the dominant population."

"Who thought this? Whose choice was it?"

"I was not part of the discussion."

Lily knew a dodge when she heard one. She let it pass for now. "Helen went to the U.S. because the G.B. wanted her to hook up with the Azá and start prepping for the hellgate. Why did you go? What was your job?"

"To learn. I went to one of your universities. The University of California, Santa Barbara."

Lily blinked at the idea of the pale, partly human Alice taking classes at an institution sometimes known as UCSB—University of Casual Sex and Beer. "Did you stay in a dorm?"

"For the first semester only. I am not suited to living with a roommate." She paused while Ah Hai rinsed her off, then started on her hair. "This is pleasant, but I do miss showers. Your world has excellent plumbing. I brought back several books about it. We do not yet have the infrastructure to implement sewage and water systems such as your world enjoys, but I have made some improvements and have plans for more. Are you planning to bathe in your clothes?"

Lily grimaced and pulled off her tunic. "How did you get to my realm?"

"I will not discuss that." She glanced pointedly at Ah Hai, who was about to pour water over her head to rinse. "I enjoyed my time at the university. Did you attend a university?"

"Sure," Lily said. Apparently Alice didn't want to talk about important stuff in front of Ah Hai. Was she paranoid, or did she have good reason to think Ah Hai might understand English? Lily couldn't make up her mind, but she went along with Alice's unspoken suggestion. While Alice went to soak in the hot pool and Ah Hai started scrubbing Lily, the two of them chatted about their college experiences.

She would much rather have asked Alice about that shield of hers. It couldn't be coincidence that the only person she'd met who had a mental shield used to have a telepathic twin. A vampiric telepathic twin who'd eaten Alice's sense of self . . . had Alice developed her shield before or after Helen cut the cord? After, Lily thought. If Helen had been as much in the driver's seat as Alice claimed, she wouldn't have let her twin develop a way of shutting down that control. But had Alice wanted to? Had her "innate drive to differentiate" made her long to shut her sister up mentally? That was a more interesting question.

Not one Lily could ask, however, not when she wasn't supposed to know about Alice's shield. Might as well talk about dorm life and algebra . . . which was as far as Lily had gotten, math-wise. Alice had taken multivariable calculus for its soothing properties.

". . . gave my textbook from that class to my grandfather. He enjoyed it, also. Ah Hai," she said, switching to Chinese as Lily eased herself into the steaming water, "I did not provide myself with clean clothing to put on after my bath. I need you to fetch some for me."

Ah Hai bobbed politely and glanced at Lily . . . who smothered a smile. "Yes, please get the honorable Alice's things for her. Do you know where to go? What she will need?"

Ah Hai knew where to go and was certain that the honorable Alice's maidservant would know what clothing her mistress required. She hurried off.

"She does consider herself yours," Alice observed.

"She was told to tend me by Kongqi. Kongqi outranks you. What did you want to discuss that made you work so hard to get the two of us some alone time?"

"I appreciate the efficiency of bluntness, but have found that few others do. First I need your promise not to repeat or reveal to anyone what I am about to say unless I give you specific permission to speak of it with someone."

"No."

"No?" Alice's eyebrows lifted a good two millimeters—more an expression of polite inquiry than surprise.

"I could promise not to reveal to anyone born in this realm what you tell me next, provided it is new information to me."

"Ah." She considered that. "A reasonable caveat, I suppose. Do so."

Lily said it all again.

"Very well. You and Cynna Weaver want very much to retrieve the children who will arrive here soon. You have undoubtedly made plans towards that end. I wish to assist you."

Lily said nothing for a very long time. Then she told Alice what she wanted.

TWENTY-TWO

WHAT *did you tell her?* Rule asked.

Night had fallen. A single mage light hovered up near the ceiling of the cell, courtesy of their jailers. A lot of people here had enough of a Gift to float a mage light or two. Lily and Cynna sat on one of the blankets, huddled up so close an observer could have been forgiven for thinking they were lovers. "I said I required proof of her intentions, and that returning my weapon and ammo would make fairly solid proof."

Cynna snorted. "Like that's gonna happen."

Lily had whispered her words as well as sending them along her mindsense. The whisper was for Cynna. Lily had decided to risk a very soft whisper now that she knew it was Fang who, through his translating charm, understood English. Well, Ah Hai might, but she slept in another cell, and neither she nor Fang had super-duper lupi hearing, and this way she only had to say things once.

Did she agree? Rule asked.

"She nodded as if she did, but she didn't actually say so. My weapon hasn't shown up yet."

And did she say why she wanted to help you rescue the children? Rule asked.

"I asked, of course. It was like I hadn't spoken. She went

back to talking about her undergraduate days until Ah Hai returned with her clothes."

Do you believe her?

"I don't know." Lily wondered if any of her frustration traveled along the mindsense with her words.

"Don't," Cynna whispered. "She's one hundred percent with them. With the spawn."

"I don't know what she is," Lily whispered/sent. "She baffles me. She didn't seem to expect me to confide in her . . . not that there's much to tell."

We need to talk about that. You said you had a way to remove the magic cage they put on Cynna and then break out of the cell. Go over that in more detail, please.

Lily had reached Rule for the second time that afternoon after she returned from her bath, but only briefly. Kongqi had sent for her to talk about—rather unnervingly—the ethics involving the use of mind magic. He wanted to know how the sentient dragons saw the subject. At least, that's what he'd said. She suspected he wanted to know what the dragons could do with mind magic, and maybe whether she could do any of those things. He continued to be very interested in how her Gift worked, how she sensed magic.

So she'd tried again after supper—and succeeded. Rule was in Liangzhou now, a city he thought was about seventy miles from the capital. Seventy miles was a stretch for her mindsense. Literally a stretch. It felt like that Silly Putty she'd played with as a kid, stretched almost to the breaking point, but she could do it. The toltoi seemed to help her hold the connection; she kept rubbing it. They'd talked long enough to catch up on most of what had happened with each of them. Long enough for her mind to start tossing out thoughts and spinning up longings. Or maybe the longings came from her body. She wanted him *here*, where she could touch him. It had been so long since she'd touched him.

Stupid mind. Stupid body. Never satisfied.

She told her mind sternly to pay attention as she explained how she and Cynna planned to bust out of jail when the time came. Next he wanted to know about the soldiers or guards. A Fist was an individual soldier, right? How many were there? How were they structured?

Not very well, she told him, and went on to outline what she'd learned. A headache was setting up shop at the base of her skull.

The Fists had a warrior ethos—their motto was "Loyalty, courage, strength"—but they weren't really soldiers. There were no wars to fight here. They dealt with crime, fires, dangerous beasts, dragons, and pretty much anything else that posed a threat. It was a high-prestige job—but as in any prestigious position, nepotism was a problem.

A bigger problem was unique to the Fists: too many Indians, not enough chiefs. What they really needed, in her opinion, were some sergeants. Li Po, the First Fist, was top dog. The Fist Seconds were the officers; everyone else was just a Fist. Fists were grouped into squads and *wǔshí*, or fifties. Squads had *gēgē*—the word literally meant "elder brother"— squad leaders who functioned like corporals, but there was no one for the squad leaders to report to except their Fist Second. The chain of command basically forced Fist Seconds to act as their own sergeants.

Two Fist Seconds were stationed here in the capital. Fist Second Fang was in charge of the guards used to police Heart's Home—the government complex—including all prisoners of the spawn. His brother officer, Fist Second Chen, led the guards who policed the city itself. The other Fist Seconds handled the guard detachments assigned to the magistrates. There were six fifties in the capital, four of them beneath the city's Fist Second and two beneath Fang.

". . . I've caught some hints that First Fist Li Po doesn't work all that hard at his administrative duties, passing many of them on to his Fist Second here," she finished. "I think there's some friction between him and Fang. Li Po ordered Fang to guard me personally, which is stupid. Fang doesn't have a proper second to handle everything he ought to be doing."

So there are two hundred guards assigned to the city, a hundred to the government complex. Do the two guard contingents back each other up in case of emergency?

"That would be up to the First Fist." Her headache was getting worse—a sign of depletion. "Rule, I'm not sure how much longer I can hold the connection."

I'd better brief you on my plan, then.

He had a plan. Thank God.

She interrupted three times as he outlined it—once to exclaim "She can *do* that?" and later to say in disbelief, "Reno is their *mother?*" And then, heart aching: "Rule." Just that. Just his name.

For much too long he didn't say anything. Then he picked up again with describing his plan. She let him finish. When he did, she said very softly, "We're going to talk about it. Not now, maybe. But we will talk about it."

Cynna gave her an odd look. She hadn't translated that part, not fully. Lily swallowed and went on more normally, "Your distraction puts a lot of innocents at risk. I don't like that."

Do you have another suggestion?

She didn't, but . . . "What does Grandmother say?"

That if we don't stop the Enemy, millions of people are likely to die.

The calculus of death made for the coldest of logic. If you accidentally caused a few innocents to die while trying to save a few million, was it justified? Military leaders would say yes, but collateral damage was such a tidy term for the spilled entrails of guilt and death. Her own training and instinct told her to protect civilians, not endanger them. "I'll think about it. Maybe there's another way." She took a steadying breath. "I've got a couple questions about the timing and the gate. You said we won't be building a gate, but reopening the one used to bring the children here, which is a lot easier. But the nodes that gate is tied to aren't stable. Or they won't be after Reno flies through that construct, which he hasn't done yet as far as this realm is concerned, but he will. The gnomes said they couldn't build a gate on an unstable node."

If you recall—his mental voice was exceedingly dry—*our Enemy will be working extremely hard to get the nodes stable.*

Lily frowned dubiously. "But when will they be stable? Reno thought it would take the G.B. between two hours and twenty hours to get them stable again after Reno flew through the construct."

We will have to hope she doesn't finish at the low end of Reno's estimate. We have no way of dealing with her if she's

*free to turn her attention to us. Our goal will be to get as far
from her avatar as we can as quickly as we can.*

He kept missing her point. "But if she's still stabilizing
the nodes, we won't be able to open the gate!"

*Ah. I discussed that with your grandmother. She says
the nodes will not be as unstable on this side as they will be
in Dis.*

"That does not make sense. How can one side be seriously
unstable and the other side okay?"

"I don't know. *She tried to explain—something about
space being elastic, but matter very stubborn—which I'm
afraid didn't mean a bloody thing to me. But reopening a permanent gate is a very different matter from building a new
one. She says mildly unstable nodes won't keep us from reopening a permanent gate, though it might affect how many
of us can use it. Reno will have to advise us about that.*

"It is a permanent gate, then?"

*Gan believes it is. If she's wrong, if it was a temporary
gate, it can still be reopened, but will collapse rather quickly.
Grandmother doesn't know how quickly.*

So they could probably open the gate. Not certainly, but
probably. And it might stay open long enough for them to get
out of here. Or it might not. "If Grandmother thinks she'll be
able open the gate—"

*Not her. Cynna. Grandmother apparently has the same
limitations regarding gates that dragons do.*

"Cynna's supposed to reopen the gate?" Lily caught her
friend's eyes, which were as startled as her own must be. "I
don't think she knows how."

"Plus I'll be depleted, remember?" Cynna said. "I won't be
able to Find my hands in front of my face at that point, much
less open a gate. Reopen one. Whatever."

Lily passed that on quickly.

A pause. *Grandmother says she can refill Cynna magically.
You could do this, too, but there is no time to instruct you, so
she will do so. She will also instruct Cynna. She says . . .* Another pause, as if he were waiting for Grandmother to finish
telling him what she said. *Cynna is to call up the clan memory
about gate building to refresh her mind on the concepts.*

"I can do that," Cynna whispered after Lily passed that on. "But we need to take the kids to Earth, not Dis. God knows I want to go to Dis. Cullen . . ." She stopped. Swallowed. "But we have to get the kids safe, not take them into the middle of a battle."

Lily relayed that.

I haven't told you about that part of . . . get to Xitil . . . dangerous, but it gives us a chance. We can't . . . for the same reason the dragons didn't open one when they lived in China.

"Wait. Your 'voice' is getting faint. I missed some of what you said. Most of it, really. What's that about the dragons?"

His mental voice remained maddeningly soft, making her want to turn up the volume. But she caught all the words this time. *When they lived in China, they didn't open a gate to Dragonhome.*

"They didn't?"

No. I have more to tell you about . . . ancient history. Dragon history. That will have to wait until . . . need to rest, but gate between Dragonhome and . . . very bad.

She wasn't sure if he was telling her to rest or saying that he needed to. "I'm missing parts of what you say. My mind-sense is getting thin and I'm not catching everything. Why can't we open a gate to Earth? Dis is not a good place to take the kids." Being full of demons and a mad demon prince, not to mention their Great Enemy's avatar.

The membrane between the two realms . . . excuse me. She says that membrane is a terrible metaphor. The whatever-it-is that keeps realms separate is brittle between Earth and Dragonhome. She . . . think of this dividing strata . . . thick, but brittle. The amount of power . . . form a gate through such strata is likely to fracture . . . think of the way very dry dirt cracks. Power would bleed into both realms . . . fires and earthquakes. Lots of power. Really big fires and earthquakes. If we opened a gate between Earth and Dragonhome, neither . . . safe for the children. Or anyone else.

"That won't happen with a gate between Dragonhome and Dis?" Lily whispered.

She says not.

"What about crossing? That's not the same as a gate, right? Gan—"

The rock wall exploded. It exploded *out*, sending chunks and shards flying out into the empty air. And also Cynna.

Lily shot to her feet and leaped the three feet between her and the huge new hole in the wall and jolted to a stop, staring.

The moon was up and nearly full. It flooded the scene with light, plenty of light to see Cynna floating about fifteen feet away and fifteen feet above the ground, her eyes wide with shock. A muscular man with braided mustaches hung in the air beside her. His *shenyi* was crimson and gold.

Zhu Dìqiú, Master of Earth. Aka Dick Boy.

Dick Boy scowled at Lily, ignoring the woman he'd hauled out to leave hanging in thin air. He shot a stream of Chinese at her too rapid for her befuddled brain to take in.

"Slower," she said, her jaw clenched tightly enough to make it hard to get the word out. Tight enough to make her head pound, too. She forced her jaw to loosen, forced herself to speak more courteously. "Speak more slowly, please. Your dialect is strange to me. I did not understand."

"You met secretly with Alice. You will tell me what you spoke of with her."

"It was not a secret m—"

Cynna screamed. Her body remained still. Rigid. Frozen in place by Dick Boy's TK, unable to react to whatever agony gripped her except with that scream. Lily thought of what Kongqi had called *jùdà téng*, a form of body magic that caused agony. And of the guard Alice had disciplined. No lasting damage, Alice had said. God, she hoped not. Dear God.

Cynna fell silent. Her head drooped forward. No other part of her so much as twitched.

"Tell me."

"We talked about many things. The translating I'm doing and—"

Cynna's tunic parted along the shoulder. A red stripe appeared on her arm. Blood, welling up in the cut that had appeared all on its own.

"Tell me."

"Th-the Codex," Lily stammered. "Alice asked me about the Codex Arcana." He didn't react. Didn't know the Latin phrase? She tried translating the name to Mandarin, though gods only knew if the cursed book was called the same thing in China. Or here. "The *Shén de Suǒyǒu Mófǎ*." The Book of All Magic, if she'd said it correctly. Which she probably hadn't.

"Do you mean the *Shén de Shū?* She asked about the *Shén de Shū?*"

Book of the Gods. "Yes. Probably. We spoke English so I'm not sure what you call it, but—"

Kongqi arrived in a thunderclap of displaced air. One second he wasn't there. The next he was hovering about ten feet from his brother. Had he teleported? Gods, could they do that?

Dick Boy's face flickered through expressions almost too fast to catch—alarm, chagrin, then a curled-lip sneer. "How dramatic you are, brother."

Kongqi's voice was a low rumble of rage. "You will tell me why you interfere with *my* prisoners!"

Dick Boy shrugged, his lack of concern an insult in itself. "I did little to the humans. A bit of blood on one, and no damage at all to the other. Shall I put the first one back where I found—oh, very well. You do it."

Cynna's arms folded up against her sides. Like a bulky arrow shot from an invisible bow, she shot back through the gaping hole in the wall. Lily threw herself aside barely in time to avoid being Cynna-struck, then saw her friend float gently to the floor.

"Shit," Cynna said, sitting up. "Shit, shit, shit."

"Are you okay?" Lily whispered.

"For some value of 'okay,' yeah." She scooted on her butt to get close to the hole and look out.

Dick Boy had crossed his arms. He sneered at his brother, his mustaches turning the expression into a parenthetical comment. "Are you worried about the stone? I will put that back when I am through."

"You are through," Kongqi told him in that deadly rumble. "*If* I allow you to leave."

"Allow?" Dick Boy lost his sneer in affronted anger. "You speak of allowing? Since you interest yourself in my actions, you will tell me—"

"I tell you nothing! These two are *mine!*"

"Your memory fails you. Prisoners belong to all of us, not just—"

"I am Father of Law! All prisoners are in *my* custody. You interfere in my territory and think you will not pay for it?"

Lily stole a glance at Cynna. Her own heart was pounding way too hard, a drumbeat of go-go-go with nowhere to go. Cynna's skin was like chalk beneath her tattoos. "You sure you're okay? You look kind of shocky."

"I don't hurt anymore. Well, except for my arm, which is aching like a fucking bad tooth. But the other . . . if that's what you felt with those pain ants . . ." She shuddered.

"I don't know that it's the same. After a certain point, though, the kind of pain doesn't matter. It's just pain, and it swallows you."

Cynna nodded. "Did you, ah, cut things off with . . ." She filled in the silence at the end of the question by mouthing Rule's name silently.

"Yeah." Not because she was smart enough to act that quickly to keep the spawn from "seeing" her using mind-speech. She'd just been too startled when the wall exploded to keep her attention on her mindsense, so it had coiled up inside her once more.

What was left of it. She'd pretty much used it up. Her head pounded miserably.

"What are they saying?"

Oh, right. Cynna had no idea what was going on. Lily whispered a quick summary. ". . . so Kongqi claims you because he's in charge of the Justice Court, but Dick Boy isn't buying that. They're exchanging insults now. At least I think that bit about breathing helium was an insult."

Dick Boy was one solid glower, his shoulders bunched as if he might spring at his brother at any moment. "You are overly fond of subtlety. Right action can be direct—and at times should be, as any but a prissy [unknown] would know."

Lily whispered the translation to Cynna.

"If I were certain you understood the meaning of [unknown], I might be offended. I fear, however, that you lack the—"

"Enough!" Dick Boy bellowed. "You will tell me why your granddaughter met secretly with—"

Kongqi roared. It was not a dragon's roar, not precisely, but no human throat should have been capable of that much volume.

Fire engulfed Dick Boy.

And Kongqi.

And winked out, both fires vanishing at the same instant, leaving Kongqi and Dick Boy without so much as a smoky smudge on their fancy clothes.

The two brothers weren't alone in the air anymore. The rest of the spawn had come.

TWENTY-THREE

~~~

FIVE Zhuren floated in the air—Kongqi, Dick Boy, and three that Lily had never seen before, but recognized from their descriptions. That meant the whole gang was here, with one exception: Zhu Huǒ, Master of Fire . . . who Lily knew as Tom Weng. Tom would still be busy on Earth right now, gearing up to steal Ryder, Toby, and the rest of the children.

Lily matched them to their descriptions. The tall, slim man in a midnight blue *shenyi* trimmed in pale green had to be Zhu Shuǐ, Master of Water and current Father of Study. His long hair hung loose, lifting and drifting languidly as if caught by currents of water instead of air.

The spawn on Shuǐ's left was, simply put, beautiful. He wore an open robe rather than a proper *shenyi,* a gaudy brocade in turquoise and magenta, over linen the palest of pinks. That had to be Zhu Shēngwù, Master of Body Magic and current Father of Wealth. Gossip said he'd used his skills on his own body, making himself into a living work of art.

Opposite Shēngwù was the only one with a beard—Zhu Tú'àn, Master of Patterns. Tú'àn wore his beard in thin braids decorated with silver beads. His *shenyi* was the color of moss, trimmed and embroidered in silver; his dark hair was pulled back in a tight bun that reminded her disconcertingly of

Grandmother. Tú'àn didn't hold a position in government right now.

He was the first to speak, in a clear and lovely tenor. Lily did her best to give a running translation for Cynna. "As the only one of us present without a governmental position, I assume the role of arbitrator. Do any dispute that this is my responsibility?" He paused. No one responded. "Zhu Kongqi, you have a grievance against Zhu Dìqiú."

"Do I need to state it?" Kongqi asked with meticulous courtesy.

"Not on my behalf." Tú'àn glanced at the others. They gave no signal Lily could see, but maybe that lack of response was the signal. "Nor do the others require it. We are aware of his discourtesy."

"I have a statement to make," Dick Boy announced.

"Zhu Dìqiú." Tú'àn gave the slightest of sighs. "It is clear you have interfered in what is your brother's rightful domain. No doubt you had reasons. Those do not interest me at this time, although I'll confess to some slight curiosity as to why you found it necessary to interfere so . . . obviously."

Impossible to be sure, given the way moonlight washed everything in silver and charcoal, that Dick Boy flushed. Impossible to imagine a dragon flushing with embarrassment . . . but the spawn weren't dragons, were they? "I acknowledge my error in damaging a building that is part of my brother's domain. I will repair it and am willing to make reasonable restitution for the offense. I do not accept Kongqi's claim upon the human Cynna Weaver." He answered stiffly.

"She is a prisoner of the Court of Heavenly Justice, and therefore in his domain."

Dick Boy lifted both brows. "Is she a prisoner? She is housed in the Court, yes, but she was given to Báitóu Alice Li."

One of the others—Shēngwù, the beauteous Master of Body Magic—frowned at him. His voice was a baritone. "Do you object? Her disposition was announced formally. You did not dispute it then, which is the proper time to bring up any perceived error."

Dick Boy's upper lip lifted in unsubtle scorn. "I fear, Brother, that you misunderstand. I do not dispute the right of the current Father of Law to dispose of a prisoner of the

Heavenly Court however he pleases. I say that he cannot both give her and keep her. She has been given to Alice. She wears no shoes. Is she not, then, *yāoqiú?*"

"All prisoners are claimed," said Shuǐ of the floating hair, "but the current Father of Law holds first claim. Your claim—and mine, and that of our other brothers—is secondary. If this were not so, each of us would have to surrender our claim on every prisoner who was executed, which would be tedious."

"But is she still a prisoner?" Dick Boy persisted. "She was given to Alice."

"Prisoners with particularly useful skills are occasionally given where their skills are needed instead of being executed."

"Yes," Dick Boy said. "Exactly. Once given, they are no longer within the Court's dominion."

"I have never considered that to be so," said Shēngwù. "If you did, why have you never raised the issue? I do not recall that you ever claimed any of the other prisoners who have been given by the court into other hands."

Dick Boy spread his hands. "But how else to consider it? A gift is not a gift if one continues to claim it. I did not raise the subject before because I had no particular need for any of the other former prisoners, and it is not our custom to interfere with the secondary rights holders. But custom does not alter my claim. As *yāoqiú*, Cynna Weaver belongs first to all of us and only secondarily to Alice. I am therefore free to exercise my claim upon her. My claim does not [unknown] that of any of you." He inclined his upper body a couple degrees in a formal, if very small, bow. "But neither does Kongqi's."

"If she is *yāoqiú*," Shēngwù said slowly, "Dìqiú is within his rights to use her as he wishes as long as he does not damage her enough to interfere with the claims the rest of us hold."

Shuǐ spoke again. "But is she *yāoqiú?* Her name was not changed. When we claim a child, the child receives a new name. Can a person be *yāoqiú* yet retain her family name?" He shook his head, making his hair sway like underwater fronds. "I think not. Cynna Weaver remains a prisoner and within the dominion of the Court."

"Prisoners do not give up their names," Shēngwù observed. "But they *are* claimed."

Tú'àn nodded. "Claimed, and yet the status of a prisoner is

very different from other *yāoqiú*. Those we claim as children
are special to us."

No one spoke, but they all looked affirming, even Dick
Boy. Shēngwù almost smiled. Shuǐ went so far as to nod, making his floating hair wave like seaweed.

"Very well," Tú'àn said. "It seems we have two points to
examine—the status of Cynna Weaver and the terminology
used for the claimed. We may have been sloppy in using the
same term for both the children and those who are claimed as
prisoners. We did so because it was a simple way to indicate
the legal status of prisoners, but it is now causing some degree
of confusion."

"I am not confused," Dìqiú stated.

Tú'àn gave him the slightest of bows. "We all know how
rarely you allow confusion to enter your mind, Brother. The
rest of us require deliberation to achieve such . . . certainty. I
propose that we postpone our examination of the second
issue—the need to differentiate between prisoners and those
claimed as children. Nor do we presently need to discuss the
manner in which Zhu Dìqiú acquired access to Cynna Weaver.
He has agreed to his error there, and the rest of us need be
involved only if he and Zhu Kongqi cannot agree on proper
restitution for the offense. I will speak to the immediate issue:
is Cynna Weaver a prisoner?

"Zhu Kongqi." Tú'àn turned to face Kongqi directly. "By
keeping Cynna Weaver in the Court of Heavenly Justice and
allowing her to keep her family name, you appear to be up-
holding the Court's claim upon her despite having given her to
Alice. Do you indeed assert a claim upon the human Cynna
Weaver?"

"I do," Kongqi said, "and I welcome the opportunity to
present my reasoning. My brothers may wish to consider the
proclamation of disposition, which states clearly that Cynna
Weaver was 'disposed into the keeping of Alice Báitóu.' This
is the wording traditionally used for a secondary claimant and
has never been considered to alter the rights of the first claimant. But is this the correct time and place for a detailed examination of this topic?"

The spawn exchanged glances with each other.

"Perhaps not," Tú'àn said. "Much more important matters will soon demand our attention."

Kongqi gave a small, agreeing bow. "But must such an examination [unknown] my primary grievance? You all heard what Dìqiú said." With the last sentence, his voice thrummed with outrage.

In other words, Lily thought, never mind the part about who gets to torture who. What mattered was that Dick Boy had said out loud that Alice was Kongqi's granddaughter.

All the spawn turned to look at Dick Boy sternly.

Dick Boy spread his arms. "I acknowledge that, in my haste and anger, I fell into error. I should not have referred so specifically to the honorable Báitóu Alice's heritage."

At last everyone had something they could agree on: Dick Boy had screwed up and had to be punished. They all had suggestions for that—suggestions that made Lily think Dick Boy was not beloved by his brothers. Lily supposed one of the spawn could regrow any of the body parts mentioned, but still . . .

"Zhu Kongqi," Tú'àn said, "you have not stated your preference."

"An affront to privacy is a serious matter," Kongqi said. "Words spoken publicly cannot be erased; therefore, the punishment must be permanent as well. None of the bodily punishments would satisfy me, for they are not permanent. Given the situation from which the offense arose, I believe a just punishment would be for Zhu Dìqiú to permanently surrender his claim upon the human Cynna Weaver, regardless of the outcome of the examination we will make later."

Dick Boy did not like that. He tried to hide it, but he was an emotional kind of guy. His very dislike made the rest agree that it was an appropriate punishment—that, and the fact that it let them end the discussion. Lily had the impression the spawn didn't much like hanging out together. They agreed to meet again in six months for the examination of the "larger issues"—how to define "prisoner," Lily supposed—and it was over. Three of the spawn zipped off, moving so fast they made her think of enormous mosquitos.

Dick Boy didn't leave with the others. Neither did Shēngwù the beautiful.

Lily let herself sink down to sit on the floor beside Cynna. Her head ached miserably. She wanted the last two spawn to go away so she could try to contact Rule again . . . though she doubted she could. The mind-stuff in her gut was too thin. She wanted a cup of coffee. A couple ibuprofen wouldn't hurt, either. And a pillow. Why hadn't she tried to bargain for a pillow? They had chickens here, right? They must have feathers to stuff pillows. But coffee . . . she sighed in pointless longing and rubbed the back of her head.

Two rocks floated up. One paused while the first settled itself with a dull crack against those still in place. The second one joined itself to the wall on the other side of the hole.

"I will assist, with your permission," Shēngwù said in his smooth baritone.

"As you please."

Lily leaned against the wall—an undamaged interior wall—and continued to translate quietly as the Master of Body Magic attempted to tease information out of the surly Master of Earth Magic while the two of them rebuilt the wall. Shēngwù floated the rocks up to the hole. Dick Boy ignored or deflected Shēngwù's oblique questions while placing the rocks, sometimes altering them. That was weird to watch; the rock seemed to melt and reform, but without heat. Eventually Shēngwù abandoned subtlety the oblique and asked directly about Lily's "secret meeting" with Alice.

Dick Boy snorted. "Information has a price."

His price did not seem to be high. He required Shēngwù to promise to inform the other spawn, then described what had happened before Kongqi showed up.

The interesting thing, she thought, was how readily Dick Boy and Shēngwù accepted that Lily had spoken the truth. Perhaps not the entire truth—they had, after all, been interrupted. But they both spoke as if they believed that Alice had asked Lily about the Codex, which they called the Book of the Gods.

As, of course, she had . . . when Lily first arrived. Which had provided Lily's inspiration for that particular lie: it wasn't entirely a lie. Maybe that had helped her fool Dick Boy. Whatever body signals he might have been using to detect lies—respiration, blood pressure, who knew?—would have been going crazy with fear for Cynna. Subtler tells should have been lost in that swamp of emotion, but if he did have some other way of detecting lies, she'd spoken a partial truth. Alice *had* asked about the Codex, just not at the meeting Dick Boy was so interested in.

Dick Boy and Shēngwù had no trouble believing that Alice was interested in the Codex. Wouldn't all the spawn be? Now that she thought about it, though, she'd met with Kongqi almost every day, and he hadn't asked about the Codex. Not once. He'd wanted to talk about altruism, the difference between sympathy and empathy, and dragons. Most of all, dragons—the ones he referred to as "the sentient dragons." Did that mean Kongqi already knew plenty about the Codex, but hadn't shared his knowledge with Alice? Or that Alice had told him that Lily knew very little, and he accepted that? Or did it mean that he really didn't much care about the Codex?

She rubbed her poor head and wondered if everyone here was insane.

"Headache?" Cynna whispered.

"Yeah."

Cynna took Lily's hand and lifted her eyebrows . . . inviting her, Lily realized after a moment, to mindspeak. Lily gestured at the nearly finished wall and shook her head. Touching skin-to-skin made mindspeech easy, but didn't make it invisible to one with the Sight. Harder to see, probably—or that's what Cullen had told her once. But difficult was not impossible. She didn't want to take the risk.

Cynna opened Lily's hand and wrote a letter on her palm, then another, until she'd spelled out, "Depleted?"

Lily nodded. "And hungry." Maybe depletion headaches and hunger headaches were the same thing. "Why do we get headaches when we're hungry anyway?"

"It's a blood sugar thing," Cynna said absently. She frowned at the nearly finished wall—or at the spawn on the other side, still discussing what Lily might know about the Codex. "Low blood sugar can make the blood vessels in the brain spasm or constrict."

Outside, the two spawn agreed that whatever Lily had told Alice about the Codex could not be considered reliable, but it would, nonetheless, be interesting data. The last rock snicked into place. And the spawn fell silent.

Gone? Lily got up to check, peering out the reconstructed window slit.

"Are they gone?" Cynna asked.

"As far as I can tell. I don't see them."

Cynna sighed. "That was weird, wasn't it? The way they kept speculating about what you'd told Alice, but they never asked you. You were right here, but it's like you were a tree."

"A tree?"

"I've been thinking about how the spawn see humans. Seems like it's kind of the way we see trees. People mostly like trees, but we see them in terms of how to use them—for shade or landscaping, or we can chop them down for lumber and firewood. And people who love trees love them differently. Some love forests. They don't worry about any individual tree, but they want the forest to persist. Another person might love the big oak in their backyard, but they'll poison or uproot any little oaks that sprout in their lawn. No forests allowed. Someone else might really enjoy studying trees, but he doesn't worry about how the trees feel. Tree feelings aren't real to him."

"Kongqi studies us," Lily said slowly. "Dick Boy is all about functionality. Using us. Killing a child means the same thing to him as pulling up a weed."

Cynna nodded. "And when other people are around, that's what we pay attention to. People get our attention whether we want them to or not. I think to the spawn, 'people' means other spawn. The rest of us are trees."

"So they didn't ask me anything because I'm just a tree and they forgot I was here."

"Pretty much."

That sounded about right. Lily lowered her voice to a whisper again. "I was thinking it might have been a setup."

"You mean that Dick Boy and Kongqi were only pretending to ignore you?"

"I mean the whole thing. It could have been a way to test me, see if I'd keep my promise of secrecy. Not that I think all the spawn were in on it," she added. "Maybe none of them were. Maybe it was all Alice. She could have said or done something to make Dick Boy suspicious, couldn't she? Knowing he'd react the way he did. I get the idea that Dick Boy is more obvious and direct than the others."

"I guess that's possible."

Cynna sounded dubious. Lily couldn't explain without saying things out loud that she shouldn't—and maybe because it wasn't clear to her, either. But it all wrapped around Alice. Alice had her finger in everything here, and she kept doing things that didn't make sense.

One thing was sure, though. They made sense to Alice.

Overhead, the single mage light winked out. Lily grimaced at the darkness. One of the most aggravating things about being a prisoner was not being in control of even the small stuff, like light.

"We should get some sleep," Cynna said.

"Yeah. Tomorrow will show up at the usual time." And tomorrow the kids might arrive. Or not.

Toby and Ryder. Diego, grandson of Ybirra Clan's Rho. Four-year-old Sandy, son of the Czøs Lu Nuncio. And three-month-old Noah, whose grandfather had been the Etorri Rho. All of them lupi. All of them born to Change when they hit puberty. All of them except Ryder closely related to the Rho of his clan . . . and that could not be coincidence. Cynna thought the rite to transfer the Change must require children with proximity to the mantle. Children with founder's blood.

And thinking about all that made it hard for Lily to settle her mind when she lay down on her thin sleeping mat. She did try poking at her mindsense, but it was so sluggish and her head hurt so much . . . Rule wouldn't panic. He'd known she was having trouble holding the connection. He wouldn't be going crazy, wondering what had happened. She hoped.

She rolled onto her side, but that was the bruised hip. A thin mat between it and the floor did not work. She sighed and rolled onto her back again and stared up at a ceiling dusted with moonlight from the rebuilt window slit. The countdown clock kept clicking in her brain. One more day until the kids got here . . . or maybe five. Or four, or three, or two . . . Between one and three days until Rule arrived. It depended on whether the boat he was on had to wait on some magistrate.

The kids might get here before he did. Rule's plan depended on him, Grandmother, and Gan getting here first.

Rule's plan was pretty damn shaky.

It was better than anything she'd come up with, she reminded herself. It did what it was supposed to: maximized their assets and gave them the best chance they had of succeeding. It wasn't the fault of his plan that their chances were so damn slim. They didn't have many assets, not when stacked up against an Old One, six dragon spawn, and an entire world.

She was not cheering herself up, was she?

Cynna's mind must have been giving her a hard time, too. She'd been doing the same sort of shifting around Lily had. Finally she sighed. "You're awake, too."

"Yeah."

"I'm just so scared."

"Yeah."

Cynna snorted. "That's it? That's all I get? No pep talk about how it's all going to work out?"

"Come on. You'd hit me if I said something stupid like that."

"That is oddly comforting." A pause. "It's a wonder I didn't pee myself when Dick Boy did the magic jujitsu to me."

"Um . . . the *jùdà téng?*"

"That thing. Yeah. I've never felt pain like that. I've given birth, but I've never hurt like that. He could have done that to me before instead of killing that little boy. I'd have cracked like an egg. Told him anything."

"That's the thing about torture. It both works and doesn't. If we hurt enough, we'll say anything to make it stop, but 'anything' doesn't mean what we say is true. We'll say whatever we think will make them stop hurting us."

Another pause. "You didn't. When they used the pain ants on you, you didn't crack."

Lily did not like thinking about that. It made her gut feel like jelly—a mooshy, quivery, about-to-fall-apart feeling. "I would have."

"But you didn't."

"Cynna. Get real. The hallucinations hit before I broke, and then I was too crazy to give Kongqi what he wanted. I couldn't even make sense of the question. Half the time I didn't know he was asking a question. His voice turned into a gong or his mouth turned into a cavern and bats flew out and attacked me." Attacked with burning, horrible bites. Ate her arm with acid mouths.

"But you said no. Over and over, you told him no."

"Did I? Yeah," she said, remembering. "It seemed like that was the one thing I knew, the one solid thing. I had to keep saying no." Say no to the monsters. That's what she'd held on to.

"I don't have anything that solid. I don't have your strength."

"Strength isn't something you have, like blond hair or a sweet tooth. You have to make it up fresh every damn time."

"What does that even mean? I have no idea what that means."

"It's what Grandmother told me a long time ago." Not long after Lily's friend had been raped and killed in front of her. "I'd heard some of Mother's friends talking about how strong I was. 'So strong to be so young,' they said. Stuff like that. It made me mad. I didn't feel strong. I felt ripped up, angry, horrible. I told Grandmother what I'd overheard and how mad it made me. She asked what I thought strength was. I said I didn't know, but I didn't have it. Nothing was easy. Getting up in the morning was hard. Going to bed was hard. So was everything in between."

"What did she say?"

"That strength doesn't make things easy. It makes things possible. And no one really *is* strong. We don't have some well of strength we can drop a bucket into and scoop some up. We all have to make it up as we go along, she said. So I asked, even you? Oh, yes, she told me. She was good at making strength because she'd had so much practice. No doubt I would get better at it as I grew older, but I must not expect to feel strong. At the times we most need strength, we never feel strong."

Cynna was quiet for several moments. "Is making it up the same thing as pretending?"

"Not exactly, though I guess you could use that if it's what you have. You make strength up out of whatever's at hand in that moment—anger, a bit of song, a sunset, a memory. Habit. Training. Stubbornness . . . that's my personal favorite. And what you've got changes, so you can't always use the same stuff. What worked last time might not work next time."

"What if all I've got right this moment is fear that goes all

the way down? And a broken arm that hurts like a mother?
And a mind that can only focus on what I don't have and won't
stop coming up with calamities?"

"You use what you've got."

A moment of silence. "That sucks."

"Pretty much, yeah."

TWENTY-FOUR

~⟶

Liangzhou, Dragonhome
Eight hours later

THE docks at their last stop before reaching Lang Xin bustled with commerce—silvery fish flopping in a net, cargo in crates, sacks, and barrels being loaded or off-loaded from various vessels. Their own boat's crew was mostly absent at the moment, either dealing with merchants or seeking refreshment in a tavern. One of the sons sat on the roof of the structure at the rear of the boat, keeping watch. Gulls swooped and called, their voices almost drowned out by the voices of people. At the other end of the pier, a small orange being darted between all those busy people.

Rule stood near the prow and watched Gan. She was *dashtu*, but he could see her. Not well; she was a person-shaped blur, visible mostly when she moved. The translation charm had somehow gifted him with that ability.

The first time it happened, a couple of cities back, Grandmother had said airily that seeing into *dashtu* was "a matter of translation, wasn't it?" and pretended not to be surprised. She'd since come up with three different explanations, none of which made sense to Rule. He didn't think they made sense to her, either.

"Take your charms off," she instructed him now.

He turned to see her staring at him. "Why?"

"Never mind. I believe this will work." So saying, she reached for the chain around his neck that held the charms, pulled it out, and wrapped her hand around one of them. "Do you see Gan now?"

He looked back at the crowded pier. "No, but with so many people that isn't—"

She released her grip.

A blurry orange figure trotted up to their boat, easily—if not clearly—visible. "Ah. There she is. What did you do?"

"Interrupted the charm that protects you from mind magic. I had not realized that it reaches into *dashtu*, but it must. I had wondered how it worked, since it does not seem to create a shield. I think it shifts hostile mind magic into *dashtu*. An elegant solution. The translation charm is interacting with it."

"That doesn't sound good."

"It is unexpected. I cannot tell if it is good or bad. Perhaps," she said thoughtfully, "it is also affected by your innate ability to enter *dashtu*."

"That makes no sense whatsoever."

"*Tch*. What do you think happens when you enter the Change?"

He stared.

"It is not the same . . . I will call it frequency. You do not use the same frequency of *dashtu* as Gan. You lose physicality; she does not. That loss of physicality prevents you from remaining *dashtu* the way she does, but it lets you emerge in a different body. This is why lupi are unique."

Rule felt sucker-punched. What she said made sense. He did not want it to make sense. He didn't know why. "I don't . . . it's not . . ."

"Rule. You go out-of-phase with the rest of the world when you Change. What is that if not *dashtu*?"

He decided to think about it later and changed the subject. "Does Gan have the folder? I can't tell."

"She has something. We will learn what in a moment."

The *chún-chún* did not ride high in the water. The boat's sides were only slightly higher than the dock; Gan jumped aboard easily. The boat rocked slightly, but the son guarding it didn't seem to notice. She trotted up to Rule and Grand-mother and sat, which put her head below the side of the boat and so out of sight of those on the pier. And abruptly sprang into focus. She had a cloth satchel slung over one shoulder and a big grin on her face. "That was fun!"

"I'm glad you enjoyed yourself," Rule said. "Do you have it?"

"Maybe." She removed the satchel and offered it to Grand-mother. "It was in the place you told me to look, but I'm not sure about the writing on the front. It all looked the same to me."

The magistrate of Liangzhou had indeed made them wait while he finished his correspondence. The delay made Rule want to pull his hair out. Or the magistrate's beard. They were close enough to Lang Xin now that he could almost justify jumping ship and running the rest of the way. But even if he had been willing to arrive in the capital as a wolf, lacking clothes, weapons, money, and those who could implement his plan, he might have a problem getting there.

People here had good reason to travel the river and not on land. Dragonhome was home to some very large beasts. Pred-ators, of course, but herd beasts could be dangerous, too. Any wolf knew that. In the United States, many more people were killed or injured by deer than by wolves and bears. And some of the herd beasts here were enormous. He'd seen a herd of *shānjiǎo*—literally translated, "mountain's feet"—from the boat and thought they were much closer than they were, his brain refusing at first to get the scale right. Surely they couldn't be that big . . . but they were.

And that shouldn't have been such a surprise in a place where dragons thrived. Dragons would need an abundance of large prey animals. Rule would like to have seen a dragon take on one of the *shānjiǎo*, but none had appeared to grant his wish before the herd was out of sight. Which, he supposed, he ought to be grateful for.

Nor would Grandmother ensorcel the beastmaster into leaving. She could have done so without damaging his mind by telling him he had already picked up the magistrate's mail.

He would have believed this and left. Rule had pointed that out more than once, finally resulting in her giving him a *look*. "You are not in charge of me, wolf. I must do some harm. I accept this. I will do no more harm than I must." Then she'd set off for the magistrate's court.

Rule had objected to her going alone. She'd sniffed and ignored him. And she'd been right in all that she hadn't bothered to say aloud. He was too memorable. Even if he'd used some of the magical ointment, his height made him stand out. So he'd waited at the boat, restless and anxious and trying not to snarl at everyone. Eventually she'd returned, not detained, jailed, or otherwise inconvenienced. She'd obtained directions for finding the magistrate's library and which shelf and folio should contain the most recent decrees. Which meant that she'd been right about that as well. It was highly aggravating.

Then she'd sent Gan to retrieve the documents she wanted.

The folio Grandmother pulled from the satchel was stiff, pale leather. On the outside was an embossed stamp of seven stylized suns set in a circle; what Rule supposed was the date was written in beautiful calligraphy along one side. Inside was a small stack of papers.

Grandmother took those out and glanced through them. "You brought the correct folder," she told Gan, "but I should have had you bring the last two. Ah, well. This may be enough." She tapped the pages together and began to read.

The plan was for her to read the stolen documents quickly so Gan could return the folio—hopefully before it was missed. Rule called on his wolf for patience as he waited. And waited.

"Ha!" she said at one point.

"What?"

"Shh." And she kept reading.

Finally she looked up. "They are expecting calamities on a specific date and time. The magistrate has been ordered to stockpile food because his city may suffer an earthquake and fires of an unusual nature soon after moonrise on the last day of the seventh moon. He has been ordered to remain in the city, but is advised to remove his family to their country estate."

Rule stiffened. "Earthquakes and fires—that's what you said would happen if a gate were opened between Dragon-home and Earth."

"Yes."

"That construct, the magical construct on Dis—Reno used it—"

"It is not a gate. He used it as one, but he said it is not a gate. I agree, although . . ." She shook her head. "I have never sensed anything like it. I had no time to study it. I do not know what it is, but it lies mostly in Dis, though with a terminus in this realm. But even if Reno is wrong about its nature, a gate between Dis and Dragonhome would not cause calamities."

He licked dry lips, checked with the sense that had no name. "Moonrise will occur about an hour after sunset today."

"That is good to know."

"The date—if they go by the lunar calendar here—"

"It refers to the seventh full moon of the year."

"Then . . ."

"Tomorrow. Yes."

LILY leaned against the rebuilt wall in her cell and whispered, "Tomorrow?"

Yes, Rule replied. *At moonrise, which will be about an hour after the sun sets.*

Lily was alone in the cell. Cynna was attending the ballet.

At least, that's what Cynna insisted on calling it. "Ballet" wasn't a good translation, as the dancing wouldn't have much in common with a style of dance born in the Italian Renaissance. "Beast dances" came closer. According to Alice, the performance would feature stylized dances representing both earthly beasts and those in this realm. Cynna thought that watching this ritualized performance would help her translate that spell. Lily didn't really understand why, except that it was all about the symbology. Alice had agreed that it was worth trying and arranged for Cynna to go, suitably guarded, of course. She'd wanted to send Lily along to translate as needed, but Kongqi had nixed that. He'd wanted to talk to Lily about ism's—nihilism, determinism, Buddhism—as well as the deal the dragons had made with the U.S. government, aka the Dragon Accords. He'd kept Lily with him until well after supper.

She'd never thought she'd long to be back in her cell, but she had, because she couldn't contact Rule until she was alone.

"That fits with what's happening with the time rate difference," she said in a whisper so soft she barely heard herself. Rule had begun using under-the-tongue speech—a type of subvocalization—when they mindspoke. It worked great for him. Not for her. She could feel the pulses going awry when she tried it, could tell that sometimes she didn't make pulses for the words at all, but she didn't know why. Her mind just didn't seem to believe she was speaking when she subvocalized. "The way it's dropping made me think things would happen soon even if I didn't know what things. It's been going down ever since Alice started telling us about it."

Let me pass that on to Grandmother. A longish pause. *She agrees. It's very difficult to open a gate when the realms aren't time-congruent. It can be done, but it's much harder. She wonders if there is a predictable cycle for the difference in time rates that they are taking advantage of.*

"I don't know. I guess that would explain the timing of everything that's happened—they needed to sync it all with the time when the two realms are nearly synchronized. But why? Why would it be so important for them to open a gate between Earth and Dragonhome? Do you think it has something to do with the magical construct on Dis?"

We don't know for certain that they're opening a gate—it just fits what we do know. How that might connect to the magical construct, I have no idea. Ah . . . Grandmother wishes me to emphasize that the construct is not a gate, but partakes of certain elements of gates. I don't know what that means.

She didn't, either. "Cynna might. Dammit, I wish she was here. She called up that memory, by the way. The one about gate building."

Good. Lily, several magistrates seem to have received the same or a similar warning from the spawn. Maybe all of them. Grandmother says that if fires and earthquakes are expected in cities all along the river, it may mean the spawn—or the Great Bitch—intend to open multiple gates to Earth. The effects from a single gate located in Lang Xin wouldn't reach all the way down the river.

"But why?" she repeated. "What good would that do them?"

I suspect it's intended to benefit the Great Bitch, not the spawn. This would be part of their deal with her. *Perhaps the main part. The amount of chaos and destruction multiple gates would cause could destroy the Chinese economy.*

"The Chinese . . . oh, yeah. Right. I guess they'd be gates to China, wouldn't they? Dragonhome's nodes don't correlate to U.S. nodes."

That was my first thought, given that fall-throughs seem to all be from China, but we can't assume that. There may be some nodes here that touch American nodes but haven't re-sulted in fall-throughs.

"Huh." Lily considered that a moment. "Maybe they have, though. Alice's grandmother was a Westerner. I originally thought that the woman must have been traveling in China when she accidentally fell into Dragonhome, but maybe not. Maybe there have been a few *láis* from the West. So we don't know whether or not the U.S. would be affected by these gates."

Oh, we'd be affected, even if none of the nodes here con-nect to nodes in North America. China has a tremendous ef-fect on the U.S. economy. On the world economy. If their economy truly collapsed, we'd likely see a worldwide reces-sion, possibly a depression. As to how that helps her . . . *our Enemy might want chaos, turmoil, and confusion in general, or she might be steering things towards a specific cascade of events. She* is *a patterner.*

Right. Lily contemplated that, decided that she couldn't read patterns, so maybe she shouldn't try to predict what the Great Bitch was trying to accomplish. Other than taking over the world, that is.

A thought occurred to her. "What if some of these dragons— the mind-blind dragons here—flew through the gates? How would our dragons react?"

I don't know, and Grandmother says she does not care to make predictions. We'll talk about this, but Lily, we have to assume this timetable means that the children will arrive to-morrow. If this—the opening of gates, or whatever it is—is scheduled for moonrise, then we have to assume the children will arrive before that.

"Yeah. Yeah, that makes sense. If opening gates to Earth is payment from the spawn to the G.B., they won't do it until they get what she promised them." The children. That's what they wanted—babies and children who could be plundered for their ability to Change. Lily closed her eyes. She was so *angry*. So tight with anger and fear and some unholy fusion of the two. Vividly she remembered how Toby had looked in the blue pj's he'd worn to bed the night the monsters came . . .

Eyes open, she told herself. Got to keep her eyes open and focused on the present. "We need to talk about the timing. About how long we'll have to hold the area around the gate." She and Rule had been separated for much of their assault on Xitil's former palace, so he didn't have all the facts. "We can't reopen that gate until we reach a moment when we—the other 'we,' that is, the ones in the past—aren't in Dis anymore." She huffed out a breath. "Did that make sense? Talking about events that are both in the past and in the future makes me dizzy."

I follow you. You're worried about the delay, the time between when the children were taken through the gate and the time when all of us left Dis. I am, too, but don't see how we can estimate it accurately.

"Cynna and I have tried. We think we've come up with an estimate for the maximum delay. She's sure Ryder was in Dis up until someone broke her Find, so that's the earliest moment the children could have been taken through a gate. As close as we've been able to figure, that was about two-and-a-half hours before Gan grabbed Cynna and yanked her into Dragonhome."

Two-and-a-half hours. He was silent a few moments. *That's longer than I was hoping. Grandmother says she cannot hold the ward that long.*

"That's what I was afraid of."

You're assuming that time is now passing at roughly the same rate in Dis and here?

"The last figure I got from Alice for the time rate difference was down to three minutes, ten seconds."

Then we will have to hope that the delay is not the maximum possible. The minimum would be about thirty minutes, based on when we arrived at the audience hall. Either way, we will need the distraction.

She couldn't argue. Much as she hated it, she hadn't been able to come up with a better idea. "Reno will be able to help.

He left through the construct right before Cynna lost her Find, so he should get here before the kids do."

We don't know if he'll travel in a straight line, time-wise, or more crookedly, the way Gan did. He might arrive five minutes from now or after the children are brought here. And once he's here, he may not act directly against the spawn.

"Because he's their mother."

Yes. But we can count on him to act against the Great Enemy, even if that endangers the spawn. Grandmother explained why. I need to tell you about that, but it's a long story.

She hoped he was right. Learning that the green dragon had given birth to the spawn had shaken her. "Maybe you should save the long story for later. I need to tell you about my idea for Gan. I started to before, but I lost the connection. Ask Gan something for me. How easy is it for her to cross to Earth from Dragonhome? Are there a lot of spots where she could do that?"

A pause, long enough to have her drumming her fingers on her thigh impatiently. Then: *She says Dragonhome doesn't have as many crossing spots as most realms. She means all crossing spots, not just those that touch Earth. She thinks this is because Dragonhome is set crooked to all the realms—a statement that got Grandmother's attention. She's questioning Gan about what that means. She . . . oh.* His mental voice thrummed with sudden emotion. *Lily, she just told Grandmother that there are always crossing spots near a node.*

"You're thinking what I'm thinking, right? There will be a node at or near the gate, so there will be crossing spots. Maybe, while the rest of us hold the area around the gate, Gan can cross with the children, one at a time. Take them to Earth."

Son of a bitch. I didn't think of—I can't believe I never thought—just a minute. Hold on a minute while I ask.

Another endless pause. When Rule spoke again, his words were crisp yet weighted, as if each word was part of a dam holding back all sorts of emotion. *She says yes, if there's a good crossing spot. There may not be, and even if there is, she may not be able to take all the children. She has plenty of power, but it makes her dizzy to cross realms that aren't matched in time. If she's too dizzy, she won't be able to cross safely.*

"The time rate difference is pretty small now."

Yes. Another pause. She could almost feel him mastering his emotions enough to continue. *So dizziness may not be a major problem. But she also says that slipping through the strata—she liked Grandmother's word for that—around Dragonhome is difficult. She isn't sure how many times she can do it without resting. She described the process as being like "trying to shit a brick, only you're both the asshole and the shit that's trying to come out the asshole."*

Lily couldn't help grinning. "Colorful, that's our Gan."

Yes.

For a moment neither of them spoke. Was he struggling with the same messy mix of hope and fear as she was? Acid drops of "maybe" dripped and burned, dripped and burned. But if they could get the kids to safety . . . well, what happened to the rest of them mattered, it mattered a lot, but once the kids were safe, they'd won. "So we try for that, if we can. It's not a sure thing, but—"

He laughed. Mindspeech was only supposed to carry words and this wasn't verbal, yet she knew it for laughter—a sensation entirely mental, too broad to call amusement, a bubbling exuberance that could only be laughter. *What about all this isn't insanely risky?*

"True," she said wryly. "And we've made it this far, so . . ." Sounds outside her cell caught her attention. "I think Cynna's back. I'd probably better go. I'll need to brief her on everything, and I don't want to get depleted again."

Of course. I love you.

She closed her eyes and sent the words back to him. Those three words were so clear in her mind . . . she didn't need to whisper, didn't need any help with them at all. And then, instead of telling him good-bye, she asked something that had been bothering her, though she'd made herself use their time to discuss more important things: "Rule? You aren't calling Grandmother 'Madame' anymore."

She told me to call her Grandmother.

A smile surprised her, sliding over her face smooth and easy. As if she were happy. "You've been adopted."

I was already part of her family. He sounded baffled. *When you and I married, I became part of her family, as she is part of mine.*

"You've been adopted," she repeated softly. She knew what this meant, even if she couldn't put it into words . . . or maybe she could. "Let me put it this way. You've been claimed."

Ahh.

Funny how a single syllable—one she couldn't even hear, strictly speaking—could hold such understanding. "Tell Grandmother I love her."

TWENTY-FIVE

~~

LILY was sound asleep when the hinges on the door creaked. She shot bolt upright, her system zinging with adrenaline alarms.

It was Ah Hai. Lily sighed, her body flooded with fight-or-flight chemicals. Reason number 122 to hate being a prisoner: no one knocks on a cell door. "You're early," she observed, trying not to sound pissed about it. There was enough light coming in the window slit to see by, but only just. The tiny cell was painted in the pearly grays of predawn.

Ah Hai nodded and knelt beside Lily's sleep mat. In silence she held out a familiar object: Lily's Glock.

Lily's eyes flew to Li Hai's face. The albino woman tapped her closed lips with a finger. Not the "shush" gesture Lily was used to, but the idea was clear. "You are to come with me," Ah Hai whispered in her dialect.

"What is it?" Cynna said, her voice bleary with sleep.

"Ah Hai wants me to go with her," Lily said softly. She took the weapon, and Ah Hai promptly dug into a pocket and pulled out two full clips. Lily took those, too, and held them out to Cynna, sending, *Hide these for me.*

Cynna—sitting up now—accepted them and tucked them under her blanket. "Where? Where are you going?"

Lily had no idea, so she asked Ah Hai.
"To the workroom of the Zhu Kongqi."

LILY had been to Kongqi's workroom many times now, often enough to wear down her fear of the place. Wear down, but not eliminate, and the weirdness of this summons brought it back full-force as she stepped out into early morning air almost cool enough to call crisp.

Ah Hai walked beside her. As usual, two guards kept pace in front and behind—but not Fang. Fang always accompanied her, but not this time. Not on the day when Rule, Grandmother, and Gan would arrive. When the children would arrive. Her mind spun out a dizzying number of possibilities for Fang's absence, all of them calamitous. She told her mind to shut up. It didn't listen.

"Where's Fist Second Fang?" she asked Ah Hai casually.

"He is not yet on duty, I think."

There, see? she told her mind. A change in the routine does not automatically signal a return of pain ants. Kongqi had a busy day planned, what with stealing the Change from babes and opening gates to Earth. He was squeezing her in at the only time available to him.

The question, of course, was why.

He had no reason to question her again. Not about anything that mattered anyway. There was no way he could have guessed at their plans. He had no mind magic, so he couldn't know she'd been in contact with Rule. He certainly didn't know about Grandmother. He wanted to talk about solipsism or the Dragon Accords some more before she was handed over to the Great Bitch to get her mind scrubbed clean. Last chance and all that. She had to quit worrying about the secrets she was keeping so he didn't sense her nerves.

And that was like trying not to think of an elephant. That damn elephant clomped along beside her all the way to the *Qī Jiā* and down its halls to Kongqi's lab.

There were no guards stationed outside it. *Why not?* her mind shrieked. Kongqi always had guards outside his sanctum. Ah Hai laid her palm on the door and whispered something so softly Lily wasn't sure she heard it. Then she set her hand on the latch and opened the door.

The door was supposed to swing open, powered by TK. Kongqi always did it that way. Lily didn't move. That might have been tactical. It might have been sheer funk.

Ah Hai paused a few steps in, apparently realizing Lily hadn't followed her. "Come," she said, using the English word Lily had grown to hate and beckoning with one hand.

She could take the guards. Lily was sure of that. But this was not the day to stage an escape. Reluctantly she entered the workroom. Everything looked pretty much the same as ever, with one exception. Kongqi wasn't there.

"What's going on?" Lily asked. "Where's—"

Ah Hai made that "hush" sign again and moved behind the door . . . standing where the guards wouldn't see her, Lily realized. The little woman closed the heavy door using hands instead of TK, then set her palm on it again and whispered at it. She turned to face Lily and whispered, "The Zhu Kongqi will be here soon. We wait for him here, where no one can hear us. First I must caution you as I was bid. The weapon I returned to you will not harm the Zhuren when they fly. They have shields that protect against projectiles."

Lily thought about that, about how fast they zipped around in the air, and nodded. They'd probably need to develop those shields just to keep bug-spatter from messing up their pretty *shenyi*. But would such shields really work against a bullet traveling at 2500 feet per second?

"Honorable Lily Yu, do you remember that I told you once about the Kanas?"

That was so far from anything she'd been expected that it took her a moment to place the name. "That's the village. Or the villagers maybe. The people where the sp—where the Zhuren were raised."

Ah Hai nodded solemnly. "I am afraid I led you to think an untrue thing. The Kanas did not all die when their village burned." She looked at Lily expectantly.

How had Ah Hai put it when she told that story? *It is said*, or something like that. Not "this happened," but "it is said this happened." "What happened to them?"

Ah Hai looked vaguely disappointed. "Perhaps you do not

know that the village of Kanas lay in a region where there is much magic."

Why didn't the woman just tell her? "High magic means . . . more people born with Gifts? More born with . . . shit!" she exclaimed in English as the light dawned. More mutations. She went back to Mandarin. "Are you saying that *you're* a Kanas? That some or all of those who are claimed—the *yāoqiú*—are Kanas?"

Ah Hai beamed. "I cannot tell you that."

"You mean you're not allowed to."

"If you were ever to meet one of the Kanas—one who was not an elder—she would not tell you who she was. However, she might choose to tell you a story."

Lily's heart pounded. She leaned in close. "Will you tell me a story, Ah Hai?"

RULE stood at the rail and inhaled deeply. Gan sat on the deck beside him, her eyes bright with curiosity, her mouth—for once—silent. She was already *dashtu*.

They were in Lang Xin at last.

The sun was high and hot, the air too humid for sweat to evaporate. The wet air trapped scents, bringing a rich mélange to his nose. There was the river itself, wet and pungent, heavy with smells of fish, green growing things, and decay. The now-familiar smells from the boat itself—wet hemp, sun-warmed wood, rice, old grease, and the mingled scents of those he'd traveled with. A thousand more scents came from the city. Peppers and ginger, anise and cabbage. The smoke from cooking fires. Sewage. Rot. Flowers. And humanity in all its sweaty, musky forms.

The docks at their other stops had been busy, bustling places. The docks at Lang Xin doubled that. Cargo of all sorts, from the bales of cotton being off-loaded from the boat next to theirs to the crates of birds a thin man was piling onto a two-wheeled cart—birds that looked like small chickens but smelled like pigeons. All sorts of foodstuffs, from fish to cabbages, onions to eels. A child of nine or ten wandered along the pier, twin baskets weighing down his shoulders, calling what Rule's translation charm whispered was, "Fresh pears!

Fresh pears for sale!" A pair of young men staggered drunkenly, arms around each other, singing loudly. The charm rendered those words for him, too. Most of them were obscene. An old woman gave the young rowdies a condemning look.

Another old woman approached Rule from the rear of the boat. "You want an apple," Grandmother informed him and handed him a large, lumpy red fruit that was certainly not an apple.

He eyed it. "What is it really called?"

Grandmother pulled a second fruit from the bag and handed it to Gan. Which must look odd to anyone watching, as she seemed to have handed it to thin air. "Píngguǒ. Which means apple."

She was in a mood this morning, wasn't she? He grinned at her, then took a big bite of the lumpy fruit. It was good, tart and crisp. More like a pear crossed with a mango than an apple, but good.

"The prospect of action makes you cheerful."

"It does, yes."

She sighed. "I suppose it is the wolf."

"Wolf and man are in accord this morning." Although he was troubled that he hadn't heard from Lily yet. Before, when he was far away, it had been hard for her to make contact. But he was here now, in the same city. Surely he would hear from her soon.

Soon. Such a difficult word. He turned over in his mind all that would happen soon, clicking off the points in his plan. And took another bite of lumpy fruit. "The people here must have named this after something familiar. Called it an apple because it's red. I hadn't realized they had apples in ancient China."

"Apples originated in China."

According to Grandmother, almost everything originated in China. "We need to get moving."

"Mei Bo will be ready soon."

The boat father was going to take them to the *Yóupiào Jú*—the Stamp Office. Regular traders like the Siji received their stamps from agents there at the docks, but visitors like Grandmother and Rule had to go to a Stamp Office. A small fee or tax was charged on all commerce arriving at or passing through any of the cities with magistrates, and a stamp was issued to show the goods were lawful. Grandmother hadn't yet paid the fee, as gems were mostly exempt, being used often in lieu of coins. But the exemption didn't apply in Lang Xin. Here she had to declare her diamonds and pay the fee.

Rule hoped the boat father would be quick. He wanted to get their plan in motion. He looked out over the river and summoned patience.

Even the river was crowded here. Sampans by the dozens. Flatboats, one-way-only crafts that would let the river carry them and their cargo downstream. Two *chún-chún* were docked here in addition to theirs. They'd already encountered the crew of one of the *chún-chún* in Liangzhou. The other was docked on the next pier over from theirs, close enough for the crew to call out cheerfully to the boat father when he finally emerged from the shed at the rear of the boat, dressed in his best clothes—still a plain tunic and trousers but made of good cloth, the blue dye still bright. He'd exchanged his usual straw hat for one rather like a sailor's with its turned-up brim, black with bright embroidery on the brim. He carried the pouch that held the official mail.

"Cousin!" the translator charm whispered in Rule's ear, and "Mei Bo, you old robber! How was your trip?"

"A good trip," the boat father called back. "No thieves, and only one dragon!"

His cousins on the other boat were suitably astonished and demanded the story.

"They don't remember that they already visited us," Rule murmured to Grandmother.

Her eyebrows lifted. "Did you doubt it?"

Actually, yes, though he wouldn't say so out loud. Rule wasn't easy about depending on ensorcellment so much. It was reassuring to know that the "forget" part of Grandmother's instructions worked. Now if the more complex part worked as well . . .

"Later," the boat father called back to the cousins who had already visited his boat. "We will lift a cup together, heh? And I will tell you about the dragon who held me in his claws. I must go, but later, we will talk!"

Lang Xin doubled everything, Rule thought as, at last, he

followed the boat father from the boat onto the dock. People, noise, the crates and nets and boxes of commerce. And the stakes. The stakes went way up the moment his foot hit the hard wood of the dock.

Mei Bo walked ahead with his daughter and one of his sons. The other son would watch the boat, a duty he'd drawn by losing at the dice game last night. The son with them wore a hat similar to their father's. Mei Ling's head was bare, her hair shiny in the sun. Both of them wore blue, though in different shades.

Rule's little group had donned their best clothes, too. He wore the least-faded of his two shirts with a new pair of trousers, ones with legs that reached all the way to his ankles. He now had a straw hat like many of the locals wore to protect his face from the sun—and shield it a bit from passing eyes. Grandmother had on a new, bright red shirt with her worn black skirt. Gan didn't wear new clothes. Because no one would see the little one, she'd donned her original clothing—her adventure gear, she called it—the khaki shirt and pants with pockets everywhere. But she'd added a new hat. It was an incredibly bright green, shaped like a beanie, with red embroidery and a yellow pom-pom at the crown. He had no idea where she'd found it. She positively strutted down the pier.

"I have been thinking," she'd told him last night, her odd little face deeply serious. "And I do not see how you could do this without me."

He could have answered so many ways. Luck would play as large a role as any one of them. Maybe larger. So would Reno, though he might put the green dragon in the same category as luck, as both were impossible to predict or manage. He might have pointed out that their success depended on all of them. On Lily, whose mindspeech gave them an edge their enemies did not suspect and could not match. On Cynna, who was a powerful spellcaster and a Rhej, able to draw on the clan memories. The spawn, for all their power, lacked Cynna's magical expertise, or Alice Báitóu wouldn't have negotiated so hard to obtain some of Cynna's spells. Then there was Grandmother. If anyone was essential to their success, she was.

Instead he'd nodded with matching seriousness and spoken another truth. "That's true. Our plan depends on you."

He'd expected her to preen. She hadn't. She'd nodded back at him solemnly, then stared out over the dark water, its ripples slicing the moon's reflection into glimmering life.

The moon would be full tonight, he thought as they reached the end of the dock. Her call was strong and sweet, impossible to ignore but not yet imperative. That song would turn from a beckoning to a demand when she rose above the horizon an hour after sunset . . . just as the gates to Earth were flung open and all hell broke out in two realms.

"I suppose," Grandmother said sourly in Chinese, "that is the line we must join?"

A line of people stretched out of the door of a small building set slightly back from the street that ran alongside the docks. Twenty or thirty people stood, chattered, scowled, and waved paper fans at their faces, hoping to stir up a breeze. Many, but not all, wore hats. A wizened old man pulled a huge pottery jar set on wheels alongside the line, dispensing cups of tea for . . . Rule paused, listening. He could hear the old man's voice, but it was too far for the translation charm.

The boat father assured her that it was, adding that "old Chen Mu's tea is very good. Only one *dìsì* a cup. We will get some tea, eh?"

"And *baozi*," Rule said in his extremely limited Chinese. He'd picked up a little more of the language with the translator charm whispering in his ear all the time. Not much, but a little. He'd developed a fondness for the bland food ever since breaking his too-long fast with them. But *baozi* did lack meat, and it was lunchtime. "And . . . *shāokǎo*?" He wasn't sure of his pronunciation of the spicy kebabs he could smell but didn't see.

After a bit of polite dithering about who would pay— Grandmother won—Mei Bo sent his daughter to obtain lunch and the rest of them headed for the back of the line. And Grandmother gave Gan the sign to leave them.

The little one scampered off, then paused, looking back at them. Rule couldn't see her well enough to make out her expression, but there was something wistful about that looking-back.

A smile was all the reassurance he could give her at the moment, so he offered that.

"It is good of you to keep us company," Grandmother was saying to Mei Bo.

"I am happy to do so, madame."

He did seem to be. Not that he'd had any choice, Rule reflected.

Grandmother continued to meet the boat father's eyes steadily. "You have been a good host on our trip. I am glad to repay a small part of your kindness." She said all that in Chinese, then added a short English phrase—"Wake up"—before going back to Chinese. "Are the *shānjiǎo* in place?"

"Oh, yes," he told her, sneaking an awed glance at Rule. "All is ready. My cousins tend them now."

"Very good. Forget that I asked about them." And, in English, "Sleep."

"I am sad that I do not get to buy a meal for you," Mei Bo said. "Did not this great swordsman of yours save my life? When that dragon . . ."

Rule!

Yes. I'm here. Rule spoke under-the-tongue so he didn't have to move his lips in public. *I'm in line, waiting to see the tax-stamp officials.*

I've got people around, too, so I'll makethisquick. Needto-tellyou that Ah Hai brought me my weapon this mornananan the ammo, then told me about theclaimed—they're the bfaffitions. And they're descenackafum thekanas. You remember whuitollu about them? The oneshooifima zhurnneistope backa?

Your words are coming through garbled, he said. *I don't know what you said.*

Dammit!

That came through plenty clear. *You have people around you? You're trying to subvocalize to use mindspeech?*

Yes. Focus . . . is . . . hard . . . when I'm . . . walking . . . andtalking. Need to . . . waitaminute.

Lily hadn't had much experience speaking under-the-tongue. That seemed to affect her ability to use it to shape her thoughts for mindspeech. He was closer to her than he had been—*close,* his wolf whispered at him, *close*—but she was still on the other side of the city, and apparently distracted by those nearby. *Is your information urgent as well as important?* he subvocalized, not knowing if she was "listening."

Both. The . . . barefoot ones . . . seemtobe slaves . . . are onourside. Ah Hai . . . saysthespawn . . . will be . . . busy . . . preparingfortheir . . . ritual. Long prep. I . . . Dammit. Igottago.

The barefoot ones? What did she mean? Frustrated, Rule was frowning as Mei Ling came skipping up, holding one of the ubiquitous string bags in one hand and skewered meat in the other. Her smile faltered.

Couldn't have that. Hating himself, he smiled at her in the way he had no business smiling at anyone but Lily. She blushed and held out the mystery meat—mystery being the key word here, as he had no idea what animal it had come from. Probably one not found on Earth, though it smelled a bit like goat.

She told him shyly that there was a juggler, and would he like to go see? Then blushed again, for of course she assumed he didn't understand what she'd said, and turned to her father to ask permission to take Wu Tŭ Ní to see a juggler. Wu Tŭ Ní was the name Grandmother had bestowed on him, claiming that it mimicked his real name closely enough to help him remember to respond to it. The naming had amused her greatly. Later he'd learned that those syllables could mean anything from rainbow dirt to local wool to vomit mud.

". . . a very good juggler, Father," Mei Ling said earnestly, "and it is not far to go, being only down the street in front of the scribe's stall."

Mei Bo chuckled and asked Grandmother if she minded if the two young people went to see this amazing juggler. He thought she needn't fear attack here, eh? And so had no great need for her swordsman. Ever since the dragon attack, he had insisted on referring to Rule as a swordsman.

Grandmother looked sour, which fit her character, but grudgingly agreed and told him in English, "Take your time. The line is long."

In other words, everything was proceeding as they wanted it to. He hadn't even had to come up with a reason to extract himself from the line. Mei Ling had done it for him. But her timing sucked. He needed to talk to Grandmother about Lily's garbled message, see if she knew who these "barefoot ones" were that Lily thought were on their side.

Lily would have to tell Grandmother about them herself. He gave Grandmother a small bow and said, "Thank you, madame."

"Yes, yes. Go on." She made a shooing gesture.

He did, preparing himself to be charming. The trick to charming people was really no trick at all. Men and women alike were charmed by those who found them charming. With some people that could be difficult, but not with Mei Ling. Shy and lovely, silly and smart, she was as appealing as a kitten. No, the hard part would be hiding his guilt.

He was using her. Together, he and Grandmother would use her whole family. "I wish I could speak to you," he murmured in a language she didn't understand. "I wish I could have the chance to explain."

She blushed happily and spoke in a language she thought he couldn't understand, telling him the day was beautiful, and he was beautiful, and she was so glad her father liked him now.

He smiled and smiled and told her she was beautiful with his eyes. That much, at least, was true.

TWENTY-SIX

GAN did not like this realm. Oh, she'd been in worse ones, but she'd never had to stay in any of them and she'd been here for days and days in spite of it having huge dragons that wanted to eat her. She might not be a demon anymore, but she was sure she still tasted good to dragons. The dragons, however, were not the worst thing about this place.

There was no chocolate.

Gan sighed in mournful near-silence so the people around her wouldn't hear. She was tired of having to be quiet, tired of no-chocolate, and tired of all these feelings she didn't understand. It was like being scared, but not about anything that was happening. About things that hadn't happened and maybe never would, and a lot of that not-exactly-fear wasn't even about her. It was about her friends. She was *worried* about them.

Gan wasn't used to worrying. She didn't like it. She wanted it to stop.

Absently she stole a sticky-sweet bun from the stall of a vendor who was distracted by yelling at a young boy who couldn't go *dashtu* and had to do his stealing the hard way. He didn't seem to be very good at it.

The gnomes kept telling her how wrong stealing was. She

didn't get it. Gnomes paid a lot of attention to owning stuff, but they thought *owning* was the same thing as *having*, which was just silly. You could only own the things you really loved. Everything else you just had—you ate it or used it or whatever. You might get mad if someone took something you'd planned to use, but that didn't make stealing bad. Right and wrong weren't based on what made people mad at you or on what made them like you. Old Woman had told her that.

That's what Gan called Li Lei Yu in her mind—Old Woman. Old Woman was special. Important like a friend, but not the same as a friend. Gan couldn't come up with words for what she meant, but for some reason she didn't want to use one of Old Woman's regular call-names.

Old Woman had had lots of call-names over the years, which wasn't surprising with someone so dense with *üther*. You didn't get that kind of density just by staying alive a long time. You had to live both widely and deeply, and Old Woman's *üther* went really deep. Like a dragon's, almost. Just now she was using three call-names—the one she used back on Earth, one that she'd made up to use on their trip, and the one her family used. They called her Grandmother.

One thing about Old Woman Gan did have words for: she almost always made sense. Like when she said that right and wrong weren't the same thing as if people liked you or were mad at you. That made sense. If Gan stole some more food and gave it to that boy who wasn't a very good thief, the boy would like it but the man she stole from would be mad. One would say she'd done a good thing and the other would say she'd done a bad thing.

Right and wrong were complicated, but that's because they were a soul thing, and souls made everything complicated. Gan's soul was very new. She'd only started growing one when Lily Yu became her friend, so she didn't have right and wrong figured out yet. Old Woman said that most people didn't. She said, "Never trust people who think they know everything about right and wrong. They stopped thinking a long time ago."

Old Woman was good at making sense of things. Good at putting words to things that confused Gan. Maybe she should ask Old Woman what to call her.

The street Gan was on was wide and full of people. Some had carts they pulled and some carried stuff on their backs, but most were just busy going someplace. Gan passed through a tall, decorated arch with a lot of other people and got a look at where everyone was headed.

It was a big, green, open place. There were a few buildings, too, but mostly it was open space. Wide open spaces gave Gan the shudders. These people had some sense, though. The paths they used to go between the buildings were shielded from above by trees, and the market—which was where most of the people were headed—had a big roof over it. A dragon could still get you in the market, but he'd have to land first, so he probably wouldn't bother. Dragons preferred to swoop down on prey from the air, not go chasing it on foot.

This must be the government place. Rule Turner and Old Woman had expected her to find the nodes in the government place because the spawn would want to have all that power close by where they could control it. They'd been right. The nodes were out in that big, open space, pulsing like twin hearts. Right in the middle of it.

Well . . . not exactly. The exact middle was marked by a tower. The tower had a red disk on top and a door in its base and was halfway between the nodes. Probably it was tied to them in some way, or why have it there? Hey, maybe that's where the gate was?

Gan squinted at the tower as if that would help, but no. She couldn't sense the gate from here. Closed gates were hard to sense unless they'd just been used. She'd have to get close to sense it. Only there was no way to do that without walking out across a lot of open space, and . . . whoops. She hopped aside just in time before a man with a long beard walked into her. Then she moved off the path so she could think without people colliding with her.

Walking across a big open space was never a good idea when there might be dragons, but it was especially not a good idea at the government place. Old Woman thought the dragon spawn sensed magic the same way she did, which was kind of like the way Gan sensed *üther*, which meant the spawn could sense Gan when she was *dashtu*. Probably they wouldn't be able to see her, but they could sense her. And the spawn were all here in the city now. She knew what they looked like, or at least she knew their descriptions. Plus they'd have more *üther* than the humans around them, being both dragon-born and longer-lived, so she should be able to spot them.

No spawn seemed to be around now, but they were probably in one of those buildings because of their plan, which was really complicated. It involved Lily Yu and gates and the Great Bitch, whose avatar Xitil had eaten, making her crazy. Making Xitil crazy, that is, not the Great Bitch, though Gan thought maybe the Great Bitch was crazy, too, and wondered if she'd once eaten someone who didn't agree with her.

Gan didn't really understand the dragon spawns' plan—or was it the Great Bitch's plan?—but she'd decided it wasn't her job to understand it. She just had to find the gate so she could tell Lily Yu where it was when Lily Yu contacted her.

Gan wished Lily Yu would go ahead and do that, even though she didn't much like it when someone talked inside her head. That was what dragons did. But maybe once Lily Yu mindspoke her, she'd stop worrying so much. And maybe Lily Yu would say she was proud of Gan. That Gan had done well.

Gan felt a little glow, thinking about that. Then she thought about her own plan.

She'd been insulted when Rule Turner wanted to make a plan for her. Did he think she needed him to tell her what to do? It was a really simple plan, too, which was insulting. But he'd said he wouldn't worry about her as much if he knew she had a plan, which had made her feel funny. Good-funny, not bad-funny. She hated worrying, but it made her feel good to think Rule Turner worried about her, even though she liked him now so you'd think she wouldn't want him to have worry-feelings. But she did. It was like a secret joke, though she wasn't sure if it was a joke on him or on her. Either way, it was funny.

The first part of the plan was for her to stay hidden in bunches of people. It was much harder, Old Woman said, to sense Gan being *dashtu* when she had people around her, especially if those people were Gifted. Their magics hid hers. Gan couldn't tell who was Gifted and who wasn't, but lots of people here had some magic, so she'd just stay in the middle of crowds as much as possible.

But no one was walking through the middle of the big, open space where the nodes were. She had to use the second part of the plan, which she didn't like because it was waiting. Waiting was boring. She'd hoped she would get another idea once she saw the government place, but so far she didn't have any ideas.

Maybe Lily Yu would contact her soon and she'd have a better idea. With another sigh, she moved into a group of people who were headed for the market.

The market wasn't a bad spot for waiting. There were people to watch, people who would hide her magic. Maybe she'd steal another snack to pass the time. She wandered around the stalls, dodging out of the way automatically before people who didn't see her walked into her.

And then someone did. A baby. It was sitting on a blanket beside a tiny stall that sold spices and herbs, and it was staring right at her.

Gan stared back, shocked. Maybe it didn't really see her? She waved at it. It made a gurgling sound and smiled and held up its hand as if it might wave back, but then forgot about that and started chewing on its fingers instead.

That made Gan want to laugh, so she made a face at it. It laughed again, or she thought that gurgling sound was a laugh. It sure looked happy. And it was too small to talk, surely, so it couldn't tell anyone it saw her. She sat down and played with the baby, making faces, doing silly things to make it laugh. That went on until it suddenly plopped forward, catching itself on its hands, and started to crawl toward Gan. And the woman who worked at the stall, who hadn't seemed to be paying any attention at all, swooped down and picked it up.

The woman was young. She clucked at the baby and said chiding things as if she was mad, but her face was happy and her voice was soft. She checked the baby's diaper and told it that it was wet.

That was the mother, Gan realized. The mother was supposed to do those things. Watch the baby so it didn't wander off. Feed it when it was hungry. Change its diaper when it peed itself. Gan felt something twist in her feelings, a strange, sad feeling.

Demons didn't have mothers. They had princes.

All life on Dis started out as bugs who either ate other bugs or got eaten. If you didn't get eaten, you eventually ate enough other lives to become a larva. That was pretty much the same as being a bug—eat or get eaten—only you were a being. Not that you could really think yet, but you knew you existed, which bugs don't, and eventually you transformed into a demon of one sort or another. Being a demon was still mostly eat or be eaten, only with sex, too, and a lot more thinking.

There was no room along the path of bug-larva-demon for mothers. No room for family at all.

She frowned at herself. Did she want a family? Why would she? Families seemed to spend a lot of time expecting things from each other and getting mad or sad when they didn't get what they expected. People got upset about their families all the time—human people, gnome people, sidhe people . . . every kind of people except demons. Because demons didn't have families.

Maybe families were a soul thing? If you had a soul, it made you want a family?

Unsettled, Gan picked a spot at the edge of the market where she could watch the area near the nodes and sat, prepared to be bored. And wished really hard for chocolate.

TWENTY-SEVEN

~

LILY sat at the battered table across from Cynna and Ah Li and thought, *Stone. Stone. Stone. Got to be stone—solid, patient. Waiting.* She did not feel like stone. Some other kind of mineral maybe. Or a combination of minerals. Dynamite, for example.

"The honorable Alice will be pleased." Ah Li's voice was rich with satisfaction. Her round face glowed with it.

Automatically, Lily translated the healer's words for Cynna, then passed on Cynna's reply.

It was the middle of the afternoon and she hadn't had one private moment to contact Rule. Sunset was still hours away, Lily told herself. They had time.

The day had started with Ah Hai waking her, then Kongqi had indeed joined them at his workshop, not at all surprised to find them there. He'd wanted to talk about sewers. Sewers, for God's sake. When she persuaded him she knew next to nothing about sewers, they'd chatted about pets. What was the difference between a pet and a slave? Sentience? Then how did she know her cat (she'd mentioned Dirty Harry) wasn't sentient? How did humans in general determine or define sentience?

She hadn't had good answers. When Kongqi finally released her, Fist Second Fang had been waiting with her usual

pair of guards. She'd tried mindspeaking Rule on the walk
back to her cell, but kept messing up. And when they arrived,
Ah Li had been there, ready for another translating session. A
long session, broken briefly by lunch. Apparently she wasn't
getting a workout period today.

But finally they'd finished. Finished as in done, *fini*, completed. The translated spell worked. Now they were waiting
for Alice to join them so she could observe their success—and
make her last two payments. She owed Cynna for her "sincere
efforts" plus the bonus for succeeding.

Ah Hai was there, too, happily scrubbing Cynna and Lily's
cell. She had no duties other than tending to Lily, and apparently no life outside of her duties. She'd been helping with the
cleaning as much as the guards allowed—out of boredom,
maybe, as much as a passion for cleanliness. Lily had suggested that she might like to do something else in her leisure
time, something just for pleasure. Ah Hai had assured her that
clean floors gave her much pleasure.

How long would Alice keep them waiting? Must be a busy
day for her, too, though Lily had never determined what Alice's duties might be. Would she even come? Dammit, she
hated all this waiting. She'd be better if she had something to
do, but there was nothing.

Lily had been part of so many failed attempts at translating
the spell by now, and she'd had to pay attention to do the translating, so she understood what kind of obstacles Cynna had had
to overcome. The biggest had been the worldview problem.
The spell language Cynna used included the four elements—
Earth, Air, Fire, Water. But Ah Li's understanding of magic
was based on five elements: Wood, Fire, Earth, Metal, Water.
The five elements were deeply embedded in Ah Li's worldview.
She couldn't believe a spell would work unless it balanced the
five elements. They were part of feng shui. Part of the martial
arts disciplines. Part of her medical understanding. People here
believed that all spells must reference the five elements. That
these elements must be balanced.

According to Cullen, the big difference between magic and
science was that science worked entirely objectively. You didn't
have to believe that pouring vinegar on baking soda would
make it bubble as it released carbon dioxide; it happened

whether or not that made sense to you. Magic combined the objective with the subjective. There were rules about magic that could be studied and learned. But to cast a spell, you had to grasp the working of the spell on a deep, intuitive level. You had to *believe* it.

Belief, Lily thought, wasn't the same as faith, was it? Faith was more like a decision you made to believe certain things, things you couldn't prove . . . which was one reason Lily had never trusted it. But belief wasn't a decision. You couldn't decide to believe that your cat was really a dog. Even if you said it over and over and insisted to everyone that you believed your cat was a dog, deep down you knew it was a cat.

How could you tell what was objectively true about magic, then? If it worked based on what you believed, based on subjective reality . . . no, wait. Spells worked that way. Gifts didn't, though, did they? Lily had been able to feel magic when she touched it when she was too little to know what magic was. And lupi didn't have to believe they could turn furry. That happened to them at puberty whether they expected it or not, which was why they kept such careful track of their children.

But her mindsense didn't act like a Gift. She'd had to learn how to use it. Was still learning how to use it. How much of what she could or couldn't do was based on what she believed was possible? Had it been hard to reach Rule when he was far away simply because she believed it would be? She had trouble using subvocalizing instead of moving her lips to organize her mindspeech, but Rule's words came through clearly when he subvocalized. Was that because, for him, subvocalization was easy to hear, so he believed he was speaking clearly when he did that?

What if some of what she believed was true about magic . . . wasn't? How much of it was subjective reality, not objectively true? She *knew* she couldn't throw fire the way Cullen did. Or fly like Sam. Or cast spells. What if—

"Lily?" Cynna sounded puzzled. Or worried. "I said your name twice."

Lily blinked. "Sorry. I was thinking."

"Deep thoughts?"

"About magic and spells and Gifts and reality. Subjective

reality versus objective. How do you know? How can you tell what is really real?"

Cynna's face eased in a grin. "Oh, you fell down the reality wormhole! Everyone does. Everyone who starts grappling with magic theory, I mean."

Lily felt a bit miffed. It had felt like she was on the edge of a big, new understanding. "Has everyone come up with an answer, then?"

"Sure. There is no such thing as objective reality. All reality is habit. Magic is anti-habit."

"Is that supposed to make sense?"

"Habit is something that persists without needing our attention. It persists whether we want it to or not, and it's really hard to change. Subjective reality is mental habits that go all the way down, deeper than we can reach or change through intention."

"I can't just call my cat a dog and believe it," Lily murmured.

"Weird example, but yeah. A step out from subjective reality is communal reality—what everyone we know believes is true. Some theorists believe that is an actual force, not just a collection of subjective realities. Might be true, but I don't see how we could find out. Cummunal reality is really sticky, but it can and does change. Then we get to external reality, which you called objective reality. That's the habits of the whole universe. Matter has really, really firm habits. The only thing that can change those habits is magic. It's anti-habit."

"Oka-a-ay. I'm following you. I think. But—oh. Company." People were on the stairs. Three of them—a mind Lily didn't recognize, Fist Second Fang, and Alice Báitóu. Alice's slick, shielded mind was impossible to mistake, and Fang's mind had grown familiar to Lily through repeated contact.

"You have succeeded with the spell, I am told," Alice said, calm as ever, as she moved away from the stairs. A few steps behind her was the unfamiliar mind, coupled with an unfamiliar face—a tiny white-haired woman wearing dusty black trousers and a pale blue tunic. Not the poorest of cloth, but not expensive, either. "I have brought a patient so you may demonstrate. Wang An Li has been examined by the Zhu Shēngwù. Let us see if you find what he did."

Ah Li spoke. "Shall I perform the spell from the beginning, or demonstrate using the ash I've already prepared?"

The original spell had been purely spoken and drew on the element of Air—which the Chinese system didn't include. In translating it, Cynna had decided the only way to integrate the five elements without disrupting the spell was to add physical components in the right balance. Ah Li wrote two key words in water on paper while she chanted; the paper was then burned in a brass bowl. Water and Fire were literally present; the brush was Wood, the paper was Earth, and the bowl was Metal. The chanting brought in Air. Ah Li didn't consider it an element, but Cynna believed it was necessary.

There was that word again. Cynna *believed* it was necessary. Was she objectively right, or was it all subjective? Anyway, the resulting ash was the output of the spell, which held both the magic and the intent. And the belief?

"It would be good to see the spell performed," Alice said.

Before Ah Li could begin the chanting and drawing, a shrill voice came from the stairs. The voice of a thoroughly aggravated old woman. ". . . treat an elder with such disrespect! Never, never did I think I would experience such disrespect. You snatch me off the street and—slow down! Do you think I can bound up these stairs on my old knees?"

A murmur from someone male.

"Keep your hands to yourself, boy! You think I don't know what you want? Maybe to throw me down these stairs?"

Another murmur.

"Ha! First you take my diamonds, then you drag me all the way across the city like a criminal. My bones ache with all the walking."

A guard moved into view, his expression wooden. Behind him, still out of sight on the stairs, another guard spoke stiffly. "We gave you a receipt for the diamonds, madame."

"What does that do for me? Eh? You will find some reason to fine me and keep my diamonds. Or maybe you think your superior will never know about them. But I will tell him, and he will take them all and leave nothing for you. Did you think of that? Do you hope that maybe I will die in my sleep before I tell him about my diamonds that you stole? And if I don't, maybe you will help that along, eh?"

With those words, Grandmother hobbled slowly into view, mounting the last few steps with precarious determination. Another guard hovered at her side, looking harassed and as if she might have been right. He might well be hoping the old harridan would die in her sleep. Soon.

Lily did not let her expression show anything more than surprise, but she had to swallow to keep down the laughter. And the relief. Grandmother had gotten herself arrested, just as she planned.

It was surely natural to stare at the newcomers, though. Cynna was. Ah Li was. Even Alice watched, eyebrows ever-so-slightly raised.

Fist Second Fang frowned at the first guard. "What is this?"

"Sir, we received information that this woman—Madame Chen Chan Ying—is the owner of a diamond mine, but has not paid the annual tax. When we asked her—most politely, sir, I assure you—she could not produce her stamp. She does not have any documents at all with her."

"Who provided this information?"

"One of the Siji, sir. Mei Bo is the owner of the *chún-chún* she traveled on, and he informed the stamp agent at the docks, who sent for us. I spoke with Mei Bo. He says that she bragged often about her mine and once let it slip that she did not pay the annual tax."

"He does not have proof of this? It is only his report of something she once said?"

"No proof, sir. But he is a carrier of the official mail."

Fang's eyebrows lifted. "A man whose word has weight, then. Who traveled with her? Surely she has a son or other relative with her."

"No, sir. She traveled alone."

Grandmother broke in, speaking in that shrill, wobbly voice so unlike her own. "And why should I not? There is no law that I must have a son. No law to say I cannot travel to Lang Xin if I choose! And no law that says I must bring all of my tax stamps with me when I travel. Who are you?" She peered at Fang in nearsighted suspicion. "I do not know you. Are you responsible for these hooligans who stole my diamonds? Seven diamonds! Do not let them tell you some other number. Seven!"

she finished triumphantly, as if the number alone proved their guilt.

"I am Fist Second Fang." Fang gave her a short bow and turned to his man. "We will have to send to the magistrate of her district for tax information. Madame Chen, where do you live?"

Grandmother launched into a story about her village, a tiny village they would not have heard of, no, for it was very small. She told them about her husband and how he died, describing his deathbed in ghoulish detail, and about the day she first arrived in this realm, a confused *lái* who was taken in by her husband's family—though he was not her husband then, of course, but they were married a year later. His family members were either saints of kindness or merciless slave-drivers—she switched points of view mercilessly—but they were not good at producing male children, for she had no male relative to escort her to the capital. Just as mercilessly she diverted Fang's increasingly impatient questions about where, exactly, she lived. She ended by accusing "them"—an amorphous group who seemed to consist of everyone in authority—of ignoring the claims of a feeble old woman with no son to protect her, and returned to her unshakable belief that the guards had stolen her diamonds.

She was enjoying herself hugely.

At last Fang extracted from Grandmother the location of her unknown and probably fictitious village, which told him who her magistrate should be. He would contact the magistrate about her taxes, he told her, and with visible relief had her taken to a cell. She went, muttering under her breath about hooligans and "seven diamonds. Seven."

Alice turned to Ah Li. "Perhaps you should simply demonstrate the results now. I can observe the full spell later. I am a bit pressed for time."

Lily badly wanted to mindspeak Grandmother. She wished someone would send her to her cell where she belonged—where she'd be alone—but had to stand there and wait while Ah Li demonstrated the spell.

"We do not know yet how long the ash will hold the magic and intention," Ah Li said, taking a small pinch of it between her thumb and finger. "But this is quite fresh, so it should work. I activate it by placing it on my tongue, where I can easily integrate it with my Gift." She did so, then moved to stand in front of the tiny white-haired woman whose name Lily had forgotten. She stared at the woman's body, then: "Ah! I see it. A tumor in her right breast, very small, not much bigger than a grain of rice. A tumor so small I may be able to destroy it." Her voice was triumphant.

Alice nodded. "Very good. That is what the Zhu Shēngwù found, also. It appears the spell works."

Ah Li beamed. "It is a most wonderful spell! I could never have found such a tiny tumor without it."

"Which means I owe you two payments," Alice said, looking at Cynna. "First I will finish making my second payment. The current variation in time between your realm and ours is approximately fifty-two seconds. The daily variability over the last thirty-one years has ranged from eleven hours and twelve minutes to thirty-two seconds."

Cynna was silent, intent, then said slowly, "In other words, the time difference between this realm and mine has never been less than it is right now."

"Not in the last sixty-seven years. We have not negotiated your bonus payment."

"No. I rely on you to agree to a fair payment." Cynna glanced at Lily, then looked back at Alice and asked the question the two of them had agonized over. Well, questions. They had a list in descending priority, starting with a couple they didn't expect Alice to answer. "What is the magical construct in Dis that touches on this realm designed to do?"

"I will not answer that at this time."

"When, precisely, will the children arrive, and what happens when they get here?"

"I will not answer that at this time."

"What is your Gift?"

"I will not tell you that."

"What will the time variance be between this realm and ours at one hour after moonrise today?"

Alice smiled a very small, tight smile. "It should be zero."

Zero. The two realms, which had varied in time by as much as eleven hours out of twenty-four, were supposed to be exactly aligned in time at the hour when all hell was expected to break loose.

"And now," Alice said, pushing her chair back and standing, "I have other duties." She held out her hand. "You have done good work, Cynna Weaver."

Frowning, puzzled, Cynna accepted her hand. They shook.

Alice held her hand out to Lily. "You have given good value for the payment I made you."

Startled, Lily hesitated before taking Alice's hand. Alice wouldn't tell her what her Gift was, but she'd let Lily touch her? Then she shook Alice's hand . . . and was really startled.

Alice's magic was strong. That was no surprise. Really strong, and it vibrated against Lily's palm in moving bands. A band of prickly heat—Fire—next to gritty Earth, next to the cool depths of Water, next to the windy motion of Air, next to something she couldn't identify, though the texture was tantalizingly familiar. Never had she felt the four elements so vividly. Never had she felt all of them in one person. And they were *moving.*

The four elements plus . . . what? She should know what that was. She should—

Alice removed her hand. "I do not know if I will see you again," she said in Chinese.

From the stairs came a voice Lily hadn't heard since she first arrived. That of Li Po, First Fist. "It is doubtful. She will go to the bathhouse now, to be prepared."

"Prepared for what?" Lily spoke in English, looking at Alice.

Alice responded in Chinese. "To be given to the Great One. You had guessed that much, I believe."

Quickly, urgently, Lily reached out with her mindsense and didn't worry about whether or not her lips moved. *Grandmother.*

It is good to hear from you, her grandmother replied. *You are upset.*

They're taking me to the bathhouse, then they're going to present me to the Great Bitch. I won't be here to get that magic cage off Cynna. Can you do that?

I had best not try. I am likely to kill her.

But—but surely you draw magic into you—

Certainly, but drawing magic from a living being is very different from drawing from a node or ley line. You will need to do it. Your process must be different from mine. Perhaps you use a different metaphor.

Metaphor? What did a damn metaphor have to do with it? *But if you can't get the cage off Cynna—*

"What are you doing?" Li Po demanded in Chinese.

Alice translated unnecessarily. "He wishes to know what you are doing, Lily Yu."

"She's praying," Cynna said. "You just told her she's about to be killed. Of course she's praying."

Li Po said curtly, "She can pray in her bath. Where is her woman? The *yāoqiú* who serves her? We must go."

What do I do? Lily sent, frantic.

We can begin the battle here and now. Or you can go with the unpleasant man and have your bath, escape, and return here to remove the magic cage from Cynna. Or you can go with the unpleasant man, have your bath, and let him take you where he wishes. He may take you to the gate. That would be convenient. We could join you there and you could remove the cage device.

If he doesn't take me to the gate—

Find out.

Right. She was panicking. That never worked. Lily took a deep breath just as hard hands gripped her arms. She'd been paying so much attention to her "prayers" that she hadn't noticed the guards who now surrounded her. Not the usual pair of guards, either. Six of them. "Where do you take me, First Fist?"

"To the bathhouse."

She managed not to roll her eyes. "And after that?"

"To the Zhu Kongqi."

"At the Justice Court? Or at the Home of the Seven?"

He scowled. "What does it matter?"

She made herself drop her eyes modestly. "I would like to know if I should bid my friend good-bye."

"Bid her good-bye? You have no time for that." Then he added that single, hateful English word: "Come!"

TWENTY-EIGHT

~

LILY stepped out of the *Zhèngyì Fǎtíng*—the Justice Court—for what was surely the last time. The usual crowds had dispersed, and the Heart of the Heart looked strange and empty with only a few stragglers hurrying along the paths. It wasn't that late, she told herself. The sun was headed down, but sunset was still a couple hours away.

She thought. She hoped. She wasn't good at telling time by the sun.

She had picked Option Three. A version of it, anyway. She couldn't let them take her to the Home of the Seven. It was one thing to try to escape from half a dozen guards, something else altogether to try to get away from Kongqi and his brothers. The spawn couldn't use TK on her directly—at least she didn't think they could. But they didn't have to. They could telekinetically clobber her with any and all nearby objects.

She had nothing with her, no weapon of any kind. Her Glock, which she'd wanted so badly, was still in her cell along with the ammo. Cynna could use it, she supposed. Her hands weren't tied, but Li Po had brought a full squad to escort her. Two guards marched alongside her, each of them holding one of her arms. The other three had their swords drawn . . . which was pretty stupid. Fist Second Fang wouldn't have made either mistake—leaving her hands unbound or assuming that drawn swords were a good way to control her. And they needed to control her, not kill her. The Great Bitch wanted her alive. What if she preferred dying to having her brain wiped? She didn't intend to commit suicide by guard, but Li Po didn't know that.

Ah Hai trailed behind them. Li Po strutted in front. She suspected he wanted the kudos for turning her over. He was the sort of officer who pushed the work off on others, then claimed the credit. But his hunger for glory might work to her advantage. Li Po had never watched her spar with the guards, had he? He never seemed to show up at the jail.

She would wait until she entered the bathhouse to contact Rule. That was as much privacy as she was going to get. Ah Hai would be there, but Ah Hai was an ally. Lily had listened to both her words and her mind when she told her story, and they'd matched. A dragon might be able to lie with his mind—she wasn't sure, but it was possible. Ah Hai was no dragon. She'd told the truth.

The truth as she knew it, anyway. It was possible that . . . oh, hey! That was Gan, running full-tilt down the pathway toward her, dodging pedestrians. Lily's step hitched. She turned it into a stumble to slow her escort briefly, give Gan time to arrive. And sent her mindsense out.

Gan! Are you okay? Did you find the gate? And then because she couldn't help it: *It's so good to see you! I wish I could hug you. I never got a chance to thank you for saving my life.*

Gan skidded to a stop next to Li Po and started walking backward, a huge grin on her face. She wore her many-pocketed khaki once more, but the hat was new. And bright. Really bright, with all the red embroidery on that shocking shade of green. Li Po kept walking, utterly unaware of the presence beside him.

Gan kept grinning fit to split her face. *I did good?*

Of all of them, Gan was the only one who didn't have to move her lips or subvocalize to send crisp, clear mindspeech. Lily wondered what that meant. *You did really, really good.*

Gan beamed. *I wish you'd been with us, but I like Rule now even though he was grouchy when he was a wolf. And Old Woman was there, so that was good.*

Old Woman? Lily sent, amused in spite of everything. *Do you call Grandmother that?*

In my mind I do because I don't have the right call-name for her. It's confusing, so it's probably a soul thing. I haven't found the gate yet, but it's bound to be with the nodes, only I can't get to the nodes. There's too much open space and people haven't gone out there so I could hide among them and the spawn wouldn't spot me. Are these the people who captured you? I've got a knife. I could stab some of them and you could get away.

It's not time for me to escape yet, Lily sent. As close as she was to Gan, she hardly had to move her lips at all. The guards either hadn't noticed or they assumed she was praying, like Cynna had claimed. *About the gate—no, crossing spot first. Did you find any crossing spots?*

I can't get to the nodes, Gan repeated. *And everybody's leaving now. Guards told them to. I can hide in the market because of the stalls there, but the spawn could see me if I go across the open space. I can't get to the nodes to look for the gate or for crossing spots.*

Gan wasn't really agoraphobic in the same way that you weren't really paranoid if people actually were out to get you. Open spaces scared her, yeah, but for most of her life being out in the open meant getting eaten. *I'm glad you waited for me. I can help you and you can help me. Now, about the gate . . .*

THEY'D watched the juggler. They'd eaten little balls of fried *niangao*, a sticky sweet Gan favored, and wandered a little farther from the stamp office to watch a shadow puppet show. Mei Ling had done a good job of keeping him away from the Stamp Office so he wouldn't see his supposed employer being arrested. And he'd done a decent job of flirting just enough to let her think she was succeeding so she wouldn't see the guilt crawling around in his gut.

He was beginning to understand why Grandmother had refused to ensorcel the boat father back in Liangzhou. Mei Ling and her father believed they'd turned Grandmother in because she was a tax cheat. They had no idea she'd told them to do so, or that she'd subtly edited their memories of her . . .

and of Rule. At the moment, those fake memories of him were dormant.

Ensorcellment had two drawbacks. The first was practical: it faded over time. How much time depended on the strength and skill of the practitioner, the type of ensorcellment used, and on the mind being ensorcelled. Some minds, Grandmother said, soaked up fantasies but rejected orders fairly quickly. Others had no problem accepting orders, but memory adjustments didn't stick. Grandmother expected her ensorcellment of Mei Ling and her family to last about twenty-four hours, but for some of them it would linger longer.

The second drawback was moral. Which meant it was complicated.

Grandmother wanted to do the least harm possible. That's why Mei Ling's family needed to believe Rule was infatuated with her—that he would end up giving her the child they wanted, and perhaps stay with them on their boat. This made it easy for their minds to accept some of the things they'd been ensorcelled into doing.

But there would be harm. Harm to a young girl. Harm to her family.

"Wu Tǔ Ní?" Mei Ling's sweet, high voice broke into his thoughts. "Why do the puppets make you sad instead of making you laugh?"

He'd let his face show too much. He smiled and used one of his few words—"*chá*"—and mimed sipping from a teacup, then raised his brows in question. Did she want a cup of tea?

She smiled back, beckoned for him to follow, and chattered away happily. The tea house was close and very respectable, she said. Her father wouldn't mind, surely, if they had a cup of tea. The assurance was for herself, since she'd assume he understood little or none of what she said.

He'd taken four steps away from the puppet show when he stopped dead.

Rule! Are you able to talk right now?

Not easily, he answered.

Then listen. Grandmother got here, but they've separated me and Cynna. They want me all cleaned up and pretty to present to the Great Bitch. I'm at the bathhouse. I can't let

*them take me into the Home of the Seven—that's where the
spawn live—so I'll need to make my break when Li Po decides
bath time is over. Have you started the distraction moving?*

Not yet. Anxiety tightened his muscles. *Li Po is the guard
commander, right? Can you get away from him? How many
guards are with you?*

Too many, but Gan's with me. She'll help.

"Wu Tǔ Ní? What is wrong?"

Rule looked down into Mei Ling's worried face. Silently he
said, *Distraction coming up.* Out loud—and in English—he
said, "Mei Ling. Wake up."

THE interior of the bathhouse was stinking hot from the hot
spring, but not as dim as usual. Ah Hai had casually released
half a dozen mage lights, saying they would be needed when
she applied the cosmetics.

Li Po had left after informing Ah Hai to have Lily ready in
three hands—a manner of telling time Lily had not mastered,
but it might mean a couple hours. Or not. The five guards remained just outside the door.

"I cannot even see your friend," Ah Hai whispered. "How
can I agree to this if I cannot see her, speak with her?"

And read her, Lily thought. That's what Ah Hai really
wanted—to use her empathic Gift to learn what Gan was like.
It was a reasonable request. "All right. She may look odd to
you, though."

A hint of a smile. "I look odd to many people. Many of the
Kanas do."

"Okay. Gan, drop the *dashtu*."

"It's not something I pick up or drop," Gan complained in
English—and apparently became visible, because Ah Hai
gasped. Lily couldn't tell when Gan was *dashtu*. The little one
looked the same to her either way. "It's more like crossing,
only without really going anywhere."

"You do look different," Ah Hai said uncertainly in her
language. "Rather like . . . you will forgive me, I hope, but you
look like the being the Zhuren wanted everyone to watch for.
One of demon heritage."

"That's me," Gan agreed cheerfully in English. "I'm not a demon anymore, but I used to be before I started growing a soul."

Lily translated for Gan. Ah Hai turned astonished eyes her way. "Growing a soul?"

They had a three-way conversation, with Lily translating what Gan said for Ah Hai. Gan explained that "you can't have a friend if you don't have a soul, so when I became Lily Yu's friend, I started growing one. It's probably bigger now because I've got lots of friends." She went on to tell about her friends in Edge—there were two, it seemed, a gnome and a human, plus five others she considered half-friends who might become real friends someday, ending with, "And there's Cullen Seabourne. He's in Dis and he might be dead, but he might not be. I don't like thinking about that. And in this realm there's Lily Yu and Cynna Weaver and Rule Turner, who used to be a half-friend but he's a real friend now. And that's why I came, because my friends really needed my help. I don't ever want Lily Yu to die again."

"Again?" Ah Hai repeated faintly, eyes wide.

"It's a long story," Lily said.

"But it is true? All this is true?" she whispered. "This Gan was a demon, and she grew a soul?"

"Yes."

"Ahhh . . ." Her eyes grew moist. "It gives me such hope. Not that I had lost hope, not ever. We were told it would be the work of generations, but . . . but if a demon can grow a soul—" She stopped, blinking rapidly.

Belatedly, Lily understood.

At its heart, the story of the Kanas was pretty simple. They had been charged by "the Great Dragon, who is not like other dragons" to raise the spawn. And they had never stopped.

The Great Dragon was Reno, of course. Rule had told her that Reno had fallen through from Dis to Dragonhome while looking for a way to enter that realm more voluntarily—and that had triggered him changing to female. Apparently Reno had been delaying that change for a very long time. Lily had thought dragons might need the help of their fellows to turn female. Turns out she'd had it backward. They needed help delaying that change.

Those Kanas who'd survived the burning of their village—which Ah Hai would not discuss—had decided they could serve best if their identities were unknown to any but the Zhuren themselves. And so were born the *yāoqiú*. The claimed.

"We did not want people coming to us, seeking favor with the Zhuren, as they would have done if it was known we were Kanas. We did not want an exalted place, but only to serve," Ah Hai had explained. What did that service mean? "Obedience, of course. The Zhuren are as the heads of our family. Sometimes we give advice. If they do not take our advice . . . ah, well. Adult children do not always listen to their elders, do they? But sometimes—rarely, but sometimes—we must act, for we see what they cannot. Their hearts have not yet grown enough."

That remained the real job of the Kanas: to help their damaged charges learn empathy. Lily spoke gently, putting it the way Ah Hai had. "If a demon can grow a soul, then the sons of the Great Dragon might grow hearts."

IN a valley tucked into the low hills around Lang Xin, the grass grew tall and lush. Despite its proximity to the city, it had never been cultivated. Nor would it be. It lay along the migration route of the *shānjiǎo*. For thousands and thousands of years, herds of the enormous beasts had followed the same route, eating their way north to the forested slopes of the Shaanxi mountains, then, as the weather cooled, slowly circling around to head back south along another route. This allowed the grass on their original path to recover.

At this time of year, the *shānjiǎo* were still a couple hundred miles south of Lang Xin. At least most of them were. About forty of the beasts had headed north ahead of their fellows and were cropping grass contentedly with a single hill separating them from the sprawling capital. Shaped like a rhino but with the bony plates and weaponized tail of a stegosaurus, they were bigger than an African elephant. Yet the huge beasts were not considered a threat.

No doubt this was partly because their meat tasted rank to humans, so the people of Dragonhome had never hunted them.

Mainly, however, it was because the placid eating machines
were so ruled by instinct that none of them had ever been seen
to cross over the hill separating them from the city. This was
fortunate, for they were highly resistant to magic and wouldn't
be stopped by the wards. That resistance may have developed
for the same reason as the upthrust plates along their spines.
Dragons considered them tasty.

Shānjiǎo were dangerous during mating season, but that
hit in late fall, long after they'd left Lang Xin behind. Or when
frightened, but they were absurdly fearless most of the time.
The pack-hunters that followed the herds, preying on the
young or the infirm, annoyed more than alarmed them. So did
the giant cats of the northern forests. Humans, they barely
noticed.

Shānjiǎo feared two things. Fire and dragons.

First one, then another of the armored beasts lifted their
heads from the delicious grass. Their snouts twitched, scent-
ing the air, for their weak eyes weren't much help.

Suddenly one of them lifted its head and let out a deep,
rhythmic groan like the call of a giant bullfrog. Others answered. All at once they lumbered into a trot, heading straight
for the hill.

SIX men and three women sat on the deck of a *chún-chún*
docked at the city's longest pier: Mei Bo, the boat father. Two
of his cousins and one of his nephews. His two sons. His sister
and her daughter. And the boat father's lovely daughter.

Rule watched the Siji sitting motionless, their eyes closed
to help them connect with beasts far beyond their physical
reach. He stood very still himself, still and straight. Hating
what he was doing to these people.

The river was on the opposite side of town from the valley
of the *shānjiǎo*, the enormous beasts that Mei Bo and his family had coaxed into starting their northern trek early this year.
Every night, under Grandmother's gaze, they'd sent out their
suggestions to the herd. Every night, they had forgotten they
had done so.

Mei Bo opened his eyes. "They come, Zhu."

Rule inclined his head once, wondering what the man saw

when he looked at Rule. One of the Zhuren, yes, but which one? Did he know what any the Zhuren looked like? Or did he only see a tall man whom he *knew* to be a Zhu?

Grandmother had crafted an elaborate ensorcellment, one that was active only after the Siji been told to "wake up." She'd told them what they were to do "when the Zhu commands." They were good people, she'd said. If she made them do a bad thing, it would damage their minds. But they all but worshipped the Zhuren. As long as they believed they were following the orders of one of the Zhuren when they called the *shānjiǎo* into the city, their minds would be not be harmed.

Other types of harm were all too possible.

Rule spoke slowly, using a short memorized speech in their language. "Good. Continue to call until you are too weary, or until one in authority tells you to stop."

He turned away, set one hand on the side of the boat, and leaped lightly onto the dock, sick with guilt. Quivering with anticipation. At last, at last, *at last* he could go to Lily.

And even that was not enough to keep him from thinking about those he left behind on the *chún-chún*. Wondering how many of them would live long enough to find out what had been done to them. And if he would ever know.

LILY had been scrubbed and rinsed. They were skipping the usual soak in the hot pool in order to have time for major primping. She must be properly prepared for her presentation—sweet-smelling oils, a fancy hairstyle, and the most formal of court wear. A quiet, barefoot woman who looked much like Ah Hai, only with pigment, delivered the garments just as Ah Hai started washing Lily's hair. When the woman left, she carried a message from Ah Hai to . . . someone. Ah Hai would not say who. "You understand, it is not for me to say 'do this' or 'do that,'" she'd told Lily earnestly. "I will ask, but another will make the decision."

Ah Hai had almost finished towel-drying Lily's hair when an old man walked up to the bathhouse guided by a young boy. He carried a walking stick and had a clean white cloth tied over his eyes. The guards told him to leave. He bowed deeply and answered that he regretted he could not obey their order, for his duties required him to be there.

He was barefoot. So was the boy.

By the time Ah Hai had Lily oiled and buffed, twelve people had assembled outside the bathhouse. All of them apologized abjectly for not dispersing as the guards told them to. All of them were barefoot.

Some of the guards were confused, some of them angry. All were at a loss what to do. The claimed were always respectful, always obedient . . . until now. Anyone else they might have struck or arrested or both, but these were *yāoqiú*. They were owned by the Zhuren. One did not strike the property of the Zhuren. One did not arrest property. Yet they would not go.

The maid who'd brought Lily's fancy clothes returned, bringing a fancy hair ornament she said had mistakenly been omitted from the first delivery. When she emerged from the bathhouse, she went to the old man and whispered something to him.

Much to the guards' relief, the *yāoqiú* began moving away. Only the blind old man saw the small, orange-skinned female hidden in their midst.

The old man led the others to the tower in the center of Heart's Home, where they settled on the ground in a large circle. Barefoot people continued to arrive in ones and twos. Some wore veils. Some wore loose clothing that muffled whatever eccentricities their bodies possessed, but other deformities couldn't be hidden. Two were dwarfs. One was severely hunchbacked. A few had no obvious mutations.

A tall peasant man sat on the dusty ground in front of We Pan Li's shop. He seemed to be dozing in the late afternoon heat, with his head lowered onto the arms he'd crossed on his up-drawn knees. With his head down, his straw hat completely hid his face. Suddenly he lifted his head and smiled. A moment later he pulled a small pot from a pocket in his pants and began smearing goo all over his face. When he was satisfied with that, he removed his shoes.

* * *

FIRST Fist Li Po was in his office in the Justice Court—a small, underground room safe from fire and visiting dragons, as were all the important rooms in the Court. In the winter it could easily be heated with a single brazier. In the summer, it sweltered.

Li Po did not like his office. He much preferred to remain at his home in the city—a large and spacious stone house with a beautiful central courtyard and one of the best libraries in the city. Li Po considered himself a scholar. If he had not read all of the books and scrolls he had collected, he was sure he would someday. In the meantime, guests were much impressed by his library.

He would much rather have been in his library now. He could read and sign papers there as easily as he could in his office, could he not? Why sweat in this hot, cramped space if he did not have to? There were underlings to carry those papers back and forth, and other subordinates to carry out the day-to-day administration of the Court. True, he did not like Fist Second Fang, but the man was competent. Irritating, but competent.

Sacrifices must be made at times, however. He needed to conduct the handover of one special prisoner himself. Not that he understood why the woman was special. Prideful, mannish—why, she fought hand-to-hand with the guards! With *his* guards. Li Po did not approve of pride in women. He did not approve of allowing them to fight with men, and he deeply resented Báitóu Alice Li for insisting that the prisoner be allowed to do so.

He disliked Alice much more than he disliked Fist Second Fang. He fantasized about someday bringing her low, but he was a realist. That would not happen. Her grandfather valued her greatly. More, he suspected, than his own grandfather valued him. The Zhu Dìqiú never sought him out. When they did encounter each other, the Zhu was civil, but no more. But he had arranged Li Po's appointment as First Fist, so perhaps he was wrong about his grandfather's lack of interest. The Zhuren were not demonstrative, after all. They valued reason above emotion.

The Zhuren also valued the prisoner who was the cause of his decision to remain in his hot office today. Li Po did not know why. In truth, he did not understand the Zhuren, but it would never have crossed his mind to disobey them.

Being underground didn't keep Li Po didn't from feeling the shudder when the wards went down.

The *shānjiǎo* had entered the city.

TWENTY-NINE

~~

AH Hai had reluctantly agreed to arrange Lily's hair in a braided style suitable for a warrior instead of the poufy bun-thing she wanted to do. In return Lily had allowed her to paint her face.

It was probably just as well she didn't have a mirror. Ah Hai had a heavy hand with cosmetics. Though she would have liked to see the flower Ah Hai had painted on her forehead—a chrysanthemum, which she insisted was appropriate for a warrior. That didn't fit what Lily had been told about mums, but then, this wasn't really China.

The outfit the spawn wanted Lily to wear was similar to the most formal court wear from the Han Dynasty. For the first time, she was given underwear—knickers and something like a tank top, both made of silk.

Everything was silk. Over her new undies went an ankle-length skirt and a long-sleeved top, both in white silk. Over that went a sort of long apron—a panel in a brilliant crimson brocade that hung down in front. And on top of everything else went a black *shenyi* with absurdly long sleeves piped in white, followed by a white sash to hold it in place. It took Ah Hai several minutes to adjust the folds of the *shenyi* just so. Lots of beautiful, hot, sweaty layers.

Almost hidden by all the finery were Lily's combat boots.

"You would look much better with the shoes," Ah Hai pleaded, holding out a pair of embroidered black slippers with thick wooden soles.

"Forget it." Lily was not leaving her boots behind. Bad enough to be forced to wear an outfit she couldn't run or fight in—though some of the layers would come off pretty quickly, the skirt was going to be a problem. She saw Ah Hai's crushed expression. "I don't want to shame your work, Ah Hai, but I need to be able to move."

She wanted to move *now*, dammit, but Li Po wasn't back yet. She'd just checked again with her mindsense. Six guards were on the other side of the door. No one else.

"You think me very silly," Ah Hai whispered sadly.

"I think you're pretty amazing. Courageous."

Ah Hai blinked. "You mock me. I am no warrior."

"You're willing to risk everything you have, everything you are, to do what's right. What is that if not courage?"

Lily was rewarded by a hesitant smile . . . and magic rushed by in a soundless whoosh that made her hair try to stand on end. The very air seemed to shimmer.

"Oh!" Ah Hai's eyes were huge. "What was that?"

"You felt it?"

She nodded. "As if the worm at the heart of the world rolled over, but the air shook, not the ground."

The wards. The wards must have come down. Lily took a quick step toward the door. Stopped. Dammit, she needed that stupid Li Po to show up. What if he turned out to be more aware of his duty than she'd thought? If he went to lead the city's guards instead of hanging around here to get the credit for handing her over . . . she needed a Plan B.

"What now?" Ah Hai whispered.

"Now," Lily said grimly, "we wait."

FIST Second Fang cursed quietly. "Is this all he sent? This note telling me to take 'all available men' and lead them against the *shānjiǎo*?"

The Fist in front of him was too disciplined to roll his eyes. He belonged to the city's guards and had carried a report from his Fist Second to the First Fist, who had written and signed a note and told him to take it to the other Fist Second, Fang Ye Lì. Then Li Po had hurried away. "Yes, sir."

He clenched his jaw. He had orders from one who out-ranked Li Po . . . but they did not include disobeying a direct order from the First Fist. Li Po was a good officer in many ways. He kept himself fit, drank abstemiously, and took his duties seriously. Unfortunately, he believed that his duties be-gan and ended with appending a beautifully drawn signature to official documents. He did at least read those documents first. Also, unlike some in positions of authority, Li Po pre-ferred competent underlings and went to some trouble to find them. But he had no interest whatsoever in actually running the Fists.

And in times of crisis, Li Po always made sure he had a scapegoat handy.

Fang knew very well what that damnably vague "all avail-able men" meant. Whatever he did, Li Po could say he had done the wrong thing, taking too many men or too few. The same reasoning applied to sending Fang to personally lead the men without establishing a clear chain of command between himself and Second Fist Chen. Li Po wanted someone to blame if things went badly.

He and the messenger were in the barracks beneath the Justice Court—a large room every bit as stuffy as his superi-or's office. All around him men were finishing their prepara-tions for the display they were to put on soon—tying dress sashes, adjusting the hang of sheathed swords. Several shot glances his way. They knew about the *shānjiǎo* invading the city, forcing the wards to fail. He'd already sent two squads to assist—the men who'd been chivvying everyone out of the *Xīnzàng de Jiā* early. Heart's Home was closed to the public now, in preparation for the arrival of an important guest.

Quickly he went over the roster in his mind, the leave rota-tion, the number of men sick or injured. With those out plus the two squads already detached and the squad Alice had taken with her, he was down a half-fifty already. He could not leave the jail completely unmanned, so there went another squad. And he was supposed to have a full fifty on display when the Zhuren's important guest arrived. Whenever that might be. No one seemed sure, but the men were to be arranged in ranks, waiting, beginning at four hands before sunset.

Li Po would have to lead the men in that bit of pointless display, it seemed. The question was, how many men did Fang leave his superior? He could play it safe and take only the remaining twenty men from his second fifty, leaving the first fifty for his commanding officer. But did he wish to play it safe?

"*Shānjiǎo* are hard to kill," he said slowly. "Arrows bounce off their plating." And if you tried to get close enough to use a sword, you risked being trampled or smashed with their heavy tails.

"Yes, sir," the Fist said emphatically. "Fire will turn them, so Fist Second Chen has some of the men using torches, trying to steer them back out of the city, but they only turn aside for a bit then come right back."

"How many have torches?"

"Sir, I think two squads. The Fist Second is worried about fire from a dropped torch. Which could happen. When one of those beasts charges you—" He stopped. Gulped.

"You have been charged, Fist?"

"Yes, sir."

It had been hot and dry for the last four hands of days, as it usually was at the height of summer. And only the wealthy built with stone. The *shānjiǎo* were undoubtedly doing a great deal of damage, but a fire would be worse. "How many squads does Fist Second Chen need?"

"He asked for a full fifty, sir."

Fang raised his brows. "He has four fifties of his own."

"Yes, sir. But in addition to his worry about the fire, Fist Second Chen is very concerned that . . . sir, the Zhuren have not appeared to reinstate the wards."

Where were the Zhuren? That was a question everyone in the city must be asking. When the wards failed briefly after the earthquake five years ago, the three Zhuren who were in the city had appeared immediately, working both to reinstate the wards and to quench fires started in the quake. None had appeared in the skies in this crisis. Not even *his* Zhu, the Zhu Kongqi.

But he knew some of what Zhu Kongqi had taken on. He should not criticize, even in his mind. "They will do so, I'm sure."

"Yes, sir." The Fist sounded as uncertain as he felt. "What I meant was that, with the wards down, the predators who follow the herds might enter the city."

Fang smiled a tight, hard smile. So be it. "I will bring the rest of my second fifty and four squads from my first fifty." Let Li Po make his show with the remaining thirty. He would do what he might to keep the city from burning.

He turned and called out, "Our orders have changed." And quickly listed the squads who would come with him.

AH Hai had grown distressed when Lily wanted to sit. She would wrinkle the silk. So for an endless period, Lily mostly stood still and sent out her mindsense. She checked in with Gan first.

Gan had a lot to tell her. First, she'd found the gate. It was set into the tower exactly halfway between the nodes. She'd found a lot of crossing spots, too, and tried to tell Lily about each one, but the short version was that the only crossing spot to Earth opened into solid rock. But Gan had found what she called a perfect spot to cross into Edge: "It opens up real close to the City! So I can take the children there and order people to take care of them and take them back to Earth through the gate!"

And that, Lily thought, was probably better than sending the kids to some random location on Earth, like Siberia or the middle of the Mojave. Gan really could order people in Edge to take care of the children; she really could command the use of the gate between Edge and Earth. There were two problems with it, though. Gan would have to make multiple trips to take all the children to safety, and Edge's time was not in sync with Dragonhome's. She couldn't be sure of "getting the time right. It's pretty tricky." Also, Gan wasn't sure the crossing spot was close enough to the nodes for Grandmother to include it in the ward.

That was a question only Grandmother could answer, so

Lily contacted her next. She was just across the compound so was well within Lily's limits, and her mind was easy to find. It didn't compel hers the way a dragon's did, but it did sort of beckon. Grandmother said she would have to see the area around the gate and the nodes before she would know how large her ward would be. Next Lily reached for Rule, and then Cynna, telling them about the gate and crossing spot.

Every one of them asked the same question: any sign of Reno?

No, she had to say each time. No big green dragons had shown up.

She kept checking outside, too, counting the minds just outside the bathhouse. Six guards. No Li Po, dammit. She checked in with Gan again. The little one was eager to chat, so maybe she found waiting hard, too. Lily let her run on a bit before cutting her off. This time, when she checked on the guards, another mind had joined theirs. A hard, almost shiny mind. One she recognized.

She hurried to the door and listened. Li Po was angry and loud about it. She heard him clearly berating his men for letting the *yāoqiú* to assemble by the tower. Why hadn't they all been sent back to their duties?

A stammering voice assured Li Po they had tried. The *yāoqiú* would not go. They claimed their duty required them to be there.

Li Po was sure they had not been firm enough. He sent one of them to tell the *yāoqiú* to leave.

Lily stepped back from the door a second before a fist, hard and imperative, pounded on it. "Come!" Li Po demanded.

For once, that word made Lily smile. She took a deep, calming breath, sent out a quick word to Grandmother—*ten minutes!*—and opened the door.

The sunlight was blinding after the dim interior of the bathhouse. There was a bit of a breeze when Lily stepped out of the bathhouse, welcome on the few bits of skin not covered by all the silk, but the sunlight was blinding. Lily blinked, took note of the position of the sun—low—and the positions of the guards.

Only four guards, all standing in a loose bunch behind Li Po. The fifth was trotting toward the circle of the claimed.

She ducked her head. "First Fist," she whispered very softly, channeling Ah Hai's docile manner. "I would ask a favor."

"What? What? I cannot hear you."

"A favor, honored Fist," she whispered, not one bit louder, her head still lowered.

He stepped closer. "Speak up, woman."

She bobbed in a not-quite bow and managed to make herself audible. Barely. "Do we go to the House of the Seven?"

"Yes. And quickly."

"Thank you," she said, bobbing again, bending her knees more deeply this time—and she uncoiled, springing at him.

It was ludicrously easy. She'd separated him just enough from the guards behind him, and he expected nothing from her but trembling submission. Instead she spun him around, seized one arm and bent it high behind his back, and held Gan's knife to his throat. "Tell them to stay back!"

"I will not—"

She pressed the sharp blade into his flesh. Not deeply, but enough to hurt. To make him bleed. Blood focused the attention wonderfully, and for all his warrior's bearing, Li Po was unused to combat.

He yelped. Then he barked, "Stand back! She has gone crazy! Where did you get that—"

"Hush," Lily told him, raising his arm a bit higher. Not high enough to dislocate the shoulder, but it had to hurt. "Tell them to lie down flat on the ground. On their stomachs."

Reluctantly he did.

"Where is Second Fist Fang?"

"He will arrive any minute with a full fifty. They will fill you full of arrows."

She moved the knife a bit higher, right under his chin, and pressed with great care. She did not want to accidentally slit his throat. "That was a lie." She knew because his mind-voice had turned to babble, which is what happened when someone tried to lie in mindspeech. "Where is Fang?"

"I do not know."

"That was half true. Not good enough." She pressed lightly with the knife.

Li Po swallowed. "It is true. I ordered him to take—to take some men into the city to help with the emergency there. The *shānjiǎo* have gone crazy. I do not know precisely where he is."

"Excellent. We're going to join the *yāoqiú* now."

IN a cell at the Justice Court, an old woman sang.

The guards dicing on the other side of the cell door were complaining about being stuck there while the others drew the exciting duty of fighting the *shānjiǎo*, which none of them had ever seen. Not that this kept them from passing on tales of the huge herd beasts. If a couple of them were privately blessing their luck at missing this treat, they knew better than to say so.

Chu Wen Shan, who had been a Fist for only nine months, was the first to yawn.

"We are boring you, Wen?" one of the others asked.

"I don't . . ." He frowned vaguely, lay his head down on his folded arms, and fell asleep.

Thirty seconds later, all five were asleep. So were the prisoners in their cells. All but one.

The bar that should have fastened that cell door was missing. No one had noticed this; no one had been able to notice that cell door at all. Li Lei Yu opened the unnoticeable door and walked out. She crossed the room briskly, ignoring the slumbering guards, and removed the bar from another cell door. She went inside and woke up Cynna Weaver.

This was not easy. First she shook Cynna, but got no response. So she emptied the water pail over her. It was half-full.

Cynna shot bolt upright. "Wha . . . what?"

"It's time to leave," Li Lei said briskly. "You are very groggy. I will help you stand."

"Jussa momen'," Cynna mumbled and felt under the blanket. She pulled out Lily's Glock and the two clips of ammo, stuck the clips in the sling that held her injured arm, and held up her free hand. "Okay. Upsy."

Cynna was ten inches taller than the old woman and outweighed her by at least forty pounds. Li Lei pulled her to her feet easily. "Can you walk? I do not wish to carry you."

Cynna blinked blearily. She didn't seem to find the possibility of being carried by Li Lei absurd. But then, she was still half asleep. "Sure." She took a wobbling step. She didn't fall, but it was a near thing.

Li Lei slid an arm around Cynna's waist and tugged her along toward the stairs. "The effect will be less on the first floor."

"Right." Cynna bobbed her head knowingly. "Th' spell would dissipate outside a radius of . . . how strong is this spell anyway?"

"Strong." Li Lei grunted as Cynna took the first step down the stairs—and nearly tumbled headfirst. "I did not wish to be bothered."

"I wish I had a sleep spell. Can make a sleep charm. Not a spell."

"It is a dragon trick. I do not think a human could use it."

Cynna looked down at the older woman. "You don't look like a dragon."

Li Lei did not answer, concentrating on getting her sleep-drunk charge the rest of the way down the stairs. At their foot she said, "You should hide the weapon and start your own spell now." And catching sight of a Fist who looked like he'd collapsed to the floor when the spell hit but was now trying to sit up: "Good. Stay here," she told Cynna, and went to the man.

She slapped his face lightly, made him look in her eyes, and told him he would escort her and Cynna to the tower.

By the time the sleepy Fist struggled to his feet, Cynna had joined them. She no longer wobbled when she walked, but her eyes were still heavy and she still clutched the gun in one hand. Li Lei wondered if she had made the *sleep* sending too strong.

"You'd better take Lily's Glock," Cynna said. "I'm too fuzzy-headed to shoot straight."

"I dislike guns. Do not shoot anyone until you are more awake. That will happen soon." She turned to the guard, switched to Chinese, and used Lily's least-favorite word: "Come."

THIRTY

~~~

LILY had perp-walked bigger men than Li Po, but she'd had the use of both hands and a pair of cuffs. It helped that Li Po wasn't much taller than her, but he was stronger. A lot stronger. If he started seriously struggling, she'd have to either drop the knife or use it. If she used it, she lost her hostage. If she dropped it, his men might rediscover initiative.

This was going to occur to him eventually. He wasn't deeply stupid. She hoped it was later rather than sooner.

The four Fists stayed flat on the ground as ordered. The fifth was still trying to persuade the Kanas to disperse. He hadn't yet noticed what had happened to his commander. Lily aimed Li Po at the tower and shoved him forward.

The tower at the center of Heart's Home was, like most of the structures, made of stone. It was round, topped by the red Frisbee that acted as a dragon alarm, and about seven feet in diameter. A narrow wooden door was set in the stone. At least thirty people sat on the ground in a large circle around that tower. Their presence was not Lily's idea. She'd told Ah Hai the Kanas were putting themselves in great danger. Ah Hai had nodded and agreed . . . and was now walking across the grass about ten feet behind Lily and her prisoner.

The Kanas had reinvented the sit-in.

They—at least most of them—didn't know exactly what the spawn were planning. The guy in charge, the one Ah Hai had contacted, probably did. He might have told the other elders; Ah Hai didn't know. But most of them knew only that their Zhuren planned some act that would cause great damage, much loss of life, and that it was part of a deal they'd made with the two powerful out-realm women who had visited the spawn.

Two? That had confused Lily, but after asking a few questions, she'd figured it out. The G.B. had been visiting Dragonhome off and on for decades, maybe as much as a century, setting this up. But she used to arrive in her other avatar, the one Xitil had eaten. Now she showed up in Ginger Harris's body. It would have looked like two different women to the Kanas . . . who considered this the greatest threat they had ever faced.

Their charge, after all, wasn't to keep the Zhuren from harm. All beings were harmed by life in some fashion. Nor was it to keep them alive. The Zhuren could handle that themselves just fine. Their charge was to teach the Zhuren to care. To connect.

These two women must have offered the Zhuren something they wanted very badly, Ah Hai had told Lily. They wanted it enough to bring great harm to the people who were in their charge. Doing such harm would damage the Zhuren, perhaps irretrievably. The Kanas assembled here because they were willing to place their bodies between the Zhuren and whatever goal they sought. They believed that those they'd served for generations would hesitate to harm them and might listen.

Hesitate. That was the word Ah Hai had used.

The Fist that Li Po had sent to disperse the Kanas finally realized something was wrong. Even at a distance Lily could see the shock travel through him as he stared at her and his commander. He exclaimed, drew his sword, and started to run.

And tripped and fell as he passed one of the seated figures, who'd stuck out a leg at exactly the right moment. The barefoot man rose, lifted the downed Fist slightly with one hand, and drove his other fist into the man's face. He dropped his victim and started running—straight for Lily. The straw hat he'd been wearing flew off his head.

Lily's heart pounded. It was all she could do to keep the hand holding the knife steady.

Li Po picked that moment to balk. He outweighed her by sixty or eighty pounds, so when he stopped moving, she did, too. "You are not going to kill me."

"Shut up."

The barefoot man ran fast. Much too fast for a human. He stopped as suddenly and gracefully as he'd launched his run, unwinded, his dark eyes shining and holding hers. Time seemed to stretch and slow, sweet as taffy, into a moment whole and perfect.

"May I?" Rule gestured at Li Po.

She nodded, then found her voice. "Please do. Otherwise he's going to annoy me into killing him."

A smile spread over his face and expanded into a grin. "That would be a shame when you've gone to such trouble to capture him."

No doubt her answering grin was as silly as his, as silly as the nonsense they said out loud while their eyes said more important things. "It would."

Rule walked up, gripped Li Po's arm where Lily held it twisted behind his back, and lifted it higher. Li Po grunted with pain, bending double in the effort to keep his shoulder in joint. Lily started to hand Rule Gan's knife, but Rule had retrieved a blade of his own from somewhere. It was about three times as large as hers. She couldn't stop smiling. "He's all yours."

Their pause had allowed Ah Hai to draw close. Rule glanced at her. "Is that—"

"Ah Hai. Introductions later."

Rule nodded. "Let's go."

They started off at a quick jog. Lily couldn't go any faster in the damned skirt. Rule had no trouble controlling Li Po one-handed. "I don't see Gan."

"She's on the other side of the tower. About all I can see of her is that remarkably green hat."

"You can see her? She's not *dashtu?*"

"I can see her in *dashtu* now. Not clearly, but she's not invisible. It's something to do with the translator charm Grandmother made me."

"She did what?" She shook her head. "Never mind. Obviously there's stuff you haven't told me yet. It's full moon. You okay?" That was shorthand for, *Are you keeping it together?*

"More distractible than I'd like, but well enough. Any sign of our large green friend?"

Meaning Reno. And it was beginning to really worry her that the dragon hadn't arrived yet. "No. On the upside, the spawn haven't shown up, either."

"Ah Wen said they left strict orders not to be disturbed. They are preparing for the ritual that will not take place."

"Ah Wen?"

"The leader of the Kanas. We've been chatting."

"Which one is he?"

"The older gentleman with the white cloth tied over his eyes." He gave a nod at an old guy sitting on the ground nearby as they jogged between two of the Kanas, all of whom were staring. "I'm guessing the government area has been emptied of people as part of the prep for the ritual. But where are the guards? I didn't expect my distraction to be this effective."

"Your distraction did most of the work. I helped. This"— she jabbed a thumb at their prisoner as they stopped next to the tower—"is the Fist commander. First Fist Li Po. He sent his second into the city to help with those big beasties you rounded up. The Fists," she reminded him when he looked baffled, "don't have sergeants. My best guess is that the remaining Fists are in their quarters in the Justice Hall, waiting for someone to send for them."

"In that case . . ." Rule spun Li Po around and cold-cocked him.

The man fell like a toppled tree, out cold before he hit the ground. Several of the watching Kanas gasped.

A laugh bubbled up in her, fizzy with delight as he reached for her and she for him. They didn't kiss. Just held on to each other, held on tight, hands touching, clutching, cherishing, and let the world take care of itself for a moment. Just for a moment.

Something tugged at her *shenyi*. "Lily Yu! Lily Yu! You can hug me now!"

She cursed, laughed, let go of Rule to bend and hug Gan, who hugged her back. Then she unfastened her sash, pulled off the *shenyi*, and untied her skirt. As she let it fall, Ah Hai arrived at a trot and began gathering the discarded garments, looking scandalized.

Rule said tersely, "Here they come."

She jolted and looked around.

He might have been referring to the Fists they'd left on the ground by the bathhouse. They'd gotten up, but weren't actually doing anything yet, however, so he probably meant the three figures approaching from the Justice Court. Grandmother, Cynna, and a single Fist were headed their way. The Fist had his sword out but pointed at the ground.

Rule raised his voice. "Quickly!"

Grandmother stopped, spoke to the guard, and started to run. So did Cynna, which had to hurt with her broken arm. So did the guard, but he ran in a different direction.

Gan shot out of the circle of Kanas, racing toward Grandmother and Cynna. "I did it! I found the gate!"

"So you did," Grandmother said. "I am pleased with you, Gan. They placed it in that tower, I perceive."

"Uh-huh. I think they tried to hide it, but I found it anyway. It's a permanent gate, too, like I said. Did Lily Yu tell you that?"

"She did. You must show me where the crossing place is."

Gan raced back to stand in a spot that looked like every other spot. It was about twenty feet from the tower. "Here! It's right here! I crossed to make sure it's safe."

"You did very well. Thank you, Gan." Grandmother stopped inside the circle of Kanas, looking around at people who were frankly gawking at her. She spoke in Chinese. "A very nice circle. Very tidy. It will get you all killed. You must sit much closer together, up near to the tower. Do not block the door. Rule, see that they don't. Lily, remove the magic cage. I will build the ward."

With that, she ignored her own orders to march up to Lily. She stopped and looked up at the sky. Whatever she saw made her hum thoughtfully. Then she pulled her granddaughter into a firm hug. She stroked Lily's hair once with great tenderness, then held her at arms' length and studied her. "You are well."

Lily smiled. "I am now."

THE technique Cynna had devised to defeat a sidhe artifact was simple enough. The magic cage drew on her own magic for power. It wouldn't allow her to use any magic that went beyond her skin. Therefore, she'd cast a spell that operated entirely on her. She'd actually discussed the spell in question with Alice. The no-pain spell was the opposite of a healing spell since it did a great job of eliminating pain, but completely stopped healing. It was a power hog, too. Set up on a loop, it was self-feeding, drawing on Cynna's magic until she stopped it.

Useless as a healing spell. Perfect for their needs now.

"Here," Cynna said, handing Lily her weapon, then pulled the two clips of ammo out of her sling. "I've already got the spell running. First time my arm hasn't hurt since I got here."

"Just a sec," Lily told her. "No pockets." She went to Ah Hai, who'd found a place in the circle already, and got the white sash back from her. She tied it around her waist and stuck the gun in it, then took the clips from Cynna. She needed to swap out the partly spent clip in the weapon for a fresh one. She had no idea how many rounds were left. But later, she thought. After she and Cynna got rid of the magic cage. She wedged the clips in the sash and made sure it was snug. Not as secure as she'd like, but it would do for now.

Cynna folded herself to the ground, sitting cross-legged. "I'm ready."

Lily took a deep breath. "Okay. Let's do it."

She sat cross-legged in front of her friend and took Cynna's hand—the one not attached to a broken arm—in both of hers.

Grandmother was standing stock-still next to the tower. She had announced that the ward could be built to include the crossing spot.

Gan—fully visible now, Lily assumed—was chattering away at Ah Hai, who seemed bemused. Rule was persuading the Kanas to move in close to the tower. A tricky bit of persuasion, that, when he didn't speak their language. Li Po was flat on the ground next to the Fist he'd sent to disperse the Kanas. The First Fist was still unconscious; his subordinate had come around, though he seemed dazed. Both were tied up. Rule had worn a length of rope around his waist under his tunic.

Lily tuned all that out and focused on Cynna's magic. It was a complex riff of textures—the fingerprint-y feel of Cynna's original magic, the fur-and-pine needles that meant lupi . . . which Cynna wasn't, but as Rhej she shared in the clan's magic and could draw on the clan's power.

She wouldn't. Not this time.

Lily had only used her Gift this way a few times, but it wasn't hard. Not for her, that is. It was going to be hellish hard on Cynna, whose every instinct would be telling her to fight, to get away, to reach for clan power to replenish the terrible emptiness. But Lily's part just took focus. Grandmother had that in spades. "I do not understand why Grandmother couldn't have done this."

"Just do it," Cynna said.

All right, then. One moment she was touching Cynna's magic. The next she was sucking it up.

Not all of it. And okay, that was a little tricky, but only a little. She had to go slowly, that was all. The tangle of looped-spell-plus-magic was separate from the rest of Cynna's magic. That was the whole point. The magic cage couldn't access that looped power, so when Lily drained all the other magic from her friend, she wouldn't destroy her friend's Gift. Cynna would still have the power caught up in the no-pain spell.

Even going slowly, it wasn't a long process. A couple minutes after Lily sat down and began vampirically draining her friend, Cynna's eyes rolled back in her head. She toppled over. Lily continued to grip Cynna's hand with one of hers and started running her other hand all over Cynna. Head, neck, feet . . . a *whoosh* and sudden blast of heat made her focus wobble for a second, but she got it back and kept pulling, going very slowly now. Had to be sure she got every drop.

She touched Cynna's other hand, ran her fingers up her forearm as much as the sling allowed . . . there it was, the spelltangle. Intact, as far as she could tell. Leave that. Push up Cynna's shirt. Check to see if . . . yes. Lily peeled the golden spiderweb off Cynna's skin.

Cynna didn't stir. Didn't wake. Lily frowned, dizzy. She felt odd, almost drunk. Buzzed on power? "The operation was a success, but the patient died."

"What!" Gan squawked, looking away from Ah Hai.

"Sorry. Bad joke. She's out cold, though. Grandmother—"

"In a moment," Rule said, squatting beside Cynna to touch her cheek. "She's busy."

Lily blinked and looked around.

The Kanas were all bunched up around the tower now . . . where Grandmother stood, eyes closed, arms outstretched on either side, looking as unmovable as the stone tower behind her. A ring of fire about thirty feet in diameter had sprung up, encircling them, the tower, Lily, Rule, and Cynna.

As Lily watched, the flames winked out. A pearly light slid up from the burned ground to meet overhead in a perfect dome—then it, too, vanished, leaving only a faint iridescence lingering in the air.

Cynna groaned. "My head . . . God, what a headache."

"Cynna." Lily started to touch her, hesitated. "You're okay?"

"No." She sounded cranky. "I've got the mother of all headaches. Otherwise, though, I feel like I'm dying. Did you get it off?"

In answer Lily held up the delicate artifact.

"Thank God." That came out not cranky at all. More like a prayer. Cynna closed her eyes, grimaced . . . "Okay, that helps a bit."

"Did it work? Did you shut the spell off?"

"Of course it worked. I still feel like shit, but it worked."

"Can you draw on the clan's power?"

"Could. Will if I have to, but I'd rather not. We don't know what's happening back home."

"Bring her to me," Grandmother said. Her voice sounded odd. Distant, as if she spoke from the bottom of a deep pit.

Cynna sighed and reached up to take the hand Rule stretched out. "Feels like my head's about to . . ." She moaned as Rule pulled her to her feet. "Give me a minute. Trying not to barf here." And added in a mutter, "Don't see why she couldn't come to me."

"Because I am balancing the node's power before feeding it to the ward," Grandmother snapped. "I cannot move from this spot."

Cynna's eyes went wide as saucers. "Son of a fucking bitch!"

Lily gave her a glance. "You knew she was going to make a ward."

"I didn't know she was going to use the damn nodes for it!"

Rule was frowning now, too. "I understand that node power is dangerous, but Cullen has used it."

"No, Cullen has used ley line energy. Even he wouldn't try to use the power from a node directly—and sure as hell not on a *ward*." She took a wobbly step, leaning on Rule. "And that, Lily, is why your grandmother didn't try to do what you just did. You don't use an A-bomb to pick up a book. It's hard on the book."

Lily unwound that and guessed Cynna meant that Grandmother was good with big doses of power, not small ones.

Rule helped Cynna walk to Grandmother, who said, "Give me your hand."

"Are you going to feed me node power?"

"Yes."

Cynna swallowed and held out her hand. Her eyes went wide again. "That's—"

"Incoming," Rule said.

Lily turned and saw six figures leaving the Home of the Seven: five Fists in their leather armor . . . and Alice Báitóu.

THIRTY-ONE

~~~

ALICE stopped a foot short of the iridescence that hung in the air like fairy dust, barely perceptible. "Quite nice work," she said, "especially considering you had to erect it so quickly. I have never seen a ward of this sort. What does it ward against?"

"Magic." Lily stood just inside the ward, her weapon drawn and aimed. Rule stood beside her.

"Ah." Alice gave the gun a glance. Her lips turned up a fraction. Being held at gunpoint apparently amused her. "I perceive that the magic cage has been removed, Cynna. I would like to know how you managed that. I assume the ward is your work?"

"Nope," Cynna said from back at the tower. "Hers." She nodded at Grandmother, who stood beside her in front of the door to the tower. Her arms were lowered now, her gaze abstracted.

For the first time, Alice looked startled. "Who is that?"

"My grandmother," Lily said. "Madame Li Lei Yu."

"But you are human and she is . . ." Alice shook her head. "I don't know what she is. Never mind. Do you realize she has powered the ward from the nodes? Do you have any idea how dangerous that is?"

"As I understand it," Lily said, "it means that if the ward gets knocked down, there's a good chance the nodes will explode."

"Which would destroy the city, killing thousands."

"Better not try to knock down the ward, then."

"I won't. The Zhuren may, however, and they will be emerging from seclusion very soon. If I cross the ward, what will happen?"

"It will stop you."

"You said it blocked magic, not people. And indeed, I do not perceive anything in it that would stop living beings."

"You have magic. It stops that magic, so you're stopped, too."

Alice shook her head. "That is not possible," she said as she stepped forward. She didn't quite bounce off the shimmering air, but she stopped very abruptly.

Back at the tower, Grandmother snorted.

"Remarkable," Alice said. "I would very much like to talk to your grandmother, but we are short on time. I need to enter."

"And we should let you in for some reason?"

"I am to bring the children here through the gate I presume you have located."

Rule growled.

"Who are you?" Alice asked him.

His voice was growly, too, and lower than usual. "The father of one of the children you wish to destroy."

"Ah. You're lupus, then?" Alice sounded mildly curious. "How in the world did you get here? But I suppose that is a long story, and we are short on time. You do not know what I wish. Unless you want the children to remain in Dis, you will allow me to enter your ward so I may retrieve them."

"You?" Lily exclaimed. "You're the one who's supposed to bring them here?"

"Yes. The one you know as Tom Weng and that other one are expecting me."

Lily bit her lip and glanced at Rule. His eyes were too black, the pupils trying to swallow the irises. Not a good sign. She slipped her hand in his. The mate bond helped him keep control sometimes. "What do you think?"

He shook his head as if he were trying to shake loose some confusion. "Not . . . feeling very verbal."

He was having trouble holding back the wolf. Hell. Not surprising with full moon night a couple eye blinks away, but worrying. She tried to think. She'd assumed—they all had—that the children had been/would be brought through the gate by someone in Ginger's group. Maybe a demon, maybe someone they hadn't seen because he or she left with the children before they arrived at the audience hall. That was the whole idea behind setting the ward the way they had: let the children in, keep the bad guys out.

She looked at Alice. "You could have told me this. You've held back information all along, yet you want us to trust you. How can we when you tell us nothing?"

"I have told you as little as possible to minimize the risk to myself. I do not wish to die. But you are currently aiming at me the token you claimed was sufficient to prove my good intent."

True, but . . . "What is the magical construct for? The one on Dis that reaches into this realm?"

"I don't know. I know what the Zhuren were told, but I am fairly sure they were deceived. I will tell you what I do know after you let me in." Alice leaned forward a whole inch—her version of great intensity. "You must let me in. The children *will* be removed from Dis. You know this. You remember it happening, and causality is not readily thwarted. If I don't go and get them, where do they go? With who, and how?"

"One of the claimed could go get them," Lily said. "We can't because we're already in that realm, but one of the claimed could."

"Those who hold them would not hand them over. They would not release the children to any but myself or one of the Zhuren. Do you wish to send the Zhu Kongqi?" She lifted in her eyebrows in delicate mockery.

"She is right," Grandmother said. And the iridescence vanished.

Alice stepped over the strip of burned grass. The Fists followed, their expressions stoic and watchful in a way that suggested they expected everything to go to hell in the next minute or two.

Rule murmured, "Keep an eye on them, will you?" To Alice he said, "Tell us about the construct."

"It is anchored in three realms—Earth, Dis, and here. The Zhuren were told this was necessary for stability, as once completed, the construct—that is a good term, by the way—will function as a massive gate between Earth and Dis. She says she wishes to flood your realm with demons. This may be true."

"It is not a gate," Grandmother announced.

"No," Alice said, "I do not believe it is, although it appears to have some of the qualities of a gate. I am not knowledgeable about gates, however, so that is not the basis for my conclusion that the Zhuren have been deceived. I based that on calculations concerning the amount of power the construct requires. I am familiar with that, as I have been balancing that power."

"That's it!" Lily exclaimed. "That's why your Gift felt so odd. It's balanced. Your Gift uses all of the elements equally."

"My Gift automatically balances the elements," Alice corrected her.

"That is so not possible," Cynna said.

Alice slanted her a look. "I am told my Gift is unique. To return to the topic, my calculations suggested that the Old One currently embodied in Ginger Harris lied about the consequences to my world once the construct becomes fully active. She told the Zhuren there would be localized fires and small earthquakes. This is only true if one defines 'localized' and 'small' in ways that defy common usage. I fear for my world. I chose to assist you, hoping that you will destroy the construct. It will bring destruction to your world, too."

"And yet," Rule said, "you have been working on the construct. Your Gift may have been essential to its completion."

"I believe we have already covered the fact that I do not wish to die."

Lily lifted both brows skeptically. "The Zhuren would have killed you if you didn't cooperate? Even though you're kin? I'd think your . . . that is, I'd think Kongqi would object."

"There used to be seven Zhuren."

That was not the non sequitur it seemed. If the Zhuren—all or some of them—had been willing to murder their brother, killing a great-niece wouldn't be a major hurdle.

"The ward is down," Grandmother reminded them. "This is not safe. She needs to leave so I can activate it."

Lily knew that Grandmother had to stand directly in front

of the gate to keep the ward powered up. She didn't know why, but it didn't matter. "Better go," she told Alice.

Alice started forward, followed by the squad of Fists. The Kanas were clustered tightly around the tower, however, and it took a moment for them to move out of the way. Lily saw Alice's gaze seeking someone, then her brow wrinkled. "Ah Li. I had hoped you would not come here."

"Where else would I be?" the healer asked, smiling.

"It is very dangerous to be here. Your skills are not replaceable."

"If it is dangerous here, my skills may be needed."

Alice sighed faintly and moved forward the last few steps, stopping in front of Grandmother but looking back at Lily as she said in English, "I will not return right away with the children. Gates must be rested between uses. This is particularly true when the realms are not congruent in either space or time."

"That," Grandmother said, "is a poor choice of terms. Gates do not rest. They do require a period of what might be called recalibration."

Alice shrugged. "It is the term I was given for the process. I do not know precisely how long the interval of rest—or recalibration—will be." She glanced to one side, where the unconscious Li Po lay trussed on the ground. "I have often wanted to do that," she commented, then looked back at Grandmother. "I am very interested in speaking with you. Perhaps later?"

"It seems unlikely," Grandmother said. "But I do not predict the future. You need to go." She stepped away from the door.

Alice told her squad to line up, single file, and to move quickly when she did. She reached out and unlatched the door, swung it open wide, then made a complex series of gestures and spoke a single word. She stepped forward . . . and vanished.

So did each of the Fists as they followed her.

Grandmother moved back in front of the door and raised her arms. The circle of fire sprang up again.

Five Zhuren raced out of the Home of the Seven. With a pop of displaced air, two vanished—and reappeared floating directly overhead.

"Uh-oh," Gan said.

The flames went out. Iridescence slid up from the ground.

One of the Zhuren above them raised a hand and hurled something invisible at them.

The fairy-dust glimmer closed overhead.

A blinding flash turned the world white. The ground shook.

About a 4.5, thought the California girl as she blinked dazzled eyes until she could see something other than smears of white light. Grandmother still stood, her arms straight out. Her gaze wasn't at all abstract. She looked seriously annoyed.

"Do not!" shouted a deep voice. "They have tied the ward to the nodes!"

All of the spawn were in the air now. Dick Boy was circling the ward slowly, studying it. Tú'àn hovered near Kongqi, who was one of the two who'd—teleported? Arrived first anyway. Kongqi wasn't the one who'd hurled the whatever-it-was with such great pyrotechnic effect, however. Shēngwù had done that. He, like Dick Boy, was studying the ward up close. Shuǐ was doing the dragonfly zip toward the bathhouse—no, he was aimed at the four Fists who must have decided that duty meant trotting toward the Zhuren.

All of the Zhuren wore pure white *shenyi* with white trousers beneath their robes and white slippers. All of them wore their hair the same way, in tight knots at the crowns of their heads. Ritual garb, Lily assumed, her lip curling at the thought of the ritual they wanted to perform.

She glanced to the west. The sun hung low now. Did they need to perform their ritual before the sun set, or before the moon rose?

Tú'àn drifted to the ground. The beads in his beard today were clear crystals. "Ah Wen," he said sadly. "Why are you here?"

The old man stood. The boy beside him popped to his feet, too. Ah Wen set a hand on the boy's shoulder and walked slowly toward Tú'àn. "You shine brightly today, Zhu," he said in a creaky old-man voice, stopping a few feet from the spawn, the ward glistening faintly in the air between them.

"Why are you here?" Tú'àn asked again, his expression as sad as his voice. "Do you defy us? Betray us?"

"We fulfill our charge," Ah Wen said gently. "We do not try

to correct every error. That is not our task. But this thing you plan is a terrible wrong and will damage all of you forever."

"We are damaged now!" cried Shēngwù. "You have always told us so. If we can assume our rightful forms, we erase that damage and regain our heritage! Perhaps then we will learn what this empathy is that you prate about, although I hope not. I see no value in it. True dragons have no interest in emotion."

Lily snorted. "Dragons are beings of vast passion."

That startled three of the spawn into turning to stare at her. They'd probably forgotten the trees could talk.

"Absurd," Shuǐ said.

Dick Boy landed several feet away. "The ward is designed to repel magic. It would, I believe, repel any being who possessed magic—either that or strip their magic from them if they did manage to force entry."

"Impossible," Shēngwù snapped. "This is, however powerful, a single ward. A ward can either block the magical or the physical. It cannot do both. Admittedly, crossing this one might be difficult for a human. It might even prove uncomfortable for one of us. But hardly impossible."

Kongqi landed about ten feet from Shuǐ. The spawn didn't like being too close to one another. It was very dragon of them. "It pains me, but I have to agree with Dìqiú. I believe you will as well if you examine the ward closely." A bit of a dig there, as Shēngwù had already studied it. "It is quite cleverly made, and as it is being powered by the nodes, beyond our ability to destroy by force. Attempting to do so might cause the nodes to explode."

Dick Boy nodded. "They nearly did. I contained the earthquake that resulted from Shēngwù's hasty strike, but—"

"I didn't know it was tied to the nodes," Shēngwù protested.

Dick Boy snorted. "And you accuse me of acting first and thinking later! As I was saying, I contained the earthquake, but I did not stabilize the nodes. Which of you did so?" He looked around. "Well?"

Shēngwù's mind was working along a different track. "If we can't use magic against the ward directly, we need another

way to reach inside. I believe purely material objects will neither affect nor be affected by the ward."

"You suggest we throw rocks at them?" Kongqi asked with
the type of politeness that sounds like an insult.

"It would probably work." Shuǐ was jogging toward them
with three of the four Fists who'd been left at the bathhouse.
The fourth Fist, Lily saw with a quick glance, was running
all-out toward the Justice Court. They'd have more company
soon. "We could kill or disable them that way. But the block
on magic will make it difficult to control our projectiles
carefully. We might also damage or kill some of the
claimed."

Shēngwù's lip curled. "Have they not betrayed us? Are they
not acting against us even now?"

Kongqi's eyebrows lifted. "You do not object to killing the
claimed?"

"If they do not leave, they must accept the consequences of
their decision. Is that not what they have always told us? That
we must accept the consequences of our choices?"

"I am unwilling to act in a manner which causes the deaths
of some of the claimed."

"We have no time to find a gentler solution. The ritual must
take place very soon." Shēngwù scowled. "This assumes that
you want the transformation to proceed. You argued against it
at first."

Dick Boy's deep bass broke in. "I think the old human
woman kept the nodes from exploding. She is maintaining the
ward."

"Her?"

"Surely not."

"It must be the other one, the one whose magic we caged."

Shuǐ said, "I have an idea." Two of the Fists with him suddenly flew up in the air a few feet and went sailing at the ward.
One smacked into it and slid to the ground, stunned. The other
went right through—screaming. He collided with two of the
Kanas, knocking them over.

Before the dazed Fist could get his feet under him, Rule
was there. He slung the man over his shoulder, carried him
quickly to the ward, and tossed him back out. "No, thanks," he
said. "We have enough hostages already."

Tú'àn frowned at Shuǐ. "Why do you toss Fists around? You are likely to damage them."

Shuǐ sneered back. "Is it not obvious? One of them had magic. The other did not. We now know that the ward will stop those with magic—and will not stop those without it."

"You suggest we throw humans at them instead of rocks?"

"I suggest we have the unGifted Fists walk through on their own."

"And I suggest," Kongqi said, moving closer, "that Dìqiú was partly correct. Only partly, because the old woman is only partly human. The ward makes it difficult to see her clearly, but what I can see reminds me of dragon kin."

Silence fell as the spawn all stared at Grandmother . . . who broke it. "It is extremely rude to speak of me as if I were not here."

"Very well," Kongqi said. "Who and what are you?"

Mischief or some more obscure motive prompted Lily to go formal. "Allow me to present to you my grandmother, Madame Li Lei Yu. In your manner of naming, she would be called Madame Yu Li Lei. Grandmother, the one who spoke to you is called the Zhu Kongqi."

She sniffed. "I shall not call him that, however. I have a poor opinion of masters. I am not dragon kin—"

"I did not think she could be," Tú'àn commented.

"I am dragon," Grandmother finished.

"That," Kongqi said after a moment, "is clearly incorrect."

"You have confused form with essence. It is a common mistake among the young. I have been dragon in the past. It is impossible to cease to be dragon. Therefore, I am still dragon. I am also human, but that is of little relevance to this conversation. I bring you greetings from your kin on Earth."

She had their sudden and entire attention.

Not Rule's, however. He nudged Lily. When she glanced at him, he nodded toward the Justice Court. Fists were pouring out of its open doors to assemble in ranks in front of the building.

Tú'àn broke the silence. "There are others like you on Earth?"

"No. There are, however, dragons. In particular, I bring you greetings from the black dragon, who is called by many names. I know him as Tsao Sun."

"Your granddaughter also claims to know the eldest." Shēngwù managed to layer courtesy, skepticism, and innuendo into those few words. "How odd that he would send greetings after ignoring our existence for so many years."

"He did not know you existed."

"And yet he sent us greetings. Amazing. Did he also open a gate through which to send you to deliver them?"

Grandmother gave him a look that should have made him squirm. "I find it difficult to believe you are as dense as you pretend. Until very recently, he knew only that your existence was hypothetically possible and considered the possibility fairly remote. Not that it would have mattered. As you are surely aware, I did not arrive here through a gate. The location of this realm has been lost for millennia."

"So we have been told," Shuǐ said in an icy voice. "And yet at least one dragon knew of our existence in very concrete terms. She did not—"

"*WE DO NOT SPEAK OF HER PUBLICLY!*" That megaphone bellow came from Dick Boy.

The Fists had finished assembling and were trotting toward the tower and their masters.

"Of course not," Shuǐ said, offering his furious brother a tiny bow. "As I was saying, the one of whom we shall not speak knew of our existence. If we are to believe Madame Yu, we must also believe that she never spoke of us to the eldest. Or to any of the other dragons."

Grandmother raised her brows. "You find that difficult to accept? You think a dragon would speak of parentage?"

"Not of their male parent, of course, but . . ." Shuǐ drifted off into frowning silence.

Grandmother spoke almost gently. "Not only the male parent. Dragons do not speak of parentage at all. It is possible you have been misled by your situation. This is not surprising. In your current forms, you are unable to undergo third birth."

Dead silence now, as though Grandmother had said something huge and portentous. Which meant Lily had missed something huge and portentous, because she had no idea what was so significant. Third birth? What did that have do with anything? Third birth was the term for the transition a dragon made from male to female so he . . . so *she* could have babies.

That thought ricochetted in Lily's head like a manic pinball, setting off lights and bells and ringing up a winning score. The spawn didn't want the ability to change into dragons just so they could turn big and scaly on demand. They wanted to be able to enter third birth. To turn female and have babies, dragon babies, not those begat upon human women.

They wanted to be *mothers*.

THIRTY-TWO

〰️

GRANDMOTHER spoke into that silence. "Are you aware that you have allied yourselves with the Great Enemy of all dragons? With one whose goal is to rob all beings everywhere of sovereignty?"

"We are not her allies," Shuǐ said coldly.

Shēngwù's voice was hotter. Angrier. "We made a deal with her. We do not ally with her. We do not *subordinate* ourselves to her in any way." The word "subordinate" fairly oozed contempt.

"Dragons . . ." Grandmother gave the word a subtle emphasis that made it seem as if she'd said *real dragons*. ". . . do not make deals with her. Dragons oppose her."

The Fists were almost here.

Rule spoke in a low voice. "Gan—get with the noncombatants."

Gan's voice came from behind them. "The what?"

"The Kanas. Stay in the middle of them."

Tú'àn stoked his beard thoughtfully. "I cannot decide which I want more: to kill her or to question her."

"I know which I want," Shēngwù said, his dark eyes hot.

The Fists arrived. About thirty of them.

"Good," Tú'àn said to them. "Those of you without magic

form up to my left. On my command, those without magic will enter the warded area. Your primary target is the old woman. Take her alive if you can."

"The Fists are not yours to command," Kongqi said coldly.

"This is hardly the time to argue over jurisdiction," Shuǐ snapped.

Tú'àn nodded. "Do not allow emotion to dictate to you. Clearly the old woman must be incapacitated so the ward comes down. Later we can—"

A few feet above the Frisbee-topped tower, the darkening sky exploded in thunder. And a *mind* appeared out of nowhere—a mind vast and powerful and compelling. Lily's mindsense flew to it willy-nilly.

The dragon alarm went off. Crimson light flooded the air, carrying the deep reverberation of a gong that did not exist.

"About time," Grandmother muttered.

That vast mind shoved Lily's mindsense away, leaving her dizzy. *Keep a distance,* said a mind-voice as chill and cutting as a shard of ice, *or you will succumb to dazzlement.*

Okay, but do you know what's going on? The spawn rule this world, and they've made a deal with the Great Bitch to—

Later. The construct is already partly operational. It must be destroyed before it becomes fully operational.

Do you know what—

The spawn shot into the air. All of them. And threw fire, brilliant and glowing, at the empty sky.

And Reno was *there.* Clearly visible, soaring in an easy circle, forty feet of sinuous green with wings—green as dark as wet moss for the most part, but brightening to chartreuse along the ridge of his spine and the tips of his wings. The orange of his frill provided a shocking punctuation amid all that grim green ferocity.

He roared.

A dragon's roar is like no other sound. First there's the sheer volume. Scientists estimated it at one hundred decibels, roughly as loud as a jet plane passing overhead at a thousand feet or most rock bands. Scientists, Lily suspected, were full of shit. But then, they'd had to estimate because no dragon had been willing to roar on command so they could measure it, so maybe it wasn't entirely their fault they got it wrong.

Then there was the deep bass of the roar. That was like being surrounded by a dozen cars with their windows down and their stereos' bass cranked up to max—a bass that traveled through her bones as much as it did through the air. Yet it wasn't all bass, no more than it was just a really loud noise. Harmonics turned what should have been a sonic assault into a sound of surpassing beauty.

Dragons manipulate magic with their voices.

The spawn went tumbling through the air, toes over heads, beautiful white *shenyi* flapping around them like ineffective wings.

Ah Wen stood, his face glowing with joy in the pulsing red light of the alarm. He lifted his head proudly and cried, "I speak for her!"

Tú'àn landed on the ground. Hard. He made it look almost like he'd intended to do so, bouncing quickly to his feet to look up at the dragon. Expressions flowed over his face like a river in flood, too fast to isolate. "H-her?"

Dick Boy had been blown backward without colliding with the ground. He, too, stared, looking rather stuffed. "*That one* is—is no longer female."

"The pronoun is irrelevant." Ah Wen's voice was now deeper, richer, and much colder than normal. He sounded like Reno—Reno as expressed through human vocal chords, yes, but very much Reno. "Once one becomes a mother, one does not cease to be a mother. You will stop this squabbling. We have little time to amend matters concerning your arrangement with the Great Enemy. Tell me this: did you intend to destroy the world I left you, or were you unaware this will happen?"

Shēngwù, who had been blown the farthest, shot forward with absurd speed, slowing to sail alongside Reno. He screamed his reply—and clearly not just so he could be heard over the gong that still reverberated. "The world you left us? The key words are *you left us!*" And he hurled another invisible something at the green dragon.

The great wings froze in place. Reno dropped like a stone—an enormous green stone.

"Stop that," Ah Wen/Reno said as Reno's wings caught air once more. The dragon rose quickly and slapped Shēngwù with one wing. The Master of Body Magic went spinning off.

"And I thought I had mother issues," Lily muttered.

"I wonder," Rule said softly, "if the spawn are teenagers."

She looked at him. "Hundred-and-fifty-year-old teenagers?"

"With all the angst and issues of a fifteen-year-old boy and vastly more power."

Cynna moved up to join them. "Don't forget the part about them being sociopaths. Can't someone shut off that alarm?"

"You knew I would leave when it became possible," Ah Wen/Reno said, the voice crisp the way Reno's always was, but not as cold. He almost sounded sad. "You were, perhaps, young for such leave-taking, but my choices were few. I explained this. Had I not left, what territory could you have claimed that was not also my territory? You wanted your own, which is as it should be. Do you not remember this?"

"You said you would return," Shuǐ said. "You have been gone for one hundred and twenty-nine years."

"I am relieved to hear that. For me, it has been two hundred and nine years. That noise is annoying." And the alarm at last fell silent, although the crimson light continued to pulse, melding its bloody color with the gold of the approaching sunset. "You have not answered my question."

"You ask the wrong question," Tú'àn said. "You should ask why we made such an arrangement. She offers us the ability to Change into our true forms. When we can be dragon in form as well as in mind, we will be able to enter third birth."

"This is not sufficient cause to destroy your world."

"A few fires will not destroy the world."

"I told them it would do more damage than *she* had admitted," Kongqi said slowly. He'd been blown almost as far as Shēngwù, but hadn't been in as much of a hurry and had just now reached them. He hung motionless in the air, his face oddly blank. "They chose not to believe this. Please explain specifically what you mean by 'destroy.'"

"I will explain, but understand that the words I use are imprecise. The construct will merge Earth with Dragonhome—"

Merge? What did that even mean? How could it be possible to merge two realms?

"—in such a manner that protections that have been in place for millennia will no longer apply. She will be able to enter Earth in the body of her avatar with her power intact. The merging process involves crushing the strata between the realms, which will create destructive forces such as have not been seen since the Great War. Because she wishes to rule Earth, those forces will be directed into Dis and Dragonhome. I doubt this continent will survive."

"What proof do you offer that this is so?" Tú'àn said coldly.

"We lack the time required to present my proofs."

"You want to stop us," Shēngwù said, voice ominously low. "You mean to stop us."

"Yes."

This time he threw mage fire. Fire that burned black, not yellow or blue. The fire that burns anything.

Most of it spattered off Reno as if it had been water. Most, but not all. Reno swirled in the air like an enormous green ribbon. His tail was burning. He opened his jaws and breathed out a single note. The flames died.

"Together!" Shēngwù cried.

This time, Shuǐ threw mage fire with Shēngwù. Two streams of black fire hit Reno at the same instant.

Tú'àn shot up in the air, calling down to the Fists, "Proceed as ordered!" Then he, too, summoned mage fire and hurled it.

So did Kongqi. So did Dick Boy.

But they threw it at their brothers.

"Back!" Rule ordered as a dozen Fists charged them.

Lily got off one quick shot and took two quick steps back—and realized that Rule wasn't retreating with her and Cynna. Instead he screamed and leaped at the sword-wielding men—and Changed in midair.

A wolf the size of a small pony landed among a dozen deeply surprised men.

THIRTY-THREE

~~

Dis

THE room was not entirely dark. Mage lights bobbed around near the ceiling, but not enough to make it really bright. But Toby didn't want to see any better. There were too many demons here.

Not monsters. Demons.

Toby couldn't put into words why some of the creatures in Dis made him think "monster" while others made him think "demon." What was the difference? But there *was* a difference, even if he couldn't explain it, and these . . . these were demons.

"Toby," Diego whispered, "I'm out of diapers and he just pooped."

He glanced at the other boy. He'd put Diego in charge of the littlest of them to give him something to do. Noah was only four months old and mostly he slept, but right now he was awake and working away at the bottle Diego held.

"You'll have to use one of the big ones." They'd had only a handful of the diapers sized for a really little baby, but they still had plenty of those made for one Ryder's size.

"I'll get it," Sandy said and scooted on his butt to the small pile of supplies the demons had dumped next to them.

Ryder reached for Toby's hands and used them to pull herself to her feet. Again. She chortled and picked up one foot and fell. Again.

There were two kinds of demons in the big, underground room their captors had brought them to. One kind stood up on two legs and had red or pink skin and no hair. Their faces looked like gargoyles, only with more eyes—two in front and two in back—and they had little horns on top of their heads and long, clever tails almost like a cartoon devil, only without the arrowhead at the tip. Instead they had a bony ridge that looked sharp enough to cut you open. Like all the other demons Toby had seen, they were naked, so he knew some were male, some female, but the females didn't have breasts. There wasn't room for breasts because that's where the smaller pair of arms grew, right out of their chests. Those arms were short and ended in hands that looked almost ordinary. The upper arms were long and thick with muscle like an ape's and grew out of powerful shoulders. Those arms ended in claws like the ones on their big feet.

The second kind of demon was built like a giant, hairless hyena, with skin that ranged from dun to black. These demons had only two eyes, but those eyes were red and glowing. They had two short rear legs and two longer front legs, plus a pair of weird-looking arms with too many joints sprouting from their chests. Those arms ended in hands, but with claws so wicked long that Toby didn't think they could use their hands for much.

A ring of fire three feet high penned Toby and the kids in the middle of the room. It was real fire, too, not the fake kind Cullen sometimes used. Toby was hot and sweaty from sitting near it, but he didn't have much choice. Their circle of floor wasn't very big.

"Such a big girl!" Toby sang out as Ryder pulled herself to her feet once more. And thought about how odd it was that he could sound so cheerful when, inside him, a beast was raging.

He needed that beast. His wolf. He might be too young to Change, but the wolf's rage had helped him. Kept him from curling up in a ball and screaming or sobbing. His dad was coming for him. He knew that. But he wasn't here yet. He might not get here in time . . . whatever "in time" meant. Toby tried not to think about that, and his wolf helped there, too.

Ryder gurgled and lifted a foot and plopped back down on her bottom. She fell every time, mostly because she always tried to walk and she couldn't, not yet. Cynna called her a born overachiever. But falling on her butt didn't discourage Ryder. She reached for his hands to do it again . . . and froze.

Toby's gaze flicked up. Sure enough, the scary woman, the one with two voices, stood just on the other side of the fire. She smiled at him. The man was there, too, slightly behind the woman, but Toby couldn't spare any attention for him. Not with *her* so close.

"Such a cute baby," the woman said in her ordinary voice. "Not that I care much about babies, but I don't object to them. And my other half—that's terribly inaccurate, by the way, but I've never been good at math. My other half positively dotes on babies. Especially girl babies. So pure . . ." She sighed in a dreamy way that sent ants crawling up Toby's spine. "You're right, you know."

Toby didn't speak. He wasn't sure he could. Even his wolf went still.

"Diego should have more faith in what you tell him. Your father is not only coming, he's here. Quite close, really. But we can't make it too easy for him. Where would be the fun in that? Time to cut those traces Ryder's mommy is using to Find you two." She pointed at him. This time her voice rolled through him like thunder. *"Midello-sha!"*

Toby froze in anticipation of whatever terrible thing she'd done . . . but nothing happened.

"All right, Alice," she said sweetly, stepping aside to reveal someone else. A woman he'd never seen before. "They're all yours now."

The surrounding fire vanished and Toby saw the woman called Alice clearly. She was small for a grown-up and really pale. Pale hair, pale skin, pale eyes. She wore a pale blue top and pants. There were five men with her. They were all short and looked Chinese or Japanese or something like that. They also looked mean. They wore funny helmets, some of them metal, some leather, and had leather breastplates strapped across their chests. They carried swords.

Toby reached for Ryder, gathering her close before standing up. "Who are you?"

"I am Báitóu Alice Li. Who are you?"

"Toby."

"Toby, I am going to take you and the other children to the next stop on your travels. It is called *Lóng Jia*. We will go through a gate—"

"No!" Automatically Toby backed up a step. A gate meant another realm. He couldn't go to yet another realm. His dad was *here*, looking for him.

"It will be all right, Toby."

All right? He bared his teeth at her. His wolf wanted to leap at her. To grab her throat in his jaws and shake her, punish her for lying. But he didn't have a wolf's jaws or teeth, and if he leaped at her, the armored men would stop him, maybe kill him with their swords.

Fight or flight. He couldn't fight. So he ran.

It was stupid. He knew that even as he pelted for the door, dodging hands that reached for him, darting around demons, pumping his legs as fast as he could and clutching Ryder tightly. Where could he go? Even if he reached that door, where would he go? But his body had decided to run and run it did, and it felt like the hidden beast in his gut gave him strength and speed and—

Movement flickered in his peripheral vision, then a blow landed on the side of his head. His head went one way and his legs the other and he landed hard and skidded on the stone floor and forgot how to think altogether.

Hands, clawed demon hands, grabbed him. He snapped at them. Surrounded—he was surrounded by enemies and he kicked and tried to bite and struggled, desperate to protect the precious burden in his arms, but there were too many of them. They imprisoned him in hard arms and pried Ryder out of his.

He screamed. And something broke.

Pain. It hurt *so much*—

Voices babbled, meaningless and unintelligible, and he was swinging between two sets of hands, one set holding his ankles, the other gripping his arms at the shoulders. They carried him back across the big room and he knew he must not let them, must not go where they wanted to take him, but the knowing was wordless. He writhed and grunted and hurt. He couldn't see through the pain, couldn't think, but was hit with a sudden assault of smells—sweat, blood, meat, copper, stone, urine, dust, and others, more than he could identify—a kaleidoscope of smells, each so layered and dense he wanted to sniff and sniff for hours. And wanted to stop breathing altogether, overwhelmed.

There was something he had to do. *Had* to. The pain pushed him, forced him to do it. And he couldn't. Whatever had broken inside him struggled and fought, desperate to *come out*. And it couldn't. Something was wrong, horribly wrong, and for a second he hung limp in his captors' grip, motionless and panting.

In that single breath of stillness he heard his father's voice saying, *There is no moon in Dis.*

These words meant something. Unlike the outside voices, which babbled and babbled, these words had meaning. They were important. But his brain wasn't working right. Before he could follow that meaning, track it down, and make sense of it, the man holding his feet dropped them. The other man heaved him up over his shoulder and took a few quick steps forward.

The world changed. It went from the dim, demon-riddled underground room to the slanted orange light of sunset and fresh green scents.

And he heard it. Heard her song. The most beautiful, most real thing he had ever heard. And it was easy, after all, to do what he must.

THIRTY-FOUR

A sword slashed Rule's side. He spun and locked his teeth in the man's thigh. Blood spurted into his mouth. He ignored how good it tasted and shook the man, throwing him into another man. Both fell. Rule jumped over them to escape another sword thrust and broke another man's ankle with a quick bite-and-twist. He dodged another sword thrust and leaped again, putting a dozen feet between him and the nearest threat so he could assess.

His side burned, but the slash wasn't deep. Neither was the one on his haunch, which had already closed. Minor damage.

The enemy had taken more. Seven of them were down, either dead or too injured to fight. The remaining six had spread out and were trying to encircle him. Sensible of them, although they were too few to hold that circle. They were good fighters, though. They might have frozen briefly when he first landed among them, but some of these men had fought beasts larger than him. They hadn't run.

Pity. He started turning in a slow circle, caught a glimpse of Lily and Cynna standing near Grandmother, several of the seated figures of the Kanas huddled nearby. Lily had her weapon out, but hadn't fired it again. He'd known she wouldn't, not with him in the midst of her targets, moving fast and unpredictably. Cynna stood with one hand raised as if poised to hurl some spell. Grandmother . . . just stood.

Where was Gan? Ah, there. He saw her blurry shape amid another clump of the Kanas as he continued to turn. The Fists had tightened their circle. Time to break it, before they charged. He picked his target but continued to turn to deceive his enemies.

Now. He dug in with his rear paws, pivoted, and leaped— going for height this time. Aiming for the empty air over the head of the shortest Fist—who swung his sword up, forcing Rule to twist in the air to keep his belly away from the blade. As he sailed past, he kicked out with his rear feet. One connected. He felt the claws catch flesh, felt the impact against the man's skull.

Only five Fists able to fight now. And he was out of their circle and able to steal a moment to glance up.

The spawn were darting around the sky like maddened mayflies. Reno was motionless. No, not quite . . . he hung in the air with his wings outspread, moving neither forward nor backward, up nor down. But he rippled.

Rule blinked. It didn't help. His distance vision wasn't as good in this form as when he was two-legged, but he didn't think the rippling was due to a problem with his eyes. Either Reno was doing something that caused his body to look like water in a disturbed pool . . . or something had been done to him.

Rule really needed to know which it was. He tried to appraise the actions of the spawn. It was difficult. He couldn't find a pattern in their darting flight, and two of them didn't seem to need to fly. They disappeared from one spot and reappeared elsewhere without visibly crossing the space between. Cullen had told him once that a few of the old adepts had been able to teleport. It was not reassuring to think that some of the spawn had discovered an adept's trick.

Most of what they did was invisible to him, but lightning arced once, blindingly visible. Elsewhere a streamer of mage fire flew out like incandescent night. But he couldn't see magic, so while he assumed other assaults were taking place, he had no idea what they were. But the battle was clearly three against two, with the larger number on the wrong side. Those three weren't behaving as if Reno's immobility meant they'd stopped him from destroying the construct, however. They didn't act as if they'd won. They continued to attack him in between attacks on their brothers, who fought to stop them.

He decided that Reno must have opted out of the fight. He would not kill his children, and his best nonlethal weapon—mind magic—didn't work on the spawn. And he didn't have time to keep stopping them from killing him, over and over, not if he wanted to destroy the construct. So he'd created some kind of shield, leaving the battle to his children while he did what only he could do.

A small sound made Rule whip around as one of the Fists came at him, sword already swinging. He darted in beneath the strike and severed the man's hamstring.

The Fists were down to four now. Surely they would . . . yes, they drew together, either rethinking their strategy or considering retreat. He wished he still had the translator charm to tell him what they were saying, but it was on the ground with his clothes, lost when he Changed.

Something was burning. Grass, his nose told him. Probably not all of the mage fire had politely extinguished itself after splattering uselessly against Reno or his children. He stole another quick glance at the sky—just in time to see one of the darting figures wink out. But this time the vanished spawn didn't reappear.

That can't be good, he thought, looking all around, both sky and ground, without seeing the missing spawn. Had it been one of the three enemies or one of the two allies who'd vanished? In their white robes they were hard to tell apart from the ground. He couldn't—

Grandmother's voice rang out. "They arrive!"

His heart leaped. The children. The children were coming through the gate. *Toby*, his heart sang, while his mind informed him that this meant that Grandmother had to move away from the gate. Which meant dropping the ward.

Things could get messy. If any of the magic being hurled overhead rained down on them—if the Fists outside the ward now realized it was gone—

And then it was.

First he heard a woman's voice. Alice Báitóu, who'd gone

to get the children. She said something in Chinese, then in English. "What is happening? The alarm is only halfway . . . oh. My."

The Kanas were between him and the tower and he couldn't *see*. And he had to. He sprinted quickly to get a view of the doorway that was also a gate.

Grandmother stood on one side of it, Alice on the other. Alice's head was tilted up, her mouth agape as she stared up at Reno. A Fist appeared in the empty doorway carrying a box tucked under one arm and a tiny baby in the other. Noah. The next one toted a young boy—Diego—followed by a man carrying a large box, then one carrying a diaper bag and another baby—

"Ryder!" Cynna screamed, and shoved her way to that Fist. To her baby.

The last Fist stepped from nothing into this world. He carried Toby. A writhing, twisting Toby, his body bucking, caught in some invisible agony, his face frozen in a snarl . . .

Oh, God. Dear Lady. Rule knew what that snarl mean, that writhing body, and never mind that it should be impossible. He forgot the Fists, the dragon, the spawn, and raced for his son.

Who was undergoing First Change.

"SHIT!" Lily cried.

Something was wrong with Toby. Rule was racing toward him and Lily wanted to knock a couple people down and go to him, too, but the ward was down and the remaining Fists— maybe twenty of them—had just realized it. One of them barked out an order to the rest and they began trotting forward. And Cynna was out of the picture for now, having grabbed Ryder and fallen to her knees on the ground, crying, hugging her baby.

Grandmother shoved the last of Alice's Fists out of the way and resumed her place, muttering words Lily couldn't catch. A moment later the fire sprang up again in a perfect circle. Two Fists were crossing the burned grass at that instant. One jumped back; the other forward.

The ward slid back in place, but eleven more Fists were on this side of it now. And headed toward the tower.

Lily set her feet and held out her weapon in her best two-handed grip. But the men charging them wouldn't know what she held. Wouldn't respect what a gun can do. She was going to have to kill people to prove she could.

Alice stammered. "H-he isn't . . . who is he?"

"He's calling himself Reno." Lily sighted on the man in the lead. The one smart enough to give orders. She squeezed the trigger. The gun bucked in her hands. The man cried out, staggered, and fell. She wanted to scream at them all to stop, not to make her kill them. She sighted again. "He's your great-grandmother."

"He's my . . . oh." Then, sharply, "Stop that!"

"Can't. Got to stop them."

"Let me," Alice said.

Out of the corner of her eye Lily saw Alice make a quick, precise gesture. She spoke a word once. Spoke it again and again, until the first five Fists had all collapsed to the ground in agony. Then, loudly, "Halt!"

To Lily's amazement, they did. Several called out explanations. Tú'àn had ordered the nonmagical Fists into action, but not them. Their orders were unclear, but they knew Tú'àn wanted the old woman. Alice should step aside.

"You are mistaken," Alice told them crisply. "Stay where you are while I sort out the situation."

Her familiar authority stopped them even as it deepened their confusion. Without an officer or sergeant, they didn't dare disobey one who'd often given them orders in the past. One who was dragon kin. But what if they were wrong? What if the Zhu Tú'àn expected them to capture the old woman without being specifically ordered to do so?

Rule reached Toby. Lily didn't know what he intended to do. He was a wolf at the moment and couldn't—shit and double shit!

Toby had vanished into the Möbius strip confusion of the Change.

"Get back!" Lily called out. "Everyone get away from the wolf." By the time she'd finished the sentence, it was no longer accurate. "The wolves."

Toby made a gorgeous wolf, most of him as black as his uncle's wolf form, but with a silvery gray mask across his face, on the tips of his ears, and on his belly. He made a small wolf, however, not as tall as other lupi, and lean, almost skinny. His legs looked wobbly and too long for his body. He was an adolescent wolf? Lily wasn't sure what teenage wolves looked like. She'd never seen one. The new wolves were kept sequestered at *terra tradis*. Which was where Toby would have been if they'd had any idea, any inkling, he was this close to First Change.

He stood on those four wobbly legs over the prostrate and terrified Fist who'd been carrying him, and his teeth were as big as an adult's and bared in a snarl. He lunged for the man's throat—

Rule body-slammed him, knocking him down. He yipped, startled, and fell at Grandmother's feet. Rule moved to stand over him.

"Alice!" Cynna cried. "Tell your men to give me the children—or at least to get them away from the wolves."

Lily grabbed Alice's arm and pulled. "Come on. It is not safe to be near those wolves."

Alice let herself be moved, but she frowned. "Aren't they your wolves? And why are there two?"

"Rule's okay. He's in control. The other one is Toby, but Toby doesn't know he's Toby right now." Lily stopped about ten feet from the wolves, keeping an eye on the milling Fists. Trusting Rule to keep an eye on Toby. "He just went through First Change. He's really hungry and really dangerous. He needs food. Meat."

"I do not have meat."

"Can you get some? One of your men—can you send someone to get him some meat? A couple of chickens, maybe?"

Alice considered that briefly. "An excellent idea. My squad will go get meat."

"All five?"

"When the Zhuren reclaim them, they will be a deficit, not an asset." Alice spoke in Chinese to her squad leader, telling him to take the children over to the group of Kanas who were sitting farthest from the tower, where Cynna would take charge of them. Then all of them were to go get chickens and bring them here.

Gan was with that group of Kanas. Or she had been—Lily

couldn't see her from here. The tower blocked her. She moved
aside several steps so she could see better. "Gan! It's time
to go!"

A small orange head popped up in the center of the Kanas.
Standing, Gan was nearly a head taller than people sitting
around her. "Is it safe?"

"No," Cynna said, hurrying that way with Alice's Fists and
their burdens. "But it's not safe anywhere right now."

The crimson pulse of the alarm suddenly shut off.

The ground shuddered. Lily's scowl deepened. "What the—"

"They are poking at the ward," Grandmother said grimly.

LI Lei did not look up. She did not need to. The spawn were
ablaze with magic, so easy to sense that she would have had to
work at it to cease being aware of them. Three of them hovered directly overhead—the three who wanted the children.
The three who had tried to kill Reno, who had no attention to
spare for them.

Two of the spawn had been defending him. She did not
know where those two were. It was rare that any task required
a dragon's entire attention. Dismantling the construct was, it
seemed, one of those rare tasks.

Li Lei knew how to tap into a node. For her, doing so was
almost safe. It could not be called completely safe, for nodes
were born in chaos and were inherently unpredictable. But
crossing the street was not completely safe, either.

She had underestimated the difficulty in tapping into twin
nodes.

The phrase referred to nodes that were physically close
enough to interact. Such twins were very rare, and she had
never dealt with them before. These nodes pulsed together like
two chambers of a giant heart. That synchronization allowed
them to remain stable, neither interfering with the other. It
also made it necessary for her to draw from both nodes at
once, to draw exactly the same amount of power from each so
she didn't upset their balance. So much she had known ahead
of time, and if the doing had proven more difficult than expected, it was still within her ability.

She had not known the spawn were idiots.

Only an idiot would poke at her ward the way they were—shaped blows of pure force. No doubt they knew the children had arrived. No doubt this made them crazed with fury and frustration. They wanted to find out how she reacted to their pokes.

This was very stupid of them. There were only three possible reactions she could have, and only one of those possibilities might have benefited them: if their pokes made her fear losing control, she might drop the ward. Since she, the ward, and the nodes had already weathered a much harder blow, she did not think much of this reasoning. The other two possibilities offered them no benefit whatsoever. Either she would lose control and everyone within several square miles would die, or she would retain control. As she was doing.

Which meant that the power from their pokes was deflected. Mostly it was deflected into the ground. And Lang Xin was situated above a fault.

One of the spawn had quieted the earth before, when that first idiot had struck her ward. He had struck much harder than they were doing now, thinking he could crack it open with a single blow. He had been wrong on more than one count. But there were three of them now, and if they were poking and prodding rather than trying to smash the ward like an egg, none of them seemed to have the sense or perhaps the ability to quiet the earth.

Li Lei did not have that skill, either. Not that she could have spared the attention to employ it if she had.

Poke, poke, poke.

The earth rumbled. A moment later it shimmied.

"Get the spears!" one of the spawn called down. "Run, fools! Get the spears!" Another one started calling out orders to Alice Báitóu, who was Reno's great-granddaughter. Alice Báitóu responded by asking where the Zhu Kongqi was. The spawn laughed and said he'd run off. Alice Báitóu did not appear to believe him. The third spawn told the Fists to forget the spears and get the children. The other two spawn started arguing with him.

Why did they want spears? Li Lei frowned at that. Did they mean to toss them at her? Arrows would be easier, surely. Her ward would not stop arrows. She wondered very much why they would send for spears instead of bows.

Distantly she was aware of Rule-wolf standing over his son, who was so suddenly and unexpectedly also wolf. Rule was growling, teeth bared. She assumed this was some kind of dominance rite and dismissed it from her thoughts. Dimly, too, she was aware of Lily standing with her weapon out and ready, and in one corner of her heart she ached for her granddaughter. Rule killed the way the tiger did, without hesitation or guilt. Lily could not kill that way, but she would do what she must.

Most of what attention she could spare from the power draw was with Cynna, however. Cynna and the children. The Fists had reached the Kanas and Gan, and the children were now in Cynna's care.

The children were why she was here. Oh, she would have come anyway if Sam had asked it of her. Or if Lily had, and possibly if Rule had. They had not needed to ask, however, because the spawn had taken children.

Li Lei could not protect all children everywhere. This grieved her, for all children should be protected, but she was a realist. Toby, however, had become hers. More, he had become the tiger's. And the tiger spirit that was her heritage, the gift and charge that had been passed down for generations from mother to daughter—or from grandmother to granddaughter, and at least once from great-grandmother to great-granddaughter—existed for one reason. To protect the young.

Cynna knelt on the ground, holding her Ryder in one arm, her other arm around a boy of four or so who clung to her. She spoke to the oldest boy—Diego, that would be—who cradled the smallest of them to his shoulder protectively. Grandmother turned a bit of her attention that way so she could listen in . . .

". . . let Gan take him now, Diego." Cynna's voice sounded raw. Tears will do that. "We want to get the babies out first."

Diego shook his head firmly. "Toby gave him to me to take care of. I have to stay with him."

Toby, Li Lei thought, was a fine boy. Very smart. He would grow into a fine man—though that would go easier if his father kept him from eating anyone. Toby would take it very hard later if he ate someone now. He'd rolled over onto his back, however, and was displaying his vulnerable belly to the huge wolf standing over him. A good sign. She hoped someone brought him those chickens quickly.

A particularly hard jab on one side of the ward followed by softer pokes drew every bit of her attention to her juggling act. The poking went on and on, with a harder jab now and then. Her ward held. Her control held. The earth shook again and again—small shimmies, but too many.

At last they paused in their poking. She blinked, noticing her surroundings for the first time after her long absorption. She was surrounded by Kanas. They stood three-deep around her.

The tiger stirred, alarmed.

The tiger was both ageless and very old. It was wise and unwise, vast and starkly limited. It was all conundrum and contradiction, and it knew what it knew. Some of what it knew, it shared easily with Li Lei—the muscular joy of movement, the wild elation of rending the prey's flesh with teeth and claws. Some of what it knew she could not touch. And some knowledge it shared, but in sideways glimpses, hard to understand.

She had no precognition herself, and she had not lived long enough as dragon to develop the ability to read patterns, a skill that awoke in them after the first few centuries.

But the tiger was spirit. Spirit was not as time-bound as flesh.

"Get back!" she ordered the people standing around her. "Do not stand so close to me!"

THIRTY-FIVE

~

TOO many people in the crowded space beneath Grandmother's ward, Lily thought, and not enough spawn overhead—which was a seriously strange thing to think, but where the hell were Kongqi and Dick Boy? She didn't buy Shēngwù's scornful answer to Alice's question. They hadn't run off, but where were they? Dead?

"Lead us to your crossing spot," she told Gan, and chivvied the people around her into following the small orange being who could save the children. She wanted the lot of them to clutter up a different spot—Gan's crossing spot. If they were really lucky, the crowd might keep the spawn from noticing it when their targets started disappearing.

The spawn were too furious to think with their usual cold precision, and they were not good at working together. Lily could only be glad of that. The three overhead had first called down contradictory orders to the Fists, and were now arguing about it. The Fists had no way to sort out which orders to follow.

Alice went with Lily. "I do not know a great deal about lupi," she said as the spawn argued overhead. "Did the stress of capture precipitate this First Change for the boy?"

Lily just shook her head, not knowing the answer or if she'd give it to Alice if she had. Toby wasn't supposed to enter First Change until he entered puberty. Rule was supposed to be able to smell it when Toby's hormones shifted, signaling that period. Admittedly, puberty was a process, not a moment, but dammit, Rule should have known.

With Toby, there was an additional fear about First Change. They'd had a strong indication that he was susceptible to the wild cancer, which was cancer on steroids, with tumors and growths overtaking pretty much all of the body. Lupi were only vulnerable to the wild cancer at two points in their lives—at the very end and right after First Change. This was why Rule had resisted creating an heir for Leidolf for so long. When he made someone heir, he placed a portion of the mantle in the man. And Rule had intended that portion to go to Toby. Some quality of the mantle prevented the wild cancer from setting up shop.

But just before they'd left Earth for Dis, Rule had given in and placed the heir's portion in a Leidolf high dominant named Mateo Ortiz. If Rule died without an heir, the mantle was lost. With it would go much of the sanity of an entire clan. So the heir's portion of the mantle was back on an Earth, where it did them no good at all.

Toby looked okay, though. He looked normal, for a value of normal that included four legs instead of two. Lily wished desperately she could smell Toby the way Rule could so that she'd know. The wild cancer was supposed to have a distinctive scent. Hell, she wished she could just touch Toby. Stroke him. But right now he didn't know who she was, and he wouldn't for several days. Maybe a couple weeks.

"WHERE'S Kongqi? And D—" At the last second she kept herself from calling him Dick Boy. "Dìqiú?"

Alice frowned. "I think the Zhu Shēngwù apparated them elsewhere. I did not know he could to do that. I had not thought it possible."

"Is apparate the same as teleport?"

"I enjoyed the Harry Potter books."

Which did not seem like an answer at all, but Lily let it drop.

Cynna was kneeling on the ground. Ryder had, amazingly,

fallen asleep in her mother's arms. The four-year-old—Sandy—leaned up against Cynna and Diego stood close, cradling Noah protectively and watching Cynna as if she held all the answers.

"You're certain you can take them both?" Cynna asked Gan.

"Doing it this way, I can." Gan nodded wisely. "They're little and Edge is easy to cross to, even from here. But not the wolf." Gan cast a quick glance across the warded area at where Rule stood beside his panting, agitated son. He'd gotten Toby as far from everyone else as possible. "I can't take him. He'd eat me."

"No, you can't."

Overhead, the spawn continued to argue, but not as loudly. Lily couldn't hear them well. At her feet, the ground gave a delicate shiver. Three-point-something, she thought, and tried to ignore how frequently it was happening because she couldn't do a damn thing about it.

Cynna looked at the four-year-old clinging to her side. "Sandy, you have to go with Gan now. She'll take you to a place called Edge. A lot of the people there will look funny to you. Have you ever met a gnome?"

Sandy shook his head solemnly.

"They're small, like Gan. They'll take care of you and Ryder and see that you get home."

Sandy's bottom lip quivered. "I want to go home. I want to go home real bad."

"You are. It will take time to get there, but you're on your way home now." She encouraged Sandy with a little push on his bottom, and the boy took three small steps to join Gan. Cynna took a shuddery breath and held Ryder out. Ryder woke up and started to wail, reaching for her mother.

Gan's eyes widened. "It's screaming!"

The ground shuddered once. Stopped.

"Babies do that sometimes," Cynna said. "And Ryder's a she, not an it."

"It's weird how you people get a sex when you're so new. You don't even get to pick."

Cynna huffed out a shaky laugh, stood, and bent and kissed her crying daughter, avoiding the reaching arms. Then she kissed Gan's forehead.

Gan rolled her eyes. "Cynna, we can't do sex now!"

"That was a friend's kiss, not a sex kiss. Now go."

"Okay," Gan said, and grabbed Sandy with her free arm, pulling him up tight against her.

Then they were gone.

Cynna just stood there, staring at the empty spot with red eyes.

The spawn didn't react. They must not have seen Gan take the children away. Lily breathed a huge sigh of relief and moved close to her friend, touching Cynna's arm. "You okay?"

"I just sent my baby off with *Gan*. Gan doesn't know how to change a diaper. She probably doesn't know which end to diaper. Not that she has any diapers, so I guess that doesn't matter."

"They're bound to have diapers in Edge, and people who know how to change them."

"I think Sandy knows how to change a diaper," Diego offered.

The boy looked so young and lost, standing stock-still clutching tiny Noah to him. Lily wanted to make everything okay for him, too. And couldn't. "You know why Gan took Sandy and Ryder first?"

"Because they're so little. I'm older, so I can wait. It doesn't seem very fair to Noah, though. He's the littlest of us."

"I cheated," Cynna said, sounding weary. "I sent my baby to safety first."

Diego frowned but said grudgingly, "I guess my mom would've cheated for me, too, if she could have."

Ah Hai was one of the Kanas in this group. She moved forward, smiling, and touched Diego's shoulder and told him in Chinese what a fine, brave boy he was.

He looked faintly alarmed.

"Ah Hai is really nice," Lily told him. "She—"

"They've decided," Alice said suddenly.

Lily tipped her head back to stare up at the three circling figures above them.

Tú'àn called down to the Fists. "Your Zhuren now agree. Two squads of Fists will go with all speed and return with the spears. The rest of you are to capture or kill the old woman. Capture is better. Go!"

Quiet time was over. "All of you Kanas, keep this spot

clear so Gan can cross back," she ordered, and started toward Grandmother at a run.

So did a bunch of the Fists. The rest sprinted away to get the damn spears—those huge iron spears she'd seen before. Spears that took two men to carry. The weapons they'd brought out when a wild dragon buzzed the city.

The Kanas who'd stayed near the tower had moved at some point. They now stood in front of Grandmother, shielding her with their bodies.

The ground moved. Another gentle quake, but it lasted longer.

Lily took up position in front of the Kanas—in front of Grandmother—and prepared to kill people. But could she kill ten men before they reached her?

No.

"Get back!" Grandmother ordered. "Do not stand so close to me!"

Lily steadied her weapon and shot a man. Out of the corner of her eye she glimpsed Rule running toward her—no, toward the Fists. And Toby ran beside him.

Lily got off two quick shots. Hit with one, missed with the other. Rule took down one man too swiftly for Lily to say what exactly what he'd done, except that it involved screaming and blood. Toby lunged for another man—

And the earth rolled like the ocean beneath her feet.

Lily didn't fall. The stance she'd been trained to take kept her knees flexed, and she rode the suddenly liquid earth as it bucked beneath her. Screams—behind her, all around her, and the sound of rock scraping. Falling. Most of the Fists fell, and someone behind her did, too, knocking into her and accomplishing what the quake hadn't. She fell as well.

So did the ward.

She felt it, a blast of power that stung every exposed inch of skin as she rolled, and she pushed to one knee and looked all around.

People were sprawled all over. The tower was missing its red-Frisbee cap. The tower itself seemed whole, but it listed slightly to one side. Someone called out to move, get away from the tower; someone on the tower's other side said something about getting the blood stopped. Lily couldn't see who was bleeding. At the base of the tower, Grandmother lay flat on the ground with one of the Kanas—a young man—sprawled half on top of her. She'd been knocked out of her position, the center spot she had to hold in order to hold the ward.

The young man moved, pushing himself off her. Grandmother didn't.

"I'll get her!" came a shout from above. "You two get *him!*"

Lily rose to both knees and pointed her weapon up. The spawn swooping down at them was an easy target, his white robe seeming almost to gather what light remained against the dusk of the sky, but he moved fast. Too fast. She fired. She fired over and over. But either she missed with every shot or the spawn could bounce bullets off his chest like Superman. He swept down to within about ten feet and Grandmother's limp body started to rise.

Two wolves leaped at him. However good his bullet repellent might be, he couldn't bounce wolves off his chest.

Toby's jaws locked on his ankle. Rule hit him higher—probably aiming for the throat, but the spawn got his arm up in time. Rule's jaws closed on that arm. For a split second they seemed to hang there, but pain or the shock of the assault must have distracted the spawn, or maybe the addition of Rule's and Toby's weight was too much for his TK to support. They fell.

The wolves lost their grips on their prey when they hit the ground a scant six feet from Lily. Rule recovered immediately, leaping atop the downed spawn while Toby was still trying to scramble to his feet. Rule lunged for the spawn's throat—and stiffened, his back arcing unnaturally, a high-pitched whine rising from his throat as he collapsed, stiff and still, on his side. The spawn rose up on one elbow, pointing at Rule, and she saw which one it was—Shēngwù, the master of body magic. Shēngwù, who'd just practiced his art on Rule.

Lily wasn't really aware of crossing the small space between them. Dimly she noticed her knees hitting the dirt beside Shēngwù, who twisted to point that finger at her. Magic swept over her, a prickling on her face, as she jammed the muzzle of her Glock against the beautiful Shēngwù's skull and squeezed the trigger, wondering if the bullet would bounce back into the barrel and her Glock would explode in her hand.

The gun bucked. Blood and brains and bits of bone flew every-damn-where.

"Bounce *that*," Lily snarled at the dead man and scrambled over his body to reach Rule, who wasn't moving—wasn't fucking breathing, she discovered as she ran her hands over him, bent, and pressed her ear to his chest, but she found no heartbeat. But he wasn't dead, couldn't be dead, because the mate bond wasn't broken, and she brought both fists down together on his chest, hoping to surprise his heart into a restart.

And the other wolf, the one who didn't know he was Toby, growled low in his throat at her, teeth bared, head down. He stood on only three legs, but he stood close. Much too close.

Rule's chest heaved suddenly. He made a hacking sound like a cat with a furball and sucked air in audibly.

"Lily!" Cynna called. "Get back! Back away. Toby's defending his Rho."

Lily didn't answer. Didn't move. She was pretty sure that movement would send Toby springing at her.

Rule shoved to his feet. His sides heaved as if the movement had been a great effort, but he stood, placing his body between Lily and his son, baring his teeth at Toby—who stopped growling and ducked his head, not in the about-to-spring way, but in submission. He looked confused. Rule looked like he was about to fall over.

A man screamed.

She twisted and saw one of the Fists on his knees beside Shēngwù's body. He was keening, grief twisting his features. More of the Fists raced up and Lily started backing away. They didn't seem to notice as they cried out, some of them calling for the master to heal himself. Until one of them screamed, "They have killed him! Kill them! Kill them all!"

Uh-oh.

That man charged straight at her, sword swinging. Lily brought her weapon up, squeezed the trigger—and ducked at the last second when her weapon failed to fire.

Out of ammo. Out of ammo because she was a bloody idiot and hadn't exchanged the partly used clip for a full one. Lily cursed as she backed up rapidly, fumbling in her sash for another clip as the man charged again. She twisted, ducked, kept moving, and saw Rule start to charge at the man's back—and stumble. And fall. Whatever Shēngwù had done to him, he hadn't really recovered.

The Fist kept coming, wild with grief and rage, which made his strikes powerful but uncontrolled. She could evade him, but two more Fists were coming up behind him.

And she couldn't find the clips. Either of them.

Dammit to bloody hell. They'd fallen out of her sash some-where along the way.

Behind her, Grandmother started to sing. It was an odd song, wordless and high-pitched, built of quarter notes. Magic patted Lily's skin with sticky fingers.

The Fist trying so hard to split her open faltered to a stop, blinking. The two Fists behind him slowed, swaying unsteadily. One by one, all three sank to the ground.

So did the Kanas near the tower, Lily saw with a quick glance around. The other Fists collapsed the same way, a gen-tle surrender to gravity as their knees folded and their eyes closed. The Kanas guarding the crossing spot lay down and slept, as did the eight-year-old boy who waited for his turn at safety, a baby still clutched in his arms. The wolves were the last to succumb, but soon they, too, slept.

Grandmother sat with her back to the stone tower, her face pale as chalk as she finished her wordless song. The only ones still awake on the trampled circle of grass around the tower were her, Lily, Cynna, and Alice. Mind magic, Lily realized. Grandmother had sung them all to sleep using a form of mind magic, and Alice and Cynna had shields against that, though Cynna's didn't work against mindspeech.

Alice walked up to Shēngwù's blood-spattered body. His head was a gory mess. His beautiful face was almost un-touched. "You are hard on my family, Lily Yu," she said quietly.

Lily didn't say, "Your family keeps trying to kill mine." No point. Instead she looked around—and up—calling out as she did, "Grandmother? Are you okay?"

"Backlash," Grandmother muttered, cradling her head in both hands. "I did not die, so it will pass. I will not be able to bring up the ward for some time."

The remaining two spawn had flown over to the Justice Court. Lily couldn't see them clearly. There was a grass fire between here and there and smoke hazed the air. She heard them, though—they were arguing again.

And she had to get to Rule. She didn't question that, just stuck her useless weapon back in the sash, tightened it, and headed for him. She did pause briefly to take swords away from sleeping Fists. One she slung several feet away; the other two she brought with her.

Not that she intended to use them. Benedict had told her that unless she trained with a sword, she was better off without one. *Use what you* know, he'd said. *You're good at unarmed combat. You can defend yourself better without a sword than with one if you don't know what to do with the damn thing.* Since he'd gone on to demonstrate what he meant by handing her a practice blade and then "killing" her three times in under a minute, she'd believed him. But at least those three Fists would wake up without their weapons.

The two wolves lay close together. She set down the swords and knelt between the sleeping wolves, putting a hand on each furry rib cage . . . and felt the slow, gentle movement of their breathing. Her own breath hitched in something like a sob. Alive. Both of them alive. She'd known that, dammit, she'd been sure of it, and yet one corner of her mind hadn't believed it until this second. As long as Rule was alive, he could heal whatever the spawn had done to him.

"Is that iron?" Cynna asked from several feet away. "It looks like iron."

She looked up, saw Cynna standing near the crossing spot. She was holding Noah and staring at the Justice Court. Lily looked. The grass fire put out enough smoke to haze the air, but she could see the two enemy spawn. One of them dipped low and grabbed one of the oversized spears from the two men who'd brought it out. He lifted it with one hand. With one bloody hand.

"The spears? Yeah, I saw them when that other dragon showed up. They're iron."

"Iron's bad. Maybe really bad."

"Why?"

"Iron—especially old iron, rusty iron—disrupts shaped magic. Spells. Which probably includes whatever Reno's doing. Not that I know what he's doing, so I can't be sure the spears could get through his protection. But they might. No, they *should*, based on what I do know."

Tú'àn and Shuǐ were arguing again. Or maybe they were giving orders to the Fists or planning their strategy. Lily couldn't hear them clearly, but she caught a few words. One of them was *fùchóu*. Vengeance.

Reno was a big, fat, sitting duck hanging there in the air, oblivious, tranced out or something while he tried to save this world. And probably their own, because if the Great Bitch could bring all of her power with her to Earth . . . Lily shivered in the heat. "Have you got anything you can use on the spawn?"

"The charms I made might work," Cynna said bitterly. "If I had them. The spawn are too far away for any of my quickie offensive spells—if those would even work on them, which they probably wouldn't. I don't know if they're as immune to magic as you are—"

"Not truly immune," Alice said. She stood beside Shēngwù's body still, about halfway between Lily and Cynna. She was watching her great-uncles intently. "They are naturally resistant to magic and can enhance this natural resistance. I do not understand how the Zhu Shēngwù was able to apparate Zhu Kongqi and—"

With a loud, percussive *pop*, Dick Boy appeared overhead. And roared. It was not a true dragon's roar, but it was ungodly loud—and in the middle of it, Kongqi popped into place close by. Both spawn were dripping wet. Dick Boy's *shenyi* was gone. Kongqi still wore his, sodden and dripping and stained with what looked like blood.

Dick Boy bellowed a name: "Shēngwù!"

"He is dead," Alice called.

"Dead?" Startled, Dick Boy looked down and scowled. "Who robbed me of the chance to slit his treacherous throat?"

At the Justice Court, more pairs of Fists emerged carrying spears. One of those spears floated up through the air into the second spawn's outstretched hand.

"Chat later!" Lily yelled up at them. "Your brothers are about to try to kill Reno!"

The two enemy spawn had seen their brothers. One of them gave a roar a lot like Dick Boy's and shook his spear. The other whizzed off—and as he did, the grass fire went out. On the ground, the Fists started jogging this way—two full squads with three extras. Thirteen of them, four still paired up so they could carry two of the spears, the rest with their swords out and ready.

Kongqi called out a word Lily didn't know and zoomed over to the Fists. He grabbed one of the iron spears and tossed it to Dick Boy—who had followed, but was still at least thirty feet back and twenty feet higher up. Then he grabbed the last spear.

"What are they doing?" Cynna cried. "I thought they were defending Reno."

"They will attempt to do so." Alice sounded certain. "The spears are very dangerous, however. They carry death. I wish the Zhu Kongqi had paused long enough to give new instructions to those Fists, however. I do not want Lily Yu to shoot any more of them."

I would if I could, Lily thought. Thirteen Fists coming, and she was out of rounds. Grandmother still sat with her head in her hands. No ward coming up anytime soon. Rule and Toby still slept. A single swordsman could slice open both their throats.

"Does anyone see my clips? I need my damn clips!"

"Not over here," Cynna called back.

She could defend Rule and Toby against unarmed men. Not against swordsmen. They would kill Rule. They would kill Toby, who wasn't *useful* now that he'd Changed. She shook Rule. He didn't stir. "Alice, can you help Grandmother get over to Cynna?" Cynna was the only one who could offer any sort of protection right now.

"No. I will assist Cynna. They will send the greatest number of Fists to retake the boy, I believe. What clips do you seek?"

"The ones you sent for my gun. They fell out. Grandmother—can you walk if I help you?"

Grandmother muttered without looking up. "Not yet. Lily, wake Rule."

Alice went on in her unruffled way as she walked over to Cynna. "I didn't send your weapon and ammunition to you. The Zhu Kongqi did."

"He—" Lily cut that off and stole a quick glance upward.

The spawn's white robes almost glowed against a sky gone creamy pink in the west, where Kongqi had intercepted Tú'àn. The two of them were dueling with those oversized spears that "carried death"—whatever that meant. Shuǐ was darting around Reno, pursued by Dick Boy. "He didn't just now change sides?"

"Surely you are aware that he has been helping you since you passed his test. The Zhu Dìqiú has, also, although his aid has been more deeply hidden."

"Dìqiú?" Lily's voice was sharp with disbelief. She shook her head. If they had a "later," they could talk about it then. "I can't wake him up, Grandmother. I've tried."

"Use your mind, child," Grandmother snapped.

Use her . . . oh. Mindspeech. Maybe she could wake him with mindspeech. Easily, fluidly, she touched Rule's mind. *Rule. Wake up. We need you. Toby needs you.*

"Did I get the time right?" Gan's high-pitched voice was squeaky with excitement or anxiety. "I kept poking until I found a time close to when I left, but I couldn't tell *how* close it is. Why is everyone asleep? Did we win?"

"Not yet," Cynna said grimly. "They're safe? Ryder and Sandy—they're okay?"

"Sure! I stayed there awhile because I could, you know, with the times being so crooked. It isn't *now* yet in Edge. It will be when I go back, but it isn't yet. The gnomes are taking care of them."

Cynna let out a single, harsh sob. "Okay. Okay, good. Here, take Noah. I'll get Diego." She thrust the sleeping baby into Gan's arms.

The Fists were nearly here. Lily kept calling Rule. She'd never tried to mindspeak someone who was asleep before. She knew the pulses of her words were sinking into his mind . . . which felt/looked softer than his waking mind. The forest colors were the same . . . no, not quite. They were darker, and there was a little smudge of solid blue right here . . .

"I can incapacitate four of them," Alice was saying. "I do not know your capabilities, Cynna. How many can you stop?"

Lily ran her mindsense over the blue smudge. It was both slick and sticky, like double-sided tape. It felt wrong, yet familiar . . .

"I don't know," Cynna said tersely. She picked Diego up. It

took both arms, and the boy was utterly limp. "I can kill some, though."

"I do not wish them killed."

"I don't wish *us* killed," Cynna snapped. "Gan—"

"I can't take him like that!" Gan protested. "You have to wake him up!"

. . . the stickiness felt like the magic that had patted her face when Grandmother sang. Yes. The blue smudge had to go. But how to get it off?

"I can't," Cynna said. "Why can't you take him when he's asleep? Noah's asleep."

Fingernails were good for peeling off tape. She thought about fingernails as she reshaped her mindsense.

"Because I'm already holding Noah and that one's bigger and he's all droopy and I can't hold him up against me! I have to have lots of him touching me or all of him won't cross with me!"

"Diego should wake soon," Cynna said, "but don't wait. Take Noah to Edge now. Come back for Diego as close to now as you can."

Lily pried up one edge of the sticky blue. The rest of it came loose and evaporated.

THIRTY-SIX

CYNNA stood over a sleeping boy and readied herself to stop a man's heart.

She'd killed demons before. Not people. Not beings with souls and confusion and loved ones and lives that they badly wanted to live. But she had no other weapon, no gentler way of stopping the men who would take Diego so that the spawn could destroy him. And no way could she let them do that.

She couldn't hold the heart-stopper spell. It had to be discharged as soon as it was invoked or it would stop her own heart. And the range was only about ten feet. So she waited as swordsmen charged toward them, toward her and Diego, the silent Alice, and the sleeping Kanas.

No, she realized—the mostly sleeping Kanas. Some of them were stirring, the sleep spell wearing off. How long until the other Fists awoke, too?

She'd fantasized about killing two of the spawn, burned and ached to do just that. Especially Dick Boy, who'd killed that other boy with such offhand cruelty, like swatting a fly. But now it seemed that Dick Boy and Kongqi were on their side, or were at least trying to keep their brothers from killing Reno. And now that Cynna could kill, she wished badly that she didn't have to.

Life was one big, fat, confusing bitch sometimes, she thought, and prepared to shout the words of the spell.

LILY was calling him. Rule's eyes opened as his nose flooded him with scents.

Lily, smoke, blood, other humans. Toby, his wolf-scent so new and surprising. The rose-flesh-and-cinnamon smell of the spawn he'd fought. The acrid sting of gunpowder and the released bowels of death.

Thank God, Lily said, her mind-voice clear and crisp. *I killed Shēngwù. Grandmother put everyone to sleep so the Fists wouldn't kill me. I'm out of ammo. She can't put the ward back up. I don't think she can walk. Cynna's got Diego. Gan's taken the other kids to Edge. Toby's asleep. Kongqi and Dick Boy are dueling with the remaining two enemy spawn with huge iron spears that Cynna thinks could break into Reno's protection, and thirteen Fists are about to attack us.*

It was an elegant and terrifying summary, completed by the time he'd lurched to his feet. His body felt stiff, as if whatever the spawn had done to him still clung, but it responded. He shook his head to clear it . . . and slid into *certa*. A single glance told him everything. That, and what his ears picked up.

They were trying to hold two points, the crossing spot and the gate. And they couldn't. He opened himself to the moon's call and threw himself into it. And Changed.

The pain was one crisp bite of agony and over. "Cynna! Bring Diego here! Quickly!"

"No! Gan—the Kanas—"

There was no time to explain. "Run!" he roared at her. He bent and slid his arms beneath Toby's new form, limp with sleep, and said to Lily, "Get the swords." The ones he'd seen next to her in that single glance. He lifted Toby. Even in *certa* his heart ached for his son, catapulted into combat and a new body at the same moment, bereft of memory, knowing only instinct and fear. They fought so hard to keep First Change from being like this!

But both thought and the ache were distant. Acknowledged, like the wounds on his own body, but only one part of the gestalt of this moment.

Cynna had obeyed and was bending to pick up Diego. Lily had the swords. Grandmother was only a few feet away. Near her, two of the Kanas were waking. One sat up. Three seconds passed as he crossed those few feet and laid Toby down next to the woman who sat, face chalky and eyes closed, leaning against the tower as if she'd fall over without its support. He turned and took one of the swords from Lily. He was not skilled with a sword, but he knew the basics. His speed should make up some for his lack of expertise—if he could move quickly. If his body had finished throwing off that cursed spell.

"Grandmother," he said tersely, moving the unfamiliar sword through a few parries, testing how his body responded. "Can you call the tiger?"

"No."

Cynna was almost here, the sleeping boy in her arms. The pale woman hadn't followed her, but stood frowning thoughtfully at the Fists about to reach her—most of whom were now swerving. They'd been aimed for Cynna. For Diego. The boy was the primary target. Did the spawn realize yet that he was the only one of the children still here?

Except for Toby, that ache in his heart whispered. Toby, who had been catapulted out of childhood and into the terrifying shoals of adolescence. Who was no longer vulnerable to having his Gift reft from him, but his life could still be taken.

Cynna slid Diego to the ground and straightened quickly. "Dammit, Rule, I can take out three or four, and Alice said she could get four—"

"Blind them," he told her and, at her obvious incomprehension, snapped, "Your light spell. The bright one. Blind them."

A grin of pure elation flashed over her face and she faced the Fists, spoke five quick syllables, and tossed a brilliant light right in the faces of the ones in the lead. They stumbled to a stop, causing most of the others to stop, too, or to swerve. Giving Rule's party precious seconds.

"Grandmother," he said, "you and Cynna have to open the gate now."

"We cannot." Her voice was thin and flat and certain.

"Then we have a problem," he said as the first rank of Fists came into view. The ones he'd heard jogging toward them when he slid into *certa*. The Fists—a full fifty, he judged—led by a man who must be Fist Second Fang.

"GRANDMOTHER," Rule asked, "can you call the tiger?"

Li Lei gave Rule's question a small part of her attention and told him no. Most of what focus she could summon remained fixed on the gate, which she studied with her eyes closed.

The gate was damaged.

It had been tied, in part, to the structure of the tower. This was not as foolish as it seemed, for the tower, too, was anchored. But that anchoring involved Earth magic, and that had been badly disrupted when power spilled and caused the earthquake. The tower had been damaged; therefore, the gate was, also. The damage seemed to be limited to the way the gate was tied to the tower. The gate still stood. It might even be usable. She could not tell. She was no expert at gates.

At this moment she was glad for eyelids, which imposed some limit on pain. Her head hurt. It hurt so badly that it almost eclipsed the pain in every other part of her body, which seemed to be circulating fire instead of blood. She had not experienced a backlash this severe since she was seventeen, when she had used mage fire in an attempt to kill an undying being. That act of desperation had not worked out well in the short term, as it had all but killed her as well as wiping out a large portion of a city. The long-term results had been surprisingly wonderful, however.

She was not at all sure the same could be said for today's act of desperation.

One does not use magic when suffering from backlash. Normally one cannot, so for most people the issue does not arise. But she had seen three swordsmen coming at her granddaughter, who had no more bullets, and Rule had still been affected by the spawn's spell—an obscenely thorough "freeze" spell, she believed, one which stopped all muscles, including the heart, the diaphragm, and those involved in lifting the rib cage with each breath. Sun knew two similar spells, or possibly three; she had chosen not to learn them. She considered it an unnecessarily cruel way to kill.

When Lily had killed the spawn who was killing Rule, she

had cut off the spell's power. The spell had immediately begun to dissipate, but it had still been present. Rule had not been able to act. And so she had.

Not with a spell. Even she could not shape a spell while suffering backlash. She had told Cynna Weaver that her ability to send sleep was a dragon trick, which was a fair description. Sending sleep was as much a part of her as walking, breathing, or ensorcellment, and so was available to her as long as she was conscious. Her singing had, however, been a working, a way to extend the reach of her sending. Without it, she could send sleep only to those close enough to touch. Such a working was not truly a spell, but it had undoubtedly worsened the backlash.

Li Lei did not approve of desperation. It was quite lowering to find that she could still succumb to it at her age. She could not raise the ward. She could not call the tiger. She was not at all sure she could stand up.

Rule spoke to her again. "Grandmother, you and Cynna have to open the gate now."

"We cannot," she told him.

"Then we have a problem."

"Yeah," Lily said, her voice tight. "That's Fang. He's brought his fifty back from the city."

Li Lei pried open her eyelids and squinted out at disaster.

Dusk had not yet drawn its curtain on the day. The western sky wore its colors gently—pink rather than flame, a soft yellow misting into pale apricot where it blended with the pink. There in the west, a dragon the color of wet moss floated in *di'shai* while his children hurtled around him, a confusion of magics and power filling the air as they tried to kill him or one another. Down here, below that soft sky, people were about to die. The wrong people, curse it. And she could not *see* what was happening. Her view was eclipsed by those who would protect her if they could.

Li Lei summoned strength and slowly, carefully, rose to her feet, one hand on the stone of the tower. There she swayed, seeking balance that had deserted her in the loudness of pain.

The Fists she'd put to sleep still slept, but others had arrived. In that first second she watched one of them fall when Alice Báitóu pointed at him. But there were more, several of them much too close. Farther off were the ranks of men Lily had called a fifty, trotting briskly their way.

Rule engaged the nearest man with a sword. Cynna shouted a series of syllables and threw light in the face of another man, making him stumble. Lily cursed and threw a rock, which almost made Li Lei smile. Lily did not like being unable to act.

Neither did she.

She thought of a monk who had died before she could speak with him again. Of a woman who had lived her entire life in a small village in Tibet, and a man she had known over a hundred years ago, a man with a laugh so full and rich she could almost have subsisted just on the wealth of that laugh. Children's faces flickered through her mind, children she had helped, had loved, where she could. And the face of her own son just after birthing, tiny and perfect, a bottomless joy. And the face of his father, wise in his way, patient, and dear. *Sun*, she thought. And *Li Qin*. Two great loves as different and as alike as sunrise and sunset. She wished the one could be here and was glad the other was not.

She had always been selfish that way. "Bah," she said, deeply annoyed by her impending death.

Rule fought two Fists now. Lily somehow dodged another one's sword and flipped him onto his back like a turtle. Li Lei wished she had seen that, but things were happening quickly now. Cynna spoke different syllables—hard syllables, edged with a darker magic. When she hurled this spell, there was no light at its end. Only death. Most of the Kanas had woken and the old man spoke, the one who had spoken for Reno, telling them to form their wall of bodies again.

"No," Li Lei said sharply. "That is death without purpose."

And some ten feet away, a small orange figure popped into view. Gan was fuzzy to Li Lei, which meant she was *dashtu*, which was good. At least one of their number would live through this.

Li Lei expected Gan to see what was happening and pop back into Edge and safety. Instead she screamed, "Lily Yu!" and started running, pumping her short legs. Li Lei's gaze flicked back to her granddaughter in time to see Lily hit the ground, having stumbled over a body—a man dead or asleep, she could not tell and did not care. Another Fist, very much alive and awake, jumped over that body and swung his sword back for a stroke.

Gan jumped at him. With all the foolish, heartbreaking courage of the young, she leaped at him—every inch of her clearly visible. Not in *dashtu* anymore, for she couldn't connect with the world in that state. The Fist reacted automatically, altering his stroke to meet this new threat.

His sword slid into the middle of Gan's chest.

And the tiger called *her*.

LILY didn't know who cried out as ten feet of Siberian tiger leaped onto the back of the Fist who'd cut down Gan. Maybe it was her. All she could think of, all she could see as she scrambled over to her friend, was the blood spurting out from the hole in Gan's chest. The red, red blood ruining the many-pocketed khaki shirt.

Gan lay on her back, her eyes huge and shocked in a face bleached of color. "Ow, ow, ow."

"Hold still," Lily said, and untied her sash. "One of the Kanas is a healer. I'll get her. She'll help you."

"He killed my heart," Gan whispered.

"Shh. Don't try to talk." Frantically Lily folded the sash into a pad.

Gan groaned, her eyes rolling back in her head.

She couldn't see, dammit. Tears were no help, no help at all. She dashed them away angrily and called Ah Hai's name, trusting Grandmother to deal with the Fists—with any and all of them—as she pressed the pad she'd made against the wound.

The sky exploded.

White blanked out vision. Blanked out sound. For endless seconds Lily hung suspended in nothing but white, as if sound along with vision had been blasted out of existence. Then she heard a buzzing, high-pitched and irritating, as if she had mosquitos in her ears. The white began to break up in drifts of coruscating color as the buzzing subsided into voices.

Someone keened. Someone wept. Others called out to one another. Lily blinked rapidly as if that might help her stunned vision recover. And realized one of those voices belonged to Fist Second Fang.

". . . immediately. I repeat: Squads Four and Six, stand down."

"The Zhu Tú'àn gave us orders to—" someone shouted. "The beast will kill us!" came from a different voice.

Fang's voice was parade-ground loud. "My orders are from the Zhu Kongqi, who has jurisdiction over the Fists at this time. You will all stand down. Those confronting the orange beast may keep their swords at the ready as you back away slowly."

The dazzlement was clearing from Lily's eyes. She saw Grandmother crouched over the downed and very bloody body of a Fist, snarling at two other Fists who began to retreat one slow step at a time. Behind and to her left, the pair of Fists who'd been fighting Rule backed up, too. They scowled as they did it, but they lowered their swords.

Above them, an enormous dragon the color of wet moss whirled. His tail lashed out, knocking one frantically dodging spawn from the air. His head shot out—and his jaws closed around another spawn. He did not swallow. Instead he spit out the spawn—and that one, too, went tumbling through the air. Lily didn't see where either one went.

A single spawn remained airborne. Lily didn't know which one. He spoke, apparently addressing Reno, though his words were indistinct.

"I speak for her!" Ah Wen called in a voice too loud and deep for an old man's body. "Zhu Kongqi, you will retrieve your injured brother. Bring him to me when I land."

This was followed immediately by a familiar cold mental voice. *Humans near the tower must clear a space for me to land immediately. Those who will use the gate should gather next to it.*

This must have been sent to everyone, judging by the reactions of those around her. The Fists blanched and looked around wildly. The Kanas seemed awestruck but obedient, beginning to move right away.

"I can't," Lily said flatly. Her hand still pressed the pad to Gan's chest. It was scarlet, soaked through with blood. Gan's face was still that terrible bleached color. Her eyes were closed. "Gan's badly injured. Did you—was that—is the construct gone?"

She is not mortally injured. My son is. Move her next to the gate.

His son? Which one?

Rule reached her and pressed one hand to her shoulder. "The construct—"

Later.

"Is it over?" Cynna asked, her voice tight. She stood a few feet away, carrying Diego, who still slept. Like Toby. Like several of the Fists. "Is Gan—how bad is she hurt?"

Lily swallowed. "The sword went right in the center of her chest. She said he killed her heart."

An enormous, blood-spattered tiger padded up on Gan's other side. Grandmother bent and licked Gan's face, purring loudly.

Gan opened her eyes, scrunched her face up in a scowl, and spoke in a thin, disgruntled voice. "He did. I'm going to have to grow it again from scratch. It's a good thing I've got a spare."

THIRTY-SEVEN

~

FANG cleared the area with a few snapped orders. The Fists he'd brought carried away the injured and the sleeping. The dead were allowed to remain for now.

Cynna laid Diego down next to the door that was also a gate. She sat next to him, cradling her broken arm with her good one. It was probably hurting. Rule moved Gan and Toby—Gan first. She gave out little squeaks of pain with every step. He settled Toby slightly apart. Eventually he would wake up and he wouldn't be safe company. Grandmother sat next to Gan and started grooming her gory fur, and Lily hurried to retrieve Rule's pants and the charm necklace he'd lost when he Changed. She'd spotted them earlier while looking for her clips, which were still missing, dammit. He raised his brows when she handed them to him—clothing was not his priority— but slipped the chain over his head and was pulling up the pants when Reno descended.

In the fading light, he looked more black than green as he reached for earth with his taloned feet, the great wings out at first, then folding. As they did, two of his sons arrived. Kongqi floated down in the usual upright position, one hand on his brother's shoulder as he guided him gently to the earth in front of Reno. Dick Boy wasn't upright. He didn't look injured. He looked dead. His eyes were half-closed, only the whites showing. His white *shenyi* was torn and bloody. It looked like he'd been struck by one of the spears.

Reno lay on the ground, half-curled around his two sons. The old man—Ah Wen—walked up and knelt beside Dick Boy. Dìqiú. Whatever. "I speak for her," he said, but his voice was quiet now. Subdued. "Jiānqiáng. I am with you."

Cynna, next to Lily, whispered, "What did he say?"

Oh. Right. Cynna couldn't understand. Lily whispered a translation as Dìqiú's eyelids twitched. Slowly his eyes opened fully. He stared up at the enormous dragon looking down at him, eyes lambent in the dusk. "Mother." His voice was weak, thready. "Can you . . ."

"I cannot," Ah Wen/Reno said sadly. "You and your brothers wrought too well with your death spells."

"I missed you." A pause. "Mother . . ." His voice was a thread now.

"I am here."

"Did I do the right thing? I tried, but . . ."

"You did well, my son, my Jiānqiáng. You did very well. I am proud of you."

His face relaxed in what might have been a smile as his breath sighed out. He did not inhale again.

Lily's throat felt tight. Her eyes burned as if she might cry, and that was absurd. Dick Boy had been a murdering sociopath. He'd killed a small child . . . and he'd loved his mother. Craved her approval. Maybe he had tried to do the right thing. Maybe he'd been too damaged to know what that was. She drew a shaky breath. And maybe she was way too emotional right now to think straight.

In the silence, two more bodies floated down from the sky—these bodies upright, alive, and bound with what looked like strands of faintly glowing air. Zhu Tú'àn and Zhu Shuǐ landed less gently, their knees buckling with the impact. Neither attempted to rise. Maybe they couldn't. Willingly or not, they knelt before the green dragon.

Ah Wen's voice was loud again, and cold. Icy cold. "You killed your brother."

Neither of the spawn replied for a very long moment. Finally Zhu Tú'àn—give him credit for guts—said coolly, "It was not our brother we were attempting to kill."

This time the silence went on. And on. About the time Lily thought she might confess to something, anything, to break it, Ah Wen/Reno spoke again. "My anger is too great for clear thinking. You will be placed in your living quarters until I am able to decide rationally what to do with you."

In the pause that followed, Lily whispered a quick translation.

Cynna did not whisper. "Did he just ground them and send them to their rooms?"

Reno must have heard. He ignored it. Nothing happened for several moments . . . "First Fist. I have placed the two errant Zhuren in stasis."

In stasis? Lily stared at the spawn . . . who were really, truly not moving now. Not breathing or blinking or—or anything. They looked like that bird in Kongqi's workroom. Hadn't he said it didn't work with mammals? "Uh—the First Fist is tied up," she said. "About that stasis thing—"

They cannot remain in stasis long, said the cold mental voice, *but they are well enough for now.* Even as Reno spoke silently to Lily, his head swung around to stare at Fist Second Fang as Ah Wen spoke aloud. "Fang Ye Lì. Your superior is dead. He was killed when the Zhuren caused an earthquake, which in turn caused the crystal topping their tower to fall, striking him. You are now First Fist."

Reno, she realized, must have been reading minds at superspeed. He seemed to have a pretty good grasp of how things were set up here.

Fang's eyes were wide. He thumped himself in the chest in salute. "Sir." A pause. "I do not know how to address you with proper courtesy."

"I am using the call-name Reno at this time. I do not use a title. 'Sir' is an acceptable signifier of respect. Have the Zhu Tú'àn and the Zhu Shuǐ taken to their rooms in the House of the Seven. I will release them from stasis when you inform me that satisfactory measures have been taken to secure them. Once released from stasis, they will be unable to perform any magic, which should make it easier for you to fulfill your duty.

I leave it to you to determine what those measures should be, with two stipulations. First, these measures must not take more than two days to implement. Second, the Zhuren are to be treated courteously."

Lily whispered her way through a rough translation, but sudden fury tightened her throat. Why hadn't he done this earlier? If it was so quick and easy for him to truss up the spawn, to keep them from using magic, why hadn't he done that right away? People had *died*. She knew. She'd killed a couple of them.

She had enough restraint not to hurl that question at Reno, who was answering some question of Fang's. Instead she reached for Grandmother's mind and hurled it at her.

"Quick and easy" is an advertising slogan, Grandmother snapped back, *not the product of actual thought. It is quick to shoot that gun of yours. It is also easy as long as you do not care where the bullets go.*

Okay, so it wasn't easy to bind their magic. But it was quick. Why didn't he at least try to—

He did. Before, they were not holding old iron. Once they took up the spears, their own protections were diminished.

As several of Fang's men moved forward to retrieve the immobile spawn, Alice's clear, calm voice rang out, startling Lily. She'd almost forgotten the woman was here. "Reno. Are we to understand that you are now in charge of the government?" Oddly, Alice spoke English.

Reno's head swung toward her. After a longish pause, Ah Wen/Reno replied in Chinese, "I have conferred with several of the Kanas. I am pleased with your efforts on several fronts, Báitóu Alice Li. I am in charge to the extent that my dictates must be followed, but I have no desire to order the affairs of this world. I will make this explicit so all will understand."

His next words might have come from a speaker mounted in the sky with the volume turned way up. "Residents of Lang Xin. I am called Reno. I am dragon. I affirm the continued authority of the Zhu Kongqi. He will be obeyed as long as his orders do not contradict mine. The orders of Báitóu Alice Li will also be obeyed as long they do not conflict with those of the Zhu Kongqi or myself. The Zhuren Tú'àn and Shuǐ have been removed from authority. The Zhuren Dìqiú and Shēngwù are dead. Official mourning will be delayed until the current emergency has ended."

"Tidiest coup ever," Rule murmured. "He just promised them continuity and stability. They'll go for it."

Lily glanced at him and let herself bask, for a moment, in the pure rightness of having him *here*. Right here beside her. "Yeah. Might may not make right, but it makes for a damned persuasive argument when it comes from a dragon."

Reno wasn't finished. He lost the amplified voice and switched to English—American English, a language Ah Wen couldn't possibly know. Lily suddenly understood why Alice had used it—to keep the exchange as private as possible. "Zhu Kongqi. I am aware that this is less than satisfactory for you. You cannot welcome my authority. I counsel patience. I still intend that this be your world, not mine. However, it is likely that in time other dragons will come, either to visit or to live, once the location of this world is known. It will be necessary to secure your territory in a way they respect. If you wish my counsel in this matter, we will have time to discuss and plan, for this will not happen soon. Events in other realms will occupy them for some time. For now, know that I do not intend to exert my authority beyond what is necessary in order to secure and educate your brothers, who have fallen into serious error in their thinking. You, however, were able to discern right action in a confused and difficult situation. I am," he said, his voice falling to a low rumble, "exceedingly proud of you, my son."

It might have been the failing light that made her think Kongqi's eyes sheened with sudden dampness. He bowed.

"We need to go," Rule said, low-voiced. "We need to get to Dis. Grandmother, the gate—"

A cold mental voice said, *Abide. Li Lei tells me the gate is damaged.*

"What?" Cynna cried out.

Restrain your panic. More specifically, she believes one of the gate's anchors is damaged. I will send Báitóu Alice Li to examine it. She has been maintaining the gate and may be able to strengthen or repair the anchor. Her Gift makes her particularly suited for such a chore. We have time for this. It will be approximately fifty-seven minutes before your past selves leave Dis. I will speak with Li Lei as soon as she returns to her usual form. She must learn how to send the correct signal through the node, or you will be unable to contact the gnomes.

Shit. Shit. Lily put both hands to her head and pressed as if she could squeeze coherent thought into it. They'd been relying on Gan to cross from Dis back to Earth to tell the gnomes where they needed their gate. Gan was down to her spare heart. "Gan can't do it?"

She can cross. Crossing does not burden her heart. Walking does. If she crossed at a node where the gnomes were not present, she would have no way of reaching them. No one else should address me until I speak to you again.

The gate was damaged. Their passage home from Dis was in doubt. Lily decided not to say any of the obvious things. "Fifty-seven minutes. How can Reno know that? How can it be right? It was late afternoon or early evening when Gan dumped me here. It must be two or three hours later than that now. Shouldn't it be the same time of day, if the times are in sync the way Alice said?" She rubbed her head. "Did that make any sense?"

"We talked all this out, remember, remember?" Cynna said. "Gan crossed time crookedly. She didn't get here at the now she left from. Not with any of us."

Lily just looked at her. Apparently she wasn't the only one who had trouble talking about it in a way that made sense.

Cynna sighed. "Just take the dragon at his word, okay?"

"Lily," Rule said. His voice sounded stiff. "If we can't leave yet, there's something I need to take care of. I need to speak with Alice or Kongqi. You said they both speak English."

She frowned at him. After a moment she realized what—and who—he was talking about. "We'll talk to Alice first."

"You don't need to—"

"I think I do."

MEI Ling was beautiful. This surprised Lily more than it should have. Rule hadn't said much about her other than she was lovely, infatuated, and very young. But Lily didn't think Rule had ever met a woman of any age he didn't find lovely in some way, so she was taken aback when faced with such glowing beauty.

Her father was pretty much the way she'd pictured him, though. Not wealthy, not powerful, but proud in his way, although deeply unsettled by the events of the day. And by his current company. His eyes were full of reproach when he looked at Rule, but he stood back and allowed his daughter to speak.

The boat father and his family had been in cells in the Justice Court. A squad of the city's contingent of Fists had brought them there about the time Reno showed up. The city Fists had somehow figured out that the Siji family had caused the invasion of the giant herd beasts. Maybe someone with a sorcery Gift had seen that the beasts were being called and been able to follow that call back to its source. Lily wasn't clear on that part. But Kongqi had agreed that they would not be held responsible once Rule explained—or confessed; there had been a distinct odor of the confessional in his terse account. He'd ordered them released.

Mei Ling had refused to go. Not without speaking to "Wu Tǔ Ní." And Rule wouldn't refuse her whatever satisfaction she might get from accusing him in person, and her father had naturally accompanied her.

Rule wasn't, Lily thought, thinking clearly. Guilt could do that to you.

She stood in front of him now, big eyes wet with tears, and asked him if it was true, what she'd been told—that she and her family had been under a compulsion created by "that terrible old woman."

Rule was wearing the translation charm. He understood her. "Tell her yes."

Lily did. This made Mei Ling's tears evaporate in a flash of anger. She gave Lily a dirty look. Lily didn't think Mei Ling had been told who she was. She turned those melting eyes back to Rule. "Then you were under compulsion, too. The old witch made you deceive us." The word she used also meant "hag" or "sorceress."

"No, Mei Ling," he said gently. "I knew what I was doing. I did it of my own will. I used you and your family. I needed . . . my son's life was at stake and I was desperate. That does not excuse me. It doesn't make what I did right."

Lily repeated what Rule said, word for word.

"Your . . . son," Mei Ling whispered. She closed her eyes

as a shiver traveled through her. When she opened them, she was staring at Lily, not Rule. "Who are you?"

"My name is Lily Yu."

"No, who *are* you? Why are you here? Why do you speak for him?"

"I am Rule's . . . the wife of Wu Tǔ Ní."

"You are a witch, too! Like the old hag!" She looked Lily up and down, clearly dismissing what she saw. "You have enspelled him."

"Lily," Rule started.

"No," she told him in English. "Let her make up her own story about it. She will anyway, and she needs someone to hate right now."

Mei Ling drew herself up proudly. She pressed one hand to her stomach. "You may be able to hold him with your sorceries, but I carry his *next* son." With that, she turned her back on both of them and asked her father, with what Lily was sure was deceptive meekness, if he would take her home now, to their boat.

As the two of them moved away, Rule spoke in a low, urgent voice. "Lily, she isn't—I didn't—"

She looked at his worried, guilty face, and shook her head. Then she took his hand. "I know that. Even if you had cheated on me—and you didn't. I know that. Everything else aside, she's only seventeen." And passionately in love with Wu Tǔ Ní . . . who was a story she'd told herself. A story Rule had encouraged her to tell, but it wasn't real.

Yet the feelings were real, even if they were fed by fantasy. Lily glanced at the retreating backs of the boat father and his daughter. She wouldn't go back to seventeen for anything. "You feel guilty, but not because you had sex with her. But you did use her, and in order to make her believe you wanted her, you had to let yourself want her. And that makes you feel like pond scum. As you should," she said, nodding approval. "It may have been necessary, but if you act like pond scum, you should feel like it. But even if I were wrong about everything and you had cheated on me . . . well, if she did carry your child, you'd know. And she'd probably be leaving with us, because there is no way in hell you'd abandon your child. No matter what it cost you, me, or the whole bloody world."

He blinked. After a moment he said slowly, "Have I mentioned lately that I love you?"

"It bears repeating."

His hand tightened on hers. "I love you."

She smiled. "I know."

THIRTY-EIGHT

THEY'D gone to the Justice Court for the confrontation with Mei Ling and guilt. They walked back holding hands. Lily couldn't make herself ask the question foremost in her mind, so she made a statement of it instead. "Toby seems to be okay."

Rule's grip tightened on hers. "I installed the heir's portion of the Leidolf mantle in him."

"You—" She stopped. "How? When? From here? You left it in Mateo. He's back on Earth."

"Right after Toby Changed. When I knocked him to the ground and stood over him, I reached, and . . . retrieving the heir's portion felt odd. Very odd. Time seemed . . . distorted. It wasn't difficult, precisely, just strange. Placing it in Toby was easy. I was surprised to find I could do it while wolf. I'd always thought the Rho had to be two-legged to install the heir's portion."

Lily was silent a moment before her mouth kicked up in a small grin. "I'll bet Mateo is really confused right now."

"I'm sure you're right," he said dryly. "He'll doubtless consider it new evidence of my perfidy."

She snorted. They started walking again. Alice met them before they arrived. "The gate is functional," she said in her uninflected way. "I am on an errand for the Zhu Kongqi now, but will return to open the gate when it is time."

"You fixed it?" Lily asked. "You're sure?"

"Quite sure. The gate's tie to the tower was frayed, but not fully severed. Such a repair was well within my knowledge and ability. The tower itself is no longer sound, but both tower and gate should hold for another six to eight uses before we must disconnect the gate from the tower so the tower can be rebuilt." She tilted her head slightly. "It is unlikely that I will see you or Cynna again after you leave."

"I . . . yes, it seems unlikely."

"That is a pity. I have grown to like Cynna, and had much to learn from her still. I do not think I like you, but you are an interesting person. I would have enjoyed getting to know you better. You were right," she added, "about the passions of dragons. I don't know what the Zhu Shēngwù was thinking to say otherwise."

Lily watched Alice walk away, her head crowded with thoughts, then turned to look at Rule. He was looking at her. "The gate's fixed," she said stupidly. She felt a little drunk on victory, or maybe it was exhaustion.

He didn't speak. His throat worked when he swallowed. After a moment he nodded, and they kept walking.

Reno still lay where he'd landed, curled around the body of his son . . . no, his sons. He'd had someone bring Shēngwù's body and lay it beside Dìqiú, or maybe he'd floated it there himself. Kongqi and Ah Wen were with him. As they passed, Lily heard the quiet drift of Ah Wen's voice, but couldn't catch the words.

When they reached the tower, Toby was still asleep. So was Diego. Not that much time had passed, really, even if it seemed like hours, but surely they'd wake soon. Next to Diego, Cynna sat cross-legged, her gaze fixed on the golden filigree spread across one thigh. She looked grim and exhausted. Next to her was a very large tiger . . . who had finished grooming herself and was now grooming Gan. Gan seemed to like it. Having experienced the sandpaper of a tiger's tongue, Lily was impressed by the toughness of Gan's skin.

They needed Grandmother to change back to her human self and learn how to send the signal the gnomes could pick up with their whatchamacallit. Presumably, she wasn't able to do that yet. Lily couldn't seem to get herself to worry about it. She was riding some sort of exhausted high.

Her head seemed to be floating a good foot above her shoulders, and walking took more effort than it should have, but that was okay. She'd survived. They'd all survived. The gate was fixed. It all felt a bit unreal, but if so much good stuff could happen, what else might be possible? Yes, they were about to embark on what the military called a forlorn hope. Four of them against a dragon spawn plus a roomful of demons and an insane demon prince . . . and that assumed that the Great Bitch's avatar remained too preoccupied to deal with them personally. If they won that battle, they still had to escape through the twisty tunnels beneath the blasted caldera. And if they made it aboveground, they had to hope Daniel was still alive and guarding their motorcycles, or they'd be facing an impossibly long walk.

Yet she found herself willing to believe, in this moment birthed of trauma and temporary triumph, that Grandmother would learn what she needed to from Reno. That Benedict and Cullen would still be alive when they arrived . . . and they were fairly sure of that much. She and Cynna had seen Jude carrying Cullen away from the fire, and Rule was sure Benedict had been unconscious, not dead. Benedict had been lying motionless so close to the cackling demon prince . . . but Xitil liked her food lively, didn't she? Meals that screamed while she ate them. Surely an unconscious Benedict wouldn't appeal to her that much.

Rule's plan was solid. Maybe the odds were against them, but the plan was solid, so maybe somehow everything would work the way they needed it to. It could happen. Why not spend this small bubble of time believing the best would happen instead of the worst? This struck her as a completely novel idea, one never before entertained in the history of the world. This world. All the worlds. *Why not?* she thought, giddy.

Rule squeezed her hand. "I need a word with Cynna."

She nodded. "I'll talk to Gan. Diego's still here." Which was shorthand for a longer thought she was too tired to lay out in words, but he either caught her meaning or was too tired himself to ask what she meant.

He went to kneel beside Cynna, laying one hand on her shoulder. "You figured out how to activate it yet?"

She continued to fuss with the scrap of gold filigree . . . the magic cage that had kept her bound for so long. "No, but Alice said she'd give me the key. Looks like I'll need it. The gate's fixed. Did she tell you that?"

Rule nodded.

Her voice was low, intense as she went on, "I only held Ryder for a minute. It wasn't enough. And I shouldn't say that because that was the one thing I absolutely had to have happen—getting her to safety. Only now that I have that, all I can think about is everything else I might lose."

"He's alive," Rule told her. "I mean to see he stays that way."

Cynna's smile was the barest twitch of lips. "Yeah. Me, too."

Lily sat on the ground next to Gan. "Hey, there. You saved my life."

"I know," Gan said, grumpy.

"Thank you."

Gan frowned at her. "Maybe now you'll come to visit me. I've come to visit you twice, and you've never come to visit me."

Lily opened her mouth to point out that going to hell, then on to Dragonhome, wasn't exactly a visit. That she'd been through a few different sorts of hell before that, making it hard to take off for a social call in another realm. And closed it again, because that wasn't the point. She took Gan's hand and squeezed it. "You're right. You're a really good friend, and it's my turn to visit you. I will, too, just as soon as we're sure the world isn't ending or anything."

Gan perked up. "You'll like Edge. The gnomes are kind of stuffy, but there's lots to do. We've even got chocolate now."

Lily smiled. "Speaking of chocolate, you should probably get back to Edge. Reno says he can teach Grandmother how to send a signal to the gnomes."

Gan's lower lip stuck out in what was definitely a pout. "The dragon doesn't know everything."

"He said you couldn't walk. Is he wrong about that?"

"I could probably walk a little bit. And the gnomes will probably be at the node, waiting for the signal."

"Which node?" she said gently. "All of them?" They had no idea which node they'd need a gate built on so they could get home from Dis. Obviously not the twin nodes, which were in the audience chamber. And not the one they'd used initially, because—according to Reno—it would be unstable. Putting together bits and pieces of what she'd been told, Lily thought that temporary gates destabilized nodes because they weren't anchored. Permanent gates were anchored, so they didn't.

Not that she had any idea what "anchored" meant. She squeezed Gan's hand again. "I want you to go let a healer help you grow that new heart."

"Yes, but . . . but it's hard to go away and miss what happens next. I want to know what happens. And you might need me."

Lily nodded. "That's true. But we'll have Grandmother with us."

The pout was back. Gan looked at the tiger. "I want you to come visit me, too."

The tiger purred.

Gan looked back at Lily. "Is that a yes or a no?"

"It means she likes the idea. Gan, will you be able to take Diego with you when you cross? I can wake him up, I think."

"I guess so, but . . . hey! What's Old Woman doing?"

The tiger had blurred. Or the air around her had. It was like looking through a window sheeted with rain, or through really dirty glasses, or as if fog had rolled in, but with a bizarrely distinct outline that shifted, moment by moment, until Grandmother sat on the ground in her usual form. She was a lot more naked than usual, however.

"I will wake the boy," she announced, "then I will learn the trick with the signal. Lily, bring my clothes." She looked down at Gan, eyebrows lifted. "Old Woman?"

"I don't know what to call you. I know what your call-name is, but it doesn't feel right somehow."

Li Lei Yu smiled. It was her good smile, the one without edges. "You will call me Grandmother, of course."

GRANDMOTHER dressed and spoke with Gan briefly. Lily didn't hear what she said, but it wasn't likely to have included "good-bye." Grandmother did not approve of good-byes. Lily asked about the backlash and was informed that when the tiger called her, the change eliminated such inconveniences. She then marched briskly over to Reno. Apparently whatever Reno planned to teach her required proximity, maybe even physical contact.

Rule carried Gan to the crossing spot. Diego—awake, rested, and clearly feeling that life was on its way back to normal now that adults were in charge again—walked there with Cynna, holding her hand and chattering away. He seemed aggrieved that Toby had gotten to Change and would therefore get to stay with the adults. Cynna pointed out that he would get to see Edge and Toby wouldn't. This clearly appealed to him.

The idea was for Diego to curl up close to Gan so that they touched all along their sides. Diego looked dubious, but he followed instructions. He and Gan were almost the same size, though Gan was heavier. Gan curled one arm around the boy, and a second later, they were just . . . gone.

"You're good with kids," Lily told Cynna.

"Yeah, who knew? I sure didn't." Cynna shook her head. "It's probably because I can relate. My inner child isn't all that inner. Mostly she's pissed off."

Attend, Reno said.

Lily stiffened and looked over at the dragon. She couldn't see Grandmother. Reno had rearranged his coils into a snaky circle, and presumably Grandmother was inside that circle. His three sons—one living, two dead—were not. The living son started toward them.

I told you I had removed the forces anchoring the magical construct to this world. This partial dismantling of the construct prevented it from completing the process of merging realms. The construct had been operating for some time, however, gradually altering the relationships between the realms of Dragonhome, Dis, and Earth. You may think of these alterations as drawing them unnaturally close to each other. With the construct no longer operating, forces will begin moving them apart once more. Be aware that the terms "close" and "apart" are crude approximations. There is no physical distance involved.

These forces will cause disruptions in all three worlds, but I believe the realms of Earth and Dis will be most affected. I lack both the data and the time needed to calculate these

*effects, and indeed, some are likely to be random and there-
fore unpredictable by any metric. However, two of them seem
sufficiently likely that I will caution you to watch for them,
should you survive to return to Earth.*

Lily grimaced. Optimistic guy, that Reno.

*There is a high possibility of a period of counter-entropic
fall-throughs, by which I mean that demons are likely to fall
into Earth. There may be only a few who do so. There may
be many. I do not know how long this period will be. There
is also a high probability that the Great Enemy achieved a
partial victory and some portion of her power will now be
available to her avatar when she is in the Earth realm. I
have no metric for determining how much or what form that
will take.*

Rule's voice was hard and low. "You mean that more of her
will be able to enter Earth?"

*No. I mean precisely what I said. More of her power will
be available to her avatar in that realm. She remains unable
to enter any of the realms. Do not interrupt again. I have one
more thing to tell you. I will do so. I will finish instructing Li
Lei and may remain in communication with her. I will not
speak with the rest of you again before you leave, which will
be in approximately seventeen minutes.*

*Rule Turner's plan for the assault on those in the audience
chamber on Dis is well constructed, given the materials and
personnel available to him. It is not, however, likely to succeed. The Zhu Kongqi and I have discussed this. He will propose to you a deal that has my support. I strongly urge you to
accept it.*

I require solitude now.

Kongqi reached them just as Reno finished. He was a mess.
His white *shenyi* was torn, dirty, and bloodstained. The tidy
knot of his hair had come down and the ends of his hair were
singed. He was also barefoot. He'd lost two brothers, one of
whom had been trying to kill him. He'd regained his mother.
None of this showed in his voice when he spoke. "Lily Yu. I
have enjoyed our conversations. If you were to visit Dragonhome again, you would be a welcome guest. Do you speak for
your party?"

*   *   *

IT was full dark when they assembled in front of the gate. Lily had lost that exhausted high and wanted it back. Her stomach was queasy with nerves and her thoughts kept straying into places she did not want them to go.

Reno had taken wing. He hadn't gone far; she could feel him overhead, but he was flying high, invisible in the black sky. He hadn't spoken to them again.

There were no motorcycles for this gate crossing as there had been when they went roaring into Dis. Benedict and Cullen weren't with them. Or Max. No Mason, Carlos, Daniel, or Jude . . . and no Gan. But everyone who had been dragged into this realm was still alive and had either left or was about to leave, and that was no small miracle.

She told herself this. Her unhappy stomach replied that this just meant they'd already had their miracle, which made things look grim for the next leg of their journey.

Lily grimaced and glanced over at Grandmother . . . and at the lanky wolf sitting next to her, panting nervously. Rule had stepped away to speak with Alice, and his absence worried the wolf.

She'd tried mindspeaking Toby. It hadn't worked. He'd snarled, clearly aware that something was messing with him, but words were still foreign to him, and words were all she knew how to send. He'd already been confused, having woken from his enforced sleep to find his fellow wolf, his leader, walking around on two legs. But Rule had settled him. He had the mantle and the knowledge of how to communicate properly, without words.

He'd also had chickens. The squad Alice had sent after them in what seemed like a different day altogether had finally returned. It turned out that she'd sent them to a specific shop for the plucked birds—one on the far side of the city. She'd wanted to keep her men out of the fight and alive. Lily couldn't fault her for that.

The chickens had helped. Toby had eaten two-and-a-half of them. Rule had eaten the other half. Raw. And before he allowed his son to eat. Lily understood why; it was necessary for the dominance thing. The leader ate first. The new wolf had to see that and wait until his leader gave him food. Rule had probably been half-starved himself, having Changed twice, so he'd needed the protein. She really did understand . . . but she hadn't watched.

Grandmother stroked the wolf's head and murmured something. Toby quieted a bit. Grandmother was his new best friend, the only one he trusted aside from Rule. Ensorcellment, it turned out, didn't require words.

". . . your 'clips.'"

And that was the other big difference between this gate crossing and the last one. Lily turned to First Fist Fang Ye Lì, who stood with one of the squads he would lead into Dis. His dragon-scale armor gleamed. His mustaches all but quivered with suppressed excitement. Fang was deeply, deplorably thrilled by the chance to enter a hellgate and battle some of the scariest demons in the realm. "Excuse me, First Fist. I was deep in thought and didn't hear."

"One of my men has found the 'clips' you were eager to regain. He brings them now."

That perked Lily up. "Good! Where—"

Fang nodded at the man sprinting toward them. "I'm very interested in seeing what that 'gun' of yours does." He used the English word for "gun," as he had with "clips." His language lacked words for either item.

"You may be disappointed," she said wryly. "This one's not all that effective against demons. I had a better one, but lost it in the battle. Still," she said, accepting the clips from the Fist, who'd arrived, "this is better than nothing."

Fang and his Fists had been part of Kongqi's plan all along. The seven squads with him had been chosen for their expertise at fighting the demons who sometimes fell through into Dragonhome. They were all skilled swordsmen, and four had strong Water Gifts. Demons were resistant to magic, but the nature of that resistance varied. Experience had taught the residents of Dragonhome that many demons were susceptible to strong Water magic.

The rest of their bennies from the deal resided in a vial tucked into a pouch Lily wore around her neck. That, and the glove on her left hand. She'd insisted on the glove. The one she ended up with was a worn leather archer's glove. It didn't fit worth a damn, which was why she wore only the one.

Alice had assured them the gate could transit this many people. It was a small gate physically, but she said that by other metrics, it could be called massive. This made it possible to keep it open longer than many gates and to accommodate the various types of mass involved in moving so many people through it.

The one thing Kongqi wanted in return was his brother. Rule hadn't liked that. He wanted Tom Weng dead. Lily understood why—Weng had been responsible for a lot of deaths—but she'd been relieved. She was a cop, not an executioner, and this was what she did: capture the bad guys and turn them over to the system to deal with. In this case the system meant their mother, but Lily didn't think this meant Weng would get off lightly. Dragons gave the idea of "tough love" real teeth.

After dickering briefly over phrasing, Rule had agreed. Fang and his men would greatly improve their odds without forcing him to make major changes in his plan. The Fists' job would be to deal with the lesser threats—the hyena/centaur demons Lily called red-eyes, and the eight-foot monsters Gan called Claws. Claws and red-eyes would not be considered lesser threats under anything resembling normal circumstances.

Rule's plan made the most of their two advantages: planning and surprise. Rule had had time to map out almost everyone's position at the critical moment. The exception was Max. None of them knew exactly where Max had been/would be, but he'd last been seen not far from Xitil. Rule had used that knowledge to choreograph a fast, two-pronged strike.

For Weng, however, events would be happening at battle speed, wrapped in smoke and chaos. He could only react, not plan. And he wouldn't know where his enemies were. Oh, he might have seen Lily vanish—he'd been close when Gan grabbed her. He might even suspect that meant that she'd crossed to some other realm. But visibility had been crap, with all the smoke. It was unlikely he knew/would know that Cynna had vanished, too. And Grandmother. And Rule. He wouldn't have time to figure out what had happened. He would not, could not, be expecting them to come through the gate from Dragonhome.

The addition of Fang's men had caused some discussion. Fang thought he and at least one squad should go through the gate first. According to Kongqi, Weng would be aware the second the gate opened. Weng wouldn't be expecting a squad from the home team, but he'd assume—he'd *know*—the Fists he saw coming through the gate were on his side, so he wouldn't react with instant lethality.

Rule was not a lead-from-behind kind of guy, but he'd ended up agreeing to this, too. Lily wasn't sure how much that had to do with Fang's argument. Where Rule went, Toby would go. Rule couldn't protect his son the way he desperately wanted to, not where they were going. But he could keep him from being one of the first through the gate.

Rule's voice rang out clear and firm. "Take your places. We'll be moving fast."

Lily's heart jumped into double time, each beat pounding *out of time, out of time, out of time.* She hadn't had a chance to talk to Grandmother privately, and she desperately needed to. She needed another word with Rule. She needed . . . to get the vial out. She shifted to stand directly behind Grandmother, who would be going through right after Rule and Toby. Cynna was now behind Lily, and the other four squads of Fists behind her. Behind them were the last two who would enter hell. They were civilians, two of the Kanas: Ah Hai, the healer, and a wrinkled old man named Ah Cheng, who could quench mage fire.

Lily fumbled with the pouch—damned stupid glove—and pulled out the stoppered ceramic vial, gripping it tightly in her gloved hand. She tossed the pouch down. No need for it now.

The dragon soaring high above their heads began to sing.

THIRTY-NINE

DRAGONSONG could work magic. This song didn't, except on the heart. Reno sang of grief and irredeemable loss, loss that would persist until the suns died and the universe drifted to an end. His song didn't have words, but that's what it meant as it reached inside Lily, gripping her by the throat and the gut as she ran through the gate.

She had never been through a permanent gate, but it didn't feel any different from the temporary kind. There was that instant when every cell in her body shimmied in an indescribably strange way, then her foot landed on the rock of a different world. She left dragonsong behind, racing into smoke and heat and the mad cackling of a demon prince.

The gate opened up near the pile of burning bodies. Demon bodies. The smoke was bad and the stench was worse. How could she not have noticed the stench the first time around? It smelled like a mix of burned hair and burned plastic with a hint of roasting flesh. For one mad second she wondered what in hell demon bodies were made of.

She couldn't see Weng from here, but she knew where he should be. She heard Fang's voice calling out commands as she ran after Rule, Grandmother, and Toby for several long strides, catching a single instant's glimpse of Ginger through the smoke. The Great Bitch's avatar stood motionless on the other side of the fire. Then she veered. Rule and Grandmother and Toby ran on without her, racing for the mountain of pink flesh Lily knew was at the far end of the room. For Xitil.

Lily aimed at a black pillar rising darkly through the smoke, the pillar where she'd skidded, twisting her ankle, knocking herself silly. Feet pounded behind her. And there were the Claws who'd been about to catch her when Gan took her out of this world—bipedal creatures at least eight feet tall with built-in weapons on each foot, each hand, and at the ends of their muscular tails. One had red skin, the other an insanely cheerful bright pink.

Behind them was Tom Weng. He was pointing at her—hurling a spell maybe. She sure as hell hoped so. His spells would bounce off. If he decided to throw fire instead, she was cooked. Magic slid off her. Fire didn't, even if it was magically generated. But Weng had wanted her alive to give to the Great Bitch. They were gambling that he still did. For him, only a few moments had passed.

"Get her!" he yelled.

He was yelling, she realized, at the Fists behind her. Good. She veered around the Claw who, after a moment's frozen startlement, had started toward her. Behind her, someone called out in Chinese. And the Claw started to wither as water splashed to the floor at its feet.

When you sucked all the water out of a body, that body died. Even when it belonged to a demon.

Lily ignored the other Claw, trusting that those coming up fast behind her would deal with him. And launched a spinning kick at Weng.

None of them could defeat a demon spawn with magic, which left brute force. Only she was immune to the spawn's magic, and Weng would take her alive, if he could. This meant she had to be the one to take him down. Rule had not liked where logic led him, but he was too good a tactician to ignore it.

Weng was fast, but so was she—and he'd had no martial arts training. He ducked her first kick, but failed to take advantage of the split second when he could have used the miss against her. She flowed from that kick into a quick side kick.

That one connected. So did the next one, and the one after that was to his temple—a blow that might have killed a human. It knocked Weng silly. He swayed. Her next kick sent him to the stone floor.

Lily was on him the second he landed. She didn't try to pin him. He was dazed, not unconscious, and the spawn were insanely strong. He reached for her throat. She fumbled with the stopper on the vial, pulling it out just as his fingers closed, vise-tight, around her throat, cutting off her breath as she poured the contents of the vial onto his face.

Téngtòng mǎyǐ. Pain ants. Dozens of them—Kongqi's entire stash—spilled onto Tom Weng's face.

His eyes widened for a split second before he began screaming. His hands fell away from her and he clawed at his face.

They had, at Kongqi's estimate, between twenty and thirty seconds before Weng's super-duper healing cleared out enough of the venom for him to think straight. She scooted back quickly and yanked open his *shenyi*, then shoved up the thin silk shirt he wore beneath it.

Cynna dropped to her knees next to Weng and slapped the magic cage on his upper belly, chanting as she did. "That's it," she said. "His magic's bound. Take him and tie him up."

Lily repeated that in quick Chinese for the Fists who'd run up behind them, adding, "For God's sake, be careful of the pain ants." She sprang to her feet.

Three of the Fists were engaged with the other Claw, their swords darting. One lay on the floor, the front of his armor dented. Several more swarmed up around them, one of them with a coil of rope.

She couldn't see, dammit. Couldn't see what was happening at the far end of the room, where Rule and Grandmother and Toby had gone. Where Benedict would be lying unconscious. Where Cullen and Jude should be, and Mason, and maybe Max.

And Xitil.

"Come on," Cynna cried, and took off running.

"Squad seven," Lily called, "with us!" And she raced after Cynna.

Cullen had set off a demon-killer bomb in the chamber.

That was the source of that pile of bodies. But it hadn't killed all of them, and those who'd survived had mostly regained consciousness. Lily heard Cynna snarl a spell, then she threw something invisible off to her right. A huge Claw staggered out of the smoke and collapsed right in front of them.

Cynna jumped over it, so Lily did, too. Three more strides and she passed out of the densest smoke—and saw Xitil. Rule. Toby. And Grandmother.

Rule was holding off one of the red-eyes with his borrowed sword. Toby may have thought he was helping. He yipped and darted in, much too excited, but he jumped back before the demon could connect. Behind him, Lily glimpsed Fang and his squad fighting three more demons.

Xitil was a lovely blend of pinks—a deep rosy color shading into soft petal-pink. She was also huge, the size of an elephant. She looked like a mad scientist's gene-blending creation, a cross between a centaur, a slug, and some bugs. Her lower body was vaguely slug-like, with a centipede's legs and a scorpion's tail. Her upper body was mammalian, with six pendulous breasts and four arms. Her neck was short, her head round and hairless, and her wide, wide mouth lacked lips. A dozen or so bright blue eyes circled that round head like a hippie's headband.

Several of those eyes were fixed on Grandmother, whom she held in two of her large hands. Grandmother stared back at her. It was terrifying. It was exactly what was supposed to happen.

Demons can't use mind magic worth a damn. Not even demon princes. And Grandmother was very good at ensorcellment.

Grandmother was speaking in a firm, quiet voice. ". . . not harm us. You want all the humans, the lupi, and our companions in this realm to remain alive. You do not want your subjects to harm any of us. This is extremely important to you."

After a moment Xitil nodded her round, bald head. She spoke in a sweet, lilting voice in a language overly full of consonants and short on vowels.

The fighting . . . stopped. Just stopped.

"Great prince," Grandmother told the demon holding her some ten feet off the floor, "you grow sleepy."

Xitil swayed. Several blue eyes closed, opened again. Some stayed closed. The big hands opened—and Grandmother fell to the floor. "Whoops," Xitil said in perfectly good English, and giggled. And collapsed.

Grandmother did not get out of the way in time.

When Rule pulled her out from under the sleeping behemoth—gasping for breath and flat on her back—she beamed up at them with what Lily could have sworn was the sort of giddy triumph she'd felt earlier. "That went well," she announced, her firmness hardly impaired by the wheeziness in her voice. "It is not even a bad break."

THE break Grandmother referred to was her wrist. She'd landed badly, but hadn't taken any additional damage when Xitil collapsed on her. While one of the Fists wrapped the wrist, Mason came limping up with Max riding piggyback. Cynna went after Cullen and Jude, and Rule retrieved Benedict, who was still unconscious. Not a good sign. He'd have healed a simple concussion by now.

Every one of the demons in the chamber had vanished. Lily figured they didn't want to be around when Xitil woke up.

The Kanas man started quenching the fires, and Grandmother gave Fang instructions. "The ensorcellment will not last. The sleep will, as long as you are not stupid. Do not try to kill the demon prince. That would only wake her, and she would not be in a good mood."

Fang answered with a small bow.

"Can you walk out?" Rule asked her tersely from beside his brother's still body.

"Of course. It is my wrist, not my ankle."

That was good, because they were running out of strong backs. Max's leg was badly mangled and Benedict was unconscious. Fortunately, Mason and Jude had only minor wounds. Minor for lupi anyway. They'd be able to walk out. Cullen—woozy but conscious—insisted that he could, too. This was blatantly untrue. He couldn't stand up. He'd gotten his throat slit at some point and must have nearly bled out before his healing closed it.

They didn't take time to explain or to hear the others' stories.

They didn't even wait for Ah Hai to check out Benedict. He was alive. His best chance of staying that way was to be well away from here when the Great Bitch returned her attention to the chamber where her avatar stood—silent, motionless, and untouchable.

They didn't warn Fang against disturbing her. He couldn't.

One of the Fists handed Jude a water skin. Jude would be carrying Cullen, and Cullen's body desperately needed fluids. If he stayed awake, he could drink as they traveled. Rule picked up his brother. Max would ride out on Mason's back.

They didn't know how far Xitil's prohibition on harming them had gone. Cynna said the demon prince could have sent her orders to every part of the ruined palace, even to every demon in her territory, but they didn't know if she had. They had to be prepared for the possibility of a fight, so Lily took point. All of the mobile lupi were carrying those worse off, so it had to be either her or Cynna, and Lily had her mindsense to give warning. She also had Benedict's Uzi and enough ammo to comfort her.

Rule would be guiding them, however. The mental map Reno had bestowed on him over a week ago—according to the time they'd lived, that is—was still as clear as ever. And they needed to leave the way he'd come, not the way Lily had. He'd left Carlos in one of those dark tunnels, alone and poisoned by spider-demon venom, unable to walk. Left him with their last grenade in case he was attacked before his healing cleared enough of the poison for him to try to make it out of the tunnels.

Lily did pause briefly on the way out. She stopped in front of Fang, her head crowded with an unsorted mess of things she wanted to say. He'd been her jailer, but an honorable one. His Fists had disarmed the other Fists in the fight at the tower. They'd fought demons here, keeping her alive so she could take down Tom Weng. He and his Fists would be waiting now, waiting and hoping the gate opened before the Great Bitch finished stabilizing the nodes. None of them knew how long either of those things would take, but Reno thought the gate would open first. Maybe.

Would she ever know if he and these men survived? She settled for thumping her chest with her fist in the salute she'd seen him give. "I have been honored by our acquaintance, First Fist."

His dark eyes flickered with surprise. He returned the salute.

THEY did not have to fight. Not once. They never even saw a demon as they walked and jogged through a dark labyrinth lit by Cynna's mage light. They did have to stop briefly where a loose pile of rubble partly blocked the tunnel.

Beneath that rubble was Carlos's body. So were the corpses of two of the spider demons. Those demons had come back, and Carlos had done the only thing he could.

They couldn't carry his body out. They did uncover enough of him that Rule could remove the gold cross he wore, and Cynna crossed herself and said a very short prayer. Carlos had been Catholic, like Cynna, and he had a grown daughter. Maybe her father's cross would be some comfort to her.

Benedict woke just before they reached the surface, and that was really good news—both because it meant he was healing and because none of them had come up with a way to carry an unconscious man on a motorcycle. He was in a lot of pain, he was dizzy and disoriented, and he had trouble remembering where they were or how they'd gotten here, even after they told him. But . . . "We need to get out of here," Rule told his brother, "on motorcycles. Will you be able to ride on the back of one and hold on to me?"

Benedict considered that a moment. "Yes." All sorts of tight things unknotted inside Lily at that one word. If Benedict said he could do something, he would do it.

Their motorcycles were waiting. So was Daniel.

LI Lei spent the first hour or so of their trip to the node considering buying a motorcycle. This surprised her. She had never taken much interest in motorized vehicles, and she was decidedly uncomfortable—bone tired, with her wrist hurting fiercely. And her cracked rib—which she had declined to mention to the others—had not finished healing.

And yet there was an exhilaration in speeding along, the

wind tangling in her hair. It was the closest she had come to flying since she ceased to be a dragon in form. She wondered if Li Qin would enjoy it. Li Qin was rather conservative about some things, but she was not closed-minded.

In the end, she decided not to decide at this time. She was a trifle giddy. She had not expected to be alive.

Li Lei had spoken truthfully to Rule about her chance of success at ensorcelling a demon prince. He was in charge of their tactics and needed to know. Rule had . . . oversimplified somewhat when he relayed that part of his plan to Lily. Li Lei had chosen not to offer Lily those details Rule had omitted. No doubt if Lily were aware of this, she'd be angry that Li Lei and Rule had conspired to take away her right to worry herself silly. Li Lei did not regret having done so.

Demons were incapable of using mind magic. That much was largely true. But Xitil was a demon prince. Demon princes were like other demons in some ways, and a different sort of being altogether in others. The princes established the "rules" in their territories, rules that amounted to natural laws. One of the rules in Xitil's territory was that everyone understood everyone else, regardless of what language they spoke. That was mind magic, and on no small scale.

Before the dragons left Dis for Earth, before Xitil consumed the avatar of an Old One and went insane, she must have had excellent mental shields. Li Lei had not needed to ask Reno about this, as it was obvious. If Xitil had not possessed very good shields, the dragons who had been her neighbors would have controlled her, and she would never have entertained that avatar. The question had been whether or not she still possessed them.

As it turned out, she did . . . but they were a tattered and decaying mess, like the rest of her mind. Li Lei had been able to slip in between the chaotic layers of shielding. It had not been easy or pleasant, but it had been possible. This had been a profound relief.

Li Lei did not have all the abilities she had possessed during her time as dragon. She could not fly, use mindspeech, or compartmentalize her mind. But she had retained some of them. Dragons knew how to share their deaths. If she had been unable to ensorcel Xitil, she would have done so. It would have been a good death, for the others would have lived. She glanced aside at the rangy wolf loping along beside them. Toby was tiring, but he had held up very well. He seemed more accepting of the others in their group now. Perhaps he was getting used to them, or perhaps it was simply that more of them smelled right, even if they were not currently wolves.

But she vastly preferred life over even the best of deaths. A broken wrist and a cracked rib were annoying, but they would pass.

At last, they reached the node Li Lei had, after discussion with Rule, selected for their first attempt. It was not the closest to Clanhome, but she was fairly sure it did not open up into solid rock or an uncomfortable distance above the ground.

On this side, the node was set in a narrow culvert or dry riverbed. The descent was shallow enough that the bikes could make it, but not with passengers. Li Lei got off, thanked Mason for driving her on the motorcycle, and climbed down the culvert, every muscle and joint in her body aching. She stopped at the node and shaped the spell she must use in her mind, then sang to the node.

It was not dragonsong, which Reno would have used. It was a translation into sounds her vocal chords could accommodate. It worked. It also took a great deal of power.

She swayed, barely able to stay upright. A firm arm went around her waist, steadying her. She permitted this, as it seemed preferable to collapsing. "The pulse went out successfully. We must wait now for the gnomes to arrive and erect a gate. I believe the Fists provided some food?"

"Rough rations, but yes." Rule smiled down at her. Then he surprised her, lifting one of her hands and kissing the back of it. "Grandmother, you never fail to amaze me. I wonder sometimes what would have happened if you'd ever gotten mad at the government and decided to topple it."

She snorted, entirely pleased with her new grandson. "I do not pay a great deal of attention to governments. Although once . . . but it was a very small country. I do not count it."

FORTY

~

THE wait for the gate to open seemed endless. They lined up along the dry riverbed more or less in order of injury. Benedict was at the front with Mason, who would carry him through. He'd passed out again as soon as they reached the node. Cullen was still weak, but he'd improved once he got some of the jerked meat into him along with a fair portion of their water. Max's leg had started healing, but badly, as the bone hadn't been set in time. He'd need surgery to straighten it.

Lily, Rule, and Toby were the exceptions to the lineup. Someone had to keep watch from the top of the short incline, and Lily could use her mindsense along with her eyes. Toby's sense of smell might be a plus, too, but he wasn't a dependable sentry. He was there because Rule refused to let Lily stand watch alone, and Toby went where Rule did.

At the moment he was sound asleep, his head on his father's thigh. Rule stroked him absently. "You should have some more of that jerky."

"Too thirsty to eat." She'd gotten down some of the sweet-spicy dried meat the Fists had provided, but she really didn't like it. It also made her terribly thirsty, and they were out of water. "You can have the rest of mine."

He shook his head and fell silent a moment. "I don't think you ever met Carlos's daughter. Her name's Raina. Raina Matthews."

"No, though I've heard Carlos mention her. I've met his father, though, haven't I? Miguel Gutierrez? He wears a beat-up black cowboy hat all the time and a squash blossom necklace. Works at the clan's construction firm."

"Miguel. Yes. He never outgrew his love for cowboys and Indians, though he alternates between calling himself a cowboy and calling himself an Indian—Navajo usually. As he hasn't a trace of Navajo blood, this annoys Benedict." Rule's smile flickered and died. "This will be hard news for Miguel."

He hurt. She could hear it in his voice and thought about telling him that they'd come out of this with far fewer deaths than they had any right to expect. But that wasn't the point, was it? "Tell me about Raina," she said instead.

Raina Mathews was twenty-five, single, no children. Her mother had named her, and she hadn't put Carlos's name on Raina's birth certificate, although she and Carlos had been living together when she got pregnant. She'd wanted him to marry her. She'd believed that Carlos had no rights to the child unless he married her. He hadn't, of course. Lupi didn't marry . . . until first Cullen, then Rule, broke that taboo. She'd kicked Carlos out the day she and Raina came home from the hospital. He hadn't seen his daughter again until she was five years old.

"I expected Carlos to be angry when I married you," Rule said quietly. "He wasn't. In his mind, the mate bond made my situation completely different from his."

After college, Raina had gotten hired at an investment firm in L.A., and she was ambitious enough to put in long hours. Carlos hadn't seen her often after that, and had been talking about moving to L.A. himself before the hidden war with the Great Bitch heated up. He'd stopped talking about moving.

"I picked Carlos for the mission because of his love of bikes," Rule said. "Loved riding them and tinkering with them. He worked in a motorcycle shop when he was younger. He knew how to fight, of course, knew weapons. He'd worked under Benedict for a dozen years. But I wanted him because he might have been able to fix a bike if one of them broke down. He brought a small toolkit with him . . . we never needed it."

Lily ached for him. For Carlos, who'd died alone in the dark. She ached for Carlos's father and for his daughter, and she said, "Did he die because he made a mistake?"

"What? No! No, he did everything right. He just took too much venom when—"

"Then he didn't die because you picked the wrong person for the mission. He died because—well, it's hell. Demons. Lots and lots of demons. I still don't see how the rest of us survived."

He smiled slowly. "That has a lot to do with your—"

"It is time!" Grandmother called. "The gate opens!"

She and Rule and Toby went through last, with her on the back of the bike and Toby loping along beside them. The moment when every cell of her body tried to draw apart from every other cell and do its own little shimmer-dance seemed longer, stronger this time—maybe because she was so bloody exhausted—but then she was through the gate and home.

Home was rough, low mountains with forested slopes—the national forest that adjoined Clanhome. Home was a whole lot of people clustered in the small valley where they'd exited, and Isen crouching beside his oldest son, who lay flat on the ground now with Nettie bending over him. Home was the shadow of a dragon cruising overhead, and the tug of a mind Lily knew well. Sam's mind.

Home smelled strongly like barbeque.

"Injuries?" Isen boomed as he ran up and gripped Rule's shoulders.

"All healed. Did they tell you—"

But Isen wasn't listening. He crushed Rule to him in a hug that may have come close to cracking a rib or two, then let go with one arm so he could hug Lily with it. "And this—" He broke off, one arm around Rule, one around Lily, and looked down at the wolf snarling at him. His bushy eyebrows lifted. "And this is my grandson, well and healthy and a great surprise. You have much to tell me."

Rule pulled away so he could crouch beside Toby and soothe him. "I do. We won't be sending Toby to Nokolai's *terra tradis*."

"No, I can see that. Leidolf does have a *terra tradis*, of course, but will you—ah, later. I will hear everything, but first you should eat and drink. We brought ribs and pulled pork from the Jolly Pig. Nettie will see to Benedict"—a quick glance over his shoulder, the twitch of a worried frown—"but the rest of you must eat."

"Coke," Lily said with great sincerity. "Coke first, then food and explanations, but you should know that the other kids are in Edge. They're fine, they're safe, and Gan will—" She broke off, startled by the sight of an unexpected face in the crowd. "Rule, your brother's here! Your other brother, I mean. Jason. And Adam's with him."

And from ahead of them in the mob came Cullen's voice, very loud. "That's him! Grab him! That's—"

"Cullen!" Isen roared. "Sit!"

Lily couldn't see Cullen from here, but she had no doubt Cullen had promptly folded and sat on the ground.

"You are injured," Isen went on severely. "You will not go chasing and grabbing people. Especially not people to whom I have given guest-right."

Cullen's voice again, much quieter: "Guest-right?"

"Yes. I, too, have much to tell," he said, speaking more to Rule and Lily now. "Though some of it should come from your brother Jason, and some from these two, whom I have named *ospi*." He waved one hand. "Come now, step forward so I can introduce you. I think Rule and Lily never met you, did they?"

Isen hadn't really brought half the clan with him. It just seemed like it. A man and woman slipped out of the crowd around them. Lily put her at five-seven, maybe a hundred thirty-five pounds. Early thirties. She was red-haired, voluptuous, and freckled, with the round cheeks that made Irish women's smiles so infectious. He was, in a word, gorgeous. Five-eleven and one sixty-five, she thought, and in his mid-twenties. His curly hair just missed being black, and his eyes were a startling pale blue. His features were beautifully symmetrical. His body might have been copied from Michelangelo's *David*.

Both of them wore jeans, T-shirts, and wary expressions.

"This is my son, Rule Turner," Isen said, "and his mate, Lily Yu. Rule, Lily, this is Michael . . . I think you prefer

Brown for your surname? Michael and Molly Brown. They stand with us against the Great Enemy and have great need of the clan's protection. Michael is . . ." He paused, then smiled a slow, canny smile. "Let us say that he is the holder of the Codex Arcana."

Ready to find
your next great read?

Let us help.

Visit prh.com/nextread

Penguin
Random
House